FIGHTING FOR REDEMPTION
Copyright © 2024 by Charli Cotner

ISBN: 979-8-9891566-3-4

Cover Design by Haya

Edited by Represent Publishing and Perfectly Write Editing Services

Fighting For Redemption

Fighting For Redemption

CHARLI COTNER

RP Represent Publishing

TRIGGERS

Fighting For Redemption

- Struggles with Mental Health
- Overwhelming Anxiety
- Subtle Manipulation
- Toxic and Abusive Relationships
- Violence

@authorcharlicotner

Author's Note

In the words of the incredible Payson Pennington: In a society obsessed with perfect facades, I desperately want to help people realize that it's okay to aim simply for a grateful heart and the strength to face another day.

CHAPTER 1
PAYSON

Enjoying the view?

Have you ever experienced one of those mesmerizing nights when everything aligns just right? Laughter fills the air, and the sky becomes a canvas of twinkling stars. You're surrounded by friends whose joy mirrors the thrill in your heart. Yet, these nights pass quickly, leaving behind a vibrant and unforgettable collection of memories.

The type of memories that linger, etching themselves into your mind and body. Every part of you feels invigorated, from the soles of your feet to the tips of your fingers, each inch carrying the echo of the night's adventures.

My arms move of their own accord, swaying above my head, when suddenly, I feel a firm hand on my skin. This isn't just any touch; it's a firm, unfamiliar grasp on my bare waist.

Cautiously, I open one eye, trying to piece together the events that led to this moment.

Crap. Crap. Crap.

Those unforgettable memories? The aching muscles and sore body? They dissolve in an instant, replaced by a tidal wave of *What on earth were you thinking, Payson?* Reality crashes over me like an icy torrent, and the realization of how the night ended with him sends fragmented memories surging back into sharp clarity.

The ride to his place was a whirlwind of shared glances and stolen touches, anticipation thickening the atmosphere around us with every passing mile. Each look, each brief contact, sent electricity dancing between us. As soon as we crossed the threshold, the charged atmosphere became palpable. In a frenzy, we discarded our clothes, creating a haphazard trail of fabric that traced our path from the door to his bedroom.

His touch conveyed both urgency and tenderness, his fingers gliding over my skin with an intoxicating familiarity. Each caress played a harmony of sensations, sparking shivers and gasps as he navigated every curve and hollow with expert precision. His hands knew my body, knew exactly where to press and tease, drawing forth responses I couldn't suppress.

Out of the blue, the gravity of reality slams into me like a frying pan to the face and I sense myself tensing up. My body coils like a spring, poised to unravel.

Payson, do NOT dwell on that memory right now.

With the blanket partially draped over me, I shift my head toward him.

I didn't.

Oh, but you did.

No, that's not possible.

Once more, I shut my eyes and pray to the higher powers, hoping this is merely a horrible dream. But then his hand withdraws, leaving a cold void where warmth once lingered. The sudden absence feels jarring, as if the air recoils from the loss.

Don't go there, Payson. Missing it would imply you cherished his touch from the start, and you most certainly did not.

He moves, and I instinctively pull the covers up, ninja-like, until only my eyes peek out. From my cocoon of fabric, I watch him turn away.

Those defined calves, that tight ass—let's not even mention the back muscles. There's just something irresistible about a man's back, the way the muscles ripple, making me yearn for another round with him. Or would it be the third?

God, I can't believe these thoughts are crossing my mind. What in God's name is wrong with me? He isn't just some random guy. Is he? How can I be sure if I haven't even seen his face?

Keep telling yourself that, Payson.

A sigh escapes me, followed by an internal groan. The urge to throw a tantrum like a kid denied their favorite candy builds up inside me. Maybe not exactly that extreme, but very close.

My gaze drifts back to his backside, and I have to admit, it's undeniably sexy. Don't judge me. Then, my eyes catch something unexpected—a small dimple, right there.

On his ass.

Sure, lots of guys could have dimples on their ass, right? It can't be that rare. Yet, as he moves, the dimple deepens as his muscles clench. I'd be laughing uncontrollably if that simple detail didn't confirm my earlier suspicions.

Crap, what have I done?

Calm down, Payson. You've been here before. He's just another guy, another casual encounter. No biggie.

Except, it kind of is.

He's my best friend's brother.

And for some unfathomable reason, he hates me. It makes no sense, but his animosity fuels my own. That, along with his cocky womanizing demeanor, makes my skin crawl. His smug smirk, his always-ready witty retort—everything about him infuriates me.

I lift my head slowly, cautiously sliding one leg off the

bed. My heart thumps, and I can hear my breathing in the quiet room. If there's ever a time for a graceful exit, it's now. I try to creep, but in my haste, I throw my other leg over too quickly. The bed creaks loudly, the mattress shifting under my weight.

I freeze, my pulse hammering in my ears. Maybe he didn't hear that. But I know better. There's no avoiding it now.

Okay, time to face the music. I have two choices: sneak out like a coward or confront him head-on.

Had you said no last night, you wouldn't be in this mess now, would you?

Yeah, try explaining that to my drunken, hazy mind—the lingering touches, the heated stares, and the banter, all while tipping back multiple shots.

Did I mention shots? I'm talking about shots like the ones in that LMFAO song.

All I wanted was a night out at the club with my best friend, Milli. Her brother got us into the VIP section. So we took advantage. Who knew NFL players partied so hard before the official season began? I sure didn't, but that didn't stop me from joining them. I had my reason to celebrate.

Summer was over, and that meant time away from Stoneton, my hometown, and my parents. The feeling of freedom was intoxicating, like the first warm day of spring after a brutal winter.

I took a quick look behind me one more time, watching his wistful sleeping face and the annoying noises escaping his mouth. A fleeting thought crossed my mind—maybe I could just put the pillow over his face and gently push down. That would solve all my problems.

Yeah, no. Jail isn't for me. No way. Do the right thing, Payson, even if it kills you.

Bending my knees, I begin a clumsy crawl, muttering quietly, "This isn't how a one-night stand is supposed to happen." In this unflattering pose, I'm all too exposed. That's when our gazes connect—his, a familiar shade of hazel that sends a jolt through me. I spring up, as does he, scrambling under the comforter in a futile attempt at modesty.

A bit late for that, buddy.

Silence hangs heavy in the air, charged with unspoken tension. This isn't the usual awkward-yet-amusing morning-after scenario. No casual greetings this time. My worst fears confirmed—he's the last person I wanted to see here. His eyes narrow with annoyance, yet they flicker with lingering desire. He tries to hide it, but his stare keeps stealing glances at the bare skin my hastily gathered clothes fail to hide.

I shake my head, disbelief mixing with irritation, as I grab my purse from the other side of the bed. "No way, just . . . no," I mutter. The room, with early morning light filtering through the cityscape, feels too grand for these moments. The tall ceilings, the expansive black California king bed, the tasteful décor—it's all a stark contrast to my typical dorm room escapades.

"Not what you were saying last night," he taunts with a smug grin, the kind that screams practiced routine. His expression, one I've seen a hundred times before, is almost laughable. Do lines like that actually work?

Did for you, Payson.

Yeah, thanks, brain. Like I need the reminder. I'm already pissed at myself. Who hooks up with someone they can't even stand?

I exhale sharply, my hand instinctively finding my hip. "Let's," I snap, cutting him off and motioning between us, "pretend this," I emphasize, "never happened." As I dress, I can feel his gaze trailing over me, triggering a rush of unwelcome flashbacks.

His touch.

His intensity.

His commands.

No, this shouldn't have happened.

Yet it did.

He stands, exuding a confidence that might attract others, but not me. Arrogance has never been my thing, even though my eyes trace his movements.

"I'd ask if you like what you see, but last night answered that," he quips, grabbing a pair of boxer briefs from his drawer. Relief sweeps over me as he covers up.

I dismiss his predictable remark. He approaches, his presence overwhelming. I should walk away, but that's not my style. I never shy away from a challenge.

Not even for this man, the one I despise with every fiber of my being.

Don't ask where the animosity between us started. Ever since I was little and spent time at the Sutton household, Luke had some distaste for me. It wasn't until our high school years it developed into something more palpable and hostile.

I've never really had a deep hatred for Luke; I've seen him be a genuine human being—kind to his family, loyal to his friends. However, when he's around women or experiences success, he transforms into an egomaniac.

He'd show off in front of his friends, throw insults my way, and act like he was the king of the world every time he scored a touchdown or got a girl to giggle at his jokes.

I remember one specific incident during my junior year of high school. Luke had just won a big game at NorthRidge University, and there was a celebratory party at the Sutton household. I was there with Milli, trying to blend into the background. Luke, flushed with victory and attention, sauntered over to me.

Having fun, Payson? he had asked, his voice oozing with

sarcasm. Before I could respond, he added, *Oh wait, you're probably just here because you have nothing better to do.*

The comment stung, a minor jab that landed hard. He was unaware that going to a party meant getting away from the toxic atmosphere at home.

Now, standing in his room, clad in my lacy, deep blue bra and underwear, the memories flood back. He's the same Luke —arrogant and insufferable. I remind myself why I can't stand him, even as I catch myself staring at his confident smirk.

A surge of confidence washes over me as the deep blue lace accentuates my summer tan, and the MagicLift bra works wonders for my figure. Standing just inches from him, our eyes meet, reigniting the intensity and raw emotions from the previous night.

A cold, hard knot tightens in my chest—*resentment.*

It burrows through my body, making my shoulders tense and my hands clench into fists.

As I let my fingers run over his chest, feeling the firmness and the faint sandy-blond hairs that match his head, I begrudgingly admit he might be a masterpiece of creation, despite my disdain for him. Pressing a bit too firmly, I'm torn between irritation at him and at myself for letting this happen. "I mean it. This didn't happen," I insist, hoping he gets the point. But his response is another infuriating smirk.

Anger bubbles up inside me, clenching my jaw. His arrogance is maddening, yet undeniably attractive, and that only fuels my frustration. My voice trembles slightly, but I hold my ground. "Do you understand me?" I demand, eyes locked on his, challenging him to deny my words.

He finally speaks, but it's not an apology or an acknowledgment—just a soft, mocking laugh that sets my nerves on edge.

"What an ass," I mutter under my breath, my thoughts a

chaotic whirlwind. "What the hell was I thinking?" A deep sense of regret settles in, knowing this night will be etched into my memory, an indelible mark I can't erase.

Desperate to escape the moment, I try to focus on something else, anything to distract from this pointless exchange. Just as I begin to step away, he catches my finger, pulling me back. My breath hitches, heart pounding, as his smirk morphs into a knowing smile.

Great, just what he needs—more ego fuel.

But before we can continue, a commotion outside the bedroom catches my attention.

What now? I crane my head, straining to catch any familiar sounds.

His eyes glint with amusement. He knows exactly who's outside. Typical.

I yank my finger free and rush to finish dressing, my movements hurried and frantic. Lingering here will only make things worse. Heading for the door, his casual warning stops me in my tracks. "I wouldn't do that if I were you," he says, leaning against his bed with infuriating ease.

Like I would listen to him. My mind flashes back to last night, and I curse under my breath. Whatever. I shake off his words and stride toward the door, my resolve hardening with each step.

But as I fling the door open, I'm met with another set of familiar blue eyes—my best friend's. She stands there, taking in the scene, her eyes wide with disbelief. Her gaze flicks from me to the disheveled bed behind me, and back again.

Behind her, her boyfriend, Miles, bumps into her, stumbling into the room. "Shit," he mutters, a grin spreading across his face as he pieces it all together. So that was the noise earlier—it wasn't just my head pounding; it was the walls reverberating with their escapades.

"Payson?" Milli finally speaks, her gaze shifting over my shoulder and narrowing. "Luke?"

My heart races as we both respond at once. "Yes," I squeak, my voice betraying my guilt with a high-pitched tone.

"Yes," Luke echoes, his voice seeping with casual indifference, as if this were just another morning.

I'm irked yet again. Luke Sutton, with his haughty attitude, always projecting the belief that he's superior to everyone else. But last night, it seems I passed his test.

Take that, asshole. My pulse quickens, a small, involuntary smile tugging at my lips before I quickly press them into a thin line.

Rein in that celebration, Payson.

Because right now, I have a more pressing issue at hand—explaining to my best friend I've just slept with her brother.

CHAPTER 2
PAYSON

"You know you don't have to stress about it, right?" Milli says calmly as we wait for our coffee at Scholar's Brew, a snug little coffee joint nestled in the core of NorthRidge University.

The café exudes warmth and comfort with its rustic wooden tables and chairs, each piece mismatched yet perfectly cohesive in the space. Soft, golden light filters through vintage lamps, casting a gentle glow that dances across the eclectic artwork adorning the walls. The bulletin boards, crowded with colorful flyers and event posters, add to the lively atmosphere.

The rich aroma of freshly ground coffee beans envelops us, a soothing balm to my frazzled nerves. It's a scent that brings back memories of Mocha Haven, my beloved hometown haunt. Though I rarely visit Mocha Haven now, Scholar's Brew has captured my heart since freshman year.

My gaze locks onto Milli. She stands out in her pink leotard and black shorts, her hair neatly twisted into a bun. The incongruity of her choice of footwear, a pair of well-worn

Converse, only adds to her distinct presence. She radiates a serene confidence, her calm demeanor an island amid the tempest of my emotions.

How does she stay so composed about all this? My mind is a whirlwind of anxiety, and I've been on edge for days. The act of packing for my first day back on campus was meant to anchor my thoughts and serve as a distraction. But it was no use; the turmoil inside me remained unchecked.

"I mean, sure, I was upset to find you walking out of his bedroom," she begins, her voice a mix of incredulity and hurt. "Especially since I thought you two hated each other. But, you know, enemies to lovers, it's such a good trope. The two main characters are bound to break at some point."

"More like liquid courage," I mutter under my breath, the bitterness of my words barely masked by the hum of the café.

"Plus, you know I'm not one to hold people back from doing what they want. What's the point? They're going to do it, anyway. Knowing my aversion to being told what to do with my life, I wouldn't do the same to you." She grabs a straw and raises a finger in the air, her expression turning serious. "But don't say I didn't warn you."

No need. I warn myself every freaking day.

Honestly, it's only been a few days since the so-called "incident" with Mr. No-Name. Everyone knows who he is, but saying his name out loud sends a surge of heat through my entire being, bringing back a flood of memories from that night.

I close my eyes for a split second and fill my lungs with air, trying to push those thoughts away. The scent of freshly brewed coffee beckons me, grounding me in the present. I need to focus: grab my coffee, meet with my advisor to discuss sophomore classes that start next week, and then head back to my dorm to review my upcoming resident assistant duties.

Honestly, I wasn't sure about being an RA, but I ended up loving it. Being an RA offers valuable experiences and skills for those pursuing a therapy degree. For instance:

Communication skills? Absolutely. I frequently engage in open communication, a crucial skill for therapy.

Conflict resolution? You bet. Handling roommate conflicts helps me develop skills transferable to therapy.

Empathy and understanding? Definitely. My background, coupled with working with diverse residents, enhances empathy—something vital for therapists.

Building community? Oh, for sure. As an RA, thriving in fostering communities translates into creating a supportive therapeutic environment.

Pursuing a major in therapy has been incredibly humbling, exciting, and well worth it. While I took general education classes like most freshmen during their first year of college, last spring I had a taste of psychology courses. Since then, I've been eagerly expecting my return to campus. Delving into the mind's complexities brings purpose. It offers a peaceful escape from the issues back home and the satisfaction of working toward something meaningful for my future.

Freedom.

Snatching my coffee, Milli continues her rant. I adore her, but she's been relentless about the situation, constantly asking if Luke and I have talked. I know she cares and wants to make sure I'm okay. And I am—besides the urge to kick myself a million times. I want to forget that night completely.

But seriously, when would I have the time to talk to him? He's an hour away.

Am I supposed to text him randomly, saying *Hey, do you fancy a rendezvous?*

Yeah, not happening. The sex was decent.

Lies, Payson. Lies.

Now and then, flashbacks buzz through my body, but I

squash them like annoying bugs. Milli treats it like a comedy show, but I saw her face when we walked out together—awkward. I just shrugged after she dropped my name, strutting out of the penthouse with a hint of pride. She's used to my walks of shame, so even though this one involved her brother—the guy I can't stand—I treated it no differently.

"Was he really that awful? I mean, he's my brother, but with the number of girls he's been with, you'd think they'd be lining up for more."

I spit out my coffee, nearly choking. She grabs her cup, and as we move to my usual seat, she lets out a small gasp before giggling. "Wait, don't tell me."

I raise a hand to stop her, cutting her off before she goes where I know she's heading. "Haven't you heard, curiosity killed the cat?"

She lifts her brows, as if to say *Your point?* and takes a sip of her matcha latte. Personally, I'm not a fan of those; I prefer my coffee black and strong, just like my personality.

"Apologies for the letdown, Mills, but no seconds coming my way," I remark, indulging in a sip of my coffee. The rich, bold flavor performs a dance on my taste buds. It's a dark roast, brewed to perfection, wrapping my senses in a comforting warmth. Despite the blazing mid-80s in late August, that doesn't deter me from getting my daily caffeine fix—the kind that jolts you into gear and powers your day, just what I need to face my advisor.

Or this conversation.

Milli raises an eyebrow, but I catch the smirk on her face before my attention shifts to observe some students on campus. Animated conversations fill the air as some huddle in small groups, while others immerse themselves in their textbooks. A few leisurely stroll by, taking in the vibrant atmosphere of the campus. It briefly transports me back to when I first arrived here last year.

NorthRidge University had always been a name I knew well, thanks to my mom's close ties with Dean Densen—they grew up together. My excellent high school grades caught her attention, and I secured a full-ride academic scholarship. I owe my attendance to my mom's connections; without them, attending this prestigious university would have been a distant dream. Otherwise, I would have ended up at a community college.

The idea of staying so close to home was a no-go. The chaos there made my body tense up just thinking about it— the shouting matches between my parents, the sound of breaking dishes, and the oppressive weight of unresolved tension that hung in the air. It felt like my muscles turned to stone, my stomach twisted into knots, and my heartbeat quickened every time I imagined staying behind, even if leaving for campus and seeing the sadness in my mother's eyes felt like a knife to the chest.

Just then, my phone pings with a message from her:

MOM

Good luck this semester, Pay Bay. Proud of you.

But her words carry an unspoken plea. She often suggests I take more online classes so we could spend more time together—her way of asking me to save her from everything happening at home with Dad.

"Anyway," Milli interjects, redirecting my focus to her. "I just never thought you and Luke would, you know," she says, casually waving her hand in the air.

"Have sex? Do the horizontal tango?" I say flatly, my voice devoid of any humor. Her eyes widen at my comment, and her cheeks take on a touch of pink.

Anger simmers beneath my already frazzled exterior, constricting my chest and causing my jaw to clench tight.

Why can't I move on? Why can't she? Move on, forget it, forget that man. That night held no significance for him. I was just another notch on his bedpost.

You'd think Milli, who loves romance books and is dating Miles Chasen, her childhood best friend and the former star quarterback at NRU, would have become accustomed to conversations like this. Last year, after Miles battled cancer and had a change of heart, he chose Milli and their love over the NFL, opting for a career in medicine. Can't blame the guy. The NFL, I mean, it's just not everyone's cup of tea. The crowds, the atmosphere—it all becomes a bit much for me.

Not the tune you were singing last weekend, Payson.

"Okay, not really the response I was hoping for," she remarks.

I shrug once more because it's the truth. Perhaps she needs a few more reminders to stop bombarding me with these pesky questions.

Don't do it, Payson. Just drop it.

"I mean, it's what went down. We had loads and loads of sex. I can still hear the low groans, him saying, 'Payson, god damn you are so—'"

Milli groans, reaching across the table to grab my hand. "All right, all right, no more questions, promise. Just tell me this isn't a recurring thing?"

My mouth gapes open for a heartbeat before my head tilts back. Laughter erupts from me, drawing the attention of a few nearby students, who soon join in with their own chuckles. "Yeah, uh, no, that ship has sailed."

More like that ship has permanently sunk, never to resurface.

Milli shrugs, her eyes flickering to me for a moment before she sips her drink. "Figured as much."

I gently nudge her leg with my shoe, savoring the light-hearted moment. Laughter from students fades into the campus rhythm. The tension that had knotted in my stomach unwinds, allowing a genuine smile to spread across my face.

Maybe I can finally get over all this . . . nonsense.

Just as I'm about to speak, a voice cuts through the surrounding chatter. "Yo, Payson."

I turn my head, and there he is, his expression undeniably replaying that memory from last year. Poor guy. If only he knew I wasn't interested at all. It was a one-time thing. I first saw him while doing RA duties, then again at an off-campus party, and, well, you get the picture. Only afterward did I realize he was a freshman on the football team and, to make it worse, Miles's mentee.

"Hey, Cam," Milli says, greeting him on my behalf.

I force a tight smile and take another sip of my drink, my gaze drifting back to the window. I let my mind wander, attempting to let those two handle the small talk.

God, Payson, why? Why must you find yourself in these situations?

My phone pings once again, and I take a deep breath, feeling a momentary relief. But when I see the message, my breath catches in my throat.

MOM

He's never going to stop.

My heart sinks, a familiar weight settling in my chest. The tentative hope I had for a fresh start this year shatters. My fingers tremble slightly as I read the message again, the words blurring. The noise around me fades, replaced by the rushing sound of blood in my ears. This year, it seems, won't be starting off as smoothly as I'd hoped.

CHAPTER 3
LUKE

Aliana's Enchanted Play Palace

Ever take a moment, wherever you are, and simply think, *Yeah, this is the dream?* At the moment, life is truly fucking amazing. I stand on a field I always dreamed of stepping on as I relive the words my dad once told me.

"Aim high, son. Even if you don't reach your goal, you'll still make your way to the NFL."

In the electrifying moment, my dad's words seem to echo around me like a personal anthem. The field stretches out before me, a canvas of freshly mowed grass, its green perfection accentuated by lines crisply painted, mapping out the gridiron battlefield. The aroma of football lingers in the air, a blend of anticipation and determination, permeating my very being.

Standing there, absorbing every detail, I feel my dad's encouragement transform into an invisible force propelling me forward. The coaches, brimming with passion and expertise, guide our practice with an intensity that vibrates through every drill. Their shared nuggets of wisdom weave through the air, shaping us for the season of challenges ahead.

My teammates burst with energy and skill, each play showcasing their grit and dedication.

As the field pulses with the symphony of movements, calls, and cheers, a profound realization washes over me. This is more than just another practice; it's a validation of my journey. My dad's unwavering belief in my dream isn't a distant echo, but a vibrant part of this moment. It's a vivid reminder that I'm on the right path, each step aligning with the grand narrative of my ambitions.

"Hey, Sutton, snap out of it! Save the daydreaming for when we're not all grinding our asses off through the Oklahoma Drill," Berry, an offensive player, commands with a fierce expression, intense eyes, and a stern voice. He means business; Berry Fisher doesn't have the luxury to goof off—he's a single dad, and time is a precious commodity for him. No room for messing around here.

"Got some big plans, Big Guy?"

He scrunches his nose beneath the helmet, and I almost burst into laughter. It's another Berry quirk—he despises being called "Big Guy." But let's be real, what else do you label a guy towering at six feet four inches and tipping the scales over three hundred pounds?

He gives a disapproving shake of his head, returning to his stance on the line of scrimmage behind our quarterback, Maddox King. He shakes his head, too, but I catch the slight upward tilt of his mouth. I'm not the only one who teases him, that's what makes our team unique. Joining a new team, connecting with fresh teammates—I thought it would be a challenge, different, you know? I figured adapting to a quarterback other than Miles Chasen, my childhood best bud, would be tough. As a tight end, understanding your quarterback is crucial for excellence. So, Maddox and I need to be one unit when the season kicks off, which has proven easier said than done.

During off-season training, things were rough. I was figuring out how he commanded the field—unfamiliar territory for me, but not for him. He's been here for three years. With time passing and June's mandatory minicamp approaching, things improved. We began learning more about each other. Preseason training camp, from late July into August, brought even more bonding. We'd grab a few drinks, play a round of golf on off days, or just chill at each other's places. And now? Yeah, we're best buds. I feel like I've hit the jackpot with my new teammates.

It felt like fate.

Living the fucking dream, man.

"Yeah, being Rapunzel," Berry grumbled.

"Wait, he has to dress up as a princess?" I try to stifle my laughter but fail miserably, turning away. He looms over me.

"Don't even. I don't have time for your antics."

"You got a braided wig and dress to make Princess A happy?" Percy calls out from across the field, his helmet barely concealing the smirk in his voice. Berry's eyes lock onto mine, and I quickly mime zipping my lips, trying to stifle the laughter bubbling up from the absurdity of dressing up after a grueling practice.

Percy continues, his tone light but knowing. "You know we love her, Big Guy. She's got us wrapped around her little finger."

I nod, a shared understanding passing between us. For a five-year-old, she wields an extraordinary power over us. Who could resist his daughter's charm? In just five months, she's captured my heart completely. I remember bringing her a donut every practice for the first month—just one of many ways she's effortlessly woven herself into our lives.

"But Daddy always says, 'Your body is like a castle. Take care of

it, okay? And getting a different donut is taking care of it.'" Then, she'd put her hand on her hip and let out a little huff, something that never bothered me or prompted further thought. However, when she did it this morning before practice, it had my mind racing back to this weekend at Club Revolve, one of my favorite places since moving to this part of Texas. I've hung out a few times with the guys, but last weekend marked the first time I let Milli, my little sister, come out with Miles when they both had some free time, on the condition that they stayed at my house afterward. He needed a break from his residency, and she needed an escape before immersing herself in her full-time schedule back at NorthRidge U. Little did I know she would bring Payson along.

The mere thought of it sends shivers down my spine, every nerve tingling with the vivid recollection of that unforgettable night. I fucking despise that it happened, yet something within me clings to the memory.

Her lips, impossibly soft, still haunt me. Each kiss feels branded into my mind, an unwanted keepsake I can't shake. Even now, the echo of her touch lingers, a constant reminder of my lapse and the unsettling pull she still has over me.

And I fucking hate it.

And those cheeky demands of hers.

"Just shut up and hurry, will ya?"

I swear, I've never had such a bossy woman in my bed. Milli's best friend, my arch-nemesis. Okay, not my top enemy, though; that dubious honor goes to someone else. Just thinking about him makes my chest tighten, as if cleat strings are cinching around my ribs.

Don't make head space for them, Luke.

I try to shake it off, rolling my head in slow circles to release the tension gripping my shoulders. But the relief is fleeting, slipping away almost instantly like an annoying bug I can't quite squash.

Payson, she's just another girl, another hookup, I remind myself, but it's useless. Her fiery personality and rebellious streak, the same traits that have gotten Milli into trouble before, gnaw at me. And it's not the kind of fire I like—it's the kind I hate. That night, after my first college game celebration, flashes in my mind, anger flaring up like I'm being doused in flames.

And let's not mention her obsession with guys.

Pot calling the kettle black, right, Luke?

Nope, there's a distinction. I don't go looking for women; they find me. And I don't stop until they're in my bed, completely satisfied.

"If anyone discloses information about Aliana's Enchanted Play Palace outside of our designated practices, I will actively pursue them," Berry warns, snapping me out of my thoughts.

Not like I wanted to keep thinking about her, anyway. Our first official game is next weekend, the first week of September. Win or lose, I'll make the night mine by getting lost in the next girl who throws herself at me, pushing aside all those thoughts of her.

It has to work. It will work. I can't stand that that night ever happened. It never should have gone that far. It was supposed to be some harmless shots, but it spiraled out of control.

I slam my fist into the side of my helmet, the pain a welcome distraction from the storm inside me. How could I have been so stupid? How did I allow myself to get involved with her? She has proven that she can't be trusted, especially when it comes to my sister. That night comes flashing back, and the anger surges, burning hot, all directed at me. I can't afford to lose focus. Not for her. Not for anyone.

"Aliana's Enchanted Play Palace? Berry, did you coin that name? It's cute, seriously. Love the big word, enchanting."

Percy's sarcasm drips from his tone, a huge grin plastered on his face.

What in the actual hell is happening? We went from chatting about the start of practice to jersey choices, then plans for drinks tonight, and now we're deep into Berry's princess-themed quality time with his daughter.

I mean, sure, weirder topics have come up. Even so, I mouth at Maddox for some clarity. He just gives me a disapproving look, leaving me more confused. In my peripheral vision, I spot Berry's five-year-old daughter, Aliana. Her strawberry hair catches the light, and her small, square leopard-print glasses sit perfectly on her petite face, strapped behind her ears to keep them in place. She kind of reminds me of Milli, ridiculously cute, making me smile despite myself.

For a moment, I can almost picture having my daughter one day. Most guys, I think, lean toward wanting a boy first, but not me. Nah, I'm all in for my little princess. That said, the thought quickly fades. Kids and a wife? Not in the cards for me soon.

One perk of being an NFL player is basking in the ladies' attention. They flock around me, their eyes filled with admiration, and yeah, I know how to work it to my advantage. At twenty-three, I have the world at my feet: a perfect penthouse, the best teammates, and I'm living the dream I've always craved. Nothing and no one will distract me from becoming the best damn tight end in the country.

I can already picture the headlines after the season: *Luke Sutton: Tight End Sensation, Rookie of the Year*

This journey is in its early stages, and I'm committed to making each moment count, showing that age should not limit one's pursuit of greatness. Attention, world, Luke is on the rise!

And you can be damn sure I am. Mark my words, nothing will hinder me this season.

CHAPTER 4
PAYSON

"Okay, so sorry, I'm here now. Apologies for the delay; it couldn't be helped," my advisor, known affectionately as the quirky cat lover, Josie, says. She swivels in her office chair like she's in a game of musical chairs before finally settling down. "I know you wanted to plan your class schedule ahead of time."

Yes, I wanted that. Ideally, a few days ago would've been perfect, but you know how it goes—beggars can't be choosers. Besides, when she called to inform me about a cat "incident" that led to her rushing to the pet emergency doctor, there was a feeling of relief. Sure, having our meeting as a distraction right after receiving that text from my mother would've been nice. But then again, a good run, handling RA duties, and watching *I Love Lucy* reruns work wonders for the mind and soul. And don't hate, it's a classic.

Sitcoms aren't usually my thing, and I'm hardly a romantic, but something about the slapstick humor in this show pulls me in. It brings back memories, sharp and vivid. Sundays were our special days—Dad and me. The smell of pancakes wafting through the house, Dad flipping them with a flourish while I set the table.

After breakfast, we'd stroll through the park, the air crisp and filled with the scent of leaves. His warm hand held mine tightly. Back home, the afternoons were a quiet symphony of rustling papers and muted conversations as Dad graded history papers and Mom prepped for the week. Their love was a comforting background hum.

Then at night, we'd watch *I Love Lucy* while Mom went to her book club, which was more about wine and gossip with her coworkers at the local winery. It's funny that Milli never knew her mom's Sunday nights mirrored our monthly margarita nights.

But now, watching the show alone, a pang of sorrow twists in my chest. Those Sundays feel like a lifetime ago. Their love, once a fortress, crumbled, leaving behind a void that the sitcom's laughter can only partially fill.

My advisor swiftly adjusts her cat-eye glasses, which are literally shaped like cat eyes and adorned with feline motifs. I nod in agreement as she types away rapidly on her computer. The next thing I know, I jump.

Dammit, not again.

Familiar chuckles escape her lips. I can't tell if she's just a true cat enthusiast or if she enjoys seeing people jump out of their seats. Either way, that confounded cat clock goes off every hour, its eyes popping out bug-eyed, startling me each time. Her office, filled with cat-themed items, creates a kitty haven that keeps me on edge.

Having her as my advisor during freshman year should have probably intimidated me, but truthfully, stepping into her office brought a wave of relief. It marks my escape from Stoneton and the beginning of a new journey.

Liberating. The taste was almost too sweet that first day on campus.

Away from the weight of everything back there, I could finally breathe without the constant struggle, the ever-present tension, or the anticipation of the next setback. It felt like a fresh start, and I was eager to dive back into college life and nothing was going to hinder me from reaching graduation.

"All right, Payson. Let me start by saying, your freshman year was impressive—no, it was downright amazing." As she expresses these words, she gazes at me with pride, and the warmth of that pride engulfs me.

It's an extraordinary feeling, my soul swelling with a sense of accomplishment. Considering the upheavals of transitioning from high school to college, coupled with changes in my home life, I had harbored uncertainties about how my freshman year would unfold. Yet, despite the challenges, Milli, Brooke (another best friend of mine from Stoneton), and I collectively decided at the beginning of our freshman year to embark on a journey of self-discovery, soaking in every experience and pursuing our goals without regrets. And so, I embraced that mindset, leading me to where I am now.

"GPA of four point oh."

Hell yeah, Payson.

I nod, a smile breaking across my face. A silent celebration.

"However," she says, and my chest tightens in the pregnant pause that follows. "It's not a significant issue." She glances my way once more, absentmindedly adjusting her glasses and waving her hand in the air. "In fact, it's genuinely fantastic news."

Ookay, cut to the chase.

"Considering you entered with so many prerequisites, you were technically—as you were aware—a sophomore starting as a freshman. So . . . " She pauses again. "It's entirely your decision, but according to your status, you're classified as a junior but returning as a sophomore. This gives you the chance to register for a clinical practicum. Typically, it's structured for junior year, with one session in the fall and another in the spring. However, a handful of students have had the privilege of selecting an ideal client to work with, allowing them to extend the experience for a whole year. Naturally, a licensed professional, in this case, Professor Kite, supervises this."

I arch an eyebrow, asking, "So, what exactly does that mean?" Shifting in my seat—or rather, the cat-themed chair (no kidding, it's an office chair with a white and pink cushion shaped like a cat paw that says *meow* underneath me).

She sighs, but there's a tinge of excitement in it. "It means you have the option to graduate earlier, a whole year ahead, actually."

All right, I'm intrigued.

"You have the opportunity to enroll in this program this year, alongside a few other courses, such as Abnormal Psychology and Developmental Psychology. Given your impressive grades from the past year, I'm confident you'll breeze through them. But the choice is yours—do you want to graduate a year early?"

Is that what I want?

Do I really want to graduate a year before my best friends?

What implications would that hold for my future?

While I ideally want to savor my college journey, I have more academic milestones ahead than most. After my bachelor's comes the pursuit of a master's degree, which takes another two to three years. Following that, there's the clinical experience/internship phase, lasting an additional one to two years, and finally, the hurdle of passing my licensing exam. Then comes the dream—a therapy office of my own, the Mighty Oak Counseling Center. I can already imagine it, causing me to unconsciously rub behind my shoulder, where a secret oak tree tattoo is located.

I have little to lose by moving a year ahead; if anything, it's a gain. Not because of finances, but because of the shift in mentality. Finally, a chance to escape the cycle that traps me, even in college. The thought of it sends a thrill through my entire being, my heart racing and my skin tingling with excitement. The possibility of my future feels closer than ever before, almost within reach.

But then, doubts creep in, swirling in my mind like a storm. My chest tightens, and my stomach knots with anxiety. What are the sacrifices? What does it mean to work with clients directly, under the supervision of a licensed professional? Where can I find clients and how long until I secure one? The questions churn around, leaving me both exhilarated and terrified.

But before I can think twice, I blurt out, "Count me in."

Her smile is dazzling, prompting one to form on my own lips. However, it quickly fades when she adds, "You'll need to choose who your client is."

How am I supposed to figure that out?

"Easy as pie, really. Promoting yourself will be a walk in the park," Milli declares, nestling into her seat across from Brooke at Amigo's Cantina & Grill. She hands us our second margaritas, and as I take the first sip, I realize this night is exactly what I needed. Not just the company of my friends, but the margarita's burst of citrusy goodness—a perfect blend of tequila, triple sec, and lime. The lively ambiance of Amigo's surrounds us, with animated conversations and rhythmic Latin beats creating an invigorating atmosphere.

Typically, our monthly margarita gatherings take place in the coziness of our dorm. Milli and I have been roommates since last year, which worked out perfectly. Brooke, loving her sorority sisters' company, repledged and now rooms at Sigma Alpha Omega. When Milli suggested in our group chat, the Stoneton Sisters, that we change venues and let someone else craft our drinks, I was all for it. While I love experimenting with margarita recipes, the idea of someone else handling it tonight brought a welcomed sense of comfort.

"Yeah, I guess you could always streak around campus yelling, 'I need a client, I need a client.'" My eyes narrow at Brooke's suggestion. She smiles and shrugs, taking another drink, pretending it's no big deal, but it is. Streaking is reserved for the bedroom only; high school homecoming pranks don't count.

"Now that's a lively idea," Milli remarks with a chuckle, sipping her own margarita.

Or not . . .

I roll my eyes, feeling the buzz of the margarita hitting me. For the first time today, I feel good.

Surveying my surroundings, I notice a few other students arriving; most of them are familiar faces because this place is a hidden gem. We stumbled upon it last year after shopping downtown for a gala we had to attend for the football team. It's our go-to spot, mostly because they don't check IDs, but we have our fake IDs just in case.

Back up, my friend. It's always necessary, regardless of the circumstances.

"No, I'm being genuinely serious, Pay," Milli asserts, her tone shifting to earnestness. Normally, I'd dismiss her quirky suggestions, but there's something in her voice this time—a fusion of seriousness and genuine care—that makes me pause. Her sincerity stirs a swirl of emotions within me, making it impossible to brush off her proposal without a second thought.

"You can utilize the student board in the library. Post there, stating that you're searching for a student who could benefit from therapy sessions. Clarify that you're not licensed, but you're still able to offer help," she suggests. Playfully nudging Brooke in the arm, she adds, "We know you've helped us more times than we can count, Pay."

It's reassuring to know she thinks that way about me, unlike a certain someone.

Payson, why are you even thinking about him?

Yeah, yeah, brain.

I know Milli has deep affection for me, and our friendship has grown into a sisterly bond. However, every time I enter the Sutton household or spend time with Milli and her family, I can sense their disapproval. Her mom's and Luke's icy stares and dismissive comments make it clear they aren't fond of me.

But why? I've done nothing wrong. If anything, I've helped Milli step out of her comfort zone. Is that a crime? They should be grateful for my help. Milli needed that extra push; their overprotectiveness was suffocating her.

"I can even lend you a hand," she offers. "I can design the flyers for the board. That's how I found out about the library needing tutor help. It really catches the students' attention."

She's right. All students must visit the library at some point. So, I'm sure they'll come across that flyer while walking in or out.

"Plus, look at you—who could say no to you?" Brooke adds.

I shrug, feeling a flicker of insecurity, but as the tangy margarita slides down my throat, it melts away, along with my doubts about tonight's bold outfit. The black leather jeans hug my legs, accentuating my curves just right. I run my fingers through my half-curled, half-bun hair—my signature look.

They keep discussing the idea, and I can feel myself warming up to their reasoning. It's not such a bad idea, especially since I have no other plans. Leaving my advisor's office in a panic, I was scrambling for ideas. The directive caught me off guard, and she insisted I find a client before the semester starts. That means I have this week to find someone I want to work with and who also wants to work with me, someone I can build a connection with. This process takes time; having cycled through therapists myself, I know finding the right fit doesn't happen overnight.

My phone pings, pulling me away from the conversation, and in an instant, the stress of the day floods back in, hitting me like a charging bull.

MOM

> Sweetie, how's it going? Classes start soon.
> Feeling excited? Maybe visit home before it
> gets hectic?

Uh-huh, yeah, Mom, I don't think so. I know she's subtly trying to rope me into helping with Dad. I'm not falling for it. I'm good. So good.

I exhale deeply and take another sip of my drink. My girls are watching me closely, their eyes peeking over the rims of their margarita glasses, clearly waiting for my response. Currently, I'd do anything to divert my attention from that recent text, even if it involves considering Milli's suggestion.

With a sigh, I finally relent. "All right, we can do it. On one condition."

They giggle like schoolgirls, their eyes sparkling with anticipation as they wait for me to spill more details. "Interviews are on the agenda," I announce with a resigned smile.

CHAPTER 5
LUKE

The sun dipped lower in the sky; it cast long, stretching shadows across Lone Star's football field. The stadium buzzed with energy, a palpable excitement in the air. On the sidelines, my heartbeat quickened with nerves and exhilaration, the reality of my first NFL game hitting me.

This place is colossal. Lights flicker on, transforming the expansive stadium into a dazzling display. The Lone Star Lions emblem dominates the scene, emblazoned on flags that flutter with pride and banners that scream for attention.

As the crowd floods in, the stands burst into a sea of vibrant blue and white jerseys. It's a party on the brink of eruption; fans cheer, kids wave foam fingers, and the smell of hot dogs and popcorn fills the air. The jumbotron comes to life, showcasing highlights that energize the crowd.

Coach Donovan's voice blasts through the speakers, doing his pregame speech. The playlist pulses with energy, the beat resonating throughout the stadium.

After the draft and endless months of grinding, the day has finally arrived. Clutching my helmet, I feel the weight of every drop of sweat, every sacrifice, and every ounce of determination it took to reach this point.

It's a surreal moment. As a kid, I'd sit in these very stands with my dad or watch him play, wide-eyed with awe during the season. At times, after exiting a game, I'd gaze at him and remark, *"Eventually, I'll be in that position."* My hands tremble slightly, a mix of disbelief and pride surging through me. No longer just another fan cheering for the Lions, I'm now the player they're cheering for.

Coach Donovan's whistle pierces the buzz, a sharp command that sends us charging onto the field. I jog out, the crowd's cheers mixing with my pounding heart. Adrenaline's on overdrive, and my vision catches the family crew on the sidelines—Milli, Mom, Dad—all here for my first game. They wouldn't miss it for the world.

"Let's fucking go!" Percy shouts, his voice raw with adrenaline as he smacks everyone's helmet, mine included. Maddox throws out orders, the O-line gets in gear, and I'm lining up at the scrimmage. The tension's thick. The ball snaps, and I'm off the line, dodging defenders like a pro. This is it—the big league, under the Lone Star banner. Time to show 'em what I've got.

I sprint down the field, the adrenaline still coursing through my body. The defenders try to close in, but I weave past them, every step bringing me closer to the touchdown area.

Hell yeah, take that, Tennessee Tigers.

The crowd's roar becomes a distant hum as my focus narrows on the goalpost.

Maddox shouts, "Fucking go, Sutton." The excitement and determination are clear in his voice and it only eggs me on. To do better.

The offensive line's blocking like a fortress, creating a

path for me to exploit. A split-second decision, a juke to the left, and I break free into open space.

The end zone is in sight.

Keep fucking going, Luke.

With every stride, the cheers swell, turning the stadium into a sea of encouragement. My heart hammers in my rib cage, my palms slick with sweat as I spot the ball arcing through the air, heading straight for me.

That's it, almost there.

The ball spins closer, my breath catches, my legs feel shaky, and I take a small step back, anticipation tightening every muscle.

Thud.

What in the fuck. The side hit from the linebacker sends a sharp, intense surge of pain through my muscles. My helmet flies off, and my head throbs with a jolt of discomfort. My vision blurs momentarily, and my ears ring from the impact. Every heartbeat amplifies the pain, making it throb even harder.

"Dude, seriously? Could you hit me any harder?" I retort, my voice edged with anger as I wince and try to steady myself.

He releases a low groan, his gaze narrowing before he mutters, "Don't get in my way, rookie, and we won't have problems," and then he darts back to the middle of the field, leaving me to take a moment to recover.

Oh, hell no. This guy thinks he can just brush off that hit like it's nothing? That he can take me out because he feels like it? *Not in my books, buddy.*

My jaw tightens, teeth grinding together as my fists ball up, nails digging into my gloved palms. A heat rises from my chest, creeping up my neck, causing my ears to burn. My thick skin usually shields me, but certain remarks burrow under it like thorns. Come on, we're playing football, right?

Collisions are part of the game. You maneuver around other players with skill and respect, something I know well.

But number twelve's self-satisfied smirk as he glances over his shoulder, the sheer arrogance in his eyes, sends a surge of fury through me. My hands itch to rip off his helmet and make him taste his own medicine.

Berry jogs over, extending his hand. I grab it, my grip vice-like, practically vibrating with rage. He grumbles, "Let it go, Sutton."

Percy slaps me on the ass before grabbing my helmet, pressing his guardian cap close to mine as he gives it a shake. "Stay sharp, tight end! We're in this together."

He shakes me, and the world pauses. My eyes wander to my family on the sidelines. Beyond them, I catch a glimpse of something—no, someone.

My sight narrows, straining to focus, but Percy's shake jolts me back, making me blink. The figure disappears, as if it never was. It must be from the hit. Pain radiates from the impact. I hear Milli scream my name, snapping me back to reality. I blink a few times, releasing a deep breath, trying to regain my focus.

"We are a team," Percy says, giving my helmet one last shake. I nod in agreement, his words resonating as he runs off. I tap my helmet a few times, muttering to myself, "Focus, Luke. This is about you, no one else."

The next play unfolds like a well-rehearsed machine. Maddox calls out signals, and the offensive line locks into position, forming a protective barrier. My muscles tense, every nerve on high alert. The sting from the previous hit sharpens my determination, my body coiled and ready to spring into action.

When the ball is snapped, a rush of energy propels me forward. My legs pump hard, muscles firing with renewed vigor as I dart through defenders. The crowd's cheers pulse in my ears, driving me onward. With each powerful stride, the end zone looms larger, a magnet pulling me closer.

Maddox releases a precise pass, and my vision zeros in on the spiraling ball. Adrenaline floods through my veins as I leap, muscles straining and fingertips reaching. Time seems to slow as I stretch my arms, feeling the rough texture of the pigskin against my fingertips. Defenders close in, their presence a looming shadow, but I clamp my fingers around the ball, trussing it against my chest.

Thud.

This time, it's me colliding with the end zone turf, but the impact is triumphant. The ground is solid beneath me, my body sinking into it with a victorious thump. The crowd erupts, their cheers crashing over me like a wave. My teammates swarm, their energy a whirlwind around me, celebrating the touchdown.

Adrenaline still coursing through me, I push myself up, a grin spreading across my face. "Fuck, yeah!"

Maddox slaps me on the back, his expression lit up with a grin. "That's the way, Sutton! You owned it!"

Berry's voice rings out, filled with excitement. "Hell yeah, Luke! That's how you do it!"

Percy, true to form, offers a hearty pat on the back. "Told you we're in this together, tight end!"

My heart pounds, muscles still thrumming with the thrill of the play, the sting of the previous hit now a distant memory.

As I turn to look at the jumbotron, my name and picture front and center, a grin spreads across my face. Pride swells within me, almost tangible. The emblem of the Lone Star Lions on my jersey gleaming under the stadium lights. The realization hits me—my first NFL touchdown.

Each step of the journey—practices, sacrifices, drive— converge here, in the end zone. My sight finds the family sidelines, where Milli is jumping up and down, her face radiant with pride. Mom clutches Dad's arm, his other one pumping the air as he tilts his Lions hat in my direction.

Atta boy. Like father, like son.

This is more than a touchdown; it's the culmination of dreams, a testament to teamwork, and a symbol of resilience. My muscles hum with adrenaline from the play. Slapping hands with teammates, their faces glow with exhilaration. This is just the start of my NFL journey.

And I can't wait to fucking see how much more I can give this season. Nothing is stopping me now.

"The best part of the NFL, right?" I mutter to Maddox, barely audible amid the club's booming bass.

My muscles relax against the plush leather of the VIP lounge, a shiver running down my spine as one of the blondes with short hair traces her nails lightly over my forearm. The other triggers a rush of tingling heat that spreads to my core. My heart races, not from the game but from the intoxicating mix of their touch and the electric atmosphere. Sure, I could get these women on my own, but being in the NFL brings certain perks. The VIP lounge is always populated with women expecting us, whether after a celebratory win or even a tough loss.

He just raises an eyebrow, taking a sip of his sour whiskey, phone in hand. His fingers flick across the screen, and I can see the concentration etched on his face as he's absorbed in his damn Kindle app.

"King, seriously? You're reading right now? In the middle of the club?" I lean in, the pounding bass vibrating through my chest, my disbelief clear in my expression.

King glances up, his eyes narrowing slightly as he meets my gaze. He takes another deliberate sip of his drink, the corners of his mouth twitching into a faint, unapologetic smile.

"Best way to celebrate," he murmurs.

I suppose everyone has their own methods for kicking back after a high-pressure situation. I noticed it during some of our preseason practices. A group of us, myself included, came here to revel in the attention and let loose, especially with the ladies. It's fascinating to observe how each teammate unwinds uniquely.

Maddox? Well, he's a bookworm. Whatever it is, not entirely sure, but that guy will whip out his Kindle app whenever he pleases. I'm not a fan of reading, but kudos to him for racking up those word counts.

Percy? He's a bit like me. He soaks up the attention from the ladies, maybe even more than I do. But here's the thing: Percy, without fail, calls his mom after every practice and now after every game. I mean, I check in with my parents sometimes, but it seems like Percy is on the phone with his mom all the time. After those calls, he's on the lookout for his next high, and currently, that involves drowning any sorrows he's got in alcohol and women.

Berry prefers to head home, especially with his daughter, and they celebrate however they like. I've heard from a few guys that they always go out for an ice cream date after a celebratory win. If I were a dad, which I'm not—far from it— I'd think that's a cute way to celebrate.

I'm comfortably sprawled in this chair in our VIP section, thanks to Maddox's connections with the club manager. The two bombshells beside me are smoking hot. One's hand slides boldly down, cupping me through my pants, while the other leans in, her breath warm and tantalizing against my skin as her lips trace a path along my jawline.

Indulgence has never felt so good.

"How's it going, P?" I ask Percy, and he just shoots me a smug grin of satisfaction. And honestly, who can blame him? The brunette in front of him is topless, eagerly waiting for him to give her a damn motorboat. Delicate fingers grip my chin, redirecting my attention forward. No one else in sight, just us, tucked away in the VIP corner away from the blinding club lights. Sometimes, security has to be choosy about who can join us. After all, we're famous, and everyone wants a piece of us.

And judging by the appearance of this new blonde—platinum, long wavy hair, those lengthy, lean legs, and that sun-kissed skin. God, she looks like—

Do not go there, Luke.

But it's clear she's interested. Her gaze has that look. The kind that says she wants me. Suddenly, my skin overheats, and my desire intensifies, my pulse quickening.

I want her.

Before I can fly off the seat of my pants, my phone vibrates. Knowing it might be Milli or my parents—the only ones I'll respond to right now—I quickly fish it out of my pocket. The blondes beside me scatter, their touch vanishing. As soon as my vision lands on the screen, my frame freezes, and a chill runs through me.

TROY

> Can't be letting players impede your victory.
> Benny never would have in his first NFL
> game.

The icy feeling in my chest ignites, spreading warmth that floods my face, sending a wave of heat around my neck. My hands shake, betraying my attempt at calm. Fuck. My jaw flexes so hard it aches, each breath slicing through the air like a blade. How fucking dare he. This is my night, my moment to celebrate my first NFL game. I don't need his jabs or constant reminders of what Benny would or wouldn't do.

You should be used to it by now, Luke.

Whatever. I refuse to let this text ruin a potentially good night. I close my phone, lifting my head to see the woman I noticed a second ago still standing there. She curls her pointer finger, signaling for me to get off the chair. There's no way I'm not doing what she wants. I know exactly what's in store once I leave this seat.

Her moans.

Her legs wrapped around me.

Her wet, dripping pussy.

I stand, my pulse quickening as the blonde scans the room, her head swiveling side to side, her eyes sharp and searching. A tremor of nervous energy vibrates through her until her stare connects with my own. In an instant, the tension melts away, replaced by a primal, hungry desire that sends a rush of heat through my body, making my cock throb like it does after a last-minute touchdown. She approaches, her breath hot and minty on my lips, making my chest pound.

"Follow me."

Who am I to refuse a woman? Particularly one who's so giving.

She clutches onto my Saint Laurent brown jacket—another perk of being a tight end in the NFL? The money, baby. Sure, I grew up in a wealthy family, with my dad making a name in the NFL, but our parents instilled a work ethic in us. Milli and I didn't have things handed to us on a silver platter. We had to prove our worth, work hard for what we wanted, and then literally present our case to our parents about why we deserved it.

One Christmas, I had to give my parents a full-blown presentation, detailing exactly what I wanted, the cost of each item, and how it would benefit my life. Did I achieve my desired outcome? Hell yeah, I did. My presentations were successful, and who could refuse their only son?

I'm one in a million, and the woman taking me from the VIP to the club seems to share that sentiment. We move through the hall, turn a few times, and unexpectedly end up in a dimly lit space that resembles a closet or storage area. My eyes scan the small area—it's not precisely my first choice for a quick fuck, but beggars can't be choosers.

My eyes become fixed on her profound blue irises, delving deeply into my soul, and for a moment, I'm transported back to last weekend. The way she made me feel, the intensity of her gaze with every thrust, intense growl, and when I came inside her—not once, but three times. Yes, the details linger, resurfacing at every opportunity.

I could claim to detest it, but truth be told, that night was scorching. The fervor, the anticipation, the lingering gazes, the forbidden touches—all of it collapsed the moment her ass was on my bed.

God, that heart-shaped ass, it fits my hands flawlessly.

And those curves . . .

And here's where we wrap up thinking about her, Luke.

Without hesitating, the woman literally throws herself at me. Her arms encircle my neck, and my hands find their way to her lower back as I lift her up. Her legs wind firmly around my midsection, her breath hitching. *I know, baby, my cock is one in a million and is craving to be inside that warm, sweet heat.*

I guide us closer to the light and accidentally bump into what appears to be an empty storage box. I gently set her down, and she removes her top, unveiling her breasts— double D's, damn. They're gorgeous, not tear-drop shaped like hers, and certainly not the color of baby pink.

Stay focused, Luke.

Still, they're delicious, fitting perfectly in the palm of my hand. I give them a strong squeeze, and she confesses, "I've been waiting for this moment."

Uh, okay? I mean, I've been waiting for a good time tonight too.

She unbuttons my jeans, and she drops her skirt, revealing some lacy, deep blue underwear.

I release a deep groan, wondering if this is the universe's way of dishing out karma, warning me I shouldn't be intimate with this woman. Because every single detail is triggering memories from last weekend.

Her hair, her eagerness, and even her underwear were nearly identical.

We hastily shed our bottoms. My shirt and jacket stay on, while she is naked as the day she was born. Her pussy is wet, and I don't waste any time on foreplay. One, because it's clear she is ready for me, and two, we're in a storage closet—whether or not it's locked, anyone could walk in.

She takes the condom from my fingertips, unwraps it, and slides it onto my cock, giving it a few pumps that draw a groan from me. I intertwine my fingers with hers, both of us gliding over my cock as she says, "Fuck me."

No need to ask me twice, baby.

With a swift motion, I lift her up, her legs instinctively wrapping around my waist. Our foreheads touch for a fleeting moment. As I move, an electric tingle spreads through my body, intensifying with each thrust. Her inner muscles contract around me, her wetness growing thicker, her moans echoing louder in the room.

My gaze meets hers, catching the glimmer of raw hunger in her eyes, the curve of satisfaction on her lips. The weight of the past events dissolves, leaving behind an intoxicating promise of a memorable night.

"What the fuck is going on?" My body tenses from a deep, stern male voice emanating from behind me. The abrupt interruption casts a shadow over the once-secluded moment, leaving an air of tension hanging in the storage space.

My initial instinct is to cover up, but if this guy is barging in on us, he might as well get a show. I continue with a few more thrusts, leaving the woman breathless. We're both on the brink of climaxing, and I'm no quitter.

I increase the pace. And the man behind us? The nerve. He grabs my shoulder, giving it a tighter squeeze than usual, and it's infuriating.

"You," thrust, "enjoying," thrust, "the," thrust, "show, man?" I deliver one last thrust, letting out a "Fuckkk," my attention solely on the woman in front of me. She's looking at the man standing behind me as if she's scared for her life.

Did this guy hurt her or something? I don't stand for violence, not one bit, unless it's absolutely necessary.

Before I can comprehend what the hell is going on, this woman is pushing away from me, and my cock instantly misses the warmth. It's clear a second round isn't happening by the way she's scrambling—grabbing her skirt, putting her top back on. In the dim light, I notice something sparkling on the floor.

Is that a fucking ring?

"I didn't come to watch a show," the guy growls, his tone rough and menacing. His palm clamps onto my other shoulder, and before I know it, I'm spun around. His grip is like a powerhouse, unyielding and mighty.

As I face him, my stomach clenches. His eyes blaze with fury, and his knuckles are bone white, trembling with barely contained rage. He's massive, towering over me like the Hulk, his presence even more intimidating than Berry's.

"I came to find my damn wife."

Out of nowhere, a powerful blow lands on my face. I stumble backward, slamming into the woman behind me. Pain sears through my jaw, radiating in sharp, jagged waves.

Instinctively, I touch my cheek, wincing at the tender, swollen skin. My fingers brush against my lower lip, now wet with blood. The dizziness sets in, making my surroundings blur and tilt.

What the hell is happening? This is his wife? I just had sex with a married woman.

A smirk tugs at my bruised lips. Well, I guess I can check that off my bucket list.

The guy moves closer to me, his feet closing in, but blondie tries to get between us, pleading, "Don't harm him, bear."

Bear? What the fuck? That's his name?

"He was lonely, it was nothing. He wanted attention."

Wait, I was the one lonely and craved attention?

Is this woman out of her mind? She's aware I didn't feel lonely or need attention. She had a clear agenda she aimed to fulfill, and now that she has been exposed, she is trying to pin the blame on me.

Oh, no way. My teammates have given me and the other newcomers a heads-up about women like her. They'd caution us, saying, *"Keep an eye out for those who try to manipulate situations. They've been through it all before and know the game."*

I'm not letting her twist the narrative. My thoughts race, keen and clear. She won't turn me into a pawn in her game. The frustration boils inside me—how can a person be so deceitful and then try to pin the blame on others? Memories of prior betrayals flash through my mind, and my resolve hardens.

I attempt to navigate around both of them, but the tight storage closet makes it challenging. However, this issue needs to be addressed here; if we move, the paparazzi will have a field day. Unfortunately, I don't get to choose my next move, as the Hulk decides for me. He grabs me by my shirt, leading us outside the room and into the empty hall. This time, it's not empty. A crowd has gathered, eagerly expecting a spectacle, and I know they're about to get one.

And, as you're well aware, I'm not the type to give up. I mean, seriously, who lets their spouse out of their sight, especially in a club? My future partner would either be by my side or we'd have a great time together. I clearly know how to please a woman, unlike this guy.

Just as my back hits the wall, the woman pleads, begging her husband to stop his threats. My focus locks onto his arrogant smile, and without a second thought, my fist crashes into his face. Blow after blow, I don't stop until my teammates find me, pulling me away. Flashing cameras capture our exit from the club.

Percy tilts his head. "Man, I know you enjoy the spotlight, but a married woman?"

I shrug. "She was asking for it." I move toward my Range Rover, Percy taking the passenger seat, and Maddox in the back. "It's not like I knew; if I did, I would have put a stop to it."

Would you have, Luke?

I dismiss those thoughts, a wistful smirk crossing my face, as I hear Maddox grumble, "Can't wait for morning."

And I don't grasp what he means until I wake up the next morning to an incoming call from the coach.

CHAPTER 6
LUKE

Coach practically bellows, "Luke, care to clarify what was going through your mind last night?" He paces back and forth, each step heavy with anger, his words sharp and laced with choice cuss words and grunts. My eyes flicker to Nat, our director of communications, standing in the corner with her arms crossed, her presence a silent testament to the need for damage control.

Her lips become taut, and that all-too-familiar gaze in her eye? It mirrors the one she wore at the end of the off-season, transitioning seamlessly into preseason. She repeatedly warned us about the importance of maintaining a consistent appearance and avoiding negative media encounters.

Shit.

My phone pings, and I check the incoming text. Opening the group thread, I grunt in frustration.

This morning, Coach called and told me to be in his office within half an hour. I had to rush through my routine—quick shower, fast breakfast. Normally, my mornings involve breakfast, team meetings, recovery sessions with Steph, our trainer, and film review to spot areas for improvement. The day usually ends with strength and conditioning and a light workout with Coach Menschen, who trains our group of four tight ends, including me.

Despite that, it's obvious that it's not happening, so I take a quick look at my phone again, and a new message pops up.

Lone Star Legends

MADDOX

Any updates?

PERCY

Was Coach difficult with you?

Especially Nat. Stay alert around that woman. She seems determined to make things difficult for everyone. It's like causing trouble is her mission.

BIG GUY

Well, it's her job. Dealing with trouble is her purpose here.

PERCY

Nobody asked for your input, Berry.

MADDOX

Exactly, Berry.

PERCY

Best of luck, my dude. You're gonna need it. I'll be there in spirit.

MADDOX

What Percy said.

BIG GUY

I told you not to go out . . . but you didn't listen.

I shake my head dismissively. Team support? Yeah, where's that at?

Additionally, shouldn't they have a meeting dedicated to them? The usual postgame session involves reviewing the last game, discussing mistakes, and addressing areas for improvement with the entire team. Exactly what I should be doing.

Coach's anger is apparent from the constant vibrating and pinging of my phone. Instead of responding to my teammates, I pause and brace myself for the impending conversation. Can it really be that bad? It was an honest mistake. No ring on her finger—how could I have known? Besides, I don't have a neon sign on my forehead proclaiming *Caution: I hit.*

Then again, you can never predict with our coach. Once, he ejected Benjamin, our kicker, and Beau, our linebacker, from a preseason game over a minor fight about who stole whose *Madden NFL* game. Sometimes, teammates play the game in our stadium's lounge area to relax after practice.

At the precise moment the door to Coach's office opens, he lets out a heavy sigh, and I make eye contact with a pair of baby blues that I know well. A little boy rushes in, heading straight for his grandpa. This scenario has occurred repeatedly, especially in the off-season when Walker would partake in our "training" sessions. Considering Coach's fondness for him, perhaps this won't lead to a stern lecture. Maybe Walker can charm him a bit before things take a serious turn?

Wishful thinking, Luke.

"I apologize, Dad. He was searching for you, and I mentioned you were in a crucial meeting." Rayne, Coach's daughter, walks in. She swiftly looks into my eyes and gives me a smile filled with apologies.

Wonderful, even she understands the impending storm. Am I the sole person teetering on the edge, anticipating the inevitable? Just waiting for him to rip the Band-Aid off brutally.

Regardless, I can handle it.

With a wide smile, Coach embraces Walker in a heartfelt hug. The love in his eyes when he sees his daughter or her son reminds me of my parents and their affection for me. Growing up in a loving household is a rare privilege, and Mills and I were fortunate enough to experience it. Even if my parents occasionally irritate me, I recognize their good intentions.

"Don't worry, Ray. I haven't seen you guys for a couple of weeks, so I can make an exception." He glances back at Walker, gently placing him on the ground, and adds, "How about we catch up when I finish my important meeting?" His gaze lingers on me for a moment.

Yeah, I get it. I know this meeting is important, but can we move on? This is holding me back from getting ready for our home game this weekend.

My fingers drum impatiently on the armrest. I replay last weekend's game in my mind, the cheers of the crowd, the rush of delivering an outstanding performance. I need that feeling again, back-to-back, for our loyal fans, of course.

"Afterward, let's go to the field. Fill me in on your Disney World trip," Coach suggests. Walker grins, and in that fleeting moment, I see the memories of his adventure dancing in his eyes, bringing a smile to my face.

Rayne goes to fetch Walker, shooting me another look—this one more like a silent wish of good luck. I understand the weight of it, especially coming from her. If there's anyone who truly understands her father, it's her. I offer her a reassuring smile, then turn to face Coach. He releases a deep sigh and utters the one word that makes me reconsider if I can handle whatever is about to come my way.

"Therapy."

"Therapy?" The word hangs in the air, my mind struggling to grasp its meaning. Therapy? For me? What for? There's nothing wrong with me. Coach must see the confusion etched across my face.

"Yes, Sutton, therapy. This isn't college ball; your actions have consequences. And I know therapy is a good route for rookies." The way he spits out *rookie* makes me roll my eyes.

"Come on, Coach, is that really necessary?"

Turning his head, he shakes it while peering out the small window in his office, which overlooks our field. Once our eyes lock again, he breathes a sigh. "It's that or you sit the next game."

Anger starts to bubble up, causing my stomach to clench. What the fuck.

"We're not talking about college ball," he emphasizes, his voice growing stronger. "Your age is not a valid excuse for your actions. You're twenty-three, Luke. You're in pro ball now. Whatever you do reflects on this team. Reflects on me."

My urge is to lash out and scream, clarifying that this is a misunderstanding. Nevertheless, that comment lingers in my mind, a familiar itch beneath my skin. It's as if I can hear that voice again, the relentless pressure.

"You're not doing it hard enough. Get it right."

"Show more effort. Benny would have."

"Benny would kill for this chance, you know?"

I'm snapped back to reality by the sound of a cleared throat. My coach's eyes fixate on mine, intense and unrelenting. Tightness grips my chest, my heartbeat races. It wasn't that bad, was it? Sure, my family's name splashes across the tabloids thanks to Dad's fame, but one mistake and now therapy? My throat constricts. Therapy is for people with actual issues, not me.

"And I won't stand to watch some rookie, no matter how

good you are, come onto my field and show you can't keep your actions off the field in check."

Each word delivers a blow to the gut. My throat tightens as I swallow the punishment. His final words drive me to the brink. "Find a therapist. This week. I want to see confirmation." He waves his hand, dismissing me like a bothersome fly.

I clench my fists tightly at my sides, my knuckles turning white. I reluctantly force a tight smile, my jaw tensed, and give a brief nod. Without another word, I turn on my heel, shoulders rigid, and march out of the office, my steps heavy with the weight of his ultimatum.

"What did Coach say?" Maddox asks while standing above the weight rack, supporting Percy during his bench press.

"Bet your ass took a beating? Yeah?" Percy remarks, dropping his barbell back on the rack.

"You wouldn't be in this mess if you just found a good book, or you know, maybe played Aliana's Enchanted Play Palace with Big Guy," Maddox suggests.

"You wish you were that cool to play with us," Berry retorts, letting out a grunt, sweat glistening on his forehead as he pumps out another bench press. The weight slams down, and he stands, approaching me, towering over with his massive size. "Told you not to go out. Literally nothing good comes of it."

"Therapy won't be that bad, plus maybe you'll find a hot therapist," Percy suggests, as if it's a brilliant idea.

I roll my eyes. Seriously? Who says that? And how did he know therapy was my punishment? He moved his eyebrows in a wiggling motion. And that tells me everything. He either overheard or cast a spell on Nat with his charm.

"God, could you imagine getting to have sex with your therapist once a week? I would totally sign up for therapy—once a week of free sex, and with someone you know? Friends with benefits, but with a therapist. Let's call it 'Benefits with Therapist,'" Percy says with a smug grin on his face.

"Dude, just no," Maddox says, shaking his head as he adds more weight to his own rack.

I'm fed up with this; it wasn't my fault. Besides, every other teammate of mine goes out or celebrates. So why can't I go out? Why can't I celebrate and let loose? What's the harm in that? Just because I got into one fight means I need therapy?

Not one fight, Luke.

Two fights—first during the off-season, due to an obnoxious fan's claim. Yet, here I am, first string for a tight end. His comments proved meaningless, but they still infuriated me enough to spark a bar brawl. It made the news, but Nat ensured only a handful, including my parents, knew about it. And let's not even discuss their opinions. Dad advised me to straighten out my thinking. My mother fussed over me, checking for scratches and bruises, saying, *"Oh, sweetie, be careful. Don't let them get to you."*

Yeah, sure. You try telling yourself that, Mom. You try ignoring the impact of significant individuals on your life, whether they scream at you in person or online. Good luck.

Still, I don't need therapy. Far from it. I just had a confrontation with a guy also known as the damn Hulk. It's all in the past, right? My self-persuasion falters as my phone vibrates, snapping me back to reality.

It's a screenshot from my family group chat.

Lone Star Rookie Tight End Luke Sutton Faces

Controversy: Allegations of Involvement
with Married Woman Raise Questions about
Player's Career.

I gulp anxiously, feeling a knot tighten in my stomach.

MOM

Luke, would you like to explain this?

DAD

Son, after your first game? I know we had
our talk, but it didn't include this sort of
attention.

What did Coach D say? Anything?
Punishment?

MOM

Knowing Donovan, he probably will have a
lot to say. Am I right, Luke?

I clutch the phone tightly, feeling my hands shake uncontrollably. What in the fuck is happening? People can't actually believe this, can they? It's only half the story. Had the paparazzi dug deeper, they would've known she made advances toward me. She found me, dragged me into that closet.

My jaw clenches and my breathing speeds up. Beneath the surface, anger stews, muscles coiled like a tightly wound spring. I feel like an untamed beast, ready to be unleashed without caring about the repercussions.

With trembling fingers, I send a text to my parents and Milli, desperate to make it all disappear like a horrible nightmare.

LUKE

Therapy.

I stash my phone away and give my teammates a disapproving shake of my head. My hand strikes a nearby bench as I utter, "Fuck off." Pointing to them in a line, I add, "None of you had to go through this, so you can't just say, 'It won't be that bad.'"

I head toward the door leading to our locker rooms, thinking, *Screw this*. Before I exit the weight room, I hastily declare, "I'm too busy for this. It's my first NFL season, and that's where my focus needs to be. Not in some silly office discussing my feelings." With that, I leave them because, at this point, talking to my teammates about this "agreement" I have with Coach seems entirely pointless.

Only a good run can improve this situation. Not therapy. I cherish running; it clears my head, allowing me to get lost in another world, much like reading does for Maddox, or Aliana for Berry, and perhaps women for Percy?

Before lacing up my shoes for an afternoon run in the warm late summer weather, I receive a text. Contemplating whether to respond immediately, I decide it might be important and open it.

BSE!! (BEST SISTER EVER)

Luke, hey, I wanted to text you separately from our group chat. I think I might have the perfect "therapist" for you. Call me later.

CHAPTER 7
PAYSON

All I want is to help others struggling under life's burdens. I yearn to demonstrate to them that life holds more than their present hardships and that therapy is not about achieving perfection but about discovering contentment. In a society obsessed with perfect facades, I desperately want to help people realize that it's okay to aim simply for a grateful heart and the strength to face another day.

But today, the last devastating blow came from yet another unsuccessful therapy interview, extinguishing my hopes of making a difference.

Milli and Brooke had helped me set up my interview space in the library adorned with leather couches, beanbags, and various comfort items, such as weighted blankets and pillows. I have to credit Mrs. Raker, the librarian, for approving it. I have the best two, most supportive, friends ever to exist.

Nonetheless, just like finding a good therapist, it was a challenge to find the right client for a task spanning several months. Just yesterday, a girl approached me for bedroom tips; a college virgin seeking self-exploration. Afterward, I needed a break and was excited to return with a fresh mindset today.

Today I enjoyed Malcolm's company, whose parents insisted on him getting therapy to improve his social skills. And while I recognize the significance of his campus social life, it didn't appear necessary to have weekly sessions for the upcoming months. These sessions were meant to be a chance for me to really test myself as a therapist, tackling a more intricate client challenge.

By the time I'm ready to email my professor to drop the class, Milli walks into our dorm room. Seeing her brings me a wave of relief. "I've been waiting for you," I say.

She tosses her bag onto her side of the room, where it lands perfectly in her egg-shaped chair that sits neatly in the corner. The chair's glossy white shell with the plush, colorful cushions inside creates a cozy nook that's distinctly Milli. My cluttered desk, already filled with textbooks and notes, contrasts with Milli's meticulously organized corner. Fairy lights above my bed cast a warm glow, softening the harsh overhead lighting. A tapestry with intricate patterns hangs behind my bed, adding whimsy to the plain walls. A plush rug with vibrant colors marks the shared space between our areas, serving as the heart of the room where we unwind after long days. As much as I adored our snug little freshman dorm, this year's setup is way better. Being an RA has its perks, such as a bigger room that offers more space to breathe and move.

Milli starts her usual evening wind down, and I'm half watching her remove her makeup at our bathroom vanity. "Why? Did something happen?" she asks, turning to face me with her face all sudsy, hair pulled back by a headband, and eyes narrowing. "Hold up. Did you snag a decent client?" She claps, sending suds everywhere, and we both break into laughter.

I pivot in my desk chair, shaking my head in frustration. I groan as I reply, "Nope, no, and nah. Really appreciate the effort and the idea, Mills, but no offense, it totally sucked ass."

Her mouth drops open, but she immediately continues scrubbing her face. After drying off, she grabs a book from her shelf—likely another romance novel—and settles into her beloved egg-shaped chair. I have to admit, that chair is pure comfort. Moving to my bed, I sit and cross my legs, enjoying the fluffy pillows and warm blankets I've carefully arranged.

"Perhaps the idea didn't suck?" she ponders, raising an eyebrow. I'm curious about her intentions because, let's face it, it was definitely a terrible idea.

With a slight tilt of her head, as if she can read my thoughts, she lifts a finger. "I get it. This week's been rough on you. But I was actually waiting for your last 'client' mishap to wrap up before mentioning this."

I furrow my brow, skepticism and unease mingling within me. "What are you talking about? Mention what?" My hands grow clammy, and my heart races. Seriously, I can't handle another out-there suggestion right now. I'm nearly at the point of quitting on the whole search for a good client. Maybe it's not meant to happen for me.

Hang in there, Payson, my inner voice urges, just when I need it the most.

As Milli sets her phone aside—she's been texting, likely Miles—she tells me, "He'll text you soon." She raises a finger, preempting my protests. "Now, before you shoot down the idea, think about yourself, your future. You need this class to graduate. This setup could be a win-win. So, please, no getting mad at me, okay?"

Later that night, when Milli is already fast asleep, her

breathing soft and even, my phone buzzes. I pick it up, my eyes squinting at the message from an unknown number, and finally realize what she was referring to.

UNKNOWN NUMBER

So are we doing this or what?

Doing what? I'm clueless.

PAYSON

Uh, might be a wrong number here? I'm not "doing" anything.

UNKNOWN NUMBER

Okay, playing hard to get, I see. Typical. I know you've been wanting this, Pennington. We are proceeding with this, whether you like it or not.

Pennington.
Only one person calls me that.
Luke.
My blood boils instantly. My heartbeat pounds in my ears, my body temperature shooting through the roof. This can't be real. If it's going where I think, I'm not on board. Has Milli completely lost her mind?

UNKNOWN NUMBER

Begging's not my style. Women do that, usually on their knees. But if you're up for this, I'm willing to make it work.

Willing to work with me?
Women groveling at his feet?
His words fade, and suddenly I'm back to that weekend with him.
His masculine scent of cologne, aftershave, and a hint of menthol envelops me. I can almost feel his lips sweep against

mine, each kiss sparking through my bones. My core burns, an intense, unquenchable flame. The sounds he made—curses, hisses, groans—fill my ears, a symphony resonating deep within me.

The grip of memories leaves me with a twisted stomach and tingling skin. The sudden ringing of my phone snaps me out of my thoughts and back into the present. Damn it, it slips right off my bed and clatters to the floor. The noise makes Milli shift in her sleep. Serves her right, considering she thought this setup would be a good idea.

Far from it, actually.

With a slight movement, I lean over the bed and stretch out my arm to grab the phone. *Unknown* flashes on the screen. I briefly hesitate, weighing my options before deciding to answer.

Come on, Payson, it's just Luke, not the devil himself.

But that's exactly it—it's Luke. He's like the devil disguised as a human.

Inhaling deeply, I click Accept and his voice, so familiar, fills my ears. He utters the name *Pennington.* That voice I despise, yet it sends a heated, tense shiver through me.

I cough to gather myself, attempting to regain control. "What do you want, Luke?" I snap, frustration bubbling beneath the surface.

I can almost visualize him wearing one of those maddeningly self-satisfied smiles. Or maybe he's holding back his real thoughts. But when has Luke ever hesitated to speak his mind with me? We're brutally honest, almost to a fault. That's why we clash so often—saying things neither of us wants to hear but needs to. Well, that and the fact that he's a complete, degrading asshole.

He utters a single word: "You." My pulse quickens. That word shouldn't sound so tantalizing, so irresistibly seductive. However, my body goes against me as I sense heat collecting in my core. I yank the covers over me, as if they could somehow shield me from his intoxicating effect.

This. Should. NOT. Be. Happening. He's never affected me like this before. If anything, he's always repulsed me.

"Don't have all day here, Pennington." The way he says my name has me clenching my fists under the covers.

"Sutton, can you elaborate, or is it too difficult for you?"

"We both know nothing is too hard for me," he snaps, his words sharp enough to sting.

I can't help but roll my eyes, feeling irritated inside. Suddenly, his voice becomes unexpectedly gentle, catching me off guard.

"I'm not certain if Milli brought it up, but I require a—uh —" he falters.

I jump in and say, "Therapist?" Milli might have been vague, but a quick dive into Google and my trusty research skills painted the full, sordid picture.

What a pig . . . Who engages with a married woman?

Luke, that's who.

He lets out a forced chuckle, the sound empty and tense. "Yeah, that."

That.

He acts as if therapy is beneath him, as if he's too good for it.

News flash, buddy, everyone can use a bit of therapy. It's called growth.

"It's not like I really need it or anything, but Coach insists," he mutters, his bravado crumbling.

"Plenty of people benefit from therapy, in tremendous ways," I retort sharply, unable to hide my frustration. "It's something you could definitely use yourself."

He lets out a grunt, as if I've just slapped him. Good. Maybe that will help dissipate all this frustration and the overwhelming feelings coursing through my body from just one phone conversation.

Put up your shields, Payson, I mentally urge myself.

Without a doubt, it's about to become a mantra.

"You need me, Pennington."

A scoff escapes me, morphing into a dry chuckle. "More like you need me; I don't need you."

"So you're telling me you don't need to pass Practicum into Clinical Psychology?"

Damn it, Milli spilled everything. She's definitely going to pay for that.

Irritation floods me like a crashing wave.

"Pennington, just admit you need me," he repeats.

"You admit you need me," I shoot back.

He sighs as if I am wasting his time. *More like you're wasting mine, buddy.* A pause lingers in the air. "Honestly, I'm not even sure why I'm wasting my time with you."

Excuse me? Didn't he call me? Isn't he the one desperately seeking my help?

Then, my brain, that damn thing, reminds me of the one thing I'm constantly trying not to think about.

He's practically my last hope.

He's my one-way ticket to freedom right now. And that thought alone has me . . .

"Fine. Let's meet. I need to see if you would be a suitable client anyway," I blurt out.

His dismissive chuckle and condescending attitude make all my sensations vanish, leaving me feeling indifferent. This is another reason I can't stand Luke—he carries himself as if he can do no wrong. Now that Mr. Perfect has found himself in trouble, who's he turning to?

Me. That's who.

"Really, Pennington? You want to go there? Drop the

drama. I know you enjoy it, but come on. We both know I'm the perfect client," he states matter-of-factly.

I tighten my grip on the phone as my heart rate increases. The room seems to shrink around me as I swallow hard, pushing back a surge of irritation. I can almost visualize his smug grin from the other side. "We'll see soon enough, won't we?" My voice sounds more fragile than I mean it to be.

We hang up with no goodbyes or see-you-laters, just a terse agreement to meet at his penthouse after his home game on Sunday. I place my phone on the nightstand and rub my temples, trying to ease the headache forming there. He even has the audacity to ask if I want to come watch him in action. I've seen him in "action" in more ways than one, and I have no intention of revisiting that—*ever*.

CHAPTER 8
PAYSON

MOM

Pay, why haven't you responded to my texts? Please call me.

Perfect timing, a message from Mom right before another issue.

Luke.

It's only been five days since we last spoke on the phone, but I've already sent multiple texts to confirm our plans for today. Since his penthouse is an hour away from campus, I need to know if it'll be worth it.

Just to be clear, this isn't about Luke's value. This is my ticket to graduation and freedom from the guilt that suffocates me every time I think about home.

I repeatedly knock on the door of Luke's penthouse, feeling like I've done it a hundred times. Despite my initial reluctance, we agreed to meet at this place that holds haunting memories. However, Luke presented interesting reasons for choosing his penthouse, which reluctantly persuaded me.

My dorm? Milli's constant presence eliminates any privacy.

A restaurant, maybe? Initially, it didn't seem like a bad idea. Nevertheless, he mentioned his coach's suggestion of staying low key until the situation stabilizes. His words, *People like me,* couldn't go unnoticed by me. Despite his annoying behavior, I had to admit he was right. A therapeutic session in such a bustling setting? Unthinkable.

We were left with only one choice: his self-proclaimed "Humble Abode"—essentially, the place he brings any woman he meets.

You were one of those women, Payson . . .

I mutter, my shame growing, "Yeah, I know." Every time I think about it, I want to dig a hole so deep that I could bury myself along with the memory forever.

As I knock again, my phone vibrates with a new message.

MOM

> I can't keep up with the Sunday Socials with my colleagues. Work is getting messy, and questions are being asked.

The words make my heartbeat thud heavily, and a cold sweat breaks out on my forehead. My hands shake as I try to hold onto the phone. My vision becomes blurry with stinging tears. I feel the air thickening around me, making it a struggle to breathe, my breaths coming in fast and shallow.

Take a deep breath, Payson.

For a moment, I squeeze my eyelids shut and rest my head against the door. Inhale, exhale. I continue this rhythm for a couple of minutes until the tension subsides.

Instead of getting tangled in a lengthy text exchange, I decided a phone call would be more effective. Maybe I could offer her some comfort, but also myself, something I've become all too accustomed to. Last year, when I started college, Mom had silently shouldered the burdens of our past. It was only after midterms and our first break that I fully realized the seriousness of our situation.

Dad wasn't getting any better; in fact, he was slipping further. And the burden that I constantly felt? It intensified, making me physically ill. I'd end up throwing up, then making up stories about food poisoning when my best friends asked.

On occasion, Mom would step out of the house to escape overwhelming situations. During those moments, I would patiently wait for Dad to relax before sitting with him, engaging in conversation about anything and everything to bring him comfort. It seemed like once Mom noticed how I could influence Dad, she started leaning on me more, using it to her advantage instead of pushing him back into a support group. And now, I'm pretty sure she's trying to pull me back into the mix, to help her out.

Before I get the chance to call her, my phone rings with her number. With Luke showing no signs of opening his door soon, I decide to answer.

What's he up to, anyway? Is he even in there? Did he forget about our session? Or worse, is he off celebrating with someone else? The idea of that makes anger gnaw at my insides. He better not be with some random chick, leaving me behind.

They barely scraped through against the Razorbacks, winning by just a field goal. As I drove over, I listened to the game on the radio. Sure, watching Luke play isn't my thing, but as his "therapist," I need to be prepared for the mood he'll be in for our session.

I turn, presenting my back to the imposing door of his apartment—or penthouse, depending on your perspective.

Sliding down the door, my gaze sweeps the hall, noting the stark absence of other doors. Classic Luke—he probably insisted on having the entire floor to himself. I remember Milli mentioning his move: how he fussily dictated his demands, unyielding in his desires, unwilling to accept a single "No."

Typical Luke behavior; I wouldn't expect anything less from His Highness.

An entire floor for just him? Check.

Six thousand square feet of solitary grandeur? Absolutely.

Several bedrooms? Check.

But four bathrooms? Who needs so many just for oneself?

Milli's words reverberate in my mind. *It's Luke, Pay. He always goes for the best. And don't forget the constant stream of guests he entertains.* That thought makes me cringe slightly, a stark reminder that I, too, am merely one of those "guests."

My phone's ring startles me, making me aware that I missed my mom's initial call. "Shit." Quickly, I redial, taking a deep breath to steady myself.

You can do this, Payson. Put those shields up.

While this mantra was originally directed toward the man who owns this penthouse, it appears equally applicable when dealing with my mom. I love her dearly, but she has a way of making me drown in guilt with my dad. Abuse marred her own childhood, yet her advice often feels misplaced. She would recount, *GG left your grandpa after enduring so much.* But when I questioned why she hadn't left Dad, her eyes would fill with tears. *"Because he's worth fighting for. We have known each other since we were kids. You'll understand someday, Pay, when you find someone special."*

I'm not exactly sure what she means by "someone special," considering I'm nowhere close to seeking such a person—there's too much happening in my life to consider being tied down. Additionally, there's always that lingering question: What if the man I choose ends up being like my father? My dad was normal, loving, even funny and outgoing, until he wasn't.

After hesitating, I finally pressed the Answer button with a heavy sigh.

"Hi, Mom," I say, trying to muster some enthusiasm.

"Hi, sweetie!" she replies, her tone full of warmth and cheerfulness. It reminds me of how Milli's mom sounds on their calls—something that used to bug me, but with my mom, it feels oddly comforting. At least, until it doesn't.

"I haven't heard from you in two weeks. That's not like you," she says, her worry seeping through the phone.

Regret hits me like a wave, and I close my eyes, feeling its weight settle in my chest. I knew she'd bring it up, but being an RA, juggling classes, and hunting for a potential client, sometimes messages slip my mind.

"My apologies, Mom," I say, my voice becoming gentler. "I have been overwhelmed with stuff. New year, new heap of responsibilities, you know?"

"You're such a busy bee," she responds, her words carrying a subtle sadness. Then she switches gears, her voice brightening again. "Anyway, do you think you can make it home next weekend?" I can sense her anticipation as she holds her breath, waiting for my reply.

I utter, "Sure, Mom," and the relief in her tone is evident.

"Oh, yay, Pay. Your dad's going to be over the moon to see you!"

But I know it's really more for her. She sees me as her lifeline, even if it's just for a few hours.

No matter how hard I try, her voice, filled with pleading, sadness, and guilt, weakens my resolve. I owe them so much. They moved mountains to get me into NorthRidge U. If spending a few hours at home next weekend is what it takes, then I guess that's what I'm doing.

"It will be nice to see you guys," I say, even though it's barely been a month since our last encounter—not that I'd mention that.

As our conversation unfolds, she updates me on the uneventful happenings in her life. Her work is steady, and she mentions skipping a few social club meetings without explaining why. But I know the real talk will come in person, where she'll make sure I understand the challenges she faces with Dad while I'm away. The sense of responsibility weighs me down, a burden she never texts about. Last year, her messages were always about Dad: *He needs you. He misses you.* Never about her own needs or missing me.

While she speaks, I tighten my grip on the phone, my jaw clenched. Her cheerful voice intensifies the knot inside me. She's struggling to stay positive, but each cheerful word serves as a reminder of her hidden emotions. A lump forms in my throat, and I bite my lip, willing myself not to cry. I want to scream, to ask why it's always about Dad. My heart aches with the unsaid words, the silent plea for honesty that hangs between us.

With another heavy sigh, I bring our conversation to a halt. It's been twenty minutes, and I'm not just mentally drained from a long Sunday of RA duties and prepping for the upcoming week, but physically too—my ass is aching from sitting on this hard floor. For all the luxury of this penthouse, you'd think they'd have more comfortable floors.

"Mom, I'll see you next weekend, okay? I need to get going."

Her response, a simple "Oh," cuts through me like a blade. Here comes the guilt, that unwelcome visitor. "Okay, sweetie. I love you. See you soon. Stay safe." Her voice trembles, and I can almost see her forcing a smile, trying to hide the disappointment.

My heart tightens. "I always do, Mom. Love you too." With that, I hang up.

Leaning against Luke's door, almost an hour has trickled by—twenty minutes waiting on Luke and twenty minutes on the phone with my mom—and I'm left here wondering if he's even home.

He asked me to meet him here, didn't he? So why the hell is nothing happening? Getting up, the anger that was momentarily subdued while talking to Mom resurfaces, now blazing like a wildfire. The last thing I need is to deal with someone else's issues, especially when they're already eating into my time.

Suppressing the need to yell, I tightly grip my hands into fists. If Luke doesn't show up soon, I might just explode.

But why am I even this upset? Why does it hurt that he didn't need me as I believed? The disappointment tears at me, leaving me hollow and betrayed.

Resting my forehead against the door, I closed my eyes briefly. If, by some slim chance, he's here and ignores me, so help me God.

"Maybe he was just busy," Milli throws in the next morning.

Yeah, okay. Or not.

I get where she's coming from, standing up for her brother and all. If I had a sibling, maybe I'd get it. But nope. So, feeling sorry for him? Hard pass, especially after he blew off my time and gas. That was a solid two-hour drive, plus the wait for him to open the door. We're talking three precious hours I could've spent relaxing with *I Love Lucy* or hitting the pavement for a run.

But nope, there I was, trudging home late, the echo of my

final, unanswered knock still ringing in my ears. With every step, I felt the painful sting of rejection. I called him twice—straight to voice mail both times. I texted him, my fingers trembling, ending with a definitive *We're done*. This whole thing felt doomed from the start. Now, not only am I client-less, but I also have to break it to Josie that the practicum has to wait until next year.

The bitterness swirls in my mouth, a harsh reminder of the consequences of not finishing a year earlier.

Here come more guilt trips.

More phone calls and texts, pleading for my help. I struggle to swallow as the lump in my throat burns with the realization.

Goodbye, freedom.

Should've seen it coming, Payson.

Yeah, a lesson learned. I glance at Milli, who's slipping into her dance gear, probably prepping for her morning practice. I arch an eyebrow. "Busy, huh? Really, Mills?" I roll my eyes as I turn back to gather my books for today's only class.

I'm pretty grateful for an advisor who lets me pick my schedule. Makes my Mondays and Fridays chill with just one class each. I start and end the week on an easy note.

With a nonchalant attitude, she casually throws her dance bag over her shoulder, but there's a slight tone of resignation in her voice. "I mean, he didn't even bother to text back. He always finds time to text after games—preseason or not. Even when he's swamped, he checks in with our family group chat," she says, releasing a long sigh. "Don't write him off just yet, Pay. He can be difficult sometimes."

I lift one eyebrow in surprise. "Sometimes?" Her laughter echoes and sparks a laugh from me too. It's a welcome shift that lifts the heaviness and frustration from last night and this morning.

Nothing irks me more than plans falling apart, especially

when I'm powerless to steer them. Last night shouldn't have hit me so hard—it's his life, his choices. Lack of control over the outcome, not managing it my way, truly angered me. Being stood up is nothing new; I can handle that. But ditching me for someone else or a celebration without telling me is unacceptable.

What an ass. What was I thinking, believing this could work?

Milli and I step out of our dorm and are greeted by a refreshing, gentle breeze that instantly lifts my spirits, making me smile.

At least the weather is on my side today.

"Yeah, not so sure, Mills," I admit. "Plus, I still need to meet with Josie and I've got class with Professor Kite soon, and she's bound to ask how things are going. I'll have to admit that nothing's progressing and I feel utterly out of control."

Milli takes a moment, contemplating, and I interject, with a touch of disgust in my tone. "I suppose I hold some authority—I can put an end to this ludicrous arrangement with Luke."

She stops me, and I can almost predict her next words. "Please, Pay, just call him later. Let your emotions settle first." Even though it kills me to agree, I nod, knowing she's right. It's something my therapist constantly reminds me.

"And what should I tell Professor Kite?"

Milli thinks for a moment, then suggests, "Tell her you have a client, which technically you do."

"I had a client," I correct her, but she dismissively waves it off.

"Just say you're meeting later this week, which you will."

Reluctantly, I go along with it. In class, I assure Professor Kite about my client meeting. Even as I speak, a gnawing unease churns in my stomach. Later, I wait for Luke's call, a text, any sign of his so-called "busyness." But as the hours slip into another day, my patience wears thin. I resolve to tell Josie I'm dropping the class. She tells me it is okay and that I always have next year.

But, gosh, it's gut-wrenching—I despise quitting. The thought of having the chance to graduate early, finally escaping my troubles at home, only to let it slip through my fingers, makes me feel sick to my stomach. My hands tremble as I try to hold back the nausea. What choice do I have when it's clear Luke doesn't need me as much? The doubt and disappointment twist inside me like a knife.

When he finally calls the next night, his voice sounds sincere, but I know better. I cut him off with three bitter words: "Save it, Luke." Then I hang up, my heart pounding.

Despite Milli's advice to wait it out, and despite Luke's barrage of texts and voice mails filled with apologies and excuses, my decision is firm. He claims he was genuinely busy, caught up in something important, but to me, it all rings hollow.

He didn't need *this*. He didn't need *me*.

CHAPTER 9
LUKE

"Just so you're aware, there's a possibility things could go wrong," Milli's voice crackles over the phone.

I shut my locker in the stadium's locker room, getting geared up for practice.

I hear her warning replaying in my thoughts, yet there is no alternative. This has to work. Coach emphasized that point very clearly earlier. *"Sutton, your ass is on the line. Make it happen. And don't think I can't tell when you're lying straight through your teeth,"* he had said, his eyes narrowing as he mimicked the *I'm watching you* gesture. That's what drove me to dial Milli reluctantly, even though asking for Payson's help is the least desired thing.

Let's remember, we're talking about Payson Pennington here.

I shouldn't be thinking about her as anything more than my little sister's best friend, someone I can barely tolerate. Especially in the aftermath of that particular night. Letting go should have been easy, just one night, but it uncovered past pain. Thinking about it always leads to frustration, tightening my chest like a defensive end's tackle. What made her act so irresponsibly?

I clamp my jaw so hard it hurts. My breath quickens, a mixture of anger and inexplicable attraction simmering just beneath the surface. My mind is suddenly flooded with the raw and vivid memory of that night, leaving me feeling nauseous.

As if I needed more reasons to be frustrated. I was hesitant to have her as my therapist because I didn't want her prying into my personal matters, trying to "fix" me.

Let's be clear, I don't need fixing.

Taking a seat on the team's bench, I let out a sigh. "Mills, what other choice do I have?"

There's a pause, and then she states, "You should know that you really upset her."

Upset her? Seriously? I only skipped a single session. Percy was the one who forced me to go to that new dive bar after the game, so it's not my fault. For starters, I'd never been there before, so I was curious. And second, we fucking won. I wanted to celebrate somewhere low key to avoid the press—Nat's instructions—especially after the chaos of our last celebration. So, I got carried away. Then, reality hit me with a flood of angry texts from Payson and Milli. Even Brooke, Milli's friend who I barely talk to, sent me a message.

Pausing, I say, "It wasn't intentional."

You didn't say that on Sunday night, a voice in my head reminds me.

Paying no attention to it, I carry on and declare, "Nevertheless, I need this as much as she does. She likes her coffee black, right?"

I sense Milli softening. Only a bit more to finalize everything. "Yeah, extra bold."

Under my breath, I mutter, "Just like her damn personality."

"Luke," Milli's stern tone breaks in, "I won't let you hurt her. She's got enough to deal with without added stress from you."

Don't we all have our own battles to fight? Still, I can't stop myself from wondering what Payson's dealing with. Is it really that bad? Sophomore year wasn't exactly a trial for me—it was parties and women all the way.

I release a heavy breath. Talking to Milli feels endless, but it's only been twenty minutes. She'd ignored my first couple of calls, understandable since I ghosted our group chat after Sunday.

But I apologized the next day, claiming I was busy—which wasn't untrue.

Just busy with a woman.

I thought the family would've moved past my radio silence, but Milli held onto it until I sent an SOS text. She was mad about the trick, but I needed her advice. I knew Payson's coffee habits from watching her at Scholar's Brew last year. She never refused a coffee I paid for.

"Milli," I moan, annoyed by the whole ordeal. It would have been easier with a random therapist—just show up, vent, leave, and inform Coach I fulfilled my role. Yet, here I am, entangled in this chaos, striving to concentrate on my first NFL season.

Milli lets out a sigh, and I hear a faint whimper in the background. "Good God, are you with Miles? Can you two not do this now?" My frustration boils over, and I can't help but snap, "Just send me the location, please."

A few minutes later, she texts me with a final message: *Don't mess up, Luke.*

I may mess things up, but she, the drama queen, is more prone to messing up.

"Sutton, how's that hot therapist of yours? Seen the goods yet?" Percy calls out from across the locker room.

My head jerks around as I retort, "Seriously, man?" His smug grin only widens.

Fucker . . .

Grabbing my helmet, I mutter the words, "It's going fine," as if saying it again might make it true.

Maddox's shoulder clap serves as a welcome distraction. "Don't mind Percy. You know how he is." His half smile is reassuring. Remember, we're here for you in any way."

Grabbing his own helmet, he says, "And hey, if you need someone to tag along for moral support at your session, just say the word."

Percy, walking casually toward us, adds with a suggestive look, "I wouldn't be opposed to meeting that therapist."

Over my dead body. The idea of Percy anywhere near Payson is a hard no. My dislike for her aside, I won't let him near her.

Maddox uses a subtle head shake to steer the conversation in a different direction. "If you want to celebrate after a win, how about some good books?"

I nod, grasping his point. We players usually handle postgame highs in the usual ways: women, sex, alcohol, sometimes all at once. It's a potent mix. But books? Definitely not my first choice. Milli's always trying to get me to read her romance novels, but I've never been interested. Romance is unnecessary in my life. Romance, who? Yeah, I'm actively avoiding it.

"Or maybe you could join me and Aliana for ice cream sometime?" Berry murmurs quietly.

My brows shoot up in surprise, mirroring Percy's reaction as he blurts out, "Whoa, Big Guy, did you just invite him to your sacred daddy-daughter post-win ritual?"

Berry casually shrugs, minimizing the importance. But coming from him, it's a big deal. His time with his daughter is precious, a fact he often emphasizes. His invitation truly moves me, reminding me of the connection I've established with this team, my newfound family.

I give him an appreciative pat on the back. "Berry, I would be honored to join you guys." Aliana is a sweetheart, Berry's a great guy, and who doesn't love ice cream? It could be the ideal ending to a triumphant game.

He brushes off my hand, heading toward the field. "The invite stands, as long as you don't fuck up practice or the game this week with your attitude."

A confident smirk graces my face. My attitude isn't that bad, right?

An hour into practice, Beau stirs things up. He replays that one painful moment from our first game—the one where my helmet flew off and pain shot through my body. Unlike in the game, where I brushed it off, this time I reacted impulsively by delivering a punch to his jaw. It hurt, but he was asking for it. Who provokes a teammate like that? Who considers it humorous to bring up this memory? Film reviews serve that purpose, not pranks from teammates.

And it doesn't end there. After practice in the showers, Beau corners me. "Grow some thick skin, you'll need it for this team," he sneers, his eyes drilling into mine. Anger flares up, transforming swiftly into a stronger force: determination. Every insult and slight is now my motivation to excel in therapy sessions with Payson. I can't afford any slipups if I want to clinch the Offensive Rookie of the Year title.

My father's shadow looms large, his own rookie year in the NFL an ever-present benchmark. However, it's Troy's text that keeps repeating in my mind like a mantra. *"Benny would have received the Rookie of the Year award. Don't let him down. Don't let me down."* The weight of those words presses on my shoulders, but instead of crushing me, it steels my resolve. I won't fail them. None of them—not my father, not Troy, and definitely not me.

CHAPTER 10
PAYSON

When Milli suggested meeting at Mocha Haven Café, my first instinct was to decline. Scholar's Brew was just a stone's throw from our dorm—much more convenient, especially after the chaotic start to my morning. A minor crisis involving my RA duties had erupted early on a Sunday, thanks to a crazy roommate conflict. As a freshman, I'd been relieved not to deal with such issues, but now, this wasn't my first time handling a situation that frayed my nerves. To make matters worse, the nagging reminder that I still hadn't secured a client kept gnawing at me, casting a dark shadow over my mood. The looming prospect of not graduating early feels similar to a tightening noose. I didn't initially feel desperate for graduation to come sooner rather than later, but once the idea was presented, I couldn't ignore it.

And right now? Graduating a year early is my lifeline—an encouraging vow of getting away. It is the difference between freedom and entrapment, between a future full of possibilities and a present weighed down by stagnation. So when I heard those three words from Milli's lips—*Mocha Haven Café*

—I paused, my heart and mind at war. It seemed like a minor indulgence, a brief escape from the chaos. A moment of peace, a personal treat.

The café, situated a mere twenty minutes from Stoneton, has always been a sanctuary for me. Its overhead string lights, plush leather couches, eclectic chairs, and corner bookshelves create a unique ambiance that is comforting. The symbolic oak tree mural behind the barista station has a personal meaning for me, reflected by the tattoo I absent-mindedly trace on my skin.

Startled by the door chime, I look up.

Standing there is not just an ordinary customer, but him —with sandy-blond hair and mesmerizing hazel eyes that could consume you.

Images of him with hooded eyes flicker in my thoughts. *"God, you know just how to ride me," he murmured, eyes locked on mine from below. An approving slap landed on my ass, his focus transitioning to my breasts—small, but enough for him. He caressed and pinched my nipples, each touch affirming his desire.*

"Don't lose your focus, Payson," I silently repeat, even as his smirk makes my cheeks burn.

He moves to order his coffee, and I freeze, realizing I haven't placed my order yet. It was odd, considering how often I used to visit Mocha Haven. It had always felt like a second home, with a staff like Mave knowing me well enough to expect my order.

My stomach churns with nerves and unease as Luke gets closer. Every interaction with him is filled with tension, each look a page of unease. Without even giving him a chance to settle, I blurt out the word "You."

With the grace of a ballerina, he twirls while sporting a sly smirk. It transforms into a show-stopping smile, causing my stomach to flutter with butterflies—no, mosquitoes, each one intent on tormenting me.

"The one and only," he declares with a wink, then eases himself onto the expansive leather couch opposite me. To anyone else, he might appear somewhat dwarfed by the leather couch, but not in my eyes. He seems to fill the space effortlessly, exuding a presence that's both irritating and undeniably attractive.

"What are you doing here?" I snap, my voice sharp like a snapping turtle's bite. Frustrated, I reprimand myself for allowing that thought to enter my brain.

He's not attractive. He's an egotistical jerk who stood you up, probably for some bimbo.

Right as he's about to reply, his name is called out by Chrissa, the barista. He signals with a finger in a *one moment* gesture, and it frustrates me more than it probably should. A plain *be right back* would have sufficed, no need for the theatrics.

While he goes to pick up his order, I can't help but notice how his worn-out denim jeans hug his ass. My mind is flooded with memories of that night—the touch of his muscles, the intensity of our encounters.

Handing me my coffee, he utters a smug grin that's impossible to miss. I grip it a little harder than normal. That comment? Unnecessary, but typical of him.

A combination of confusion and slight irritation fills me as I peer at the coffee he passed to me. How did he possibly know what my favorite is? Sure, black coffee isn't a tough guess, but still. I shake my head, taking a sip, hoping the caffeine will inject some clarity into this bewildering situation. From my perspective, it was going to be a lot of nothing. Not after the mess he'd made.

"I know I fucked up, and I'm sorry for that," he admits, his gaze finding mine. A momentary sparkle in his eyes softens and disappears quickly.

Did he mean that apology?

Taking another drink of my coffee, I allow its soothing sensation to fortify me as I prepare to speak my mind. I meet Luke's unwavering eye contact as I assertively state, "We're done. Before it even started."

He narrows his eyes, but I couldn't care less about his reaction. He samples a bit from his drink—some green smoothie that looks unappetizing. I mean, peas and green beans are one thing, but spinach and chunks of avocado? No thanks. And seriously, who orders a smoothie at Mocha Haven Café, of all places? It felt like an insult to them. Just another reason to hate Luke Sutton.

After setting down his smoothie, he briefly glances out the window. It's a beautiful day, the kind I spent running. To avoid the heat and humidity, I prefer early mornings or late nights until the weather cools. It's the perfect way to break up my days.

"Okay, I deserved that," he says, and I give him a skeptical look. His low chuckle echoes, sending a strangely irritating yet enjoyable tingle down my spine, forcing me to stand taller and appear unaffectedly confident.

I watch his fingers move through his hair, admiring how effortlessly he achieves that tousled look. Regardless of my emotions regarding him, I cannot deny his allure. That night comes to mind again, when my hands . . .

"Pennington, we can make this happen," he declares out of nowhere, snapping me back to the present moment. The way he stresses my surname irritates me, as if that alone could persuade me.

"It will not work," I counter firmly.

"Yes, it will," he insists.

A sigh of annoyance escapes me. This is a complete waste of my time. I've been down this road before with him, and I'm not keen on repeating it. Against my own advice, I still find myself asking, "Can you give me one reason why it should?"

I catch a glimpse of desire in his hazel eyes as he looks at me. His gaze roams across my body, staying in certain places for too long, causing goose bumps to give me away.

Curse him and my deceitful body. Does he believe he can make me reveal all my concealed emotions and expose my hidden truths? Yeah, I think not, even if it feels that way.

"We need each other," he states simply.

"Not enough," I snap, rolling my eyes. "You've tried that line before."

He mimics my eye roll with exaggerated annoyance.

Such a drama queen.

With a suggestive gesture toward his body, he asks, "What do we need to do to make this happen?" As much as my body aches for all the things that body offers, my mind remains steadfast.

"No," I state emphatically, my tone infused with irritation. My anger and hurt build up, ready to erupt at any moment. But before he can respond, I cut to the question that's been haunting me. "Why were you unable to attend our session last Sunday?"

He shifts his eyes toward the window, his nose scrunching up—a telltale sign of his nervousness.

Nervous tic, noted.

His eyes find mine once more. "Like I mentioned, I had other things to do," he says, attempting to sound casual.

Yeah, too occupied wasting my time.

"Mind elaborating?"

His refusal to meet my gaze only heightens my irritation.

"This is exactly why I was hesitant about this whole arrangement," I say, my words cutting through the tension like a blade. His head snaps up, his lips forming a tight, angry line as I continue. "Therapy requires extensive communication," I emphasize, motioning between us, "and a substantial level of trust."

He stares at me intensely, biting his bottom lip so hard that I half expect to see blood. Eventually, he blurts out, "I was with Percy at a bar."

A bar? That's his excuse?

"Okayyy," I say, dragging out the word.

Shifting uncomfortably, he hesitates. "Time slipped away from us."

I leisurely sip my coffee, relishing the heat that fills my body as I battle the temptation to react aggressively. The audacity of this arrogant, inconsiderate man. Abandoning me outside his penthouse after a lengthy car ride? Unbelievable.

"Just to clarify, you think spending time at the bar was more important than our scheduled session?" I ask, my voice cold.

His face contorts with rage as his stare becomes more penetrating. "It's not what you think," he counters, his vocal cords quivering with barely restrained anger.

"Then how is it?" I challenge, my voice rising with indignation. "From where I'm sitting, it seems like you're showing me that my time doesn't matter. That you'd rather be at a bar than getting the help you supposedly need from a therapist. That you can't even—"

"I wasn't at the bar the whole evening," he sharply interjects, his frustration matching mine. "I had a few drinks with Percy, but then fans arrived and suddenly it was 1 am and I was handling an angry crowd."

With an exasperated sigh, I roll my eyes, audibly murmuring, "And I wonder why."

Does he really expect sympathy from me now? Not a shot. His constant excuses only serve to increase my irritation.

"Just to clarify," I utter, carefully placing my coffee down and intertwining my fingers. The room is tense, the air thick with unspoken resentments. "You won your game against the Razorbacks," I continue, watching his every move. His nod comes across as an insult. "Then you and Percy hit the bar around eight because the game ended at three?" He nods again, but his eyes narrow as if he's already tired of my questions.

"You had a few drinks," I state, my voice full of contempt. Annoyance flashes in his stare as he nods once more. "And got your ego boosted by some fans," I add, emphasizing *ego* just to see his reaction. His eyes draw in further, a clear sign I've struck a nerve. "And then what? You left with these 'loyal fans'?" His gaze shifts to the window, evading my eyes, and he nods reluctantly.

I exhale. "Let me guess, those loyal fans were women?" At my words, his head jerks up, his jaw clenching tightly. His expression a mask of barely contained fury, his cheekbones stand out in stark relief. The palpable animosity between us accentuates his fury, highlighting his defined cheekbones. Under different circumstances, I might have admired his looks—those infuriatingly perfect cheekbones, not to mention the dimple on his . . .

Unfortunately, the only person I see is someone I can barely stand.

With gritted teeth, he finally confesses, "There were women there, happy?"

My laughter is bitter and scornful. Happy? Hardly, but nothing surprises me with Luke.

"Really? Am I supposed to be happy that you spent the night at a bar, getting cozy with some washed-up NFL wife wannabes? I thought your career was more important to you. The career you've supposedly dedicated your life to?" I sneer.

His eyes become thin slits and his expression grows darker. "Screw you, Pennington. My career is important. I've worked my ass off to get where I am today." A deep crimson blush spreads across his face, and I can feel my own rage igniting.

How did I think this would work? We can't even have one conversation without wanting to attack each other. As I'm about to wrap up this toxic exchange, he unexpectedly throws me a curveball.

"Interview me."

I almost choke on my coffee, causing some to spill down my lip. I brush it off, experiencing a sudden wave of warmth as his gaze follows it.

"Interview you?" I echo, incredulous.

He looks away briefly, then meets my gaze with a penetrating expression, leaving no doubt about how serious he is.

I bristle at the thought of Milli sharing so much with him, but I'm also taken aback that he went through the trouble of finding out about my favorite coffee shop. Yet, the irritation overpowers the surprise.

"Interview me," he repeats. "I'll answer questions you have. If you decide I'm a client you can work with, we schedule our sessions. If not," he sighs, running his fingers through his hair in a gesture that's almost vulnerable, "well, then I guess I'll have to figure something else out."

A glimmer of pity sparks within me, a minuscule, almost imperceptible feeling for him. I understand the anguish in his voice. Something deep within urges me to set aside my reservations about working with him, yet the idea makes my skin crawl. Therapy is a bitter pill for anyone to swallow, let alone someone in his high-profile position. Being an acclaimed NFL tight end, finding a therapist who won't sell your secrets to the tabloids must be a nightmare.

I sigh heavily, my words burdened with resignation. "Okay, Sutton, impress me," I say, maintaining a poker face while he grins smugly.

The notebook I brought, initially meant for homework after my meeting with Milli, now seems like a godsend. The plan is long gone, but at least it's present for this session.

While grabbing my notebook, I catch Luke exchanging a glance with Mave, who's busy clearing a nearby table. He's wearing that infuriating, arrogant grin—the kind that likely makes women swoon over him. He nods at her, and I cringe inwardly. "Does that really work on women?" I can't help but ask, my tone dripping with sarcasm.

He responds with a satisfied tone, glancing at me over his smoothie. "You tell me."

I roll my eyes, muttering with barely concealed irritation, "In the words of Benjamin Franklin, 'He that can have patience can have what he will.' So, I'm trying to channel my inner patience right now." Luke's gaze flickers over me briefly, his expression unreadable, but he remains silent. With a sigh, I slip on my cheetah-print reading glasses.

Luke's eyes hold a flicker of surprise as he continues to look at me. "You wear glasses?"

I steal a quick glance at him before refocusing on my notebook, trying to find a blank page.

"It's hot," he remarks casually. His voice annoys me like nails on a chalkboard, and I can't resist rolling my eyes, knowing deep down it's a backhanded compliment.

Shields up. Shields up. Shields up.

I dive into my interview questions. "What brings you to therapy?" His dismissive laughter makes my skin prickle, but I force myself to continue. "Seriously, Sutton?"

With a mocking surrender, he raises his hands, intensifying my frustration. "You're up, not me," I snap, observing the faint blush on his face.

He hesitates for a moment before deciding on his words, and when he speaks, his sincerity catches me by surprise. "Does anyone truly know why they need therapy?" He shrugs, adding, "Honestly? I'm here because Coach wants me here."

"What are your goals for therapy?" I ask, trying to keep my tone neutral.

He pauses, pondering, before he says, "I haven't really thought that much about it. As you can see." I nod, my jaw tightening like the strings of a drawn bow at the memory of him not showing up for our first session. "Thinking about it, it would be straightforward. To do what it takes to make sure I reach my yearly end goal."

I observe him intently and then ask, "What exactly is that goal?"

With anxious energy, he twiddles his straw, the empty smoothie cup showing his unease. "Rookie of the Year."

With a raised eyebrow, I hear him chuckle lightly, the warmth of his laughter a stark contrast to how this discussion initially unfolded.

"Yeah, I know it's a big goal. However, my dad earned the award in his first year in the NFL, and I admire him."

My vision narrows, skepticism warring with a grudging respect. The way he opens up, sharing this piece of himself, irritates and intrigues me.

His entire focus is on his future.

My entire focus is on my future.

We share a similarity in that regard.

He adds, "Besides, it's something I must achieve, or else—"

"Or else what?" I interject, my tone unintentionally sharper. He halts, biting his inner cheek, as if struggling to hold back his words. After a tense moment, he shakes his head and exhales deeply, the heaviness of unspoken fears.

Clearly, he's keeping something to himself. I get it, I do. Sharing what's going on inside your brain and talking about your emotions can pose a challenge during therapy. Particularly if you have a strong dislike for the person you're confiding in.

"Let's move on to the next question."

Once again, our eyes connect, and I'm drawn to broach the subject we both avoid, but he won't allow it. I reluctantly take a sip of my coffee, which has cooled down, and cringe at its bitterness.

"Why do you think you need therapy, aside from your coach telling you that you do?" I ask, pushing the interview forward. He's already passed, if I'm being honest. That minor hiccup he made? Yeah, it has me itching to know more, to have him share the pieces that I'm willing to put together.

He glances over at Chrissa, who's clearing a table nearby. His eyes briefly soften, followed by a slump in his shoulders, making the burden of his thoughts apparent. "I suppose I need to work on my temper," he admits with a heavy sigh. "On the field, it's a completely different story than what I had imagined."

Vulnerability permeates the charged air, lingering in his expressions. I inch forward, longing to make eye contact and uncover further details of his story. "Why is that?" I ask gently, sensing this is where he might shut down. His gaze swiftly shifts, and walls appear to reconstruct before me.

With a twitch in his jaw, he struggles to control his emotions.

"Do you understand the weight of the world on your shoulders?" His voice breaks, his hands clenching the table's edge with such intensity that his knuckles pale. "Like every move you make is being scrutinized, every pair of eyes eagerly waiting for your next step?" He catches his breath, then lets out a profound sigh. "And every second feels like it's shaping your future."

He shifts in his seat, his leg bouncing. "I need that control," he says, continuing. "Whenever a player makes a derogatory comment about your game," he stops, "it makes you feel like you need to retaliate . . . "

I nod, sensing the heaviness of his words between us.

"God, that sounds so shitty," he says, his voice tinged with frustration. I sway my head, trying to clear my mind of the painful memories his words have triggered. The memories of my dad's uncontrollable rage, and the sense of powerlessness as he unleashed it, still haunt me. I am all too familiar with the pain of losing control. That's why I'm desperately holding onto control.

"I get it," I whisper, my gaze fixated on his.

Silence.

While I sit here and listen to Luke opening up, I feel something stirring inside me. He nailed that spontaneous interview effortlessly. Against all expectations, he's demonstrating a willingness to be vulnerable and share his deepest struggles, an essential milestone in therapy. This realization stirs something in me, a mix of professional satisfaction and personal curiosity.

Where will this lead?

I'm unsure, but there's a small ray of hope. It's a start.

CHAPTER 11
PAYSON

Approaching my childhood door, an unsettling sensation churns in my stomach, a clash between my thoughts and instincts that leaves me on the brink. It's that gut-wrenching instinct, whispering that danger lies in wait behind the familiar wood. Every fiber of my being screams to turn back, but an invisible force grips me, drawing me inexorably forward. Each step feels heavier than the last, laden with the weight of memories and foreboding, each one dragging me closer to the trouble that undoubtedly awaits.

"Let it go, Nancy! I'm not drunk, and there's no need to send me to a meeting. I'm perfectly fine the way I am," Dad protested vehemently.

Mom turned abruptly as we entered the house. We'd just come back from our Sunday ritual at the Sunrise Café & Brunch Spot in Stoneton instead of having our usual big breakfast at home.

The outing had started well. We ordered breakfast, and Mom asked about my English Literature and Composition class, which was easy thanks to my high school English teacher, Mrs. Fenson. We talked about the debate club, a passion of mine that gave me an adrenaline rush and a refuge during Mom and Dad's tough times. Dad nodded, showing interest and occasionally asking questions, even mentioning the latest episode of I Love Lucy.

Then things changed. The young server paid extra attention to Mom, which Dad took as flirting, even though the guy was closer to my age. I knew Mom would never flirt with someone my age, especially in front of Dad. Dad's questions turned angry, but Mom tried to calm him with, "It's okay" and "I love you, baby," though I could see the tension in her eyes.

I kept quiet, but as we were about to leave, mayhem erupted. The server, thinking it would be amusing, left his number on the tab meant for me, not Mom. Dad didn't know and refused to listen. His rage was palpable as he stormed through the door. Intervening was necessary to prevent a messy situation.

I hurriedly moved forward and softly held Dad's face. The whites of his eyes were red from anger. I saw the warning signs: Harsh words aimed at Mom and me, especially Mom. His jaw clenched, fists white-knuckled, as if ready to punch a wall. I'd seen this before, ending in a hospital visit and a broken hand. Those two months of Dad's healing were a reprieve for us.

After that, it seemed like Mom almost wanted Dad to hurt himself, hoping it would make him less abusive. It was a futile hope. We needed him in a support group, not just Band-Aiding the problem.

"Daddy, please, listen to Mom," I begged. "She means well."

He pulled away, teeth grinding. "Good intentions, my ass," he muttered, rubbing his eyes again. I knew if I didn't act fast, things would spiral out of control.

I had one last trick to calm him down, and I was desperate. I held his hand firmly, ensuring he met my unwavering stare. Despite being smaller, he never crossed the line with me. Although I had intervened for Mom in the past, her current state of anxiety, concealing bruises under long sleeves during the sweltering Texas summer, suggested further levels of violence in my absence.

I gripped his hand and shared a wordless glance with Mom, my determination evident.

"Let's go outside, Daddy," I coaxed. He paused at the door, his face a battleground of rage and restraint.

Destroy. Destroy. Destroy.

The urge to annihilate everything—Mom, himself, our family— was strong.

Gently tugging his hand, I unleashed my secret weapon: the irresistible Payson puppy dog eyes. He exhaled deeply and stepped outside with me. Sunlight bathed us as we walked to Time Walk Heritage Park, where Dad, a history teacher, came alive. This park, a blend of whimsy and education, offered a chronological adventure through history with immersive experiences and interactive displays. Here, Dad's troubles vanished, replaced by pure joy.

It hurt to realize Mom and I couldn't give him this peace, but I accepted it. If this was his temporary healing, I could set aside my own feelings. As we entered the park, his transformation was profound, like a man reliving a cherished childhood memory. His jaw relaxed, and the stress melted from his hands. Relief draped over my shoulders like a comforting blanket, knowing once again I had been the anchor for our family.

Being snapped back to the present, I couldn't resist the overwhelming pull that made me burst in without knocking. The scene before me left me breathless. In a rush, my parents darted around the kitchen island, their faces tense with rage and fury. My childhood home, once a comforting refuge, now felt like a cramped jail due to its modest size.

The initial observation is a hole in the wall, proof of the reoccurring outbreak of violence. I look at my mom and my heart shatters as I see a welt forming under her eye. A lamp table lies askew, a beer can tipping over beside it, its contents spilling out like the chaos that has engulfed our lives.

Guilt floods my body like a venomous snake constricting

its prey. I should have been here sooner. I could have prevented this. The thought of my mom relying on me to help with my abusive father fills me with a desperate sense of urgency, but also a deep, gnawing hurt.

Why does this burden fall on me?

Why can't I end it completely?

Normally, I'd take Dad to the history park to defuse the situation, but it's already dark on this Saturday night. Walking after a long drive is unappealing, but leaving my mom alone with him is unbearable. She knew my schedule well enough to wield it as a tool for guilt-induced persuasion, and as irksome as that was, I understood the urgency. If I didn't return, the situation could deteriorate rapidly. I'm here, and it's a good thing.

With caution, I gradually move closer to my dad, ensuring that every step is measured and every move is calculated. The room is brimming with a noticeable tension that seems to stretch every second. The puzzle pieces come together as he holds a wooden spoon. It looks like Mom may have attempted to flee from him, and he probably forcefully grabbed her wrist, resulting in the spoon hitting her in the eye. Amid the chaos, she could have fought back, causing the table lamp to fall and the beer to spill.

His eyes flick to me over his shoulder, and an icy shiver runs down my spine. A storm of tumultuous anger and sorrow brews inside me, threatening to overflow. I can feel the weight of my heart pressing against my rib cage, like a bird trapped in a cage, desperate to break free. Yet, I cannot afford to falter. Not now. Never. Despite the harsh reality, I need to be strong for my mom. The anguish I see in her eyes gives me determination, so I move closer. However, my dad's attention returns to Mom, and I observe him fidgeting, becoming more restless.

My pulse quickens and my hands become sweaty as I

move closer to him. A part of me wants to leap at him, to shake the sense into him, to scream at him, to leave Mom alone, to suggest a support group might be his salvation. But he's my dad, Dex Pennington. But that doesn't stop me from wishing he'd seek help. My inner therapist is urging him to seek professional help and address the underlying issues that caused this. It remains a mystery, one that even my mother won't disclose, only commenting that *"it happens to people who are unhappy."* Yet, I remember a time, before high school, when I'm sure Dad wasn't unhappy.

"Don't," he advises.

Even though I'm tempted to reply with a cutting, "Stay away, Dad," I decide to take a more gentle approach as I get closer. "Daddy, I returned for the weekend."

Approaching someone engulfed in fury isn't wise, but I'm driven to remove that spoon from his grasp, to catch his full attention and pacify him, to inject some reason into this turmoil. Taking one more careful step forward, I approach him and am immediately overwhelmed by the pungent smell of beer, causing me to feel nauseated. It's time to drive the point home. "Buddha taught that holding onto anger is like grasping a hot coal to throw at others."

As my hand reaches for the spoon, in a split second, Dad whirls around and seizes my wrist, his grip tight, verging on painful. "D-Dad, p-please let go," I breathe out in a whisper. "Please. You're hurting me." His grip is iron, and for a moment, fear and panic surge through me like icy water. His eyes reveal the unleashed anger simmering within him. But then, slowly, almost imperceptibly, his hold loosens. I retract my hand, my wrist pulsating with the memory of his grip.

Mom's expression portrayed sheer horror, with wide eyes and glistening tears. I fight back my own tears, refusing to let myself lose control. I have to be strong. Strong for my mom, who has endured far more than I realized in my absence.

Strong for my dad, to help him find calm, to focus on the positives, to aid him in battling his inner demons rather than feeding them. Remorse drives me to be here, attend online classes, and be present for moments like this.

With gentle strokes, I soothe my wrist, anticipating the bruises that will appear tomorrow—a mosaic of black, blue, and maybe a touch of red.

I can sense a tinge of regret in my dad's eyes as he observes the anguish on my face. His anger and bitterness momentarily fade away, allowing me to see the father I remember, with softer features. Before his emotions or mine can spill over, I reach out with my other hand, quietly taking the spoon from him and placing it behind him on the kitchen island.

In the background, Mom silently shakes her head, conveying a clear message. Focus on Dad first. I briefly shut my eyes, take a trembling breath, and then look directly into her eyes. Our wordless exchange, filled with unexpressed thoughts and mutual suffering, flows silently between us. I am her anchor, just as she is mine.

"Hey, Dad," I say, my voice steady yet trembling. "How about we watch some *I Love Lucy* reruns?" Wordlessly, he nods and moves toward me. I flinch instinctively but compose myself quickly enough that he doesn't notice.

While I genuinely love my dad, situations like these make me wish I didn't have fear toward him. The transition from idolizing a parent to dreading their enigma is both strange and painful. Yet here I am, longing for the opposite of fear— for love, support, encouraging words.

He wraps his arm around me in a side hug and affection- ately kisses the top of my head. "I missed you, Pay Bay," he murmurs. His love comes back to me for a moment, and I embrace it, regardless of how long it stays.

An hour later, the house has quieted down. Dad's snores

create a temporary silence in the living room, following the storm. Mom has just showered and wants to make me dinner, but the chaos of the night has taken away my hunger, leaving me with a desire for nothing but to escape. It's become a routine now, a desperate need to flee after each explosion.

Mom's trembling fingers gently graze my face as she approaches, leaving a soft kiss on my forehead. A nostalgic kiss, a whisper from my carefree childhood. Her voice cracks as she murmurs, "Thank you, thank you, Pay Bay."

In these moments, a torrent of emotions floods me—gratefulness for being here, but also a consuming guilt. What if I hadn't been here? What if I couldn't protect her next time?

Questions whirl in my mind, unanswered and haunting.

Why doesn't she leave him?

What turned him into this monster?

What fuels his rage so violently?

Why doesn't my mom fight harder? For herself? For me?

Night after night, my heart shatters further, torn between love for my mother and the worry that I won't be sufficient to rescue her.

I made an attempt to restore some sense of normality for the rest of the night. Typically, I would go to parties, experience brief moments of joy, and attend therapy sessions, but my pain ran much deeper than that. The therapist in me knows this isn't the healthiest way to cope. I should lean into the discomfort, confronting the chaos within. But the chaos outside—the endless turbulence at home—has driven me to seek solace elsewhere.

Against my better judgment, I find myself doing exactly what I shouldn't. I find myself at The Cozy Corner Pub, a quaint spot just outside Stoneton. I used to come here during my freshman year, back when life seemed simpler, more manageable. Luke mentioned it to Miles last year, and now, the memories pull me back. The pub is a cocoon of comfort, with plush chairs and couches arranged in inviting circles. The dim lighting, a collection of lights in various sizes and shapes, casts a warm, intimate glow. At the front, two large leather couches await patrons eager to lose themselves in the music of local bands.

Perched at the bar counter, I watch the bartender skillfully mix my second spicy margarita—a guilty pleasure. The heat of the drink mirrors the fire I feel inside, the relentless burning of guilt and frustration. While I enjoy margarita nights with friends, tequila is my true love. My go-to is a spicy, extra-dirty margarita, mirroring the upheaval in my life.

I feel the buzz, a brief diversion until it fades away, and suddenly my phone vibrates. Reaching into my purse, I pull it out to find two new messages waiting for me.

MOM

Pay, when are you going to be home, baby? It's getting late. Wanted to catch up.

Sorry, Mom. Not feeling it right now.

PAYSON

We can catch up tomorrow, I promise.

LUKE

Hey, Penny, are we still on for tomorrow?

Penny? What the hell? Just as I begin to consider a reply, another vibration interrupts.

LUKE

Get it? Your last name is Pennington.

You know the saying about pennies, right?

Oh, enlighten me, please.

LUKE

They're time consuming.

Get it? Counting and handling pennies is time consuming. And, you, Payson, consume much of my time. So let's make tomorrow quick, yeah?

Time consuming? That's rich coming from him, Mr. One-Hour-to-Prep. Remembering all the times we've waited for him to emerge from Milli's bathroom, often using her hair products, is almost comical.

I'm inclined to speak my mind and put an end to our "arrangement" right away. But I remind myself to stay strong, for the sake of my future.

Just breathe, Payson, just breathe.

This is exactly what I do as I send my next text and search for a distraction for the night. My eyes land on Garrett, the bartender. I thought a spicy margarita would suffice, but my wrist hurts, and Luke's nonsense adds to it all. And before tomorrow's challenges, I need this—a momentary diversion.

PAYSON

Be ready by 6 pm

Almost immediately, another message comes in.

LUKE

My game won't finish until around three-ish, maybe later if we go into OT. Additionally, there are interviews, press conferences, and the need to shower. Might not make it by six.

PAYSON

If you don't answer the door on the first knock, we're done. I'll see to it that your ass gets kicked.

LUKE

Oh, baby, don't tempt me with a good time.

. . .

Before he can finish his sentence, I decisively shut off my phone. A knot tightens in my chest as I resolve to leave the past behind. Tonight is about forging fresh memories with someone new—a tall, green-eyed vision named Garrett.

I down the last of my spicy margarita in one go, the fiery liquid burning a trail down my throat, the tangy lime making my lips pucker and my senses ignite. The alcohol mingles with the adrenaline already coursing through my veins.

Out of the corner of my eye, I notice Garrett watching intently. My heart races, excitement coursing through me, briefly overpowering the lingering pain from earlier tonight.

With a slow, deliberate motion, I lick the lime juice and salt from the rim of the glass, savoring each sensual flick of my tongue. Ben's heated gaze meets mine, his eyes filled with desire, longing, and want. And tonight? I'm ready. Ready to satisfy his longing, lose myself in his touch, and feel alive again.

CHAPTER 12
PAYSON

Strike one. Strike two.

Being stood up once is infuriating, but twice? Totally unacceptable. My second knock lands harder, each thud echoing my mounting frustration. Anger bubbles up inside me, and I wrestle with the urge to get even, to send Luke an excuse so airtight he'd have no choice but to believe it. The hangover from last night's excesses is pounding in my skull, begging me to retreat to bed. However, a stubborn voice in my head relentlessly insists on pushing forward.

I have to do this. If last night is any sign, I need this. I need to remember the bigger picture.

"Luke, I swear, if you're not behind this door . . . " My threat fades away as the door swings open and I am left speechless, my breath caught in my throat. My heart races as my vision lands on his wet, messy hair, and my fingers itch to run through it—don't, Payson. My gaze drifts down to his abs, and I swallow hard, my pulse quickening at the sight of each defined muscle against his tan skin. It's not like I haven't seen Luke before; that one night is still a vivid blur in my memory. My eyes betray me, tracing the contours of his body and lingering on the V-shaped dip that disappears beneath the waistband of his shorts. Heat rushes to my cheeks.

"Taking a stroll down memory lane, are we?" Luke quips, his smirk devilishly taunting. My hand automatically tightens into a fist, imagining delivering a swift punch to his groin, wiping that smug expression away. Rather than decline, I put on a fake smile and accept his offer of a Michelob Ultra, as expected.

I don't really need a drink for this session, but the thought of it taking the edge off is appealing. When our fingers briefly touch, there's a spark that brings back memories of that night. Our eyes meet, and I see the same turbulent memory mirrored in his. It's like the past has awakened within us, a tangible tension in the air.

God, what is wrong with me? I don't want this. It happened once, and will never happen again. I tighten my grip on the beer bottle, the cooling sensation bringing my nerves down a touch. Maybe it's just pre-PMS hormones playing tricks, making his touch feel more intense than it should.

I inhale deeply, trying to concentrate as I approach the brown leather couch. One hour a week with Luke—strictly professional, no physical contact, no unnecessary frills. This is simply about graduating early and him keeping his spot on the team to receive Rookie of the Year.

When I settle and let go of my bag, I lose eye contact with Luke. Moving away from the couch, I cautiously watch him from behind. "You're always on guard, you know that?" He comments softly.

Yeah, kinda have to be.

I choose to ignore his observation, not wanting to admit that it's become a reflex, especially around those with a temper. He returns, and I catch a whiff of his scent—familiar and intoxicating, bringing back a flood of memories I'd rather forget. The beating in my chest intensifies, the silence between us thick with unspoken words and unresolved tension.

When I spot the plastic bag emblazoned with the Mongolian Wok 'n' Roll logo, my excitement is clear. My stomach rumbles and Luke's hearty laughter shatters the silence. Despite knowing that his laughter shouldn't have an effect on me, it still reverberates in the room and penetrates my bones.

"Is your stomach a garbage disposal, Pennington? That was loud as hell."

I roll my eyes, refusing to let him see how his remark stings. Bringing the tantalizing aroma with him as he approaches, he acts nonchalant, as though it's no big deal that he's brought my favorite food from a much-loved restaurant. He must have had insider information, probably from Milli. It's a sweet, thoughtful gesture, so unlike what I'm accustomed to. Maybe it's a ploy to lighten the seriousness of our session?

I eagerly grab the bag from him, unconcerned about seeming desperate. He pulls back, and to someone watching, it may seem like a small fight, but to me, it's a display of power. With a low growl, he finally releases me, and I loathe the sensation of heat between my thighs caused by that single sound. Swiftly, I slap away his hand from the spare egg roll.

"I just played a brutal game; we barely won. I need the extra protein," he says, his voice hard and unyielding.

I shrug indifferently. "Tough luck, Sutton. You also lost your temper again." His expression shifts from relaxed to serious, but I remain firm. Tough as it may be, this is why I'm here: to help him.

We settle into our respective ends of the couch, each absorbed in our meals. Every now and then, our gazes meet, and I struggle to tear mine away from the sight of his bare chest. It's incredibly distracting, especially when it's Luke.

I push myself to focus on my meal, prodding it with my fork. "Are you familiar with the concept of a shirt?" I can sense his self-satisfied smile, enjoying my uneasiness. Wordlessly, he rises, and I sigh in relief.

Suddenly, I'm choking on my food, coughing violently. He's quickly at my side, patting my back and handing me water. After a few sips, I gasp out, "Really?" while pointing at his shirt that reads I'M TACKLING MY ISSUES, ONE PLAY AT A TIME.

With a smile and a shrug, he returns to the couch beside me. "Do I look that good you almost died of choking?" he quips. I respond with a playful nudge of my foot against his ribs. His hand catches my foot, and I freeze.

Baby, hold still for me, I want to try something, Luke's voice echoes in my memory. I'm suddenly back in his room, the weight of him pressing me into the bed, his hands gripping my foot. A shiver shakes down my spine as he explores a new position, his intense focus sending my heart into overdrive.

Back in the present, I yank my foot away, the connection between us snapping like a rubber band. My chest tightens with a mix of longing and regret. This whole situation feels akin to a ticking time bomb.

We stay silent while the TV commentators are engrossed in what they call Luke's "toddler tantrum." The term captures my focus, causing me to glance at him and notice the strain in his grip, the tightness in his jaw, and his attempts to relieve the mounting pressure by cracking his neck.

In a brief moment, he evokes memories of my father, with that same intensity held inside, but in a much younger guise.

I want to urge him to let go, to breathe, to not let the demons win. However, I am cautious with my choice of words. "Does that bother you?"

This is the point where our therapy session truly starts. Luke may not be aware yet, but this is the perfect opportunity to explore the root causes of his behavior.

His head rotates, his piercing gaze firmly fixed on me, a flurry of unanswered questions swirling in his penetrating look. In mine, a demand for answers. He is as guarded as a kite caught in a relentless wind, a feeling I know too well.

When did it begin?

What fueled it?

Mr. Sutton, from my limited interactions, seemed like a decent man, especially when I saw him with Milli. Mrs. Sutton was merely tolerable. I never wronged her, yet she treated me like an unwelcome pest from the start. Therapy taught me a valuable lesson: to overlook those who try to diminish you in order to elevate themselves.

"Does it bother you?" Once again, I gesture toward the TV where they're discussing Luke's conduct on the field, particularly his attitude and behavior.

His attention returns to the screen, accompanied by a slight head shake. "It's not them talking about it that bothers me; it's that they're saying it's me."

"What makes you think you're not the one in those videos?" I dig deeper.

His stare swiftly moves to the floor, his breath wavering as he inhales. With each exhale, his shoulders sink, revealing the unmistakable signs of his inner turmoil.

He darts his eyes toward the TV, consciously avoiding making eye contact with me. It's a classic tactic used to avoid accepting a painful truth, a clear act of evasion. He lets out yet another sigh, this time filled with frustration. "Yeah, that's me, obviously. Same eyes, same hair, same name," he concedes, his voice brittle with tension. Yet, he suddenly ceases, fixing his gaze on me, a glimmer of defiance kindling in his eyes. "But it's not really me."

But it is him. Perhaps not the person he dreams of becoming, but in that instant, it was him. I want to tell him, but I restrain myself. His reluctance to fully acknowledge the truth is similar to a thread, barely holding together the fabric of his self-perception. I lean forward, intent on gently pulling at that thread.

"How would you describe yourself?" I ask. With little acknowledgment of my question, he shifts his gaze back to the TV.

"What do you mean?" he responds with a touch of disinterest.

I paused briefly before elaborating, "Who is Luke Sutton, deep down?"

A self-assured smirk appears on his face. "An amazing tight end, a force to be reckoned with, and a hit with the ladies," he replies, throwing a wink my way. I shake my head, but he presses on, clearly enjoying his own bravado. "A son, a brother. I love sports, not just football. Hockey, golf, baseball —you name it, I'll watch it. And yeah, I'm pretty damn good at all of them too."

Okay, Mr. Hotshot.

He's listing all the surface-level stuff, but he's missing the point. He's only describing roles and interests, not the deeper traits that shape his character and motivations.

"Right, okay," I say, shifting gears to probe deeper into the root cause of his outbursts. They seem to occur primarily on the field, apart from that one notorious incident off-field. Understandably, emotions run high during games, and yes, men will be men. However, that doesn't fully explain why Luke's irritation flares up so rapidly. There's something specific triggering him.

I delved into his history with football. "When did you start playing football?" I ask.

"Around four," he replies.

"Did you enjoy it, or did you feel like it was an imposition?" I continue.

"I love it, and it loves me back. We've got a really good thing going," he says, finally taking his attention away from the TV as the sports commentators discuss next week's games. Our gazes connect, indicating a readiness to engage in a deeper conversation.

As he grabs a blanket and lights the fireplace, while answering my never-ending questions, the atmosphere changes. Despite the Texas heat on a late September evening, the cozy couch and crackling fire create a warm and intimate setting. It feels too much like a typical date for my liking, so I ignore those notions and concentrate on the task at hand.

I drink some water in an attempt to calm my mind as I wait for him to return. Curling my legs to the side, I make space for him, resting my head against the couch, the blanket snug around my shoulders. When he peeks at me, I can't ignore the piercing focus in his intense gaze—heat, or perhaps anger?

My heart pounds erratically, each beat echoing in my chest like a drum. Panic flutters in my stomach, and I clench my fingers around the edge of the blanket, desperate for something to ground me. Why do his glances affect me so much?

Taking a deep breath, I pull my shoulders back and straighten my spine.

Shields up, Payson.

With a cleared throat, I gather the courage to ask the final, crucial question of the night—one that has been on my mind since our session started. "Did you like all your coaches growing up?" His eyes wander away from mine, dodging the question.

Strike one. His eyes reveal a hint of discomfort, suggesting his hesitance to open up. Nonetheless, I persist. But all he offers is a noncommittal shrug and a vague, "Yeah, mostly."

Strike two. *Mostly*—that phrase alone is telling. He didn't give a straightforward yes or no. Right as I'm about to ask more questions, he gets up and begins to clear our food from the table in the living room. His voice interrupts my train of thought. "I think it's time for you to go."

His abrupt end to our session stings more than I expected; recognizing self-denial in someone else isn't difficult when you've navigated those waters yourself. Luke might know that I attend therapy, but he's likely unaware that the struggles he's facing now mirror ones I've contended with. Opening up, placing trust in another person, can be an intimidating journey.

"Just like that?" Irritation bubbles up as I throw the blanket off with unnecessary force, being pushed out the door so soon. He just shrugs, standing up and putting the blanket back in its rightful place as if nothing happened.

Seriously, he's just going to ignore me? I tightly grip my hands, fighting to control my anger. Briefly shutting my eyes, I see his figure fading into the distance. Clenching my teeth, I remind myself that it's just the start. He will have plenty of chances to be more vulnerable and express himself. If anyone knows it takes time, it's me. However, now, that knowledge brings little solace.

Not wanting to bother with this conversation anymore, I hastily gather my belongings, my hands trembling slightly as I shove them into my bag. I hesitate at the door, looking back at Luke, longing for any indication of regret or eagerness to interact. But he remains motionless, his posture tense, a silent testament to his internal struggle.

Right as I'm about to say goodbye, he stops me with a shake of his head, saying, "Save it for next week, Pennington."

Sighing, I close the door and lean against it, pressing my head back. As I take a deep breath, a chilling thought pierces my mind: *What happened to him?*

CHAPTER 13
LUKE

Let it out all on the field, boy.

"Fucking hell!" My phone slips out of my hand and slams into my locker, creating a loud clang that triggers a series of reactions from the surrounding lockers. Compulsively checking my phone has become a habit, one born from an inexplicable premonition that messages like these will arrive before a game or during halftime. True to form, my teammates showed up in disarray and dismay following the disastrous first half. Despite it being only our fifth game of the season, today's game felt as if we were being thrown into the deep end.

A string of misguided throws, botched catches, and various errors had caused us numerous setbacks, including my own. This mutual struggle reminded me of our pregame ritual, where Coach insists we lay bare our concerns and challenges that could sway the game. It unifies us, yet today, it felt like we were more scattered than ever. I was more scattered than normal. And it pissed me the fuck off.

During our first session, my so-called "therapist" looked like she had walked straight off a movie set—blonde, sharp, and drop-dead gorgeous, with an uncanny resemblance to Scarlett Johansson. She was on a relentless hunt for one thing: vulnerability. She chased after it with the tenacity of a cat hunting a mouse, and I wasn't going to surrender easily. Nevertheless, she had this exasperating skill for getting past my barriers, asking probing questions that seemed more like casual discussions than intense interrogations. At first, I was oddly grateful for that; it made opening up seem less daunting—until it didn't.

This is Payson Pennington. The last person I wanted to reveal everything to. Vulnerable or not, one question from her during that first session had me on edge all week. Unease constantly gnawed at me, much like a persistent ache.

It made me doubt if this was right, but then when Troy randomly texted me after everything that happened, asking about the coach's thoughts on Rookie of the Year, I knew it was and responded confidently, saying, *I've got it covered, just like a winning hand in poker.*

Midweek, a text message from Payson popped up, asking if we were still on for our session tonight. It would've been easy to cancel, to claim I'd moved past needing any help. I even typed out my excuse. But who was I kidding? After that text from Troy, I realized I needed her guidance, whether my ego liked it. My chest tightened with a mix of anger and reluctant acceptance. Recollections of past rage about her stirred, but I knew deep down that I needed this—needed her.

"You guys look like pussies out there," Coach D's frustration is palpable as he hurls his clipboard across the room, narrowly missing Percy.

Percy feigns a look of wounded shock, which only seems to deepen when Maddox quietly retorts, "We aren't female genitalia." My eyes roll at Maddox's literal interpretation of Coach's coarse language. Inopportune time for vocabulary lessons.

Meanwhile, my phone vibrates incessantly in my locker, each vibration a ghostly reminder of another message I can't bring myself to check. The longing to escape from those persistent messages and unleash repressed fury, to let go of this chaotic energy, is almost too much to handle. My anxiety manifests physically—I massage my neck to relieve tension and grip my helmet tightly, knuckles turning white.

Coach D interrogates us with a tone of disbelief. "What the hell was that performance?" He reminds us of our standards: no fumbled balls, no missed catches. The moment he makes eye contact with me and says my name, it's a sudden return to reality. He lectures on the differences between college football and the NFL—a domain replete with increased stress, effort, and the demand for absolute control and dedication. This transition, he implies, is a test of our ability to handle pressure, to transform adversity into strength in the game. For me, the field has forever been my arena for confronting challenges head-on.

"I want a turnaround this half," he insists, his tone firm, his eyes sweeping over us as if we are errant children needing correction. We nod in unison, a silent pledge to meet his expectations. His voice grows louder, more commanding as he reminds us of their record the previous year compared to our current standing. "What the fuck was our record last year?" he challenges.

The room remains quiet until Big Guy defiantly responds with "Thirteen to four."

Coach D retrieves his clipboard, adjusting his hat with resolve, mirroring the determination he demands from us.

"That's fucking right. Let's keep it that way. We've already won four games this season; keep it fucking going."

Berry shouts, "Who are we?"

We chant back, "Stars! Stars! Stars!" lifting our helmets high. Just as we're about to start the second half, something else captures my attention. The urge to sneak a quick glance at my phone makes my fingers twitch. I crave those messages, needing them to feel grounded, to perform better on the field. It's addictive—the ritual is a cornerstone of my focus, both on and off the field.

While everyone else rushes out, I stay behind, knowing they're fully focused on the game, giving me a moment alone. Opening my locker reveals the message I was expecting.

TROY

Let it out all on the field, boy. Stay focused—
what you do during the game matters to me.
To Benny.

Fuck. Knowing I have no choice, I channel that frustration into the game. I tap into my inner beast, allowing it to fuel my performance. My catches are nothing short of spectacular, contributing to two touchdowns that secure our victory. Some confrontations occurred, opponents were shoved to the ground, but they didn't mind. In the grand scheme, we prevailed despite minor skirmishes. That was all that mattered.

And now it was time to celebrate, Payson Pennington style.

"We will not start this session with you shirtless, again." Payson's voice, thick with exasperation, fills the room from the screen perched on the hotel bed.

With reluctance, I begrudgingly grab my travel bag from the floor. "As you wish, Your Royal Highness," I comment, my voice oozing with sarcasm.

With an exasperated sigh, she comments, "Looks like we're off to a great start."

Thanks to an away game that caused chaos in our schedules, we had to downgrade our Sunday session to a video call a week later. This was the only time that worked for both of us, despite my yearning to join my teammates in celebrating our victory. Berry's words in the locker room echo in my head: *Therapy's good for you.*

I move back to the bed with a tee that boasts I'M THE REASON THEY CALL IT A "TIGHT" END—a shirt that nearly causes Payson to choke again when she sees it.

"Your humor is really something, Sutton," she states, annoyed, lounging in her silky pajamas. Her top slid down her shoulder, revealing glimpses of her smooth skin and the curve of her cleavage.

My hands ball into fists, my nails digging into my palms as I try to calm my breath.

Fuck, get it together, Luke.

I shift uncomfortably, every muscle in my body tense. The memories of Payson and Milli stumbling into my childhood home that night, completely intoxicated, flood my mind and amplify my frustration.

"Quit staring," she quips, her tone full of that familiar sass, and damn if my cock doesn't twitch. Good thing I was behind my phone.

"Stop giving me a reason to," I shoot back.

She pauses, mid-motion, her expression widening in surprise. "What's the game plan, Penny?" I ask, trying to steer the conversation away from the turmoil inside me. Her gaze locks onto me, and I press my lips together to stifle a laugh. Hearing it out loud, after our texts, feels oddly exhilarating.

She raises a finger, signaling me to hold on.

"Really, Pennington? What could be more important than this?"

With a crisp, definitive click, she shuts her laptop, her eyes connecting with my own as she reclines in an egg-shaped chair—definitely Milli's. Her entire attitude transforms into a combination of annoyance and amusement. "Relax. I was just finishing up some RA duties. You wouldn't believe it, but the freshmen this year are even more ruthless than last year's class," she remarks, shaking her head in disbelief.

Pausing to sip my protein drink, I raise an eyebrow, slightly amused.

Letting out a deep breath, her gaze momentarily falls to my lips before returning to mine. With a firm tone, she cautions, "Don't even say it."

I can't help myself. *I'll show you ruthless*, I mouth with a sly grin, observing her eyes track every word formed on my lips.

Rolling her eyes dismissively, her cheeks suddenly blush pink, interrupting my teasing. Is Payson Pennington blushing? It's a sight to behold and, annoyingly, one I find too damn irresistible for my own good.

The sound of her voice slices through the tension. "So, are you going to explain that stunt you pulled earlier tonight?" The atmosphere abruptly changes, becoming serious and intense.

I offer a casual shrug. "Can't say I know what you're referring to."

She leans forward, momentarily preoccupied, and her leopard top straps slide down her shoulders, yet again.

Good Lord. "Penny, this is a therapy session. Act like it."

She stares into my eyes briefly before glancing at her own reflection on the screen. In one quick movement, she pulls her straps back up, causing her face to turn a deeper pink and drawing attention to the small scar above her eyebrow. I wonder how she got it.

"Care to explain why you're deflecting our conversation already?" she questions, reaching into the mini fridge. The quick movement provides a momentary distraction, revealing Milli's bookshelves in the backdrop.

"Nope," I respond, letting the *P* pop a little. Frustrated, she shakes her head and immerses herself again in her questions about the evening's events. I dodge, insisting it was nothing significant.

With a licorice sticking out from her plush, thick pink lips, she asks, "What was the best part of tonight's game?" My eyes linger on them for a beat too long, and her snapping fingers pull me back to reality. I mentally slap myself.

"Aside from scoring two winning touchdowns?" I flash a smirk. She rolls her blue eyes.

"Well," she replies, "I'd say the halftime locker room pep talk."

Curiosity consumes her eyes as she gazes at me, eager to uncover the mystery of what occurred. I dismiss her silent inquiry with a casual, "Let's just say it kicked my ass into high gear for the second half." More like the text did, but I don't mention that.

"Luke," she warns, her tone low and serious. "I'm not joking. I will end this agreement right here and now if there's any hint you're using drugs."

My eyebrows furrow. "Wait a minute. Who mentioned anything about drugs?"

With a resigned exhale and narrowed look, she confesses, "You made it sound suspicious."

I shake my head. "Yeah, no, I've never touched drugs. Not my scene at all."

Over the video, she stares at me intently, her gaze piercing and seemingly anticipating a confession about my hidden druggie. But I'm serious, and the joke's on her.

Changing the topic, she asks, "So, what's the real story from tonight?"

I shrug. "I had to put some opposing players in their place—they were asking for it."

"Right, because violence is always the answer," she says with a sarcastic edge.

When playing, it sometimes feels like that. Like everything you want boils down to making those around you proud, pushing you to do whatever it takes.

"How was it growing up with an NFL dad?"

"Amazing," I respond right away, my voice becoming lively as memories flood my mind. The image of my dad on the field is etched vividly in my memory, his movements and the game's sheer energy. I knew I wanted that. Four was the age most coaches started taking kids, and I was ready, eager to dive into the world of football.

"When did you know you wanted to join the NFL?"

"Honestly? Since I can remember. The first time I stepped on the football field in my practice gear. It was like it was meant to be." I catch sight of Payson biting her damn pencil, lost in thought. "Sounds cliché, I know."

"Not really," she says gently, her expression softening. "We all possess a passion. It's up to each person whether those passions become something more. The way you just lit up talking about how much you love football and how much it means to you shows me it's not cliché at all."

Her words seep into me, warm and comforting, like sunlight breaking through clouds. She's right. But every time someone says, *You just wanted to follow in your father's footsteps,* it's like a hot coal igniting inside me. It's not just anger; it's a fierce, proud defiance. Damn straight, I did. I love the game as much as he does, even if sometimes it feels like I'm struggling with that.

"Did the thought of quitting ever cross your mind?" Her question hits me like a punch, and I almost blurt out, *No, why would you ask that?* But deep down, a small, nagging part of me remembers.

There was one time. That year was overwhelming—too much grief, sadness, guilt, everything. I thought about giving up. Then I got that text after one of my high school games: *You owe Benny this.* Those words snapped me back, reminding me of my promise. Whenever Benny or a text is mentioned, guilt overwhelms me.

"Maybe once, but the thought disappeared as quickly as it came," I say, giving her the short version.

"Why?" she asks, her intense stare searching mine.

Making Benny proud is my top priority. I need to make my parents proud. I have to move past that part of me, even though it haunts me every game.

I try to give off an air of unconcern. "Because it's what I needed to do to move forward. Live my life. Do what I love."

She narrows her eyes and carefully examines my words, causing my stomach to knot up. She nods and shifts to a series of straightforward questions. They flow effortlessly, simple and clear, but my mind is anything but calm. My thoughts race, tangled in the emotions I desperately try to suppress. The memories of my past mistakes claw at me, their grip suffocating, making me wonder if I will ever truly break free from their hold and find peace.

CHAPTER 14
PAYSON

Come on, you love this attention.

"Do you think it was wise to have returned home last weekend?" Lori, my therapist, asks through the car's speaker. I'm parked outside my dorm, eyes closed and lost in thought, an hour having slipped by.

I pause, my throat tightening as the memory crashes back. My timing had been critical—too critical. Without my arrival, the consequences for my mother, my father, and myself might have been dire.

I always place my safety last, a habit that gnaws at my conscience.

My fingers tremble as they trace the dark bruises encircling my wrist, each touch a raw sting. The bruises should have faded by now, yet they persist, a constant reminder. Concealing them with long sleeves or bracelets has become routine. Each painful reminder pulls me back to my mother's ongoing ordeal. I empathize with her deeply, yet I cannot condone my father's actions.

A sigh escapes me as my eyes flutter open, revealing the sight of a few students, slightly unsteady on their feet, making their way into the dorm. As their RA, I should probably step in, but tonight, my heart's just not in it. It's Saturday, after all, and they're clearly out there making memories, something I wish I could say I was doing too.

"Sounds like you're unsure?" my therapist ventures, her voice carrying a note of gentle probing.

I shrug, a gesture lost in our phone conversation, but unnecessary for someone who understands me as well as she does. I can almost hear her preparing to conclude our call or perhaps shift the conversation elsewhere, given my reluctance to dive into the topic. Despite my reaching out to her, my responses have been anything but helpful, dodging her questions as skillfully as I've been ignoring my mom's persistent messages this past week.

Pay Bay, we didn't get to catch up. How about this weekend?

That's a definite no from me.

Payson, darling. Perhaps it's time I visit you? A change of scenery might be nice.

As tempting as it is to welcome her escape from Dad, even for a short while, today's circumstances make it the least appealing option. I adore her, but specifically today, I simply crave silence or enjoyment.

"Let's take a moment to discuss Luke," she suggests.

The mere mention of his name sends a thrill down my spine, pursued by a sinking dread. Our interactions over the week had been minimal, which didn't surprise me, but what truly shocked me was his midweek locker room selfie with his teammate. The caption stated, *Proudly skipping a night out for light reading with Maddox. You should be proud.*

As soon as I saw it, I couldn't understand why he thought I'd care if he missed a night out with his friends, likely ending with some wannabe future Mrs. Sutton. The thought dug into me like a splinter, sharp and relentless. Did his text provoke my thoughts on what could have occurred if he had gone out? Or was it about his supposed commitment to his word count?

The phone grew tighter in my hand as frustration coursed through me. Why am I irritated? "What about him?" I ask, my voice tense.

"What are your thoughts on him?"

Normally, I'd have a straightforward critique: arrogant, insufferably confident, yet annoyingly charming and unexpectedly thoughtful.

Deep down, I'm curious to uncover more about Luke, beyond the persona he projects. Choosing my words carefully, I settle on, "He's okay, a bit too sure of himself, but has his moments of kindness." And that's pushing it.

With a light laugh, she notes, "Sounds like someone I know." I dismiss her comparison with a shake of my head, even though there might be a sliver of truth to it.

"And why did you choose him as your client?" she continues.

"For my class," I respond, my answer short and clipped. But the truth is more complicated. Taking him on as a client is about what lies beyond this class. The prospect of escaping everything the moment I graduate.

"Okay," she drawls, the word stretching out, signaling the imminent end of our call. I don't blame her. Here I am, giving her short, stonewalled answers. The irony isn't lost on me—I used to get mad at Luke for his curt responses during our sessions, yet our last meeting revealed more about him than I ever expected, and in a good way.

"How about we chat about this later?" she suggests, pausing briefly. We agree on the next session, coordinating around her being back in Stoneton and juggling video calls during my school schedule.

I release a weary sigh, the weight of the week's academic grind pressing down on me, compounded by this morning's exhaustive ten-mile run meant to clear my head—a fleeting reprieve interrupted by another message from my mom.

After the call with my therapist, I finally summon the energy to respond, guilt prodding me forward.

PAYSON

Can we postpone? Maybe next weekend?

MOM

Of course, sweetie. See you then.

It adds yet another task to my already crowded mental list. I mutter a silent curse, lamenting the now-busy next weekend. A sudden tap on my window jolts me. Startled, I peer outside and see Milli's beaming face, her dance attire shimmering in the streetlight, and Brooke, holding a DIY margarita kit. It's time for our monthly ritual: DIY Margarita Night. Milli waves a HAPPY BIRTHDAY! banner with exuberance.

I rush to open the door, my fingers trembling as I reach for the banner. Their laughter bubbles up, filling the night air, fully aware of my aversion to grand birthday gestures. Memories of my thirteenth birthday flash through my mind—a family dinner turned sour, an argument erupting, my dad's temper flaring, and me, retreating to my room or stepping in to play peacemaker.

I fake a smile, attempting to let go of the past and allow their happiness to bring me into the present.

"Come on, you love this attention," Milli teases, dancing across the parking lot. Her laughter is infectious, brightening my mood and coaxing the first genuine smile of the day. It's hard not to get carried away by her spirit, even as some students cast curious glances her way. Brooke chases after her, both of them a spectacle of joy. I prop myself against my car, noticing the tension of the week dissolve.

They pull me along, their enthusiasm unyielding, and before we know it, we're navigating back to the dorms. An hour later, we're concocting a spooky margarita, inspired by our tradition of DIY cocktails themed to the month. As we chat and laugh, we brim with plans to venture out to a new club in Dallas. Was I in the spirit for birthday festivities? Hardly. The thought of navigating Saturday traffic for over thirty minutes to Dallas, a city I'd be visiting anyway by tomorrow, was far from appealing. Yet, the prospect of dancing the night away and shedding the week's stress, especially without the responsibility of driving, was too tempting to pass up.

Riding the wave of tequila-induced euphoria, we huddle together, our arms linked as we assess our reflections in the bathroom mirror. The verdict is unanimous: we look stunning. Milli, in her signature leather skirt and bodysuit, paired with Converse; Brooke, casual yet chic in jeans and a graphic crop top; and myself, seizing the occasion to don my annual birthday purchase—a lavish ensemble that I indulge in each year despite my usual aversion to celebration. My choice this year is a striking aesthetic: an emerald-green velvet blazer worn open to reveal a matching lace bra, coordinated with a skirt of the same vibrant hue, all complemented by sleek black open-toe heels.

With a final approving look, we set off for The Neon Nightshade, a name as enigmatic as the place itself. Its meaning becomes clear as we approach, greeted by an array of vivid neon lights that dance like disco beams in the night, signaling the promise of an unforgettable evening.

We breeze past the bouncer, our fake IDs in hand—just one more year until they're nothing but a memory. Milli, a constant ball of energy, charges forward and collides with Miles, her arms extended. Their embrace, effervescent with love, brings a shy grin to my face; it nearly sparks a flicker of longing in me.

Almost. Brooke's elbow gently nudges me, bringing me to the present. I catch the hopeful glint in her eyes, silently wishing for her boyfriend to surprise us by showing up, despite the slim chances given his track record. Honestly, she deserves better; he's barely attempted to visit, showing up just twice last year.

Brooke nudges me once more, her eyes fixed on the bar—the main attraction that brought me here. Mischievousness dances in her eyes as she smirks and gestures for me to come along. We weave through the crowd and secure our drinks. As I lift the tequila to my lips, I feel the burn, but it's familiar, a reminder of the fun we've already had tonight. I avoid beer, wary of the hangover it promises.

The club's grandeur catches me off guard as I scan the room. A massive chandelier dominates the ceiling, casting a shimmering glow across three levels. The upper two are likely VIP sections, but we're content on the ground floor. The dance floor sprawls before us, pulsating with energy.

Out there, amid the throng of dancers, I spot Milli. She's lost in the music, moving with freedom that makes me smile. Beside her is Miles, his hat perched on his head—a subtle yet powerful statement about his ongoing chemotherapy treatments. Despite the sweat and heat, he wears it with pride, and his resilience tugs at my emotions.

Turning to Brooke, who's absorbed in her phone, I announce my intention to dance. Receiving no response, I grab her phone, capturing her attention as I declare, "It's my birthday, bitch."

She breaks into a grin, and with an encouraging slap on my ass, she's ready to dive into the festivities. "In that case, let's go dance," she says, enthusiasm lighting up her eyes.

We walk together toward the center of the dance floor as "Low" by Flo Rida, featuring T-Pain, plays. I find myself naturally syncing my body with the music, twirling and dipping in perfect time. As I lift myself up from a low sweep, I am immediately drawn to the mesmerizing green eyes before me.

"Greetings, handsome," I quip, letting my fingers dance across his chest and up to his shoulders. In one fluid motion, he pulls me close by encircling his arms around my waist. We dance in sync, immersed in the music and the crowd for multiple songs. The bright lights cast a sheen of sweat on my face, and my heart races, fueled by the rhythm and the intoxicating proximity.

Leaving him with a kiss as the music fades, I head back to the bar for another drink. My eyes catch sight of Miles and Milli, locked in a heated exchange, while Brooke dances with abandon, seemingly without a care. Little do we know, the night is just beginning to unravel.

"Enjoying your birthday, princess?" Milli teases, Miles standing close, his arm draped protectively around her.

I reply with a halfhearted smile, "It's actually not too terrible."

And it really isn't. I never usually care to celebrate my birthday, so I wasn't sure what to expect. Yet tonight, it feels nice to let loose and forget about all the responsibilities waiting for me tomorrow.

Milli's laughter fills the air, a joyful and contagious sound. There's a brief exchange of words between her and Miles, and I can't help but feel they're scheming. My unease grows as Milli's clasp tightens around my hand.

I look at Miles, silently pleading for any hint about the situation, but he only shrugs helplessly, making me feel tempted to kick him. I feel a knot of anxiety in my stomach as Milli tugs me along, making me stumble slightly as I struggle to keep up. Moving upstairs, the crowd thickens and the heat becomes more intense. Beads of sweat form on my forehead as I give Miles a pleading look, but he only grins, clearly aware of Milli's scheme.

The second floor unfolds with various VIP areas, each hosting its own small gathering. We head toward one that's relatively quiet, save for a few guests. Curiosity quickens my pulse as we enter a dimly lit, private room. Between two plush chairs, there's an oddly placed stripper pole in the center.

The buzz from my drinks is making everything amusing, and I can't stop laughing, overwhelmed by a surge of giddiness. "Why are we here?" I ask, spinning around to take in the secluded room. Through the window, I watch the lively scene outside—club-goers engrossed in their own conversations and laughter, oblivious to our slight deviation.

Facing Milli and now Brooke, I open my arms in a soundless question, my heartbeat still fast, a smile teasing my mouth.

"Remember our version of truth or dare? The one with a twist?" Milli asks, her eyes sparkling with mischief. A shiver runs down my spine, a knot tightening in my stomach—I practically invented that game. But I just nod, masking my anxiety with a tight-lipped smile. Brooke's fingers weave through mine. "And do you recall that night we all shared our wildest fantasies?" Her voice is a seductive purr, stirring a whirlwind of memories and emotions.

I'm breathless and nodding again, allowing her to guide me toward the pole with ease. Milli's excitement radiates off her like a child on Christmas morning. "Come on, Pay. This is your chance to live out one of those fantasies," she urges, practically bouncing on her toes.

The center of my being pounds deep within me, each beat reverberating through my entire body. I hastily assess the room, my gaze flickering to the clueless partygoers outside. My hand encircles the cool, metallic pole, and for a moment I can feel an exhilarating rush in my veins, pushing me to embrace the moment. Nevertheless, the harsh reality hits me, causing me to abruptly withdraw my hand and shake my head vigorously. "Absolutely not," I speak out, my voice strong despite the lingering adrenaline.

Undeterred, Milli grabs my hand again, guiding it back to the pole. "Remember? You wanted to experience this—performing a dance for an audience," she insists, her steadfast tone compelling me to confront my fear. My caution battles with the anticipation stirring within me, the war between hesitation and desire playing out in my trembling hands.

Brooke chimes in, "We're daring you to strip. Just for us."

With a resigned sigh, I give in. "Okay, but on one condition—I pick the song."

Milli's eyes sparkle as she hurries to play my selected song, "Pony" by Ginuwine. I twirl my curly hair, creating a half-up, half-down look, while my fingers graze the pole. A tingling sensation runs up my neck like the first sip of champagne, bubbling with anticipation.

"You'll need this," Brooke says, handing me her drink. I gulp down the liquid, sensing a wave of courage rushing through my body.

Milli dashes back in, cueing the song. The atmosphere shifts. It's just the three of us in this secluded space—plus the invisible audience beyond these walls. At this very moment, the club and its onlookers vanish, leaving just us, this challenge, and a fantasy becoming reality.

With the music embracing me, I hold onto the pole tightly, allowing it to guide my movements in harmony with the alluring beat. With my eyes shut, I surrender to the melody, my legs gracefully encircling the pole. I tilt my head back and immerse myself in pure pleasure. From the sidelines, Milli and Brooke's cheers fuel my confidence, their support underscoring their invaluable friendship.

The dance flourishes, guided by the melody, and I finally grasp Milli's fervor for it—the empowering fusion of music and motion. It's euphoric, like floating on cloud nine, and I wish I could linger in this bliss indefinitely. But as the song concludes and I cautiously lower myself, the atmosphere of the room changes. Catching Milli's and Brooke's gaze, a touch of apprehension infiltrates my euphoric state. Their expressions are a confusing mix, something I can't quite decipher.

Feeling both curious and slightly nervous, I sneak a glance behind me. Previously absorbed in their own thoughts, the crowd now directs their full attention toward me. Self-consciousness engulfs me, until I spot someone in the crowd—Miles. Right beside him are those unmistakable hazel eyes—*Luke's*. The world fades into the background as my heart races, leaving only us.

A fiery passion fills his eyes as they scan me up and down. His intense gaze makes my skin tingle. For someone who professes to hate me, his stare reveals a fascination that contradicts his words.

However, in the bigger picture, none of this matters. It's merely Luke. His judgments, his views—they're irrelevant. His presence here, witnessing me embrace a cherished fantasy, should be insignificant.

Keep convincing yourself of that, Payson.

Milli shrugs casually as I refocus my attention on them, while Brooke's laughter fades as they leave the room before me. With confidence, I stride toward Miles and Luke, fixing Luke with a pointed look.

"Impressed?" I taunt.

"I've seen better," he claims, yet there's a mischievous

glint in his eye as he fishes something from his pocket and places it in my palm.

A penny.

Just a cold, singular penny.

Rage courses through me as I tightly clasp it, the unforgiving metal piercing my flesh. It wasn't as if I had performed for a tip. With a precise flick of my wrist, I turn and make my way down to the ground floor, feeling the heaviness of his words with every step. The alcohol swirling through my veins only fuels the fire, intensifying the sting of his mockery.

Out of nowhere, he grabs my wrist and halts my movement. When he catches my flinch, his face tightens and a look of concern flashes across it. I quickly pull away from his grasp, dodging his worried gaze.

Determined to escape to the bar for another drink, I notice Luke surpassing me, proudly demonstrating his athletic ability as he loudly commands the bartender to stop serving me.

I turn my head sharply toward him, narrowing my eyes. "What the hell, Luke?" I snap, the words cutting through the air. I groan softly, not due to alcohol, but because of the uncomfortably close man in front of me.

With deliberate slowness, he anchors me with his hands on my waist, reminiscent of a predator closing in on its prey. My breath catches as he whispers in my ear, his warm breath sending shivers down my spine. He says, "You'll be crashing at my place."

I pull away, noticing his clenched jaw and tense lips. The way he holds onto my waist is both pleasurable and painful, making my skin burn and throb. Our eyes connect and I state, "I have no intention of going back to your place." Memories of that night want to resurface.

With a stronger grip on my waist, he makes me gasp and presses my chest against his solid frame. My breathing quickens, mirroring his, and even though I despise him, I am consumed by the impulse to forcefully kiss him.

A few beats go by as we stare at each other, faces inches apart. When he moves closer, I instinctively close my eyes, my heart skipping a beat, imagining the touch of his lips on mine. Just this one time.

Wetting my lips, I patiently wait, and then I'm met with the statement, "There's no alternative for you. You're drunk, and you're with me tonight."

Letting go of my waist, he quickly seizes my bruised wrist, leaving me feeling unsteady again. I retreat and begin to rub it. He briefly shows empathy in his eyes, but it quickly disappears as he throws me over his shoulder and we walk past some enthusiastic fans. With a determined stride, he guides us through the crowd.

"Put me down, Luke!" I plead, pounding my fists against his back, but it's futile; he's built like a wall of muscle. He just shakes his head, his jaw set. "Shut up, Penny. You're going to cause a scene, and we both know that's the last thing Coach D wants."

W-what? He did not just tell me to shut up. He did not just blame me for this. He's the one who hoisted me over his shoulder like a damn sack of potatoes. My nails dig into his shoulders, and he winces. "If you keep it up, you'll be sleeping on the floor," he menacingly remarks as we exit the club.

He finally puts me down, and the heat I experienced in the club vanishes, replaced by a burning fury. Luke stands before me, pissed off at my birthday celebration. No one asked him to be here, least of all me. I'm not in need of a knight in shining armor. And Luke? He's more like a dark cloud hanging over my night.

With frustration, he sighs and runs his hands through his hair. "Did you really think I chose to be here? I have a fucking game tomorrow, but your reckless ass is being irresponsible." He mutters the last word, though I catch it, fueling my fury.

"Irresponsible? I was enjoying my damn birthday! How is that irresponsible?" I scream, throwing my hands in the air. There's a look of annoyance on his face as he shakes his head.

"Whatever," he says, looking away dismissively. "Right now, all that matters is Milli. I owed her a favor, and as much as I hate this, it looks like you're stuck with me tonight. Brooke bailed early, and Milli's off with Miles."

Each of his words ignites my simmering rage, piercing the air like burning embers. A night that should have been filled with joy has turned into a battlefield, with Luke at the center as an unexpected enemy that I am ready to face.

'Next thing I know, we're speeding through the bustling city, the neon lights a blur outside the car window. The tension between us is electric, like crackling static. We enter his penthouse, knowing that if it weren't so late and I didn't have to be in Dallas tomorrow—or today—I wouldn't be here. While removing my high heels, something unexpectedly strikes my face. I look down at the object he threw at me, now at my feet. The unmistakable scent of his cologne, aftershave, and a hint of menthol wafted from the oversized Lone Star T-shirt. The temptation to bring it closer, to take a deep breath of him, is a struggle. Yet, I refuse to give him the gratification.

A faint throb pulses between my thighs, and I let out a quiet whimper. Damn him.

I raise my eyes and find Luke with a smug grin on his face. My jaw twitches, my hands forming tight fists. Oh, he thought this was funny, did he? My blood boils, the heat of anger flushing my cheeks. Extending my black heel, I raise it high and share a knowing smile with him. "Don't test me, Sutton."

With narrowed eyes, his fading smirk gives way to a defiant glint. "You wouldn't. You need me too much."

A bitter laugh escapes me, filling the silence with a harsh and grating sound. "Yeah, no, I don't." But the truth gnaws at me, a painful admission I can't ignore; I do need him.

With each step he takes, our breaths intertwine, the closeness causing the rhythm in my core to throb like an unyielding drum. "That's not what you were saying months ago." He maintains a poker face.

With a huff, I reach for my phone, contemplating whether to call an Uber and escape back to the dorms. Just as I'm about to act, his hand locks onto my wrist. He notices the lingering bruise on my skin, the colors a mix of dark blue and faded yellow.

When our gazes lock, for the second time tonight, concern storms in his eyes, silently questioning the story behind the mark. His intense stare is almost unbearable, and I desperately want to shield myself from the vulnerability it exposes. Yet, before I can pull away, his thumb gently brushes over the bruise, sending a war of goose bumps along my arm.

Clearing his throat, he softly suggests, "You can stay in the spare bedroom." His gentle touch on the bruise creates a flutter in my chest, and despite my resolve, I'm mesmerized. My realization that I've been holding my breath comes when he finally releases my hand. Reality comes rushing back as I exhale, and I oddly yearn for the comforting touch of his warmth once more.

Payson, that's not what you want.

After all, I am his therapist. Certain boundaries must not be crossed. I refuse to cross those boundaries, not with him.

"Thought the floor was calling my name?" I say with a

hint of sass, annoyed by the intense emotions in my body. It's easy to blame the alcohol, but I can't overlook the effect Luke has on me. *More than one.*

With a shrug, he says, "I don't want to deal with a tired, cranky therapist after my game tomorrow." He heads to his bedroom, carrying my pounding heart and swirling emotions with him. Just before disappearing, he looks over his shoulder, his hazel eyes catching the hall light, revealing flecks of gold and green that seem to pierce right through me. "Don't say I never did anything nice for you, Penny," he adds.

I clench my lower lip, tempted to reply, *Nice?* Instead, I sigh and go explore the guest bathroom, a place where luxury meets tranquility.

Picture a bathroom that goes beyond mere practicality, transforming into a sanctuary of tranquility and visual pleasure. Inhaling deeply, I shed my outfit and slip into his shirt, which cascades down to my knees, surrounding me with the scent of Luke. Tension fills my body as my thoughts wander back to that unforgettable night. The feel of the soft fabric on my skin instantly brings to mind Luke's touch on my waist tonight. His heated eyes burning with intensity, desire unmistakably simmering beneath the surface. I'm not blind to it. I shouldn't feel this sudden warmth spreading through my legs or the sly smile tugging at my lips, but I do. I can't afford to get swept up in this—I know the consequences all too well. Yet, here I am, teetering on the edge, drawn in by the irresistible pull he exudes.

Startled by footsteps, I quickly open my eyes and tightly grip my discarded clothes. Exiting the bathroom, I make my way to the guest room and arrive just as someone knocks on the partially open door.

Unsure whether to feign sleep or confront him, I find myself drawn to the door. In the soft light, Luke stands shirtless, his chiseled muscles gently gleaming.

Does this man not own enough shirts?

His lazy gaze slides down my body with a deliberate slowness that sets my skin ablaze and makes my heart pound. My body responds instantly; sweat beads on my forehead as the heat rises under my skin like an unstoppable wave.

His gaze drifts across my chest, each breath causing my breasts to rise and fall, the fabric of my thin shirt doing nothing to hide my peaked nipples. He fixates on my bare legs, delicately following the shape of my thighs. Every inch of his scrutiny feels like a physical caress, igniting my nerves.

My cheeks flush crimson, and my heart pounds so loudly that I'm certain he can hear it. He licks his lips, possibly unaware of the action, creating a dull ache that blooms low in my abdomen, an ache both unfamiliar and intoxicating.

When our gazes meet, the air shifts abruptly, creating a charged silence that becomes more and more unbearable. The room contracts, tension building between us, filled with unsaid words and intense longing. His intense, dark eyes capture my attention, making everything else disappear.

Each step he takes sends a jolt through me, my muscles tightening in anticipation. His fingers reach out, softly embracing my jaw, tracing my features with a featherlight touch, he then sweetly tucks a stray lock of hair behind my ear. His warm breath and hazel eyes make me feel dizzy.

"Luke," I whisper.

In a single heartbeat, my carefully constructed walls collapse and are carried away like petals in a wild wind. My heart halts, every part of me on edge, ready to welcome the kiss I'm convinced is coming, ready to lose myself to the moment, to him. But then he catches me by surprise with a soft, meaningful kiss on my forehead.

In a low voice, he murmurs, "Happy birthday, Payson." My eyes drift shut, his words causing my chest to squeeze. My body melts into his touch, a sigh escaping my lips as I revel in the unexpected tenderness, feeling cherished and protected in a way I hadn't expected.

Softly, he kisses me again, his lips lingering as if he wants to forever remember this moment. When he steps back, his eyes hold a depth that both startles and mesmerizes me. And then he's gone, just like that. The door closes, along with my heart. A storm of emotions churns within me, unanswered questions tugging at my soul as I sink into the king-size bed.

Why did he do that?

CHAPTER 15
LUKE

I'd be lying through my teeth if I said I slept like a baby last night. I was constantly battling with the sheets, just like a kid avoiding the bedtime monster. One second, I was about to doze off, and the next, my cock was hard and my mind racing, reminiscing about that club scene with a blonde knockout in an outfit that screamed *trouble*.

Not that I should've cared, but damn, it was challenging not to.

A groan slips out of me, promptly halted by the unmistakable noise of someone tiptoeing across my floor. Despite its newness, the creaky boards are now a hidden blessing. Is she attempting a stealthy getaway? As if I'd let that slide—after the night we'd had, a simple "thank you" would have been the least.

I have every reason to be angry with her. Acting as if the consequences were insignificant, she got recklessly drunk. Memories of Milli from years ago resurfaced on her birthday —her slurred speech and dependence on me.

My chest tightens, a storm of emotions swirling inside

me. I yank a pair of boxers and shorts from the drawer, my hands trembling with frustration. Each motion feels heavy, weighed down by the mess inside my head. I move to the door, steadying my breathing, the wood cool against my palm as I crack it open. There she is, her golden locks tied up in a messy bun, retreating to the guest room, shutting the door behind her.

While crossing to the guest room, I hear a faint stream of curses from the other side—clearly, she is not happy about being in my place. But honestly, being here, in this penthouse, isn't exactly a hardship; most women would envy her spot right now. Nevertheless, I gently knock on the door and am met with immediate silence. It's almost comical how she tries to pretend she's somewhere else, as if she can escape me, especially with her unmistakable scent still present. That scent is reminiscent of a comforting hug from your favorite coffee shop on a chilly morning. The perfect combination of robust coffee beans, smooth vanilla, and a touch of cinnamon.

"Don't stay silent now, Penny," I comment, heading to the kitchen. It's only 8:00 am, but the hostility between us is already evident. To divert my attention, I concentrate on making coffee and immersing myself in my pre–game day routine. Mornings are for fueling up—carbs for energy, protein for muscle repair.

The coffee machine sputters to life, and I slam the pans down on the counter, louder than necessary. The guest room door finally swings open, causing my muscles to tense against my will. Her soft footsteps echo on the floor. I pour the first cup, facing away from her, hoping the ritual of coffee-making will calm me. Instantly, she grabs the coffee, defying her hangover.

She takes a sip, her mouth parting with an infuriating

little noise—half sigh, half moan. It's a sound that's both maddening and arousing, and I absolutely detest it.

Her gaze meets mine. "You sleep okay?" I ask, trying to keep my tone casual.

Sauntering to the kitchen island, she shrugs with a mix of defiance and effortless sensuality in her movements. Not that I should be noticing. This is Payson—her sexiness is the least of my concerns. But it's impossible to ignore her, especially when she's only wearing my shirt.

"Skipping pants today?" I comment, unable to keep the edge out of my voice. With each sip of coffee, she savors it like she's savoring my discomfort. She has no makeup on, her hair is in a messy bun, she's sipping from the coffee cup, and her hard nipples are showing through my T-shirt. It's damn hard to focus on anything else, and I hate that too.

The way she caresses the cup's edge and holds it, followed by a slight lick of her lips, drives me crazy.

Get yourself together, Luke.

She stands abruptly, setting her cup down with a defiant clink. "Like I would ever allow you the pleasure of seeing more," she snaps, her words dripping with sarcasm and disdain.

Silently, I hold back a comeback, yet internally, I'm reliving that night.

I divert my focus back to the stove, cracking eggs with a fervor that exposes my inner conflict. Every motion is purposeful, nearly forceful, as I fight the urge to let my gaze wander to her once more. Last night's memory haunts my thoughts, the burning touch of our skin, the restraint from pulling her into bed. I knew it wouldn't end well. I must keep my focus on the prize, not become distracted by her.

"Breakfast will be ready shortly," I call out.

The sound of her voice fills the air, accompanied by the

rustling of her purse. "No worries, I'll just catch an Uber to campus."

The words land on me like a blow, bringing me to a sudden stop. Without thinking, I grab her wrist, the very same one I held last night. Her body tenses as her gaze meets mine, vulnerability briefly concealed by stubbornness.

I notice faint marks encircling her wrist. My jaw clenches, rage simmering at the thought of another person hurting her. The fury churns in my gut, mingling with an unidentified feeling, more primal, more protective.

"Stay," I utter, the word slipping out with a roughness, more of an order than a plea.

Surprise flickers across her face. I try to downplay my emotions by shrugging casually, as if her being here doesn't unravel me.

Returning to the stove, the sizzle of eggs offers a feeble distraction from the overpowering intensity in my penthouse. "Going back to campus and then coming back here doesn't seem very practical." I stress the importance of practicality rather than desperately wanting her to stay.

Without hesitation, she resists. "I need to leave, I've got homework, I need my lap—"

I cut her off, pivoting to face her. "Use mine."

She widens her eyes, then narrows them. "But my clothes—"

Yet again, I interrupt, stepping closer. "You can wear mine."

Annoyed, she huffs, but I cut her off before she can argue. I place a plate with fruit, eggs, and toast in front of her. With suspicion etched on her features, she flicks her stare from the plate to me. It's almost comical, like she thinks I've laced her breakfast with some sort of evil substance. I conceal a laugh, maintaining my tone firm as I urge, "Eat."

Her eyebrows shoot up. "You don't get to order me around, Sutton."

I click my tongue, a teasing edge slipping into my voice. "Seems you followed my directions well enough before." Her ears turn a deep shade of red, and she looks away, flustered. That small victory tastes sweet.

With my meal in hand, I join her on the island, and the thick atmosphere makes it almost feel like there's an additional presence in the room. With each bite, we silently negotiate a tentative truce. After a few minutes, I'm up and moving through the house with purposeful strides, preparing for game day.

"The laptop is on the nightstand in my bedroom," I yell from the living room, my mind already ticking off my mental checklist. With a mischievous grin, I add, "And if you need a new outfit, you know where to find mine." She rolls her eyes, but I don't miss the blush that spreads from her ears to her cheeks.

I casually mention, "Feel free to grab anything from the kitchen."

I hear her whisper something that sounds like "Of course," but I ignore it and move closer to her. Instinctively, she moves to the back of the couch, her eyes widening. I delicately raise her chin, feeling the touch of her bottom lip against my thumb. A soft whimper escapes her, soon transforming into a fierce glare. A smirk crosses my face as I take pleasure in her reaction, perhaps more than I should. Leaning in, my lips brushing her neck, I whisper, "Take a shower—you could use one." Her eyes flash with anger and something else I can't quite place.

Full of adrenaline, I head toward the door with my heart racing. I yell, "Later, Penny!" I can envision her reaction vividly: shaking head, hand on hip, lips tightly pursed in pure indignation.

Fueled by the lingering image, I step outside, ready to take control of today's game. Nevertheless, a disconcerting tug persists, reminding me of the mixed emotions I'm wrestling with.

Payson

My lungs remember how to breathe as the door shuts. It's as if his presence alone had them on lockdown.

What the hell is going on with me? With him?

How did I end up agreeing to stay at his luxurious penthouse, wearing his shirt, and having breakfast together like a normal couple?

Because part of you wanted this, whispers a voice within my thoughts.

But did I really want this? My parents, once an ordinary couple, now serve as a warning of love's bitter side. Alarm bells should ring—this situation is a glaring red flag by my standards. Although my gut is urging me to escape any suggestion of a romantic connection, I can't ignore the fact that there's something occurring between us, even if I'm hesitant to fully accept it.

I stretch lazily, taking a deep breath while the morning sun shines through the tall windows, casting light on the cityscape. The view from his couch is stunning, with a sea of tall skyscrapers that I never thought would give me a sense of belonging. However, waking up in this place, far from Milli's snores and the never-ending freshman drama, fills me with a peacefulness I didn't know I needed. It's a much-welcomed relief that I'm going to fully embrace.

I consume the breakfast Luke prepared, and it's surprisingly good. The meal was basic but far superior to anything the university cafeteria serves. Next, I treat myself to a lavish, leisurely bath in his deep vintage tub with plenty of bubbles, because a little self-care is always beneficial before getting back to the demands of homework and a session with Luke. Later, despite the lingering effects of last night's chaos and a bothersome hangover, I prepare a new mug of coffee, get Luke's laptop from his room—resisting the urge to snoop— and make myself comfortable on the couch. Right at that moment, my phone starts vibrating. Probably Milli checking in.

Yet, my heart plummets upon seeing the message.

MOM

Can't wait for this coming weekend, sweetie!

I squeeze my eyes shut, a groan escaping my lips as my head falls back against the couch. Damn, I had completely forgotten about her visit. What are we going to do? North-Ridge isn't exactly sprawling, and with me living in a dorm, it's not like I can host a sleepover. Nevertheless, I need to think of a solution. There's absolutely no question that she needs this, needs me.

PAYSON

Me too, Mama. Can't wait to see you. XOXO.

MOM

[Sends a selfie] Will the cool kids you chill with even notice this?

The picture causes my chest to tighten. Her bruised eye is glaring back at me, a cruel reminder. My eyes shut, and my fingers find a bruise on my body that looks the same. Anger and frustration rise, conflicting with the guilt consuming me. I pace the living room, trying to shake off the restless energy.

I can see past her attempt at humor, understanding it as a

thin disguise for her profound sorrow. I have a strong feeling she'll send a message tonight, regretting not being able to join her friends for their weekly wine and gossip. The guilt eats at me, urging me to grab her, shake her, scream, tell her to stand up to Dad, to choose herself. However, each time I bring this up, it ends up causing more harm, and she insists that she can take care of it or that everything is okay. Every single time, the words stab me deep like a knife.

Yet, for now, I send a message in the hopes of offering her solace, even though I am miles away, my heart throbbing with each word.

PAYSON

No, Mama. You look beautiful as ever.

MOM

You're right, I do, don't I. It adds character to my complexion.

Her message holds my gaze, my hands quivering. Confusion swirls within me. How can she endure this for so many years? How is she able to easily ignore another blow to her skin? She deserves better.

With sadness, I bring the conversation to a close, sending one last message.

PAYSON

I love you, Mom.

The photographs displayed on Luke's mantle immediately capture my interest. In the midst of the photographs featuring his family and friends, one catches my eye—a nostalgic snapshot of Luke and Miles during their time at NorthRidge University. Additionally, there are a few pictures of a younger Luke, proudly displaying medals around his neck.

I carefully lift the final frame, studying a photo of Luke, probably at the age of twelve or thirteen. I see him standing with a child his age and an older man, both of whom I don't recognize despite knowing Luke since childhood. All of them have jerseys that read *Mighty Mavericks*, and the older man's jersey is labeled *Coach Maverick*. The older man, likely one of Luke's coaches, looks so proud, and it brings a small smile to my face.

Luke consistently speaks highly of his coaches, and this guy is no different. This picture beautifully showcases a moment that made him feel celebrated and supported. It ties back to what I learned in psychology—how past experiences and relationships shape who we are and how we interact with others.

I quickly send Milli a text with a photo of the picture.

PAYSON

Hey, got a quick question for you.

Milli's response is almost instantaneous.

MILLI

Hit me with it.

PAYSON

Do you recognize this guy?

Her reply comes with a teasing undertone.

MILLI

Still at Luke's, I see ;)

PAYSON

Mills, focus. Who is he?

MILLI

Yeah, that's Troy. He used to coach Luke back in the day.

PAYSON

Was he around a lot during Luke's childhood?

The man's proud look at Luke and his friend as he lovingly rests his hands on their shoulders indicates a strong, familiar connection.

MILLI

Mostly during Luke's childhood.

PAYSON

Did Luke get along with him? Was he a good coach?

MILLI

What's with the interrogation, Miss Detective?

Her comment makes me laugh.

PAYSON

What about the boy?

MILLI

Oh, he and Benny were inseparable, grew up together, shared daycares—the whole package. They were almost impossible to separate.

That information made me even more curious. What happened to Benny? Where is he now, and what happened to the coach? Is he still in contact with Luke?

Nevertheless, I refrain from probing any deeper. Given my role as Luke's therapist, these questions are directed toward him, and Milli may not be able to provide the answers. So, I simply reply with a noncommittal, "That's sweet."

Milli's response was a brief "Yeah," followed by a promise of catching up later.

Even after closing the texting app, I find myself thinking about the coach in the photo and pondering his significance. Something inside me is fueled by an intense interest to learn more directly from him. Unable to wait, I do a quick search. When I look up Troy, I immediately close Google, realizing I should wait for Luke to provide me with his information.

I lose track of time as I delve into my coursework, using Luke's laptop to access the school database. Eventually, I pause and search for food. I end up with lunch meat and chips—not the epitome of health, but my cravings aren't leaning toward anything labeled *healthy*, especially not in the aftermath of my period. Diets aren't my thing, especially during hormonal chaos.

After eating, the temptation of another luxurious bath proves too alluring to resist. "Why not?" I reason with myself, fully aware that such indulgence isn't a regular luxury in my life. And considering it's Luke's penthouse, the water bill isn't my concern.

Feeling rejuvenated from my bath, I casually make my way into his bedroom, using the excuse of needing a fresh shirt, even though the one I've had on since last night feels anything but fresh.

I can't help but notice the details of his room once more. My fingers unknowingly trace the surface of his dresser as I select one of his Lone Star shirts to slip into. I look up at the TV above me, then out of the floor-to-ceiling windows where the sun is setting. The thought of living this every day, going to sleep in a luxurious bed, surrounded by the sunset, and having the choice of TV or tranquility, fills me with fascination.

A girl's got to satisfy her curiosity, right?

Without any hesitation, I quickly hop onto his precisely

made bed, my smile getting bigger as I realize Luke took the time to make it. It's surprising, considering I half expected him to have a housekeeper for such tasks. Maybe he's more into domestic chores than I thought. As I recline on the bed, letting my legs kick freely in the air, a childlike glee takes over. This bed—it's like lying on cloud nine. I can't resist making myself comfortable, just for a little while. Luke won't be back for hours. Why not enjoy a moment of pure bliss?

What starts as a single episode of *I Love Lucy* quickly spirals into several, and before I realize it, my eyelids droop heavily. The TV's gentle hum fades as sleep takes over.

The bed moves beneath me, and a sound I recognize, full of taunting, breaks through the haze. "My bed that comfortable, Penny?"

As I slowly open my eyes, the blur gradually clears, and there he is, smirking at me. My stomach flutters. My cheeks burn with embarrassment, yet I can't look away.

He takes a seat next to me, and the air becomes heavy with a strange sense of comfort that feels just right. Moving is not something I want to do, and he seems to pick up on this, staying in close proximity. As he strips off his shirt and slides into bed in just his boxers, a surge of heat and nerves dances within me. With a simple action, he darkens the room by turning off the TV.

I'm left breathless and unable to break my gaze. Why does he never fail to be so damn attractive when he's not wearing a shirt? Moving back, my heart starts pounding as I fight to maintain professionalism. My mind goes blank when his strong hands encircle my waist, effortlessly pulling me toward him.

What is happening?

I lightly tug, feebly resisting, but he simply chuckles. A fire ignites within me, fueled by the rich sound that spreads through every part of me. "If you're in my bed, you stay in my bed," he murmurs, his voice commanding. But he quickly warns, "Don't overthink this. I had a rough game and I just need this right now."

I'm the one he needs?

Given everything between us, I should be the one to take back his demand, especially considering the boundaries and unspoken rules. His touch, so bold and full of arrogance, should cause me to retreat. However, I feel myself melting into him. The warning signs in my head regarding the significance of this intimacy are overshadowed by the sense of safety his embrace provides. His hold doesn't feel like a cage; it feels like a refuge, leaving my emotions tangled.

In the dark, before I doze off, I whisper, "Who is Coach Maverick?" His response comes with a gentle tightening of his grip, pulling me closer as if I'm his lifeline.

"Someone of no importance."

If that's true, then why is he given a place of honor on your fireplace?

CHAPTER 16
PAYSON

What in the hell just happened?

"Honey, you could've just told me," she says, the word *just* faintly stern, "if you didn't want me over this weekend." Her words linger in the air as I steer my Kia into the nearly deserted parking lot of the movie theater just outside North-Ridge. The emptiness doesn't surprise me—it is Sunday morning, after all, and most people are likely busy with their own lives, be it college studies, work preparations for Monday, or family duties.

The scarcity of people is somewhat relieving. It feels like there's more space to breathe, less worry about the conversations my mom might start in the presence of strangers.

Turning off the car, I reach across the middle console to take her hand, exhaling deeply. "It's not that I don't want you here, Mom," I assure her, and it's the truth. I'm genuinely glad she's here; she needs this escape, even if it's just to visit her daughter at college. After she missed our planned visit last Saturday, it became clear she needed this trip more than ever, especially considering my dad's likely influence over her decision. I didn't ask about what he said or what happened, but her split lip said it all.

Seeing it again floods me with regret like a tidal wave. Tears threaten to fall as my throat constricts and my eyes burn. I fight to keep them at bay. The purpose of this visit is to uplift her and give me a break from my demanding studies and tonight's session with Luke. Our last encounter, I ended up in his arms, but I scolded myself for crossing that boundary and left in the morning.

Professional boundaries exist for a reason.

While heading toward my mom, my phone vibrates in my pocket. It's probably Milli, wondering where I've disappeared to. Before leaving our dorm, she asked about Luke's efforts. I knew he was trying, but it still wasn't enough. It was evident that he was keeping a secret, especially given his behavior at the last game. His recurring "toddler tantrum" indicated that I needed to stay alert and find out what was truly bothering him in order to help him.

As I checked the message, my mom held my hand, and we walked together, hand in hand, like a couple in their golden years savoring a leisurely stroll.

LUKE

[A photo of his game day essentials neatly arranged on his kitchen counter] Game Day Ready: Check

I shake my head at the randomness of Luke's text. Our usual exchanges are brief and revolve around scheduling our therapy sessions. This week, Luke has been unusually open, discussing everything from his favorite TV show, *Dexter*, to sharing a shirtless photo of himself relaxing on his bed. Believe me, those abs are seriously impressive. That bed . . . it's not just any bed. It's the one we've shared intimately, cuddled in, and, well, you know. Such an image would naturally make anyone's heart flutter.

Another message pops up on my phone, accompanied by a photo of Luke decked out in his game-day finest.

LUKE

Game Day Outfit: Locked In 🔒

The shirt he has chosen is just visible beneath his suit, declaring BREAKING THROUGH DEFENSES, ON AND OFF THE FIELD.

I burst out laughing, halting both me and my mom as we're about to step into the cinema. "Seriously, where does he find these?" I mutter.

"What's so funny?" Mom looks at me, curious. I nervously bite my lip, stealing a glance at Luke's photo on my phone. He looks . . . annoyingly charming—handsome, even bordering on sexy.

Wait, sexy? God, Payson, pull yourself together. This is Luke Sutton we're talking about. He's a client, for heaven's sake, and let's not forget, you're supposed to dislike him. Despise him, even.

But do people who hate one another cuddle each other?

I respond with a small smile and say, "Nothing," while she gets our tickets for *Under the Same Starlit Sky*, her beloved movie. It's precisely the rom-com that caters to hopeless romantics— not my usual choice, but I'm here for her. She deserves to trust that love can be different from the twisted version she witnesses with my dad. Even though I understand this, it doesn't stop the knot of anxiety twisting in my stomach. The idea of settling down, getting married, and starting a family terrifies me because it might reveal that the person I thought I knew is actually a stranger. That's why I avoid getting too close to men.

My phone vibrates with a new message while my mom is busy. Seizing the moment, I sneak a peek.

LUKE

Attitude Ready?: Damn straight, baby.

Warmth rushes to my cheeks as I try to keep my composure, resisting the urge to melt at the mention of *baby*. It's not even directed at me; it's just his ego flaunting the word. Two weeks without seeing Luke due to away games and my RA duties, you'd think I'd have time to forget how his arms felt. Yet here I am, my heart betraying my better judgment, pounding a little faster at the mere thought of him.

"Who's got my Pay Bay all lit up like that?" Mom probes, snapping me out of my thoughts. I freeze, torn between the urge to spill everything and the need to keep my professional distance. I'm his therapist, and he's my client. The task should be easy, but my body reacts with nervousness and uncertainty.

Putting my chaotic thoughts on hold as Mom goes to the bathroom, I hastily send a response to Luke.

PAYSON

Cut the selfies, Sutton. Focus on your game.

His reply comes almost immediately.

LUKE

Oh, Penny, I know you like them. No need to pretend you don't.

Before I can react, another message pops up.

LUKE

Worry not your pretty heart. I'm on it.

PAYSON

Really now? And how's that, Einstein? You haven't even gotten my legendary advice in two weeks.

LUKE

Well, enlighten me. You're the therapist,
remember?

Against my will, a smirk begins to tug at my lips. I shake
my head, trying to keep my focus as I navigate the snack line
with my mom. Taking the lead in ordering, she allows me a
brief moment to send a final message to Luke.

PAYSON

Keep it simple. Overthinking is our worst
enemy.

LUKE

Expert advice. How is that supposed to
help?

I let out a sigh as we take our seats in the dimly lit
theater. The usual pre-movie chatter fills the air, but my mind
is lost in another world.

PAYSON

You can't let it take over. Not the anger, not
the fear, not that shadowy beast lurking in
the corners. Think ahead—what comes after
tonight's game? Picture it. The
consequences of your actions, whether good
or bad, will catch up with you when the game
is over. How would you like to feel in the
end? Victorious? Regretful? On top of the
world? Decide how you want to feel
postgame and let that guide your actions.

I pause, the words on the screen blurring slightly. My
fingers hover over the keys, searching for the right sentiment
to close our conversation.

I am snapped back to reality by the sound of my mom's voice. "You know you can tell me anything, right, Pay?" my mom asks gently as I stash my phone away, her eyes searching mine.

I give a noncommittal shrug, my shoulders barely lifting. "Yeah, I know. There's not much to tell. I have to complete a clinical, and Josie, my advisor, set me up with this opportunity for the year." Part of me wants to tell her about the chance to graduate early, but I know that will bring a flood of emotions I'm not ready for. "That was just a client messaging me," I murmur, trying to sound casual as I glance away.

My phone vibrates, my fingers lingering over the screen.

She gives me a look, her eyes softening before she playfully nudges me. "Oh, is this client a guy?" she teases, her voice lilting with curiosity. I released a gentle laugh, my lips forming a subtle smile. She's a true hopeless romantic, my mom. The hopeful look in her eyes pierces my heart, every teasing nudge a constant reminder of her own love life's emptiness. The passing guilt, momentarily buried, resurfaces, weighing heavily and feeling oppressive.

Will this feeling ever fade?

Will I always be burdened by this?

I softly grasp her arm and rest my head on her shoulder. "Let's just enjoy tonight, okay? Watching a romantic movie was your idea, after all."

Her laughter rings out, free, enveloping me like a warm blanket on a frosty night. It's comforting, hearing her laugh like that. "All right, but don't think I'll drop this subject," she warns, popping popcorn into her mouth. "The idea of my daughter getting a crush on her client isn't something I can easily ignore."

At the mention of a crush, I immediately sit up and meet her gaze directly.

Her eyes gleam mischievously as she munches on popcorn, popping in another piece. "Oh, come on, Pay. I saw how you lit up reading those messages. You looked just like you did when you believed in Santa Claus."

Is she serious? A crush on Luke? That's about as likely as discovering a new galaxy.

She turns back to the screen as the trailers play, a nostalgic smile creeping onto her face. "Remember how you had a crush on Santa? It was adorable, even if it was mostly about the presents. I haven't forgotten how your cheeks would turn that cute shade of pink every December at the mere mention of his name."

I shake my head but smile as I steal some of the popcorn. Before I realize it, the credits roll, and we're back in the car again.

"I know today was meant for just us, but I heard your phone vibrating nonstop during the movie, Mom." Just then, the screen lights up, displaying two missed calls from Dad and seven new messages, all demanding her location, activities, and reasons for not being home. My chest tightens, not with shock but with sorrow for her.

I give her a questioning look. With tears streaming down her face, she vigorously shakes her head. Biting her lip, she winces upon touching the split. I softly clasp her wrist. "Mom, why did you keep him in the dark about where you were going?"

Her voice quivers as she speaks. "B-because he didn't—" She pauses, and I rub her back, urging her on. "He didn't believe me. According to him, you didn't have time for a movie." How could he say that? Our time together is always precious to me, even if it occasionally feels burdensome.

"You're aware that's not true, Mom, right?" I mumble.

With each nod, her tears fall quicker. I pull her into a hug from the side, our heads leaning in close. "I'm aware, my love," she whispers, her voice heavy with emotion.

Inside the car, her subdued weeping fills the silence. The fear of being stuck in a similar situation with someone I love? Yeah, that churns in my stomach, making me cling tighter to her.

"Mom, you can't keep doing this. You need to leave. You can't keep living this way."

She trembles and sniffs, shaking her head while muttering, "I understand, I understand."

But does she really? One fact is undeniable: She has to be the one to set herself free, to determine when it's time to walk away from all of this.

"This is the best way to treat your body like a castle, right, Daddy?" says the little girl at the table opposite us, her voice dancing across the black-and-white checkered table. I smile, savoring another spoonful of my Emerald Mint Chip, as she dives into her own sundae.

Luke's loud laughter fills the air in response. "Ali, are you wielding your charm to sway your big teddy bear dad again?" he teases.

Berry responds to Luke's jest with a shake of his head. "Seems to work on you, doesn't it?" Aliana grins as she looks up at her father, affectionately nicknamed Berry or Big Guy by Luke. He had mentioned this nickname when I met him outside his penthouse before we headed to Dream Scoops.

"Didn't you once declare donuts the ultimate way to treat your body like a castle, Ali?" Luke quips, taking a generous spoonful of his Rainbow Ribbon Vanilla ice cream. Surprisingly, he seems to favor the colorful mix of berry, citrus, and tropical flavors—a side of him I hadn't expected. Each session reveals more layers to Luke, moving beyond the egotistical playboy I once knew. That part of him is still there, but now I'm discovering another side.

His interactions with Aliana for the past hour have been nothing short of captivating. His patience is remarkable; his eyes sparkle with intrigue every time she recounts her adventures in early preschool, and they soften to a tender gaze when she affectionately calls him Lukie, causing my heart to expand in warmth.

With an exasperated yet adorable eye roll, she emphasizes her point by emphatically saying "Nope" with a dramatic *P*. Waving her finger with all the earnestness a five-year-old can muster, I barely conceal my amusement at her next admission. "I said it to get donuts from you."

Surprise fills Luke's eyes, then he bursts into laughter, his smile spreading wide and genuine. It reminds me of the variety of smiles my mother has—there's the obligatory *I'm here, are you happy?* smile, the ones she forces in polite company, and then, my favorite, her *free spirit* smile. That last one radiates contentment, a signal that she's exactly where she wants to be. Watching Luke now, his smile mirrors that rare, unguarded joy of my mother's free spirit smile. Clearly, he wants to be here with Aliana and Berry.

After the movie ended, a message had popped up from Luke. It felt like a lifeline, though my initial enthusiasm for our planned session was dampened by exhaustion. I was on the verge of canceling, but Luke's suggestion completely turned things around. "How about an ice cream session?"

How could I possibly resist? Ice cream was an offer too

sweet to decline, and the prospect of meeting one of Luke's teammates, along with his daughter, was a bonus. The way they interacted felt heartwarmingly familiar, reminding me of my bond with my dad. Luke brought up how their ice cream outings were a treasured tradition, similar to the rituals my dad and I shared. The comparison evoked a sense of nostalgia, but Berry quickly brushed off any sadness with a lighthearted sigh and a pat on his belly.

Berry is striking in his own right—towering at six feet, eight inches and built like a linebacker, with brown hair and eyes a unique shade of blue-gray, his arms adorned with an array of tattoos. Yet, to his little girl, he is a gentle, giant teddy bear. The adoration in her eyes every few moments makes that abundantly clear.

With a mischievous smile, Luke teases, "You're more of a donut person than an ice cream person, aren't you?"

She pauses, spoon hovering in midair, mulling over her answer, then replies with an effortless shrug, "Well, technically speaking . . . " and I can't help but grin. The idea of a five-year-old weighing in on matters with the word *technically* is hilarious. "Donuts have the breakfast slot because Daddy says ice cream is for those extra special days, like when we win at games. If there was ice cream for breakfast, that'd be my pick." She gives another shrug, delivering her final verdict with the confidence of a seasoned debater. "So, no, Lukie, in this case, ice cream takes the crown over donuts."

Suppressing my laughter with my spoon, I observe her gracefully standing her ground. Her spunk and logic are utterly adorable. Feeling a wave of camaraderie, I decide it's only right to back her up—we girls need to stick together, after all.

"Aliana, you've got a point, and I'm on your side. Ice cream for breakfast sounds like a dream. And really, donuts are just circular cakes, if you think about it." I hear Luke groan beside me, but I smile as her eyes sparkle with joy at my solidarity.

Then she beams and says, "I like you." It's such a spontaneous, sincere remark. I never seek approval, especially not from a child, but her warm voice makes me smile more.

"I like you too, Ali," I respond, adopting Luke's affectionate nickname for her—it just feels right.

She returns to her ice cream, but between bites, she casually comments, "You're pretty too." Her words hang in the air as she looks to Luke for his opinion. "Lukie, do you think she's pretty?" Anticipation causes my cheeks to burn, and Luke's intense gaze gives me a pleasant sensation of butterflies in my chest.

His response catches me off guard. He keeps his eyes on me, speaking each word with a weight that quickens my heartbeat. "Absolutely, Ali. She's beautiful." She nods, as if affirming a well-known fact, and I focus all my effort on not letting my heart leap out of my chest.

Why is my pulse skipping like this? Luke's straightforward declaration that I'm beautiful shouldn't send my heart into overdrive.

Luke's gaze doesn't waver, his intensity making it impossible to look away.

"Lukie, is she your girlfriend?" Aliana's innocent question snaps me back to reality, causing me to almost choke.

Luke shakes his head while Berry's teasing voice interrupts the moment. "He wishes. All right, Aliana sweetheart, time to pack up."

Aliana pouts, her disarming cuteness almost enough to sway anyone in charge. "But why? I'm not done with my ice cream yet."

Berry chuckles, a mix of affection and firmness in his voice. "You're done for now. Plus, it's way past bedtime."

With a dramatic sigh and an eye roll, Aliana finally gives

in to her dad's direction. Yet, she can't resist throwing in a heartfelt plea. "Can Payson come over to play at my Enchanted Play Palace, please?" Her earnestness is hard to ignore as she dramatically drops to her knees on the parlor's checkered floor, her small hands pressed together in a hopeful gesture, capturing the attention of everyone around us. It's clear that Berry is uneasy with the situation, his eyes practically pleading for help.

Overwhelmed with emotion, I found myself kneeling at Aliana's level, holding her small hands. Looking into her hopeful eyes, I respond with genuine warmth, "Visiting your Enchanted Play Palace would be a privilege."

She is filled with pure happiness, her face glowing as she embraces me in a sudden hug. Stepping back, she gently tucks a strand of hair behind my ear and whispers, "I think you've made my night."

My gaze drops to the floor as I take a moment to breathe deeply. Then, I pull her into another hug, closing my eyes to murmur, "You've made my night, too, Ali."

Feeling Luke's eyes on me, I hesitantly open mine. I see him studying me attentively out of the corner of my eye. His gaze is revealing, as if he's seeing parts of me I've never willingly shown, making me feel exposed in a way that's entirely new, beyond any physical sense he's witnessed. After a final tight hug to Aliana, I rise to my feet, and as Berry ushers his goodbyes, Aliana wraps Luke in a hug before grabbing her dad's hand. Together, they skip out of the ice cream parlor, leaving behind the echo of the doorbell as they leave.

For a moment, the parlor feels emptier, quieter. I catch a glimpse of Luke, his intense gaze fixed on me, and I can't help but wonder what thoughts are running through his mind. He signals toward the empty chair, inviting me to take my seat again. I find a comfortable spot, and when he resumes his seat, he deliberately positions himself closer than before. My thighs involuntarily tighten as his knee grazes against mine.

I divert my attention to my ice cream while Luke subtly intertwines his feet with mine beneath the table. It's a simple act, yet it feels surprisingly right.

"You like Aliana." Luke breaks the silence between us.

I nod, agreeing with his accurate observation. Aliana is undeniably charming and enjoyable to be around.

"She thinks you're pretty too," he adds with a warm chuckle. I find myself biting my lip, trying to understand why the sound of his laughter makes me want to close my eyes and remember it forever. It's just a laugh, not a profound revelation of his deepest fears or joys.

But somehow, it feels like more. It feels like he's opening a door, inviting me to see something deeper. My heart quickens, the ice cream abandoned, as I gaze at him, seeking the same sincerity in his eyes that I feel awakening in mine.

"She's right, you know." My mouth opens but then closes a second later when he continues, "Come on, Penny, it's not like this is the first time someone's called you pretty." True, many have said as much, but not Luke Sutton. Not that it should make a difference that he finds me beautiful.

But it does.

At that moment, our calves make contact. Is he aware of what he's doing? Surely, it's not every day that someone casually rubs their leg against someone else's. Does he realize how this feels? I certainly do, and I hate to admit it, but I enjoy it.

Shields up, Payson.

I'm trying, really trying. However, he's making it incredibly difficult, as every session with Luke seems to evoke some kind of emotion from within me. I steal a quick look at him, noticing a faint smile forming on his mouth. My resolve falters as my heart stutters.

My eyes drift back to my ice cream, an attempt to ground myself. "You gonna fill me in on last weekend since we didn't have our session?" I ask, trying to keep my voice steady. "We technically have to make up for two sessions in one."

"Not sure what you're talking about," he replies, his voice a familiar nonchalance.

It takes all my strength not to whip my spoon at him. *Stop playing this game,* I want to scream. These short, evasive answers won't get us anywhere. Rather, I shake my head and relish the final mouthful of my ice cream, prolonging the unavoidable confrontation.

As my leg inadvertently drifts away from his, the sudden absence of his warmth is instantly noticeable. His reaction is immediate; he turns to face me more directly, pulling my chair and me in it to the point of touching knees again. The sudden proximity sends a rush of heat to my cheeks, a mixture of surprise and something deeper. I'm trying to keep a calm facade, but my heart is racing and revealing my true emotions.

"Don't bullshit a bullshitter, Luke," I say. His eyes narrow, a hint of defensiveness—maybe guilt?—crossing his face. "Just because nothing happened on the field doesn't mean nothing happened elsewhere." I had watched the highlights of his game on my laptop, balancing RA duties. His performance was good, but his posture in the first half and the drastic switch in the second half were noticeable. He was a completely different person.

"It wasn't terrible," he says nonchalantly, yet his eyes reveal a hidden emotion.

"What's your definition of 'bad'? Because from where I'm standing, habits don't just disappear. You have to work at them, convince yourself that there's something better waiting on the other side of what you're going through," I counter. "What about tonight?"

He gives me a piercing look. "Caught the highlights," I say, forcing a light tone.

There's a mischievous smile on his lips. "You missed my game, again? I'm wounded, Penny." His laughter is sharp, like the edge of a broken glass, masking the hurt I recognize all too well—the same way my mother uses to hide her pain behind forced humor.

I give a shrug, explaining, "I had other things to attend to during the game."

His face momentarily drops, his shoulders slouching slightly to reveal the pain before he conceals it with a stoic look. Like a switch, a sly grin forms on his lips—a classic *I told you so* look.

"I listened to your advice tonight," he states, lightly bumping my arm.

I clear my throat. "That's great . . . What finally convinced you to listen to my advice?"

Hesitation fills him as his eyes intentionally avoid meeting mine. This momentary pause suggests that his next words could be a pivotal point in his journey. This kind of behavior is something we've been studying in my abnormal psychology class. It shows underlying anxiety or internal conflict.

He finally says, "I ignored a text I usually receive during halftime."

A text?

Why dodge a text?

He notices the questions in my eyes, but I interrupt before he can clarify. "Okay, you skipped a text." I pause, trying to piece it together. "This is a regular thing? Getting a text every game at halftime?"

"Pretty much," he concedes. My look sharpens, urging him to open up more. "They occasionally occur before a game, but halftime is when they mostly happen."

The fact that he gets texts is one piece of the puzzle, but it doesn't quite fit. I probe further, aware of the gravity of this unveiling.

"So, these texts," I tread carefully, choosing my words with precision, "are they meant to uplift you? To offer support during your games?"

He laughs, but there's a bitter edge to it. He shakes his head and states, "No, they do the complete opposite."

I pause, absorbing his admission, trying to make sense of it.

He receives a text both before and during the game. It's clear that checking his phone each time sets something off in him. Anger, perhaps? Is that why I noticed the shift in his demeanor during halftime tonight? He must be aware—after all, he mentioned taking my advice and ignoring the texts before the game.

"So, the texts are detrimental, then?" His eyes avoid mine, and I see a muscle clenching in his jaw. His discomfort speaks louder than words.

Drawing from my therapy experiences and memories of my dad's barely controlled anger, I instinctively reach out and gently place my hands over his fists. Our eyes drop to the connection. Maybe not my brightest move, but it's too late to second-guess. Rather than dwell on the impulse, I focus on my thumb gliding across his hand, causing his eyes to close and his body to unwind.

Did I just calm him down?

"I am proud of you," I note, my words weighted with genuine admiration.

He maintains eye contact for a moment, his face revealing a range of emotions before he breaks our gaze. My words may not have been what he wished to hear, but they were needed. My pride in him isn't just about following my advice;

it's about his courage in facing challenges, showing bravery and determination.

Once more, our gazes intersect before he averts his eyes, confessing, "They convey a mix of discouragement, encouragement, and demand." He sighs. "It's hard to describe. They're addictive—I want to read them, yet want to resist. It feels like there's a disconnect between my body and mind. There's this part of me that craves the messages, believing they somehow boost my performance, while my conscience urges me to ignore them."

"Then why not do it?" His eyebrow arches, questioning my demand, and I clarify, "Block the texts."

Frustration fills his voice as he exhales deeply. "I can't."

I press forward, determined not to give up just yet. "Is it that you can't, or you won't?" The challenge hangs between us, a gauntlet thrown.

I see the same fierce intensity in his eyes that my dad has when he's at his angriest. Gripping the table's edge, his knuckles become pale. Without another word, he pushes his chair back so forcefully that it screeches against the floor. He abruptly stands up and walks away with tense shoulders, every step filled with tension.

What the hell just happened? The air crackles with the aftermath of our exchange. I stand there, torn. I could let him walk away, let him stew in his anger, but what good would that do? He needs direction, a way to channel this storm. But he's also my ride, and I can't just let this end unresolved.

A wave of determination courses through me. I need to follow him, remind him of his choices, and confront the underlying issues head-on. The door swings open, and a frigid gust immediately engulfs me, freezing me in its grasp. I shiver, hugging myself for warmth, and step out into the night, following his retreating form.

Approaching Luke's Range Rover, I find him leaning against it, head bowed, shoulders tense. I hesitate, unsure of the best approach. Closing in, he lifts his head and his eyes meet mine, locking our gazes together. In his eyes, a tempest of emotions —anger, confusion, frustration—rages on. Although my pulse is quickening, I trust my intuition that Luke is harmless.

His penetrating gaze leaves me speechless, and the entire world seems to vanish except for the two of us. My heart hammers as he pushes off the car, his breath mingling with mine. "Fuck, Payson," he says softly, his voice sounding strained.

Without warning, his lips forcefully meet mine, filled with urgency and desperation, leaving me breathless. His hands cup my face, gently anchoring himself. His tongue teases mine, exploring my mouth slowly. He gently nips my lower lip, then moves his lips down my exposed neck, sending jolts of pleasure straight to my core.

God, each touch of his tongue etches a mark on me, a brand no one else could meet. The sudden realization drenches me like freezing water. I gasp and take a step back, feeling a physical pain from losing his touch.

My hand covers my mouth—this shouldn't be happening. But it is, and I want it to continue. I want to get lost in the sensation, to drown in his touch.

"Shit, I'm sorry. That was out of line," he says, his voice rough with regret.

However, his eyes reveal a contrasting narrative, reflecting the internal turmoil I am also experiencing. He tries to pull me back but then stops, letting his hand drop.

"You're right, it was," I respond, stepping back, trying to create space. However, he moves closer, his presence an unstoppable power.

"But I wanted to," he confesses, his cheeks flushed with a rosy hue that sends a familiar flutter through my chest.

Curse him. Why is he saying things like this, acting in ways that stir such confusion? This isn't the way things are supposed to go.

"You shouldn't have," I assert, pointing a finger to emphasize the boundary between us. "You and me? This is supposed to be a professional, therapeutic relationship."

He pauses, his eyes darkening as he seems to acknowledge the gravity of my words. For a moment, I believe he grasps the significance. But then he steps closer, and I retreat instinctively.

With each step he takes, I match it backward, my voice firm. "No, just stop right there."

He smirks, finding amusement in the situation, while I am far from amused. "But I don't want to," he protests, his tone challenging, playful.

I release a sharp exhale, my frustration boiling. "Well, that's too bad."

I stand my ground, refusing to succumb to this irresistible force. But then he unexpectedly bumps into me, and I nearly topple over. He firmly holds onto my waist, providing support, keeping me steady against a car. With the sudden contact, a surge courses through me, setting every nerve ablaze with heat.

My thoughts are racing, overwhelmed by panic. What if the car alarm goes off? But he seems oblivious to such concerns; his heartbeat thunders as loud as mine, his breath featherlight against my lips. I resist the urge to push away, determined to avoid a repeat of this situation, but my body rebels, wanting his lips on me again. Against all logic, his lips find mine once more. With one intoxicating stroke of his tongue, I'm entranced, giving in to the moment as he effortlessly lifts me.

This couldn't be happening. It felt surreal, being wrapped up with Luke Sutton on the hood of someone else's car—

something straight out of a wild fantasy. Rather than pushing him away, I was drawing him closer, wrapping my arms around his neck, and intertwining my fingers in his hair. Our kisses were fervent, our teeth sometimes colliding in our eagerness. His lips brush my throat, his hot breath murmuring, "You feel this too."

Like a warning sign, the flickering parking lot light signifies the risk of our vulnerable embrace being seen by others. Trying to regain some control, I aim to distance myself, but he only draws me closer, lifting me so my legs automatically circle around him. Our hearts beat in unison, our breaths quick and shallow.

Desire fills his eyes, like a brewing storm ready to unleash. But I could also see the conflict there, the same battle raging within me. Both of us had a strong desire for it, but with high stakes and set boundaries, this was about our future, not emotions.

After gently placing me back on the ground, he playfully taps my ass, guiding me to the passenger side of his Range Rover. I turn to look at him, my mouth hanging open, while he shakes his head and smirks.

Climbing into his vehicle, I can sense the electric tension between us. In an instant, his hand slides to my thigh, a possessive movement that sends anticipation rushing through me. In other situations, I might have withdrawn, but the sense of comfort and safety it brings is strangely reassuring.

Back at my dorm, those words echoed in my mind: *I know you feel this too.*

But what is he really feeling? Despite my fears about relationships and men, here I am, ready to dive into uncharted waters. I'm not impulsive, but the notion that our kiss or my touch could completely alleviate his anger is . . . bewildering and utterly intoxicating.

CHAPTER 17
LUKE

Does she know that, Luke?

Percy calls out from the back patio, "Hey, Sutton, you up for a burger or steak?"

Nursing my beer, I lean back, feeling the cool glass against my leg. "Steak, for sure," I answer, giving my abs a contented pat. "Gotta maintain the temple," I add with a smirk, the corners of my mouth curling up.

"One burger won't bring down the temple," Maddox counters.

He's got a point. But whenever I'm with Payson, my diet tends to go off course. Just thinking of her name sends me back to that ice cream parlor. Her smiles, her laugh, the way she's . . . so effortlessly herself—it all tightens something in my chest, like a vise squeezing my heart.

Had she always been like that?

I remember the fleeting glances across our neighborhood pool, her eyes always carrying a challenge that made my pulse race. Whenever we saw each other in the hallways of high school, my stomach would tighten and I'd clench my fists to maintain my composure. Our lives have been intertwined like the roots of an ancient tree since childhood, but it wasn't until that night with Milli that she caught my attention.

That night, everything changed.

Suddenly, my thoughts shift to the memory of our kiss. Can I really classify it as a kiss? A kiss happened last year at the bonfire—innocent, simple. What we shared was more consuming. Even the thought of it makes my blood race, like a drumbeat echoing in my ears.

How can something so wrong feel so impossibly right?

The mere idea should set off warning signals, making my heart race with anxiety and my hands tremble with apprehension. But truthfully? Her ability to pacify my inner chaos, quelling my raging emotions, has had a contradictory impact. Instead of fear, there's an irresistible magnetic force that ignites every nerve. It has only heightened my desire to immerse myself in the comfort she provides.

Maddox's voice jolts me back to reality. "Daydreaming much?" he teases.

I look at Berry and Percy by the grill, shrugging. The scent of fall permeates the crisp afternoon air, and autumn hues splash the trees around Berry's mansion. The sprawling property, complete with a white picket fence and horses, speaks of luxury. "Cupcake," he calls one horse, supposedly for Aliana, though Berry's likely never ridden it.

Maddox's blue eyes question as he leisurely sips his whiskey sour. I respond with another shrug, sipping my beer. Rayne's soothing voice interrupts the silence. "Luke, you up for another?" She holds out a Michelob, her presence a steady comfort.

"Yeah, thanks, Ray," I reply. She and I share a smile, but the moment is interrupted as Walker and Aliana crash into her legs, full of energy.

"Be careful, sweetheart," Berry calls out softly as he

enters through the French doors. His gaze, fixed on Rayne, holds both concern and another emotion. Rayne's cheeks turn pink as she brushes her black bangs aside, momentarily losing her usual composure.

Rayne exudes a motherly grace that's hard to miss. Despite her youth, her maturity shines through our conversations. With her bobbed black hair and bangs, she stands at a petite five foot two and has a face that is both charming and enchanting. I wouldn't have pictured her with Berry, but then again, I've never seen him with anyone. The only woman he's ever mentioned was Aliana's mom, who passed away when Aliana was young.

Rayne coughs to break the tension of Berry's piercing gaze. While nuzzling the children's backs, she looks at them with such tender maternal affection that it's as if she's speaking directly into their hearts. "They're fine, Berry. Trust me, I'm used to it," she reassures him.

Berry hesitates, then lets out a huff that sounds just like Payson's exasperated sighs. Fuck, even the smallest things my teammates do keep dragging her back into my mind.

"All right, babies, outside you go. It's too nice out to stay in," Rayne chimes, nudging the kids' backs playfully. Their laughter fills the room as they scamper off, leaving Maddox and me exchanging glances. Percy, with his ever-curious mind, would probably dissect the interaction between Berry and Ray. But me? Nope, uncovering my teammates' possible romantic relationships is not on my to-do list.

"So, your therapist, huh?" Maddox interrupts my thoughts with his voice. My head snaps toward him, and he chuckles. I narrow my eyes, sensing my heartbeat racing. With a casual flick, he runs his fingers through his reddish locks. "Luke, man, you're like an open book sometimes," he comments, smirking. Crossing my arms defensively, I shift my weight. He takes another sip of his drink, his eyes meeting mine. "Do you think we haven't noticed the changes since the therapist entered your life?"

Really? Have I changed that much? Sure, some things have slightly shifted, but seeing my teammates taking notes . . . it means a lot.

Anxiously, I tap my fingertips against the beer glass, swallowing hard. It's just one game, not an entire season of transformations.

Maddox leans in, curiosity piquing his tone. "What was her name again?"

"Payson," I snap back.

"Ah, Payson," he muses. "Did you know her name signifies 'The Pillar of Wisdom?' Quite fitting."

I nod. But he doesn't stop there.

"Beautiful name, for a beautiful person," he adds, eyes gleaming with mischief. My cheeks become hot and red.

"And, according to Percy, the beauty isn't just in the name," he notes.

"Percy?" I ask out loud.

Maddox shrugs. "Overheard him talking to Natasha."

Why would he ask about Payson? I know he uses his charm on Nat whenever he can, but the idea of him wanting to know more about Payson makes me grip the beer bottle tighter. A sudden pang pierces my chest, and my hands tremble with tension.

Fuck, what is this feeling? Jealousy? Is this what jealousy feels like?

I avert my gaze from Maddox, soothing my chest and shifting my focus to Percy, who's engrossed in a conversation with Ray and Coach. There's no way he's into Payson, right?

Shouldn't matter, Luke.

Right, like missing the Lone Star team tradition shouldn't matter, yet it does. Being the rookie, the team's tradition of gathering with family and friends at someone's place was a novelty. Ideally, I'd have brought my parents or Milli, but their schedules didn't align, leaving me to navigate this first gathering solo. And the notion of inviting Payson as my plus one? It crossed my mind, sure, but I dismissed it as swiftly as I would down a shot of tequila.

I inhale deeply, feeling my upper body rise and fall heavily as I try to compose myself. My sight flickers back to Percy, noting that well-known grin on his face. My gut churns while a bead of sweat trickles down my brow. I brush it off hastily, my hands still shaking.

As I shift my attention back to Maddox, I blurt out, "Yeah, she's been helping me in sorting through some issues." Our conversations twist and turn in unexpected ways, and damn if it isn't impressive—how she gets me to open up about my past. It's like being under some spell. One moment, I'm guarded, then suddenly I meet her gaze and confess secrets I vowed never to reveal. This is Payson Pennington we're talking about. I'm still trying to figure her out. She's nothing like what I expected, and I can't decide if that's thrilling or terrifying.

"That's solid, man. As long as she's making a difference for you, right?" Maddox says. At that moment, my phone vibrates in my pocket, and I give a nod.

Percy settles into the third brown leather chair across from us, completing our circle. The chairs encircle a central table positioned near the French doors and within easy chatting distance of the kitchen bar stools. Observing Berry's home, I'm struck by its farm chic aesthetic—a surprising discovery from a guy I had pegged as *the big guy* type.

It's a reminder—you never really grasp the essence of someone until you step into their personal space.

A lesson I'm learning with Payson.

With a beer in hand, Percy leans in as Ray returns to us, offering refreshments. Then, out of the blue, Percy comments, "Did you notice the glances shared by Berry and Rayne?" The question catches me off guard, almost causing me to spill my beer toward him.

I catch a glimpse of Maddox, and he's shaking his head, clearly thinking the same thing. Percy scans our faces, then lets out an exasperated sigh.

"Don't tell me you haven't noticed the undeniable attraction between them." He smirks, sinking further into his seat, legs casually spread out. "Do you think they're . . . you know?" He wiggles his eyebrows mischievously, and I have to suppress my laughter by biting my lip. I glance at Maddox again, the same barely contained amusement gleaming in his eyes.

Honestly, for someone who's twenty-nine, you'd expect a bit more . . . tact? Even at twenty-three, I refrain from assuming about others' private lives. But then, Percy and I are cut from a different cloth, sharing little more than a love for football, nightlife, and the company of women.

Thankfully, the conversation about Berry and Rayne fizzles out. Once again, my phone vibrates, causing my pulse to instantly accelerate. The rush of excitement hits me every time her name pops up on my screen, and I scramble to check it. At first, our texts were simply routine check-ins for our Sunday sessions, but recently, they've evolved into something else . . . more.

PAYSON

Missing our Sunday session?

A grin tugs at my lips.

LUKE

[Picture of Percy] He's my stellar substitute for the week.

Percy narrows his eyes as he squints at my phone. "What

the hell, man? You snapped a photo of me?" His mock frown quickly dissolves into laughter. With a shake of his head, he places his palm on my shoulder. "That better have been for some knockout." He chuckles.

Definitely a knockout.

Payson's messages roll in, one after the other.

PAYSON

Another teammate of yours?

He's sort of cute.

Think you could hook your girl up?

Hell no, I internally protest. My jaw clicks, and I grip the phone a little harder. There's no way I'm playing matchmaker for her with anyone here. She's . . . she's off-limits.

Does she know that, Luke?

Well, no. But maybe I could just hint that none of these guys are available. I mean, it's not completely false; some of them are taken.

Before I can reply, my phone starts vibrating once more.

PAYSON

Think I'll get to meet the entire crew before the season wraps?

LUKE

Definitely. But Percy is off limits.

And don't even think about it—I'm not setting my girl up with any of them.

Technically, she is my girl. My therapist. Same thing.

LUKE

Seriously, Penny, did you message me just to bust my chops?

PAYSON

Sutton, am I detecting a hint of jealousy?

I roll my eyes. There's that damn word again. I am not jealous, right? Sure, that nagging ache in my chest is back like a pesky bug you can't swat away, but being jealous of another man with Payson . . . I don't know.

Maybe it's not that absurd.

I observe Berry and Rayne's kids laughing while chasing each other in the backyard, then I respond.

LUKE

Jealous? Me? Ha! More like protective. I'm just trying to keep the team in line. Women spell nothing but distraction.

PAYSON

Coming from our very own poster boy, Mr. Infidelity.

I exhale sharply at that jab. That label stings. It's not me. Despite never really discussing that slipup with Payson, she's clued in—probably Milli's doing. But it was a one-off. A lapse. History not to be repeated.

LUKE

Not funny.

PAYSON

You're right. I crossed a line.

Can I ask you something?

I hesitate before responding.

LUKE

Are you asking as a friend, or are you playing therapist?

PAYSON

We're friends?

Both, actually.

LUKE

Wait, Penny, are you asking to be my friend?

PAYSON

Don't hold your breath, Sutton.

Oh, you mean like I did when I kissed the hell out of you?

It's the reply I really want to send, imagining her reaction. My fingers hover over the keys, itching to type it out. I can almost see her biting her plush lips, or that infuriatingly radiant smile lighting up her face—the one I've been seeing more often lately.

Seeing a different side of her at the ice cream parlor—a nurturing, caring person who I hadn't noticed before—hit me hard.

Good lord, talk about a three-sixty on my damn thoughts. I attempt to clear my mind by running my hand through my hair, but her smile continues to haunt me.

"You're blushing like a schoolgirl," I hear Percy mock. My cheeks burn even hotter at his words. I nonchalantly brush off his remark, attempting to appear unaffected. Why should I care? I don't. Besides, any redness on my cheeks is probably from the alcohol. It never fails to make me feel warm and flushed.

Just as I'm about to respond to Payson, my phone vibrates. I'm hit with a familiar wave of anticipation, similar to the excitement of game days. My heart races and my fingers tingle with the uncontrollable urge to check my phone.

TROY

[Picture of Payson and Luke on a stranger's car, locked in an intense kiss] Looks like your focus isn't quite on the game, huh? Who's the blonde?

In that instant, a raging inferno of anger consumes me. How dare he? When did he earn the right to meddle in my life beyond the field? My heart tightens and my breath comes in sharp, uneven bursts. Why is he reaching out now, of all times? We had a clear agreement that I've honored, and he was expected to do so as well.

Game day reach outs only. No random texts, no checking in.

My temples throbbed like war drums, and the pain in my clenched jaw was excruciating. Just as I'm about to hurl my phone across the room, a calming presence interrupts my brewing storm. Coach places a steady hand on my shoulder, his touch grounding me momentarily as he announces that the food is ready. With a sigh, I reluctantly close my messaging app and join the rest of the team. Despite my best attempts to stay calm, his message's audacity keeps my anger boiling, ready to explode like a volcano. And then, amid Coach's briefing on next week's home game, another message comes.

TROY

Maybe I need to visit Dallas.

Like hell he will. My fingers twitch, itching to punch something, anything.

The anger doesn't subside as the evening wears on; it clings to me, a heavy, suffocating shroud. There is a single solution I know could calm my inner turmoil, a way to silence the beast within—an hour's drive away.

CHAPTER 18
LUKE

My tires crunch into the gravel of Payson and Milli's dorm parking lot. While parking, I hear that familiar voice that instantly calms my pounding heart. My hands, which had been shaking nonstop, finally steadied after I left Berry's house.

How does she do that? How can her voice penetrate the icy barrier within me, granting me the ability to flow like a serene river under the warm sun?

"Wesley, get your ass back to the dorms now!" she shouts. I survey the empty parking lot. I ease the door of my Range Rover shut with a careful nudge, not wanting to interrupt what appears to be Payson in full RA mode. Leaning against my car, I cross my legs and settle in for the show. I wish I had brought popcorn—watching the mix of confusion on the guy's face and Payson's barely contained fury is more captivating than the latest episode of *Dexter*.

"I don't care!" she seethes. "I specifically mentioned to you less than a week ago that bringing weed into this all-girls dorm is prohibited."

Oh shit, weed? This guy has some nerve.

The only light comes from the overhead lamps and the faint glow of dorm windows, casting long shadows around them. She's aggressively pointing her finger in his face, but he remains unfazed, staring back at her without blinking, even as she snaps her fingers close to his gaze. She lets out an irritated laugh while shaking her head. It's clear that the guy is high, and she knows it all too well.

In an attempt to hold back my laughter, I bite the inside of my cheek, but the humor dissipates as he gets nearer to her. Instinctively, she recoils as fear crosses her face and he forcefully clutches her arm. Although he lacks muscle, his height makes him appear intimidating. I hesitate, hoping she can handle it, but then she wrenches free and pokes him in the chest, demanding, "Don't touch me!" and he grabs her finger.

That's my breaking point. When a woman says don't touch her, and you do, that's when I step in.

No one is allowed to lay a hand on her.

Within a split second, I'm on the other side of the parking lot, tearing the guy from her. "What the fuck, man?" he protests.

I laugh, but there's no humor in it. "She told you not to touch her."

When I move closer, he immediately backs away, his eyes widening in realization. My reputation isn't a secret around campus—four years at NorthRidge U, now making waves in the NFL. "You're Sutton," he stammers.

Tapping my chest, I confirm, "Yeah, that's me. When a woman says don't touch her, you don't fucking touch her." My jaw clenches, teeth grinding as my anger from minutes ago surges back, my palms itching to become fists.

Right as I'm going to act on impulse, I feel familiar hands encircle my waist, gently but firmly holding me back. Her presence is calming, yet insistent. His gaze shifts, tracing the link between us, then rises to meet mine, analyzing.

"He's not worth it, Luke," Payson whispers in my ear. Her tone is gentle but unwavering. The thought of him getting away with it bothers me. She's faced too much already, battled shadows no one should confront. While I may not know everything, I can sense the pain that haunts her, just like mine.

Then, a disturbing thought emerges—could he be the cause of that bruise I observed? Has he hurt her before?

Payson senses my inner struggle and finds solace by pressing her forehead against my lower back, her warm breaths soothing the turmoil inside me. "It wasn't him, just let him go. He's high and not thinking."

Her words do little to quell the fire inside me. No state of mind excuses laying hands on a woman who has explicitly said no. But when she tightens her grip on me, her silent plea brings to mind the bigger picture. Hitting him might satisfy my anger, but it won't benefit us, especially Payson. She shares a campus with this guy, and my actions could disrupt her peace more than mine.

"Luke," she murmurs, and I release my grip, letting the anger fade as uneasy calm takes its place. "You better keep your hands to yourself. If I hear of you touching her again, consider this your final warning."

With a cowardly expression, he raises his hands in mock surrender and heads toward his dorm door. His hands shaking, he fumbles for his key, replying, "Y-yeah, got it." His parting shot, "It was all in fun," earns him nothing but my scornful laugh.

"Fun, my ass," I mutter under my breath.

A gentle squeeze on my waist catches my attention. When I finally turn to face her, her expression is hard to decipher—gratitude, perhaps, or something deeper, but the pull of the moment distracts me as the space tightens between us, an undeniable force drawing us together. My emotions surge, causing me to embrace her and exhale a breath I didn't know I was holding.

She leans back just enough to meet my stare, her beautiful blue ones resembling the color of the lake in Stoneton. My favorite. With her chin on my chest, her touch brings a feeling of security and reassurance. "Thank you," she utters.

The way she says *thank you* has a different impact on me, like a sudden rainstorm during clear weather. Wouldn't any good man have done the same thing?

Her brows knit together, clearly puzzled by my presence on campus when I should be back in Dallas. I catch myself tracing the scar above her eyebrow. Before she can say anything, I blurt out the truth: "I just wanted to see you," I confess.

And fuck, I like it.

This is not how things are supposed to go with her. It was supposed to be a quick few months of sessions. Reach my goal and be done. But with each session, each moment spent in her presence, questions about that night years ago flood back. When she walked Milli straight into her room, right next to mine, both their breaths mingling with alcohol. It felt like a slap to the face—they drove home drunk, something that didn't sit well with me, given my experience. But the more I get to see Payson, be around her, it's like the girl I saw all those years ago isn't the woman I'm seeing now.

I absentmindedly caress her cheek with my thumb. Her skin is soft, warm under my touch. Her eyes softly close, and in that moment, an overwhelming impulse to kiss her, to lose myself in her, sweeps over me. My heart races, my breaths become rapid, and my hand shakes slightly. I remember our last session and how her intense stare was filled with craving, but it wasn't enough.

I inch forward, each heartbeat bridging the distance between us. I tenderly cradle the base of her neck with my hand.

Her eyes open, and as they do, our gazes lock and her eyes become glossier. The air thickens. Her lips slightly part, but then, a soft clearing of the throat beside us breaks the spell, and I blink, the moment slipping away.

"Join me for a ride?" she asks, a trace of mischief in her voice.

I let out a little laugh, narrowing my eyes. "A ride? At 8 pm? Where exactly are we going?" Darkness has long fallen, thanks to daylight savings. She nods toward something behind her, though her Kia is nowhere in sight. She laughs, light and carefree.

"You'll just have to trust me, won't you?" she declares. Our fingers interlock unexpectedly. To any onlooker, we might seem like a couple. We're not, but I have no intention of letting go. She guides me toward the sidewalk, and before long, I see a black and red golf cart. Her idea of a ride finally clicks, and I can't help but smile.

Releasing my hand, she sprints to the driver's seat and pats the space next to her. With her bottom lip caught between her teeth, I fight the temptation to lean in and meet her lips with mine, longing to feel their touch. She sends a cheeky wink my way, sparking laughter from the core of my being. I rush the final few steps and leap into the cart, causing it to rock slightly.

She gives me a playful elbow jab. "Easy there, tiger."

I casually drape my arm behind her and get comfortable, a smirk playing on my lips. "Oh, Penny, you should know I'm not the type to go easy," I retort, watching as her cheeks glow softly in the dim light. The sight makes my heart skip a beat, my pulse accelerating as I see that beautiful shade of pink tint over her high cheekbones.

I don't usually react to girls like this, but I'm not interested in analyzing it right now.

I just want to savor this—whatever this is.

She rolls her eyes, trying to play it off. "So, where are we off to, Captain Penny?" I let the smirk linger before adding, "Aside from a ride on me, that is."

Her response is an obnoxiously loud snort that makes me grin from ear to ear. She nudges me, causing the cart to veer slightly. I grab the handle above me, raising a brow. "What the fuck was that?" I ask, steadying myself. She shrugs nonchalantly.

"You deserved it."

Shaking my head, I can't resist teasing her. "There's no denying we both know that was your favorite position," I say, emphasizing her preference that night.

I watch her as her eyes sparkle, clearly recalling that night. For a few moments, we observe students wandering around campus. A part of me misses this—the campus, the college atmosphere. The shift to reality is substantial, and although I wouldn't alter it, a lingering nostalgia persists.

"Played a good game on Thursday, didn't you?" Payson notes, pulling me from my thoughts.

I shrug, grinning. "Yeah, I did." She's not wrong; I was on fire. "Did you catch the game? It was incredible. Those three touchdowns? I was unstoppable." My gaze tracks her every move, looking for any flicker of reaction. Her face, however, remains steady and directed on the path ahead. "Come on, you've got to admit you're impressed," I prod, my pride clear in my voice.

With a slight lift of her eyebrow, she presents a subtle challenge. "Oh, really? And what makes you say that, Mr. All-Star?"

I sit up straighter, feeling the need to make her proud. "First of all, it was my best performance in an NFL game."

"And the second?" she interjects quickly, breezing past my prideful admission, eyes glinting with amusement.

"Second, I kept out of any scuffles, no clashes on or off the field."

Crossing the street, we pause outside a dormitory on the outskirts of campus, where her smile radiates warmth like a burst of sunshine. Parking the cart, she turns to me and retrieves what seems to be a blanket from behind. I quickly snatch it, surprising her. Her laughter rings out. "Absolutely not, I'm freezing."

Her laughter fills me with warmth, and I can't help but smile. "Really? It doesn't feel that cold to me." Granted, it's the middle of October in Texas, and there's a crispness to the air signaling the onset of fall, but her cropped long sleeve emblazoned with *NorthRidge U. Residential Assistant* isn't exactly made to keep her cozy. As she reaches for the blanket again, I instinctively wrap my hands around her waist, lifting her onto my lap.

She has a wide-eyed expression as she clutches the blanket tightly. I expect her to slide off my lap, but she surprises me by stretching her legs across the seat. With a subtle movement, she gracefully covers herself and partly covers me with the blanket. While getting comfortable, she asks, letting the question hang in the air, "Why do you think you played your best that game?"

"I listened to your advice again." Her eyes narrow suspiciously. I squeeze her waist, and she jumps a little, causing my cock to twitch the moment her ass makes contact. She breaks into a smile. "You just like hearing that I listened to you, don't you?" I tease.

She shrugs and says, "It's nice," before pausing and adding, "Luke Sutton, an NFL tight end, enjoys listening to his therapist, Payson—" I gently squeeze her waist, then swiftly turn her to straddle me, holding onto her legs. Her breath hitches as she feels how hard I am.

Sorry, babe. Nothing I can do about that.

Our eyes meet again, reigniting the tension from before. Her soft breath brushes against my cheek, urging me to confess, "I only concentrated on what happened after the game."

She nods. "How did that feel?"

"Good, I suppose." She raises an eyebrow. "It was just one game, Penny."

She lightly pushes my chest and says, "Still, it's better than nothing, and that means things are progressing here."

I can't control my smile. "Maybe. Who knew listening to you would help me?" I playfully tease, my hand casually moving toward her thigh. I detect a slight increase in her pulse, causing me to carefully grip her leg. She jerks—a reaction of surprise or something else, I can't tell. I continue to soothe her leg with my hand as I probe. "Why do you react so strongly when someone touches you?"

I'm aware this question might be too personal, crossing the boundaries of our usual interactions. After all, these sessions—though this moment isn't officially one—are meant to focus on my progress, not delve into her reactions. But curiosity gets the better of me.

She lowers her head, her fingers delicately entwining in a silent, anxiety-filled dance. With a gentle touch, I guide her chin to meet my gaze. When I peer into her mesmerizing eyes, a feeling emerges from the depth of her sorrow and determination.

She clings to my arms, as if in need of reassurance. With her captivating blue eyes locked onto mine, she whispers in a barely audible voice, "My dad."

Her dad. The words struck me with the force of a lightning bolt, revealing a painful truth in an instant.

The source of her flinches, her unease with touch, even with me. A powerful sense of protectiveness rises within me, longing to erase those dark memories. As we sit snugly in the golf cart, she tentatively entwines her legs around my waist. The proximity is scorching with a greater intensity than any previous shared moment, even more so than the unforgettable night.

Her breathing falters, a delicate tremor interrupting. She gasps out, "Luke."

"Payson," I murmur. My thumb softly traces a path along her cheek as I brush a strand of hair away from her face. "You can trust me."

And she can trust me. While we may not see eye to eye and the past lingers, I would never breach her trust or expose her private information. I came here tonight to release the pent-up anger Troy stirred in me, knowing she could calm me.

Her throat visibly struggles against the knot of emotions, making her swallow hard. With a slow nod, the tension in her shoulders eases slightly, a subtle yet meaningful change.

My hands gently frame her face, the face I've longed to see with each passing day. Her eyelids close and her lips delicately separate. The urge to kiss her, which has been building up all evening, suddenly bursts into flames. I can't hold back; my lips crash against hers. At first, she becomes rigid, her mouth sealed.

Fuck, this is so wrong.

Suddenly, she pulls away, and in the next moment, we're consumed by a storm of a kiss. Tongues clash, teeth dance, intense as never before. Wild, untamed.

With each deepening kiss, the divide between us seems as vast as an uncrossable ocean. Craving more contact, I shift her slightly, positioning her so she's sitting directly on my hard cock. Her lips release a soft whimper as she gives in, her hands instinctively reaching for my neck. A flood of desperation and elation surges through me, quickening my heartbeat. Empowered by her response, I use my hands to direct her touch, bringing her closer as our bodies move in sync. With our lips never parting, her sweet ass grinds against me, her hips moving back and forth with the perfect friction. She moans, and I love that I get to hear and taste it. I slide my hand down, cupping her ass, reveling in the way she arches her back and exposes her neck.

"Fuck," I growl, my lips leaving hers to plant kisses along her throat. The thought of feeling her skin under my lips has haunted me all week. I want to mark her, to feel her pulse race under my touch. Being here, feeling her response to every touch, I don't hold back, not even for a moment.

"*Luke,*" Payson moans, her voice thick with desire. The piercing sound ignites a fire within me. If I hadn't already surrendered, that one moan would have been my downfall. Her voice, my name on her lips, is becoming a melody I crave.

"We shouldn't be doing this," she weakly protests, her wavering voice revealing her lack of conviction.

"Let's be more professional," I tease with a grin. Despite her words, she continues to rock her hips against me, and I can't suppress the smile spreading across my face.

"Should we? Yeah, we should," she murmurs, but it sounds like she's trying to convince herself more than me. But neither of us makes any move to stop. Instead, she wraps us both in the blanket, as if creating a secret world just for us.

Her hips maintain their rhythm, moving us back and forth as she clings to my neck, her fingers digging in like an anchor. I explore her back with my hands, the thin fabric allowing me to feel the heat of her skin.

Payson

Oh God, my clit is throbbing to the point of pain. My heart races, and my fingers twitch, fighting the urge to slip beneath the elastic of my yoga pants. Just a moment's relief, I tell myself, might clear the haze of desire clouding my judgment. Yet, his hands draw me nearer, and I rub against him, sensing that familiar hardness that craves my touch.

Professionalism is overrated, don't you think? Before I realize it, he's placing me right beside him. A whimper slips from my lips, and he chuckles in response, a low and teasing sound. "Just a sec," he murmurs. However, that "sec" seems to last an eternity until he finally commands, "Lie down."

"Lie down? Where?" My brain swirls with questions, but he's already guiding me gently onto the golf cart's backseat. It might be a tight fit, but it can hold two—that's what's important, isn't it? Stepping away momentarily, he folds my knees up, resembling a birthing position, and his eyes lock with mine, dilated with lust, erasing any uncomfortable thoughts.

His hands caress my legs, causing goose bumps to form. Our bodies entwine, the intensity of the moment heightening as he positions himself between my legs, our heat merging together. He exudes tension, every muscle in his body tight with anticipation.

Leaning closer, his stubble grazes against my sensitive skin while his mouth moves along the hollow of my throat. The world outside fades away, leaving just the two of us in this heightened state of desire. His lips find mine again, and this kiss is electric, a desperate clash of lips and tongues that leaves me breathless.

Then he's pulling away, sitting across from me. Propping myself on my elbows, I give a questioning look and ask, "What are you doing?" That smirk of his, the one that's as infuriating as it is undeniably attractive, flashes across his face.

"This," he utters, and all of a sudden, I'm moving nearer to him, sinking onto the seat. Just as I'm about to anticipate his next move, he places the blanket I brought for our RA rounds over me.

"You said you were cold, right?" he teases. I'm completely at a loss for words, my mind in utter chaos. The presence of him, right above me, is causing my thoughts to go haywire, thinking about things I shouldn't even be considering or wanting.

He slightly opens my legs, and I instinctively attempt to close them. When our eyes meet and he softly pries my legs apart again, an intense heat engulfs me, leaving no room for resistance. Thank God for this blanket, and no students are really aware of what's happening, but there's no stopping them from hearing—

I let out a gasp when Luke's fingers make their way under the waistband of my yoga pants. My body arches into his touch. A silent plea for more. I barely utter his name, and he reacts with a deep, guttural sound, which instantly arouses me.

This is insane. This shouldn't be happening.

How can I resist when every fiber of my being says yes? His touch grazes over my underwear, drawing out a low moan from deep within me.

He emits a low and husky chuckle. "Feeling impatient, are we?" His words remind me of that night, of all the promises left unsaid.

The sight of his smirk makes me crave his fingers inside me. His fingers perform wonders around my waistband. They move so slow it's torture, but the kind you don't want to end. When my pants reach my heels, the leather seat beneath me sends an involuntary shiver down my spine.

"Luke," I groan, infusing that one word with a mix of frustration and longing.

"Look at you, baby," he whispers, and I almost roll my eyes at the nickname, not caring about anything but his touch. His purposeful fingers make my heart dance like a drum solo. With each stroke on my clit, igniting all my senses, he softly adds, "Begging for my touch."

Part of me screams I should be freaking out. We're on a golf cart, out in the open, in a parking lot that's only pretending to be deserted. Surrounded by the ghosts of my daily life, where I'm supposed to be in charge.

But then, he's pushing one finger—two, finding that exact spot that sends me sky high, and any thought of where I am or what I should be doing evaporates. All embarrassment and worry dissolve into pure, undiluted pleasure.

"Oh God . . . Luke . . . " slips out as my foot nearly slides off the seat, slick with sweat.

"That's it, ride my hand." His voice is a low command, dripping with confidence. I open my eyes slightly, my vision blurred by longing, and catch him watching his fingers slip inside me, then withdraw with an enticing, teasing force. His fingers work magic, rubbing that sensitive spot, making my toes curl and turning my loud cries into quiet, desperate whimpers.

Words fail me, and honestly, I don't want them. Instead of battling against the overpowering wave inside me, I surrender and flow with its rhythm. My back rises from the seat as my hands tangle in his hair, probably yanking it way too hard, but he doesn't seem to mind. In fact, it seems to drive him even more.

I desperately gasp for air, my eyes clenched shut as my climax reaches its peak, the orgasm pulsating through my entire being. The intensity causes my head to fall back as the waves crash and transport me away from reality. A nearby enthusiastic cheer momentarily distracts me, but Luke remains unaffected, prolonging the overwhelming pleasure I feel.

"Right there, baby," he breathes, his mouth inches from mine, his words a warm caress on my tingling skin as his fingers continue their magic. When he finally removes them, my core instantly misses their touch. Our gazes lock, and I notice his fingers glistening with my desire. Daringly, he raises a brow and brings them to his mouth.

There's no chance he's actually doing that—

My mind goes blank as Luke sensually puts his fingers in his mouth, his eyes fixated on mine, relishing the taste of me.

God, that's so hot.

He withdraws his fingers from his mouth, making a popping sound. "See, Penny? I told you I'd be the one you're riding," he says, winking. I can't resist laughing, swept away by the moment. I straighten up and make an effort to control my hair, which probably resembles a nest of birds. He helps me pull my bottoms up, his eyes glued to his fingers as they graze my thighs.

Next, his eyes wander in my direction, his fingers tenderly cradling my neck as if it's his lifeline. His touch makes me lean in, and suddenly I realize—this man, with his wild, stubborn, and overly confident self, awakens something powerful within me. Whenever I'm near him, I feel butterflies in my stomach, my skin tingles, and his intense gaze takes my breath away. It's overwhelming in the best possible way, and I can't decide if it's exhilarating or terrifying.

CHAPTER 19
PAYSON

"Jetting off for the weekend, to New York no less?" Milli says. Her eyes gleam with interest as she shifts in her cozy nest in the egg chair of our dorm.

In an instant, October was gone and November had arrived. One would assume that after everything that transpired between Luke and me, our sessions would be fraught with awkwardness, each encounter a potential minefield of unexpressed thoughts and suppressed longing. But strangely, we've navigated through the tension, finding our rhythm once again, perhaps even better than before. Luke has peeled back layers of himself, and even as we sidestep the one unspoken topic, I can sense his readiness to face it.

Since that unforgettable encounter on the golf cart, I curiously find myself eager for our sessions. I know I should be cautious of the feeling that overtakes me when I stare into his deep, hazel eyes, but I can't help it. My pulse quickens and my palms grow clammy whenever he's near.

Something I never thought would happen around him. *Luke Sutton.*

While I may feel that way, he doesn't know that, nor will he. That golf cart adventure was a one-off—a boundary I've reiterated in our recent sessions.

Next to me, Brooke carefully holds out glasses filled with our creation—a cranberry orange margarita. With each sip, the tart sweetness eases my preflight nerves.

"Why not? It sounds like a blast, and it's Thanksgiving break. It's the perfect chance to escape before we're all buried in finals prep come December," Brooke suggests with an enthusiasm that's hard to ignore.

Milli gives a halfhearted shrug, cautioning, "Just don't enjoy yourselves too much." Her eyes drill into mine, probably wondering why on earth I'd zip off to New York for the weekend with her brother—or, to be more accurate, the Lone Star team. Though, to be honest, I'm not even sure where Luke and I stand now. Not enemies, not exactly friends? But somehow things feel right—like we're exactly where we need to be.

With a deep exhale, I collapse onto my overstuffed suitcase, wrestling to close it tightly. It's pretty clear I'm not a seasoned flier—the wear on my luggage says it all. Packing for this New York weekend has been a guessing game. The city's cold weather had me unsure about what to wear, plus there's the game. Luke and Coach Donovan convinced me to watch the game, while casually remarking, *It would be good to see your client in action.*

If only he knew the scale of what I have observed of Luke's actions.

Of course I agreed, because again, he is the one flying me out for a so-called client. And, not only will this be my first NFL experience but also my first time seeing Luke in his element, all happening in New York—a city I haven't visited yet. Just the thought fills me with excitement, building up my anticipation for what lies ahead.

"Why are you going again?" Milli's curiosity floats over her margarita glass as I engage in one final tussle with my suitcase. Triumphantly, I pat the suitcase and brush my hands together, declaring silent victory over the packing ordeal. With all the essentials (and a little extra) for the weekend packed, I leisurely make my way to my desk chair and partake in the margarita sipping tradition.

"Given that I've never been to New York, it seems like the perfect time to make the most of it. Especially now, with the holiday lights and magic," I muse, soaking in the very idea of the city's festive glow.

Brooke chimes in with a nod, "It must be amazing with all the decorations. Honestly, I'm a tad envious." We share a laugh, the atmosphere light and easy.

"And is that the only reason?" Milli probes further, her gaze fixed on me.

I pause, aware that jumping to *because of your brother* may create a strange perception, both for her and for myself, as I navigate through uncertain emotions.

Using two fingers to emphasize, I move on to my second point. "I must admit, I was initially hesitant. Luke and I haven't always been on the best of terms," I confess, drawing a chuckle mixed with a snort from Milli.

"That's certainly a unique perspective," she jests, and I can't help but acknowledge it with a playful eye roll.

Moving forward, I admit, "He's been surprising me lately. I can't share too much due to client/therapist confidentiality, but I will say that knowing this is happening has meant a lot to me, you know?"

"Sort of like validation?" Brooke interjects.

Meeting her gaze, I nod. "Yeah, it did. Hearing that feedback was incredibly affirming. It felt like confirmation that I'm on the right path." The pride that bloomed within me hearing those words from his coach, echoed by Luke himself, was a profound moment. Even though Luke and I have more to accomplish, I couldn't resist doing a victory dance when I went back to my dorm that day.

With an encouraging smile, Milli assures me in her warm voice, "You're aware that B and I are proud of you, aren't you?"

The smile on my face is real, and I truly appreciate their support.

My girls have always had my back, supporting me through everything and encouraging me to pursue my goals and dreams. They are my constants, the ones I can always rely on. While I wish I could count on my parents' support and hear them say they're proud of me, I learned long ago not to expect too much.

Brooke, ever the enthusiast, claps her hands, sparking the next question. "So, what's the plan while you're there? Did his coach give you the itinerary?"

I take another leisurely sip of my margarita before answering. "Not in so many words, but I've got the gist of it." Their simultaneous eyebrow raise prompts a laugh from me. "Well, the adventure starts with me catching a ride on the team's private jet tomorrow morning."

Brooke's eyes widen. "Ooh, private jet experience? That sounds amazing."

I nod, trying to play it cool, even though deep down I'm slightly freaking out. "Once we land, the team can finally unwind for the rest of Saturday," I add, as the act of sharing my itinerary solidifies the reality.

"Game day follows. Luke noted that their routine varies slightly for away games, but overall, it's business as usual for them." They nod, our drinks nearing their end, and I rise for a refill, not missing a beat in our conversation. "As for me and Luke, we'll fit his session in around the game." Typically, we save it for later, but considering the energetic vibe of game days, doing it beforehand might be a better idea this time.

I bring them fresh drinks and place the margarita pitcher back on the makeshift bar in our dorm room setup. Settling back into my chair, Brooke states, "That comes across as a relaxing weekend."

While biting my lip, I feel my heart flutter in anticipation. It really does sound perfect, and I couldn't be more thrilled. I should feel more guilty about not going home for Thanksgiving, knowing that Mom will be alone with Dad. However, when I informed her during our FaceTime conversation that I had a commitment with a client and couldn't attend, she expressed that she understood. Then she started to stir up unnecessary drama, hinting that my client might mean more to me than just work.

"I still can't believe his coach is letting you go, and even footing the bill for everything," Milli marvels. Honestly, neither can I, but who would pass up a complimentary adventure to New York, especially one that includes a session with Luke? Certainly not me.

"I'm just as surprised as you, but think about it—his coach must really believe in Luke's potential. Otherwise, why go to all this effort? Luke's even mentioned how much he appreciates his new coach, especially for encouraging him to pursue therapy."

Milli's eyebrow arches, showing doubt. "Are you serious? He said that?" For a moment, I wonder if I've overstepped, sharing something from our sessions. But then I remember— Milli is his sister, and this insight, just once, might actually be reassuring.

"Yep." I allow the *P* to pop, creating a momentary lightness that momentarily disguises the seriousness of our conversation.

Milli's smile spreads, a soft acknowledgment of the

progress. "That's great. Luke really deserves a coach who sees his value. It hasn't always been smooth sailing for him." There's a brief flicker in her eyes, a shadow of something more, before she averts her gaze.

That hesitation, the sudden avoidance—it sparks my curiosity. What's she not saying? The therapist within me longs to probe deeper. Yet, this isn't the time, nor the setting, and prying wouldn't be fair. Especially not on margarita night, and certainly not without Luke's consent.

Milli clears her throat and playfully shifts the conversation, saying, "Well, lookie here. Seems like giving him a chance is paying off, huh?" Her words carry a hint of *I told you so*, but she's not wrong. Despite a few crossed lines, a secret we're both keen on keeping, giving Luke a chance has benefited us both.

"Anyway," I continue, steering the conversation back. "His coach has noticed improvements, and with the season ramping up toward the Super Bowl, missing sessions isn't an option. As his therapist, I couldn't agree more." It's a delicate balance, but it's clear that everyone involved is invested in Luke's success, both on and off the field.

"But can't you just do a video call for the session?" Brooke asks.

I respond with a nonchalant shrug, my stance on the matter clear. "Yeah, we tried video calls once, but it's just not the same. Therapy, at least in my view, thrives on face-to-face interaction. Being in the same room allows for a deeper connection, a more tangible sense of presence and empathy. Over a screen, it's just . . . different, you know?"

She nods.

Just as they start talking about something else, my phone vibrates, grabbing my attention.

LUKE

Ready to join the mile high club?

I roll my eyes at his message, but a smirk still pulls at my lips. Really, the mile high club? This is not a situation from a cheesy romance novel.

PAYSON

Mile high club? Huh. What's that?

LUKE

It's instant access to me. Duh, Penny.

My heart skips a beat and I blink, trying to process his words. I absentmindedly play with my margarita glass, but I'm brought back to the real world by another notification.

MOM

Haven't heard from you in a bit. Give your mama a call soon? Love you, Pay.

I sink into my chair, closing my eyes. The weight of her concern makes my chest tighten. College is supposed to be a time to get away, to discover myself, to get free of everything, but here I am, tethered by invisible strings.

I gently press my temples, hoping to alleviate the mounting exhaustion. Her words, carefully disguised as concern, often imply that I have to resolve the troubles. But my heart's not in it—not today. My mind is elsewhere, tangled up in the excitement of New York. I can almost feel the city's energy pulsing through me, a stark contrast to the quiet desperation in her text.

As I get ready to send a brief response to temporarily relieve her anxieties. I pause, my fingers lingering above the screen, burdened by a sense of duty, until I finally send the message and release a long exhale.

PAYSON

Hi, Mom. I miss and love you too. I will call soon!

It's a temporary Band-Aid, but it's all I can offer at the moment.

Returning to Luke, I delve into our playful back and forth.

PAYSON

Oh, bummer. Here I was thinking it meant all access to your team. After all, you did mention getting to know them better by season's end . . .

LUKE

Don't even think about it, Penny. You're mine.

His words hit me. *His?* Warmth courses through me, beginning in my chest and rising to my cheeks. I can feel my heartbeat thudding as I reread the text he sent. I glance quickly at Brooke and Milli, but they're engrossed in something on Milli's phone, unaware of the storm brewing inside me.

Just as I'm about to respond, another text from Luke appears.

LUKE

Penny, you're mine. They can go find their own damn therapist. I have dibs on you.

My breath catches in my throat like a snagged thread. It's a powerful sentiment packed into a few words, sending my heart into a confusing flutter. How do I even respond to that? My fingers waver above the keyboard, unsure and hesitant.

The sound of a throat clearing snaps me back to reality. I lift my gaze and see Brooke and Milli observing me with a curious and amused expression. "Your face right now . . . "

Brooke begins, her voice trailing off as if she's savoring the moment.

Milli, with her keen observation, notes, "You look surprised, flushed, yet you're smiling." Their words hang in the air, a perfect capture of my tumultuous state.

I try to mask the flurry of emotions Luke's messages stir within me, but the effort feels surprisingly futile. Typically, I take pride in hiding my emotions, but with Luke . . . he's a different story. Each message and interaction lately is a surprise, making me uncertain which version of him I'll come across—the charming yet maddeningly self-assured man, or the unexpectedly gentle and considerate one who brings to mind a loyal golden retriever. If I'm honest, both sides of him have grown on me.

Trying to avoid the topic, I respond with an indifferent shrug, causing Brooke and Milli to burst into laughter. I notice Milli's gaze lingering on me briefly before she looks away and focuses on her phone, leaving me to my own thoughts.

Opting for a light but pointed reply to Luke, I swiftly type out my response.

PAYSON

> Yes, I'm your therapist. But remember, I'm not anchored down, and I do have eyes. All claims are no longer valid. That includes yours on me, Sutton.

I set my phone aside and decide to fully enjoy the company of my closest friends. This weekend, Luke would have my full attention, and the mere thought of it fills me with a mix of excitement and anxiety as my emotions battle silently. Nonetheless, Luke, with all his complexity and unexpected charm, could wait.

CHAPTER 20
PAYSON

Deal? Deal.

Sweat drips from my palms as my heartbeat pounds in my ears. A whirl of nerves goes through my body, reminiscent of when you were a child looking up at a huge roller coaster. It looms before me, a behemoth of a Boeing 767, easily swallowing two hundred to three hundred people in its belly. Considering its size, it's no wonder it can transport an entire NFL team—fifty-three players, coaches, medical staff, support crew, and occasionally even executives and owners.

As I breathe in, the scent of jet fuel and tarmac fills my lungs, causing my stomach to twist in knots. And, yeah, I know this because pouring over NFL game details became my late-night obsession after margaritas with the girls. I searched thoroughly to ensure that I wouldn't be caught off guard or appear clueless if I ended up in a conversation with one of Luke's teammates.

I'm startled by the sudden heaviness on my shoulder and instinctively pull away, only to hear a low chuckle. I swivel, my sight locking onto the source, and I'm floored. Wow, just . . . wow. Before me stands a man whose attractiveness could surely cause a momentary lapse in faith. I blink, hoping to reset the scene, but no, he's very much real, looking dashing in a suit, with what appears to be his weekend bag in tow.

Standing there, a smirk dances on his lips, as if he's privy to a joke only he understands, and I have to restrain myself from knocking that smug look off his face. Would it make him any less gorgeous? Doubtful. His eyes glisten with a mix of arrogance and amusement, catching the light in a way that makes them almost hypnotic.

The truth slowly sinks in—I have just realized that this person is one of Luke's teammates. He was in one of the pictures Luke sent me. I feel my breath catch and my pulse race. He observes my response, his smirk growing wider, and tilts his head slightly, almost challenging me to speak up.

Once again, his unexpected tap on my shoulder startles me, causing me to jump involuntarily. Despite expecting it, the surprise is as fresh as the first. He responds with a reassuring squeeze, a gesture that somehow steadies me. I muster a smile, tight with nerves, as he gestures toward the plane, leading the way. "Must be your first time flying private?" he inquires, voice tinged with a hint of amusement.

I'm rendered speechless, only able to nod in response, completely overwhelmed by the exclusivity of this experience. How many can claim the luxury of a private flight?

He laughs—a rich, enveloping sound that instantly draws my thoughts to Luke, the very man I find myself instinctively searching for the moment we board the private plane. And, oh, the sight that greets me . . . It's my first time laying eyes on a Boeing 767 up close, and I'm utterly taken aback. Its immense size and vast interior make it feel like entering a whole new world—an extravagant and exclusive realm I never knew existed. My eyes wander, drinking in the vastness, the rows of plush seating, and the polished aisles.

Suddenly, my attention is drawn to *him.*

In the labyrinth of seats, there he stands by his designated place on the plane. He has that disarming, sweet, almost puppylike expression that cuts straight through to my core. Leaning effortlessly against the window, dressed in a suit, his presence brings a flush to my cheeks. It seems to be the uniform here. Reluctantly, I scan the cabin filled with identically dressed men. Grown men, each exuding an air of polished charm that leaves my knees feeling like jelly.

I'm pulled back to the present by a strong squeeze on my shoulder, and the blonde with the mischievous smile is still there. "Wanna sit with me?" he suggests, tapping his thigh as if to indicate the seat's comfort, his eyebrow arching, a mischievous smirk playing on his lips.

I can't help but smile back, amused and a bit charmed—he's definitely got game. Yet, before I can even formulate a response, a voice cuts through the moment, firm and unmistakable: "She already has a seat."

"Screw off, Sutton. She's your therapist, not *your* girlfriend," the voice beside me snaps, irritation flickering in his eyes.

"Percy, she's not *your* girlfriend," comes the swift, implication-laden rebuttal, the words sharp and loaded.

Ah, Percy. The name seems almost too gentle for someone of his . . . stature. Is this a common theme among them?

I narrow my eyes, glancing back and forth at both of them. Percy's jaw contracts, a muscle twitching just below the surface, as Luke's knuckles whiten while gripping the seat's edge. Their eyes meet, and then they both turn to look at me, the plane filled with palpable tension.

Why did Luke care so much about Percy? Was he jealous?

"Nice to see you again, Payson." Berry's voice, warm and filled with an easy familiarity, pulls my attention. Catching his teddy-bear smile, I can't help but smile and wave in return. In my peripheral vision, I notice a flicker of annoyance—or is it something deeper?—cross Percy's face as his hand retreats from my shoulder. Suddenly, the air feels easier to breathe, not because I minded his touch, but because Luke's subtle swallow betrays his discomfort at another man's hand on me.

"Dude, what the fuck, you know Payson?" Percy's confusion is almost palpable. He pauses, gears turning, before the real question dawns on him. "Wait, what do you mean nice to see her again? When did you see her last?"

"Enough with the questions, Mr. Detective," Luke interjects as he pats the seat beside him, an unspoken invitation hanging between us. Berry simply shakes his head.

"As much as I've enjoyed this, my seat is calling my name," I announce, surprising even myself with the declaration—my first words amid the lively banter. Percy's eyebrows shoot up, but his signature smirk quickly returns, eliciting a chuckle from me. I hadn't realized how silent I'd been until now. But just as I turn to head to my seat, something—or rather, someone—comes barreling into my legs.

Aliana.

I chuckle softly and say, "Hello, sweet girl," as she clings onto my leg.

As I head toward Luke, a flight attendant assists with my bags, leaving me with only my carry-on. I definitely don't miss the way her eyes roam over Luke.

Really? I'm right here? But then, without fail, I sense his piercing gaze following my every move, the intensity reflected in his eyes sending a ripple of awareness through me, though it is short-lived.

Percy, positioned across from us, slaps his thigh in a repeat gesture, his confidence undimmed. "Don't worry, Pay baby, you'll be sitting here by the end of the weekend," he declares with a wink.

Pay baby? That's new. His audacity is so bold that it's hard for me to hold back a snicker.

Suddenly, my phone pings, briefly distracting me before airplane mode disconnects me from the world.

> **MOM**
>
> Hey, baby girl, got a second? Would love to talk.

Actually, the timing couldn't be worse. Guilt pierces through the emotional chaos within me.

She shares a picture of her bruised arms. Every mark tells a silent story of her suffering. Next, there's a photo of her face, specifically a bruise just below her cheekbone, and a word in a story I'm too scared to say out loud.

I barely stifle a gasp as tears threaten to spill when I hear Luke joke, "Someone's popular this morning." In a panic, I close the message thread, my heart racing. My eyes shut tight as I draw a deep, shaky breath, desperately trying to steady myself. The guilt of not being there to protect her courses through my veins like poison, eating away at my soul. It's sharp and unyielding, gnawing at my bones with the ferocity of a beast, making my stomach churn.

Trembling, my hands struggle to hold onto the phone. My grip tightens, my knuckles turning white as the tremor spreads through my arms. Each pulsation of my core reverberates like the pounding of war drums against my rib cage. The air is heavy and suffocating, making it hard to breathe as I struggle against waves of nausea.

Oh no, the feeling of vomiting is getting stronger quickly. My mouth waters, and I swallow hard, forcing the bile back down. I can't afford to break down—not here, not now. *Hold it together, Payson,* I silently urge myself, mustering every bit of strength I possess. But I don't have to; the next moment,

Luke's hand is wrapping around mine, and my body softens, relaxing in his touch.

"Penny, are you okay?" he asks, his sincere tone stirring the tears I'm trying to hold back. It's just a simple question, but he knows something is wrong. He's paying attention.

I casually peek at Luke and force a grin, nodding. Empowered by his touch, I text my mom with my free hand, the phone feeling heavy in my clammy grip.

PAYSON

Hey, Mom. I won't be available now but can chat later. Love you.

Right as the announcement to prepare for takeoff is made, my mom texts me saying she loves me and will have two pumpkin pies for me this weekend. I chuckle, momentarily relieving the tension in my chest.

Luke's hand slips from mine, finding its place gently on my thigh. His hazel-brown eyes meet mine, overflowing with concern and questions. Instead of letting his curiosity take over, he clears his throat, a gesture I'm grateful for.

My heart clenches with an unexpected pang of loss as his hand slips away from my thigh. I miss the heat, the firmness, that reassuring touch. Instead of a warning, I feel an odd sense of comfort wash over me. Safe. It's not a feeling I ever associated with Luke, not with our tangled past. I still don't understand why Luke hates me so much—if he even does anymore. The past few weeks have painted a different picture.

We had summers filled with playful pool shoves, laughter echoing against the water, and those fleeting, accidental brushes of our hands that sent a strange warmth up my arm. I treasured those moments, even if they seemed insignificant to him. So what changed? What twisted those memories into something bitter and jagged?

Was it something I did, something I said, or was it just the inevitable drift of people growing up and apart? Because from where I stand, it feels like the whiplash of my parents' relationship. My dad was loving, caring, everything my mom needed—until he wasn't.

I'm hauled back from my brain's meandering by a scent that hits just right—deep, bold hazelnut laced with that kick of cinnamon.

Coffee.

It's my refuge, the one constant capable of soothing my inner chaos.

Luke hands me a coffee cup emblazoned with *Mocha Haven*, and instantly, I smile. It's not just because I'm about to enjoy my first cup of the day, but because Luke, of all people, is the one who brought it. For me.

Seriously, where is the self-centered man I've been interacting with? My heart's doing somersaults over here, not quite knowing how to process this . . . thoughtfulness. It's uncharted territory for me, having someone go out of their way like this. From getting my favorite snacks to watching *I Love Lucy*, and now this—making sure I always have coffee. And not just any coffee. Mocha Haven. He had to have gone out of his way.

With a confident smirk, he quickly dismisses it as if it's no big deal. However, for this girl, coffee is everything before the crack of dawn.

"I figured it could help calm your nerves a little," he explains, and I arch an eyebrow. "I heard from a little bird that you've never experienced private flying." A.k.a. Milli had told him. "I wanted to make sure you enjoyed it. Plus, I know how much you love coffee."

Score: My heart: 0 / Luke: 1

Damn him for being so considerate. A girl could get used to this.

A grin breaks across my face. I take a sip of the coffee, and wow, it's like a taste of pure heaven. My eyes involuntarily close and I let out a pleasurable moan. The warmth fills me, giving me a burst of energy as I open my eyes, only to find his gaze already on me. My lips. I find myself licking them, maybe a tad too suggestively. We shouldn't be going down this road. I shouldn't. Yet, whenever Luke Sutton is around, my body acts on its own accord.

Can't this guy just revert to his old self already?

Then again, a tiny voice in my head reminds me that perhaps he has always been this way, and I'm only now discovering his true self.

With each sip, the warm liquid brings a sense of relief as it flows down my throat. Luke's throat clearing catches my attention, and I look at his hands. There's a deliberate slowness to their movements, with fingers tapping nervously on the armrest before adjusting in the seat. A smirk tugs at the corner of my mouth. I sip again and sink comfortably into my chair, feeling the plush cushion beneath me.

A murmur catches my attention. "Oh, yeah, this weekend's gonna be interesting." Percy's eyes gleam with a secret knowledge, his lips curling into a conspiratorial grin.

"Perc, shut it. Buckle up," Luke chides, his voice firm. With a shake of his head, his hair falls into his line of sight, and he hurriedly brushes it away with a rough hand.

Then, out pops a redhead from behind a seat, one hand extended while the other clutches what seems to be a Kindle. "Hey there, I'm Maddox, nice to finally put a name to a face," he greets with a grin.

As I spot another one of Luke's teammates, a smile lights up my face. Apparently, Luke's been chatting about me, huh? Our hands connect, and the handshake lasts a bit longer than usual. My pulse quickens and a faint heat rises to my face from his touch. In the midst of our handshake, I detect a faint growl beside me, promptly concealed by Maddox's chuckle.

"Nice to meet you, Maddox," I offer, my voice steadier than I feel. With a friendly nod, he retreats to his seat. Luke, meanwhile, shoots Maddox a half-serious glare before turning to secure his seat belt. While everyone finds their places, including myself, Luke's coach approaches, offering a strong handshake and a confident grin. "I'm Coach Donovan. Just wanted to say thanks for all your support with Luke."

I take a moment to straighten myself, feeling a mixture of pride and nervousness. "Nice to meet you, Coach Donovan. It's been a pleasure working with Luke."

Nodding, his eyes crinkle at the corners. "He's mentioned you quite a bit. I know working with this guy can be one tough nail." A few of us chuckle, the sound lightening the atmosphere. He continues, "But we appreciate your dedication." I smile and nod again, feeling a warm flush rise to my cheeks under Luke's steady gaze.

The coach walks off, and I glance at Luke, who shakes his head with a slight smile, amused. With ease, his hand finds its place on my thigh again, fingers tracing soothing patterns, as if it's the most ordinary thing. In a blink, the next two and a half hours on the plane go by and he doesn't move his hand once.

Once we touch down in New York, everyone follows the drill, exiting the plane and heading to a lineup of vehicles, each seeming to match its owner in size and style. Drivers stand by, ready to whisk away their designated player.

Just as I'm about to grab my suitcase, Luke reaches out and takes it for me. He nods toward a sleek, black Range Rover—exactly the type of car he has at home. Go figure.

"Good lord, woman, what's in this thing?" Luke grunts as he hoists my suitcase toward the vehicle. Suppressing a laugh, I choose to shrug casually.

"A lifeless body?" I suggest, trailing behind him.

While passing our bags to the driver, he gives me a fleeting glance and a smirk. "Honestly, Penny, wouldn't put it past you. But," he pauses, lifting a finger for emphasis as we settle into the back of the Range Rover, "next time you're plotting a murder, count me in."

I quirk an eyebrow—because, really, who tosses around murder plots so casually? But then he lets out a chuckle.

"Come on, you know I'm a *Dexter* fan." True, he's mentioned his affinity for the show a few times. So, maybe a penchant for serial killer dramas does lend itself to a certain . . . creative thinking?

Shaking my head does nothing to quell the goofy grin stretching across my face. The longer I'm around Luke, the more I notice how effortlessly he brings out my smiles. It's a kind of effortless happiness that feels both terrifying and thrilling.

With a mischievous sparkle in his stare, Luke gently bumps his shoulder against mine. I let out a light giggle and playfully swat at his arm. His hand quickly catches mine, his fingers intertwining with mine, causing a pleasant shiver to run up my arm.

I try to shake off the feeling, but it lingers, my mind racing. On one hand, I love that I can smile around him so easily, that I can feel this light and free. But on the other, I can't help but wonder why. Why is it so effortless? Is this how my mom felt with my dad before things took a turn?

As the engine roars to life, Luke settles into the car and wraps his available arm around my shoulder. We begin our journey away from the airstrip, racing through Times Square. Taylor Swift's "Welcome to New York" plays, setting the soundtrack as the city lights blur outside the window.

I sense Luke looking at me, his fingertips delicately

tracing patterns on my neck, causing goose bumps to appear. I shift my gaze, locking eyes with him.

"First time in New York?" he asks, his voice a low murmur over the music.

I nod, smiling shyly. "That obvious?"

He chuckles. "Yeah, but it's cute." He gives a little shrug, his fingers now playfully teasing at the collar of my jacket.

My cheeks flush, not just from his words, but also from how touchy he's been today and the way his eyes have followed my every move. It's as if he fears I might bolt if he looked away even for a second. Sure, maybe I would have at first, but now? I enjoy being here, around him.

I raise a brow, and he chuckles.

Luke leans in, and I catch myself staring at his lips—oh, how I long for his touch on mine.

Payson, shut it down now.

Then, there's the idea of his hands, exploring.

Half teasing, half serious, he says, "Then it's settled. I'm your tour guide?" Before I can respond, he adds, "Well, Penny, you haven't been to New York. I've been, multiple times, might I add. So it's a win-win."

"A win-win, huh?" I say, teasingly. "Only if I get to pick the spots."

He laughs, and it bursts through the air, genuine and infectious. His laughter draws a smile from me that feels as real as the heartbeat thudding in my chest.

With a pout that I find unexpectedly adorable—and completely different from the Luke I thought I knew—he retorts, "Then you wouldn't need a tour guide."

My lip finds its way between my teeth, a nervous habit, especially as his eyes darken, tracking the movement to my mouth. My spine tingles and my heartbeat races as his gaze intensifies.

"Another deal?" he echoes, a slight grin appearing as he

reminisces about our past pact. We had a surprisingly good ending to that session, with me indulging in my favorite Mexican takeout and us laughing together on the couch while watching an *I Love Lucy* rerun.

"What kind of deal are we talking about this time?" I ask.

With a gentle touch, he grazes my jawline and tucks a loose strand of hair behind my ear. His touch is light, almost hesitant, but it sends a jolt straight to my core, making my thighs instinctively close.

"How about this: I choose a few locations, and you choose a few?" My response is a beat too slow, so his finger traces my jawline again, pressing for an answer. "Deal?"

I pause, captivated by his parted lips and thoughtful lip bite, until I finally agree. "Deal."

With that smirk of his, he suggests, "Shall we seal this deal with a kiss?"

I chuckle, rolling my eyes. "You wish," I shoot back.

But then, almost too soft to catch, he murmurs, "I do."

CHAPTER 21
LUKE

"Is this what it means to be a New Yorker?" A grin spreads across my face as I watch Payson twirl like a graceful ballerina lost in her own world. Her arms carve elegant circles in the air. Against the backdrop of New York—its vibrant lights, the festive glow of early Christmas decorations, the dreary canopy of clouds, and the sea of bustling people—it all feels . . . mesmerizing.

Observing her, a warm feeling fills me. How is it that I once hated this woman, despising her because of the past, yet that bitterness appears so distant now? In this moment, she brings an unexpected sense of joy. Her carefree and spirited movements stir a strange sensation inside me. Maybe, just maybe, I'm starting to see her in a new light. Is it really possible?

It's possible that, in the past, I made an error in judgment. However, I recall vividly what I witnessed and what I was told. Despite the confusion, my thoughts on this woman have been completely transformed in the last few weeks.

Payson halts her spinning and meets my gaze, her face

beaming with happiness. "Join me!" she beckons, offering her hand.

I pause briefly, but then she bravely reaches out and holds my hand. As our fingers intertwine, the gentle warmth of her contact feels both unfamiliar and comforting.

We continue to walk through Times Square, the buildings towering exactly as I remember from my last visit here with my family for Christmas. It wasn't too long ago, yet it's a city my parents treasure, a sentiment Milli and I have learned to embrace in our own ways. However, this afternoon with Payson—seeing the relentless joy lighting up her face—I find myself cherishing these moments even more.

When we arrived at the hotel, we were relieved to see that we had been given separate rooms—thankfully. The only problem? Our rooms are connected by a shared space in between. And the simmering sexual tension between us? Yeah, it's almost at its boiling point. I continue attempting to push aside these . . . feelings. Is that what this is? Freaking feelings for her? It's as if my brain, body, and all other parts of me are in a state of constant warfare. Yet, every time she gives me that *I want you* look, the one I catch every now and then, I'm tempted to throw all caution to the wind and relive that night of us tangled in the sheets.

And those secretive glances she gives away? Well, they tell me everything. She wants me, craving the same things I do. Yet, the complexity of our situation demands that I remain on my best behavior for the rest of the season, even if my body hasn't gotten the memo since that night on the golf cart. Talk about torture.

"Did you know that Times Square earned the nickname 'The Great White Way' in the early twentieth century?"

Her words come as I arch an eyebrow. It's possibly the most random piece of trivia under the sun, but Payson has been dropping historical facts like breadcrumbs for the past hour. Who would've guessed she was such a history buff?

She laughs, a sound that tugs at all the right strings in me. "It was named that because it was one of the first streets in the United States to be illuminated by electric lights, making it a dazzling spectacle at night."

Just as I'm about to respond, she interrupts with, "Did you know Times Square was heavily affected during the Great Depression? Many theaters had to close or turn to burlesque shows, leading to a decline in the area?"

Maneuvering through the crowd is no easy feat, but we eventually stop in front of a well-lit café named Blue Bottle Coffee. Payson confidently surveys the entrance, appearing to give her approval. "This is it."

It's probably one of those must-visit places on her list. Considering the fact that it's a coffee shop, it's not all that shocking. Payson has a knack for discovering beauty in everyday locations, transforming a basic cup of coffee into a cherished moment. It causes me to see the ordinary through her perspective, transforming it into something extraordinary.

Before I can even read the sign, which has a bright blue coffee cup symbol, she takes hold of my hand. With ease, our fingers interlock once more, and she guides me toward the coffee shop. Inside, I'm unable to resist soaking in the atmosphere alongside her. The aroma is a combination of strong coffee and hazelnut filling the air, the buzz of activity unmistakable. It's New York, after all. However, there's a certain quality to this place that reminds me of a scene from *Friends*—cozy, familiar, and with a minimalist aesthetic that adds to its charm.

Payson's enthusiasm leads me to the counter, where a tempting assortment of baked goods, fudges, and mini bundt cakes entices all passersby. The barista greets us with a warm, knowing smile, asking, "What can I get for the happy couple?"

Payson's response is almost funny—her eyes quickly widen and a faint blush appears from her neck to her cheeks. I successfully hold back a laugh, opting to smile. There's no point in correcting the barista; it would only make Payson feel more embarrassed than she already seems.

The moment Payson releases my hand, I immediately notice the absence of her touch—the warmth, the subtle electric feeling that runs through me whenever she's near. Without skipping a beat, she diverts my attention by asking for fudge and a cup of coffee. She looks in my direction, expecting me to order. I politely ask for some water, she playfully rolls her eyes with a slight shake of her head and a quiet "Boring."

We snag a spot by the window, thanks to Payson's fondness for people-watching, as the barista gets our orders ready. Our orders are delivered quickly, and as Payson takes her first sip of coffee, she closes her eyes and lets out a soft moan of satisfaction.

Is her goal really to ruin me?

"Must you always make that sound when you drink coffee?" I note, catching her eye roll and that little smirk that screams she's full of sass today.

Acting as if it's common knowledge, she fires back, "Uh, yeah, of course, it's coffee."

With a wry smile, I gaze out at the hustle of Times Square. This time of year is different—warm enough to enjoy the outdoors, with a festive atmosphere. Honestly, if you're going to visit, now's the time.

"Why all the history trivia?" I probe, taking a sip of my water, the cool liquid soothing my dry throat.

With a casual shrug, she traces her fingers along the rim

of a coffee mug adorned with the phrase ESPRESSO YOUR-SELF. "My dad," she mutters softly, a sigh escaping her lips. Instantly, a warm smile appears on her face, her pupils softening, as if a cherished memory just brushed her mind. "He teaches history."

"Really?" I say, my curiosity piqued. Payson and I may have grown up in close proximity, but I never made an effort to explore her family background.

"Ever heard of Time Walk Heritage Park in Stoneton?" she asks.

I nod. While jogging and driving out of town, I've caught fleeting glimpses of old signs and worn paths that imply hidden stories.

"It's a place my dad and I visit often. Well, we used to." Her eyes drift away, lost in the echoes of time spent and moments shared.

Used to? There's a heavy, unspoken meaning that hovers between us. I'm torn between prying further or giving her space to unravel her thoughts in her own time. My curiosity wins out. Leaning in slightly, I venture, "You don't go there anymore?"

She shifts uncomfortably and gazes out the window as she grips the mug, her knuckles white against the ceramic. However, just as I assume she's withdrawn, she unexpectedly reveals a glimpse of her inner world. "It was our thing, you know? Still is, in a way . . . just, different now." A laugh that's more of a scoff escapes her, a bitter edge to it. "Sounds ridiculous, doesn't it?"

Quick to ease her self-consciousness, I assure her, "Not at all. You don't need to explain, really."

Honestly, she doesn't need to. It's way out of my lane, but pretending I'm not eating up every word would be playing it too cool. Discovering Payson's vulnerability, despite all the grief I've given her, feels like finding a treasure. Against all odds, she's revealing her true self exclusively to me.

With a quick shake of her head, she quickly dismisses her own vulnerability. Continuing on a different note, she mentions, "Growing up, our thing was him sharing a history fact every day. Be it about the Civil War, some state's backstory, or whatever."

"It's actually really cool," I pause, "to have something to share with a parent, something you both like and enjoy talking about." And it is—genuinely.

For me, it's football with my dad. We could spend hours discussing games, players, and strategies, while also exploring topics beyond sports. It's a connection I wouldn't trade for anything. Not everyone gets that kind of bond.

I steal a glance at Payson, her gaze far-off yet softened by the memories. "It really was." A beat. "Is," she corrects, swift as a reflex, then waves it off like it's nothing. But it's far from nothing. Her expression, the discreet gulp as she suppresses emotions—every sign points to a soul overflowing with emotions she's struggling to control.

I nod, experiencing a twinge of empathy. "I get it," I gently reply. "Football is what my dad and I bond over. But it's more than that. It's our time together, a way to connect beyond the everyday stuff."

I detect a flicker of melancholy in her stare, and it hits me how much this conversation matters to her. It's more than just sharing facts about history or football; it's about the connection, the shared moments that shape us.

For the next hour, we navigate to calmer waters and discuss the everyday things—her school experience, the challenges of being an RA, particularly when it comes to that person I encountered during my previous campus visit. She assures me all's well, and I notice how her eyes light up when she talks about all the things she's learning in her new psychology classes. It's in these moments that her passion and kindness shine through, and I can't help but admire her resilience.

Without warning, she starts clapping her hands together, seemingly forgetting her earlier sadness. "So, what's the next stop, Mr. Tour Guide?" she asks, her tone filled with playfulness. I raise a brow.

Her laughter echoes around us, a sound I've missed more than I thought. I had a moment of worry that discussing her dad might overshadow the day. But here we are, still standing, still laughing. You only have one opportunity to see New York for the first time, and I want to make it unforgettable for her.

Yeah, call it absolutely cheesy or whatever, but it seems like the right decision. Just as we're about to leave the café, Payson heads toward the bathroom, and I manage to grab some fudge to take back to the hotel. She demolished it earlier like it was the last piece of sweet on Earth, so it's got to be solid. Later, it'll be my turn to dive in.

As we stop outside the coffee shop, her excited gaze meets mine. It makes me grin, my heart stutters like a derailed train, and yeah, my palms are suddenly a sweat fest.

Man, get a grip, Luke. It's just Penny.

But that's just it, isn't it? *It's Penny.*

"Where to now?" she asks.

Even though I initially planned to go to Central Park, something better just came to mind. Neither of us has been to this spot before, it's the perfect blend of fun and historical —a place we can explore together for the first time.

"How about a behind-the-scenes tour?" Her eyes sparkle with curiosity. Without a second thought, I reach out and hold her soft hand; my pulse quickens at how natural it feels.

Why does she make me feel this way? I should be repulsed, should be pushing her aside. However, uncertainty consumes me. What if I've been wrong about her? What if she isn't who I believed her to be? What if the fluttering in my chest is real?

CHAPTER 22
PAYSON

The hotel bathroom is pristine with shiny marble and spotless mirrors, yet my hands shake as I clutch the vanity. I observe my reflection, noting the strain on my face and the constant shifting of my gaze. My heart is pounding like crazy, and I press a hand to my chest, trying to calm it down. It feels as if the universe has taken a positive turn, but I'm on edge, expecting something bad to happen.

It's not a big deal.

But it is.

My day with Luke yesterday ended at the New Amsterdam Theatre; it was a dream come true for history lovers. And the best part? Luke managed to persuade the actual tour guide to allow us access to the rooftop garden. Imagine this: the city lights twinkling below, gentle snow falling in the background—it was nearly perfect, just like a scene from a Hallmark film.

Nevertheless, after that magical evening, I gave my mom a call to see how she was doing, but she didn't respond. Anxiety began to take hold because she never fails to reply.

Hours passed with no call back, and I even texted her and got nothing back. Worry consumed me all night as my mind raced, conjuring up various worst-case scenarios. What if something had happened to her? What if she needed me and I wasn't there?

This morning, a heavy weight of unease settles in the pit of my stomach, causing breathlessness. I attempt to suppress the thoughts, but they persist, unforgiving and relentless.

Just let it go, Payson.

I know I need to, but it's hard sometimes.

Taking a deep breath, I try to calm myself, nervously wiping my sweaty palms on my jeans. Things will figure themselves out—today, in the future. I have to believe that. Despite the worry caused by my parents' situation, I must focus on my bigger goals: excelling in my course, graduating ahead of schedule, and becoming an exceptional therapist. This NFL game is just another hurdle along the path.

A knock at the connecting door cuts through the silence, making me jump. "Penny, I know you're in there," a familiar voice says, causing my pulse to quicken.

A smile appears on my face as memories come rushing back—him uttering those same words in his penthouse the day after my birthday. It feels like a lifetime ago.

I jump once more as another knock rings out. "Really, is that necessary?" I mutter under my breath as I storm to the door, frustration and a flicker of anticipation bubbling up. Why am I so nervous? I fling it open, and there he is. Not just Luke, but a barely there Luke. No shirt, just a towel hanging dangerously low. I catch myself lingering on his impeccably flawless, water-kissed skin.

Longing floods over me, my hands wanting to caress him, to follow the water clinging to his body. But I glue my hands to my sides, my heartbeat thumping in my chest. Our eyes lock, and the world just . . . pauses. We're stuck in this electric moment, eagerly waiting to see who will make the first move.

Then he wildly waves one hand while miraculously holding two coffees in the other. The scene is almost humorous, but it only heightens the tension between us. Why is he always so effortlessly charming?

Observing the two cups again, I arch an eyebrow and, with a toothbrush poking out of his mouth, he attempts to make his point. He mutters, "Is this some sort of new fashion statement? Cause I dig it, Penny."

My eyes roll, I'm literally in jeans, white sneakers, and one of my NRU sweatshirts, with a high ponytail. He stretches his hand, probably aiming for my hair, but I catch his wrist in time. His skin is wet and warm under my touch.

Just like my body, yet in different areas.

Our eyes meet, his eyebrow quirks, and then that grin—the one I'm supposed to dislike but secretly adore—spreads across his face, sending that all-too-familiar rush of heat through me.

Releasing his wrist, I quickly grab my hat from the bathroom vanity and head straight back to his room. With a nod of his head, he takes in the view of my room. "Not as cool as mine, but it's all right."

Fueled by curiosity, I grab a coffee from the holder and enter his room, eager to see how his space measures up.

Luke Sutton's place is, predictably, a suite—because of course it is. It's got everything: a kitchenette, a dining table for four, and even a couch. Seriously, who needs all this space for just two nights? Nights that are meant for nothing more than sleeping, at that. With my hands on my hips, I spin around to face him, only to see him signaling with a finger and throwing clothes at me.

Does he have a habit of throwing clothes at women? He pulled the same stunt that night at the club. Maybe it's a habit from all his fleeting encounters. The thought of him being with other people, those jersey chasers, their lips touching his, their hands exploring his irresistible body—it creates a pressure in my chest and makes my stomach churn.

Is this jealousy? It's an emotion I don't recognize well. Yet, Milli would confide in me, describing these exact feelings whenever other women got close to Miles. No, this can't be happening to me. That would mean I care about him more than I'm willing to admit, and that's simply not an option.

You do care, Payson, my inner voice teases, but I shove it aside.

"What do you think?" His voice snaps me back to reality. I close my eyes, attempting to tame my chaotic thoughts. What in the world is going on with me? Opening my eyes, I stifle a laugh, biting my lip and watching him. It's no use—he's wearing his new therapy shirt that says TACKLING PROBLEMS ON AND OFF THE FIELD. Then he does a ballerina spin that mirrors one of Milli's, ending with a bow, and it's just . . . ridiculously adorable.

His antics draw a reluctant smile from me, the kind that starts slow but spreads until it's unstoppable. It's disorienting how much I enjoy this side of him, the carefree and playful Luke, which contrasts with his usual cocky attitude.

I shake my head in an effort to calm the heat building inside me. "You're such a dork," I manage to say, my voice catching.

Our gazes collide, causing a sudden hitch in my breath. "But you like it," he admits with that familiar, stomach-fluttering smirk.

Maybe I do.

My pulse quickens as I shift my focus. Why does he have to be so . . . everything? I clear my voice, struggling to gather my wits. "Don't flatter yourself."

He inches closer, causing my eyes to instinctively narrow.

There is an instinctual urge to retreat, but I stand my ground, rooted. Our breaths mingle as he reaches out and a lock of my hair grazes my lips. His touch lingers, his thumb softly brushing my lip, creating a slow and deliberate caress that sends shivers down my spine and sets my nerves on fire. I'm irresistibly drawn to the magnetic field he's generated, tempted to nibble on his finger and witness his response.

But the spell breaks as quickly as it was cast. He casually moves away, strolling past me and sitting on a bar stool as if we're just friends. How does he do that? Pretend as if he didn't just shock the whole room with a single touch. I'm left here, trying to steady myself as my skin tingles and heart races.

Before I can bring myself to face him again, my eyes land on the clothes he'd flung at me. Lone Star team gear. A hat, a scarf, and a jersey emblazoned with *Sutton* and the number eighty-eight across the back. I inhale deeply and turn toward him, raising the merchandise with a questioning look.

While shrugging nonchalantly, his voice takes on a low and almost tender tone. "It's cold out. Figured you'd need the hat and scarf." I raise an eyebrow, holding up just the jersey. While he tries to keep his demeanor relaxed, I can't help but notice the smug grin creeping onto his face. "There's no question who you're rooting for today, baby."

Baby? Good lord, this man and his towering ego—it's enough to drive anyone crazy. It can be infuriating half the time, but in moments like these, a different feeling stirs within me, causing an aching desire.

He's midway through a coffee sip when I pitch my voice higher, "Ready to start?"

He smirks, leaning forward on his elbows, invading my personal space once again, making it a challenge to even take a breath. "Are *you* ready?" he teases, knowing exactly how he affects me.

My throat tightens, and I can feel every swallow magnified by my tension. Nodding, I make a conscious decision to avoid sensitive discussions right from the beginning. I've noticed a pattern with Luke where if I ease into our conversation with casual questions, he tends to be more willing to delve into the tougher and more profound questions afterward.

"Who are we playing against today?"

"The New York Cyclones," he responds, his gaze fixed on mine.

"Are they any good?" I manage, keeping my tone light.

A glint of pride is visible in his eyes as he confidently asserts, "Yeah, but we're superior."

"Are you confident in your chances of winning?"

Impatience colors his response. "Doesn't that answer your question?"

Whoa, okay, what was that about? Where did that attitude come from? I dismiss it and continue on. "Are your parents going to be watching?"

"No." That's unexpected. Since when don't his parents watch his games? Reading my mind, he says, "They're busy with weekend plans but will catch the replay."

"Anyone special then?" I ask, aiming to ease the strain that has shifted from playful to strained. My question really strikes a nerve. His jaw tightening is a clear indication that someone is expected to show up at the game. But who?

Just as I was about to speak, his phone made a loud ping on the table, interrupting me. From my vantage point, I can't see the screen, but Luke's explosive response tells me everything I need to know. In a swift move, I reach out and catch his wrist, preventing him from doing something drastic. Our gazes connect, leaving me torn between pressing forward or withdrawing. While his irritation was obvious, a piece of me needed answers.

In a hushed tone, I question, "Are those the game day texts?"

It's not uncommon for him to have them. Over the past few weeks, he has been consistently informing me that they are still arriving, possibly even more often than usual. They are persistent, and it makes me curious about who the person is behind the screen. Every time I get the chance to ask, either our session ends or Luke, like he does best, shuts down.

His intense gaze grows stronger as he struggles with the decision to be vulnerable and reveal the truth. With a louder-than-usual thud, he exhales deeply and places his phone back on the table. "It's nothing," he mutters, withdrawing his hand from mine and nervously playing with his hair.

"It's definitely something," I rebut, my frustration clear as I clench my jaw. Sure, his teammates and coach have been singing praises about his progress, and I've noticed improvements myself. But here I am, racing against time to earn credits before winter break, and there's Luke, eyeing the Offensive Rookie of the Year award as his season's crowning achievement. I'm painfully aware that achieving such heights requires more than just physical prowess on the field; it demands mental and emotional strength off it too.

His fingers fidget on the table as his nose wrinkles with each vibrate from his phone. The desire to grab it is overwhelming. But deep down, I know that would cross a line. I breathe in heavily, fighting the urge, and stand up, my legs feeling unsteady.

Meeting his gaze, my heart sinks. Where is the Luke who had been effortlessly open with me over the last few weeks? This tense, almost desperate person wasn't him. There's anger simmering beneath me, directed not only at him but also at the circumstances. If he thinks I'll stay and have a session with him acting like this, he's got another thing coming.

I inhale slowly and deliberately, sensing the tension in my rib cage. In Psychology 101, I quickly learned that working with an angry client is not possible. I've witnessed this behavior previously, and it always ends badly.

I push my chair in, partly out of politeness and partly to keep my fingers busy, preventing myself from either slapping him or shaking the answers out of him. "I'm leaving," I declare, my tone trembling with suppressed rage. He stares into the depths of my gaze, devoid of his usual confidence, making them appear empty. But then he stands and approaches me, his movements slow and deliberate. "You can't just walk out of our session, *Pennington*."

When did we go back to last names? The formality hits me hard, like a punch to the gut. The way he speaks, a combination of contempt and power, reminds me of a familiarity I thought we had overcome.

My eyes tighten, my voice icy as I retort, "Actually, I can leave. It's not like you're compensating me for my time." His audacity ignites my temper further, my hands clenched into fists at my sides. I'm here because his coach specifically requested my presence on this road trip to assist a player.

"It doesn't matter. You being here is about helping you pass a class," he counters.

My frustration intensifies as I struggle to maintain control. Luke and I were never the model of friendliness, but I felt a shift in the past month, a possible breakthrough. There were more laughs, more smiles, more . . . just everything.

"Let's not forget, I'm contributing to your career," I say, making my stance clear with my hands firmly planted on my hips. "I can retake the class, find another client. For me, it's not a significant loss."

My words seem to strike a nerve, his eyes widening. But frankly, I was past caring. His gaze shifts behind me momentarily before returning, his nostrils flaring, fingers tensing into his palm so tightly I half expected to see blood. I now realize I might have pushed too far. The signs were all there; he was a ticking time bomb in need of a moment to defuse.

This very session was imploding before it could even properly begin. Turning away from him, it seems we're both at a loss for words. Out of nowhere, his hand tightly grasps my shoulder, swiftly spinning me around to meet his gaze. Not only does the sudden touch startle me, but it also ignites a fire inside. Without thinking, my hand shoots up, ready to defend myself from the sudden intrusion into my personal space. Consent in such interactions is one thing; being caught off guard, quite literally blindsided, is entirely another.

He wraps his hand around my wrist and pulls me in so close that our breaths intertwine, creating an intimate moment amid the chaos. The look in his eyes, once devoid of life, now shines with a softer intensity. Did he truly think that by being physically close, with a strong but gentle hold, he could ease the tension? That his earlier, almost aggressive stance would somehow make me forget the urge to push back, to defend my ground?

His hand rises toward my face, causing an involuntary twitch as the intensity of the moment overwhelms me.

"I won't hurt you," he whispers, his fingers tracing a path down my cheeks, along my jaw, to my collarbone, finally resting at the nape of my neck. His touch sends my heart into a frenzied skip.

The fire in his stare softens, turning into an almost pleading look, as if he were trying to communicate something beyond words, his body language a silent testament to his inner conflict.

He closes his eyes and leans in, his forehead touching mine, causing me to do the same. I feel his breath intermingling with mine, creating a bubble of shared air that makes everything else fade into the background. Perhaps for the first time since I'd entered the room, I sense him truly relaxed. A wave of calm washes over me too.

"Yes, it was the usual game day texts," he admits with a hushed voice.

I choose to remain silent, allowing him to feel my presence through our shared breath and space. In this quiet moment, I understand that I have a role beyond being his therapist. I am someone here for him, someone to calm him, someone who truly cares.

"I tried not reading the messages like you told me," he confesses. It was something we discussed in the last session. I recommended that he approach the game with a focused mindset, paying no attention to the texts until it concluded. "It's been kind of freeing. Seems like it makes a difference, not seeing them until after."

I softly affirm, "That sounds like a positive thing."

A heavy sigh escapes him, carrying the burden of unexpressed thoughts. "Is it really?" he questions, doubt lacing his tone. "I mean, right now, not reading those texts . . . they might be helpful, but they . . . " He hesitates, his fingers intertwining nervously.

"They what, Luke?" I urge gently, my voice a soft nudge against his uncertainty.

When he opens his eyes, his usual bravado is momentarily absent, leaving them raw and exposed. "Those texts," he starts, his voice slightly shaky, "are the only thing that alleviate the guilt I feel every single day. They remind me of what I did, what I caused. Because of that, they push me harder, on the field and off." His eyes squeeze shut again, like a door slamming against a painful memory, and his voice falls to a whisper. "I despise every one of them, but I can't stop reading them."

I pause, the weight of his words settling heavily in the room. Luke had really let me in more than he had in months. The entire beginning of November, we tiptoed around this exact subject. Now that we were diving headfirst into it, I was completely shocked, lost for words. His vulnerability and honesty were heart-wrenching and revealing.

Maybe we are more alike than either of us realizes. He looks like a lost little boy trapped in a man's body. While I could sympathize with him, I struggle to condone him allowing this to continue. As his therapist, it wouldn't be right. But as someone who is starting to care for Luke, someone who has a father stuck in a vicious cycle, it's like I am seeing it all over again. And while I may not be able to help my father, maybe I can help Luke.

Or at least do my damn best.

Right as I was about to say something, he says, "I know how bizarre it sounds, believe me. Saying it out loud, it sounds . . . fucked up. But—" He exhales deeply, a sigh that carried the heaviness of years. "It's the truth. I've been getting these texts since my sophomore year in high school."

My eyes widen. Sophomore year? That's nearly as long as I've dealt with never-ending guilt. Feeling like whatever I do isn't good enough. This was clearly one of the things he was struggling with. I can see it in his expressions, in the little hints he has shared over months of our sessions. The confession lingers in the atmosphere, dense and tangible. My heart aches for the teenage boy he was, navigating the storm of anonymous messages, and for the man he has become, shaped by their relentless presence.

Luke

It's impossible for me not to watch as her thumb glides over mine, calming my frustration. Our eyes meet, her expression filled with curiosity, pushing me to reveal more, inviting me to open up further. Her hand quivers gently in mine, her breaths shallow and filled with anticipation. At this pivotal and delicate moment, I understand that she deserves my vulnerability after all this time. My chest tightens, and I swallow hard, offering what I can, here and now—a step toward her, letting her see the real me, beyond the rage, beyond the game.

"The messages are almost always the same, but somehow they have gotten worse, more persistent, some proudful, some discouraging." I force a chuckle, even as the laugh rings hollow, my throat tightening. "Some are about Benny. What Benny would want, what Benny would have done."

Payson's eyes twitch at the mention of Benny, a flicker of recognition perhaps. Her brows curl in, knitting together before smoothing out again as if she's forcefully pushing the thought away. It makes me wonder if she knows who Benny is. There's no way. And Milli couldn't have told her because she doesn't even know the whole story, only the surface level of what happened all those years ago.

I pause, the words caught in my throat. My palms grow clammy, and a knot forms in my stomach. I've always been the strong one, the one who keeps it together. But with Payson, the need to shield her from my battles against the need to let her in, to let her see the cracks.

"Can I ask you something?" Payson's voice is barely above a whisper. Her gentle tone and the concern in her eyes tell me she's being cautious. I'm grateful for it. Her calmness acts as an anchor, steadying the storm inside me.

I nod, and she continues, "Do you only ever feel that guilt

go away when you do what those texts tell you to do?" I look down at our intertwined fingers, pausing to think before nodding again. She nods, too, as if she's sharing part of my burden.

"What emotions do you experience after successfully completing what the texts mention?" she asks, leaning in slightly.

My response is quick and to the point. "Fucking great." I release her hand, my fingers balling into fists as a rush of conflicting emotions surges through me.

"How long does it last?" she asks. "Like, how long do you feel great for?"

I'm taken aback by her question, and my shoulders immediately tense up. Honestly, I have no clue. I follow through on the texts, feel great on the field. Yet, when not on the field, it's as if everything vanishes. I'm back to square one. I release a heavy sigh.

Unexpectedly, she throws me a curveball by asking, "Have you considered blocking them?" The echoes of her words hang in the air, evoking a sense of déjà vu from that evening at the ice cream parlor.

"Yeah, but I have thoroughly researched it. The person will know if they are blocked."

She nods thoughtfully, her fingers tapping lightly on her knee as if she's piecing together a puzzle. "Have you ever considered completely disregarding the texts?" Payson asks, not waiting for my answer as she pushes on. "I get you can't block them, but have you ever just let them be unread? Like, completely delete them without even looking at them?"

Just as I'm about to respond, she starts pacing the room. My gaze involuntarily follows her, captivated by her determined stride.

"How about we experiment for today's game?" she suggests, her voice cutting through my haze.

Payson continues her rhythmic pacing, a dance of nervous energy, before halting just steps away. With her hand on her hip, lips slightly pursed, she strikes her signature thoughtful pose. Her finger rests against her lips, making her look damn sexy in therapist mode.

"Let's try something different for today's game—no phone usage," she suggests. Her nod suggests she's convinced this will work, and honestly, she's got me intrigued. "From now till after the game, leave your phone here. Don't bring it to the game, not on the bus, nothing."

"SUV," I correct her briefly.

She rolls her eyes but continues, "It'll give you some space to breathe."

Will it really, though? My heart races, my palms become sweaty. It's already challenging to ignore texts during the game and check them later. Now, she wants me to delete them? Anxiety surges through me at the thought. I picture Benny's face, the disappointment that might follow.

"It will be like an 'out of sight, out of mind' kind of deal," she explains, gesturing vaguely. "You know, like that—"

Her words blur as I wrestle with my rising panic. Each thump of my heart reverberates in my ears, overpowering her voice. Drawing nearer, her face softens. "I know it's hard," she says gently, placing a reassuring hand on my arm. "But maybe it's exactly what you need."

By raising a finger, she makes it clear. "For one, he won't know since you're not blocking the texts."

He.

How did she— Right, the moment I slipped, mentioning *him.* My brain does a quick rewind, but that's not the crux of the matter.

Next, she raises two fingers to highlight her second point. "Secondly, you're completely disregarding them. It's not like he'll know you didn't read them, unless you have your Read receipts on, right?"

I nod, confirming that's not an issue. Exhaling deeply, she seals the deal on our experiment by clapping her hands together.

"So, your phone stays right there." She points toward it lying innocently on the table. It might as well be shouting my name, every fiber of my being urging me to grab it, to dive into whatever world Troy has crafted for me this time. Yet, at my core, I am aware that this is necessary—not just for my career but for me personally. This is step one.

"You'll be apart from your phone—"

"For the first time," I cut in. It's true. Even though I didn't read Troy's message after our last session, my phone was still in the locker room. It was still by me, calling me to read them.

Her eyes widen slightly, but then she nods. "You'll head to your game, stick to your pregame routines, and then play. Afterward, you come back here, shower, and . . . " she gestures vaguely, her expression twisting almost in distaste " . . . do your post-victory thing."

The way she hints at my usual post-win routines, those nights of fleeting connections, strikes a chord. But truthfully, I haven't gone clubbing in quite some time and it's . . . refreshing.

But what really gets me is her confidence in the winning game ritual—her certainty that we're going to win. It's more than just motivating; it's sexy as fuck.

The realization hits me like a slow burn—somehow, everything she does, every gesture, every expression, seems to become . . . well, irresistibly sexy?

A smirk finds its way onto my face as she wraps up her point. "All while ignoring those texts."

I'm on board, at least in theory. "I can try all of that."

Her smile is a brief flicker of victory until I add a layer of complexity to our little experiment. "But what about after? After the postgame celebrations? Those messages will still be there, waiting on my phone." There's a pause, heavy with unsaid thoughts as she meets my gaze. Then, she tucks a strand of hair behind her ear, a clear signal she's wrestling with what to say next.

My impatience and genuine curiosity push me to urge her further. "Spill it, Penny." It's obvious she's holding onto an idea, maybe another piece of this puzzle we're trying to solve together.

Biting her plump pink lips, I feel a chill down my back as she nervously proposes, "What if you let me delete them?"

I gasp, my eyes grow larger, and I sense a tightening in my chest. Is that even an option? To allow her to delete those messages as if they never existed? He wouldn't get a Read notification, and there'd be no alert that I blocked him because, well, I wouldn't have.

"Delete." The word feels foreign, heavy, as it tumbles from my mouth, sparking a rush of guilt inside me. How can I consider letting her press that button, exposing her to his words, his name? Guilt gnaws at me, the idea of burdening her with this bitter pill to swallow.

But I know this is the moment to test the waters, to see if stepping back from those texts will change the game for me. As I deliberate over tonight's match, a part of me clings to the fragile hope that I won't regret this choice. I approach Payson, feeling a flutter of nerves in my chest as our faces draw inches apart.

"Okay, but under one condition." She stares at me for a moment, and a smirk plays at the corner of my mouth, masking the storm of anxiety and anticipation beneath the surface. "How about we turn this into a deal?"

Her lips curve into a knowing smile that sets my body on

fire. "And what would I get out of this?" she counters, her eyes sparkling with amusement and something deeper.

The air between us crackles with an almost touchable electric charge. My gaze sweeps over her, lingering on every detail, as if trying to memorize this moment. My heart pounds as I lift my hand, my finger lightly tracing her lips, feeling the softness of her skin. My thumb gently pulls at her lower lip.

Leaning in close, my lips touch her ear. "You'll have to be patient and see for yourself." The promise hangs in the air.

Turning on my heel, I force myself not to look back. With every step I take toward the door, doubt weighs heavily on me. Am I truly ready for this? And more importantly, is Troy?

CHAPTER 23
PAYSON

Good luck, Lukie.

"Can you believe it? This is the most awesome thing ever, right?" Aliana bounces beside me, her eyes wide and sparkling with joy.

My pulse quickens as I nod, caught up in the contagious energy surrounding us. Cheers fill the arena as the crowd's chants echo through the stands. Our faces are bathed in a colorful kaleidoscope as the jumbotron blazes with vibrant hues.

A thrilling feeling surges through my body, from fingertips to stomach, as excitement builds. I've spent numerous Friday nights at Stoneton High and cheering for the North-Ridge University Panthers under the lights. But tonight feels different—alive in a way I hadn't anticipated.

"Grandpa is amazing, don't you agree, Al? Look, look, he's definitely coming up with a brilliant plan, isn't he, Mom?" Walker's enthusiastic voice cuts through the chatter, his little hands tugging at Rayne's shirt.

Looking down at him, I can't help but smile at his earnest expression. His excitement is tangible, mirroring Aliana's enthusiasm. At five, Walker is the spitting image of his grandfather, with sharp blue eyes and a magnetic charm that promises he'll be quite the heartbreaker one day.

I find myself looking back at the field, where Luke is surrounded by his teammates. His focus momentarily breaks to seek me out in the crowd. In that moment, our gaze connects and the noise fades away. The intensity of his stare silently has a grin tugging at my lips despite myself.

I silently urge him to understand my unspoken plea —*Focus, Luke*. Yet, I can just about hear his teasing response, *Oh, Penny, I'm focused, all right,* sparking a flutter in the pit of my stomach, his words landing exactly as he intends.

With a shake of my head, I signal to him that I'm watching him, my fingers shifting from my eyes to his as a warning. He replies with a mischievous wink, and although I can't see it, I'm confident a smug smile is hiding beneath his helmet.

From the field, the rallying cry travels through the stadium, "GO, let's freaking go!" Luke's team huddles briefly, hands slapping backs in solidarity before they scatter. And who, among all, decides to make a beeline for me?

Luke stands out unmistakably at the heart of the field on the fifty-yard line. And, wow, he's breathtakingly striking, with a powerful build and a vigorous presence that commands attention. I've seen him in action before, but being this close to the field and to Luke himself feels completely different.

Slowing to a jog, he approaches the barrier that holds back the eager crowd itching to join the fervor. With the helmet in his hand, the world narrows its focus on us, blurring out everything else like clicking cameras and staring eyes. With just one look from his hazel eyes, everything else fades away. My pulse quickens and warmth fills my cheeks as he edges closer, a small grin playing at the corner of his mouth. "Are you prepared to witness me completely dominate our experiment?"

For a split second, I'm lost, until it clicks—he's talking about our conversation from the hotel room. To be honest, I have no idea what he has in store, but the way he gazes at me, with a sparkle in his eyes, makes my heart race. He's up to something daring, and I'm caught between thrill and worry. As much as the idea unnerves me, I can't help but want him to seal the deal we made. My fingers grip the barrier tighter, the cool metal grounding me amid my swirling thoughts.

What am I even thinking? But deep down, I know. This experiment—it's a trial for something new, a potential breakthrough for him. Perhaps not a complete solution, but a step forward.

Right as I'm preparing to speak my mind, Aliana beats me to it. "Good luck, Lukie. You're going to be incredible."

Luke's attention swiftly turns from me to her, his eyes gleaming with adoration. Then, he does something that just melts my heart; he lowers himself to her level. Instead of glancing down at her, he deliberately meets her gaze, making their moment the entire world. He playfully taps her nose and says, "Thanks, Al." He catches my attention, winks, and says, "Did you hear that, Penny? I'm going to be incredible."

He rises, and I roll my eyes, despite the smile wanting to come out and play. Suddenly, he leans in close, and for a moment, I wonder if he will kiss me. But at the last minute, he opts to drop his lips to my ear. "Can't wait to cash in on that deal." His gaze dances over me, deliberately avoiding direct eye contact, and suddenly I feel a burning sensation throughout my body.

Aliana's voice pierces through the haze in my mind, loud and distinct, saying, "Daddy! Good luck, Daddy." It's like a splash of cold water, jolting me back to reality. I released a trembling breath, attempting to regain my composure.

Pull it together, Payson. But honestly, what's the use? Luke is headed back to the field, yet he keeps sneaking glances at me. In an attempt to grab his attention, I playfully call out, "Hey."

With his helmet in hand, he pauses and raises an eyebrow, questioning. I flash him a grin. "Wishing you luck, Lukie." That grin of his, the one that used to drive me nuts, wishing I could wipe it off his face? Now, it glows against the backdrop of the night, like the last brilliant star refusing to be outshone.

The sound of someone clearing their throat nearby interrupts my focus on Luke. When I look around, I see four pairs of eyes focused on me. With a bitten lip, Aliana is trying to suppress her smirk while her eyes shimmer mischievously. Walker shakes his head, his grin widening in amusement as if he's savoring a secret joke. Rayne's gaze is scrutinizing, her slightly furrowed brow undermined by a subtle smile. And Berry? He's wearing that familiar grin, his eyes moving between me and Luke as if he's solving a puzzle.

I swallow hard, my pulse quickening. "What? Is there something on my face? My teeth?" I blurt out.

Rayne is the first to break the momentary silence, her lips forming a wicked grin. "What was that about?" My eyebrows furrow in confusion, but she only laughs and waves her hand nonchalantly. "Good lord, woman. That. All that . . . chemistry. You and Luke? I swear, the tension was so thick you could cut it with a knife."

My cheeks flush at her words, a nervous flutter in my chest. Aliana's sincere and wide-eyed question interrupts the conversation. "Didn't you say you're not Lukie's girlfriend?"

Berry jumps in, saying, "Not yet, sweetie." That's his

second nudge about Luke and me, suggesting something more, a label that's far from reality.

You sure about that, Payson?

Walker's sudden question catches me off guard, his curious expression lighting up his small face. "Mommy, does that mean Berry is your boyfriend?"

Wait, what? Are those two an item? I dart my gaze back and forth, observing their mutual shock. Yet, Rayne's lips twitch, revealing a faint smile that exposes her unease. Ah, now it makes sense. They're not together, but that doesn't mean Rayne hasn't noticed Berry's attractiveness.

It's a bit of a silent drama unfolding before us, and honestly, good for Rayne. Yet, Berry seems utterly clueless of her interest. His facial expression tightens, his lips pressed together so firmly they resemble stone. With a cleared throat, Rayne grabs everyone's attention, bending down to the kids' level, she speaks with a gentle yet firm voice.

"No, Walk, Mama doesn't have a boyfriend." Her gaze flicks toward Berry, heavy with unspoken words, but he remains oblivious. His expression is a stone fortress, as if even a penny thrown at him would bounce off without leaving a mark.

With a tender smile forming on her lips, she looks back at her son. "He's just here to say hi to Aliana, kinda like how Papa comes to the sidelines to see us sometimes." Walker nods, a glimmer of understanding in his gaze. His small shoulders sag just a bit, a shadow of sadness crossing his face. It's subtle, but enough to pique my curiosity about his dad's story.

It's not like I would know or anything. Jumping into this NFL wives and girlfriends scene feels like landing on an alien planet. First off, getting chauffeured here by Luke's personal driver? Fancy stuff. My stomach did a flip as soon as I stepped out of the car and was whisked off to the sidelines. I had a feeling that Luke was behind it, making my heart skip a beat.

Without saying a word, Berry leans down to kiss Aliana's forehead and sends a grateful glance to Rayne. Rayne just acknowledges it with a smile that lingers a moment too long.

Our eyes meet, and I raise an eyebrow, wordlessly asking a question. Rayne mimics my expression, playfully wagging her finger after rolling her eyes. Unbeknownst to her, I have a knack for understanding people. It's as clear as day: She's got a crush on Berry.

"Boooo, that was fucking garbage!"

"Seriously, ref? Are you even watching the damn game?"

"Hello, blind much? That was a flag if I ever saw one."

Looking at Rayne, her eyes widen in surprise as she protects Walker and Aliana from the overwhelming energy of the crowd. Each child is partially concealed by her, with one ear against her leg and the other covered by little hands, amusingly but effectively trying to tune out the lively chatter around us.

When halftime arrives and the whistle blows, Rayne's reaction is a combination of awe and skepticism. "Kinda makes you think we're smack in the middle of a WWE final, huh?"

I chuckle, because let's be real—it's spot on.

Automatically, my eyes track down number eighty-eight as he sprints toward the stadium tunnel. His eyes connect with mine briefly, causing a surge of longing that leaves me breathless and my heart beating with fierce intensity.

"Mama, can we grab some ice cream?" Walker hits Rayne with those super-effective puppy dog eyes. It's a look I've seen Aliana pull a handful of times. And hey, who can blame them? If I were pulling that move, though, I'd be lobbying for a spicy margarita, not ice cream. No offense to ice cream lovers, but when it's in the low forties? Ice cream's a hard pass. A bit of tequila, though, now that's my kind of body warmer.

With her arms extended, Rayne motions for the kids to lead the charge toward the snack counters. Just as she's on the verge of speaking, Aliana jumps in with her revelation. "You know, after every victory, my dad and I celebrate with ice cream?"

Walker's eyes ignite with the brightness of Christmas lights, bouncing his surprised glance from his mom back to Aliana. "You've got to be kidding me, that's totally unfair," he exclaims, his voice tinged with awe and a hint of jealousy.

Unfazed, Aliana casually shrugs and says, "Ice cream is our way of celebrating." She then emits the softest, most charming huff, declaring, "And really, it's the ultimate way to treat your body like a castle."

Walker's gaze sharpens on her just as we line up to order. Concession stands at high school games or NorthRidge University don't have much to offer. But here? It felt like a whole new culinary universe appeared before me, each stand luring me with its mouthwatering treats. Chinese cuisine waves its aromatic flag, Mexican dishes promise zest and flavor, and pasta? My stomach answers with a hungry growl. I'm leaning toward a hearty, cheese-laden New York pizza paired with a beer—my compromise for the lack of spicy margaritas.

Walker sassily responds, "You're not exactly treating your body like a castle. My mom says broccoli is the real way to treat your body like a mansion." He pauses, mulling over his next words. "And, it's apparently a direct route to a woman's heart." With a shrug, he adds, "Who would've guessed? Greens being so . . . cool?"

Oh, these two are something else. I'm not usually around kids much. To begin with, our family gatherings are intimate —my mom only has one sister, and my dad is an only child. Moreover, my aunt, uncle, and two cousins reside far away in California, which means there aren't many young children in my everyday life. Even though Jebson and Jordan aren't exactly little anymore, both being in high school. And then, there's the fact that I've never really felt drawn to spending time with kids or imagined myself working in a daycare. I was perfectly content helping out at home or at Mocha Haven Coffee Shop whenever they needed an extra hand.

While Aliana gives Walker a skeptical look, I find myself doubling over in laughter, struggling to suppress a snort and covering my mouth hastily. Oops. My face must be turning an impressive shade of red, but luckily, no one seems to notice. The kids are lost in their own world of debate, and Rayne just shakes her head with an eye roll, clearly used to their antics.

"Do they always bounce off each other like this?" I whisper to Rayne, nudging closer as the line creeps forward.

Amusement fills her crinkling eyes. "Not really. Today's kind of special—they don't usually spend this much time together."

My mouth forms an *O* of astonishment, and she lets out a soft laugh at my reaction.

"Yeah, you'd think they were inseparable, especially with Berry and me always at the games back home," she muses, her gaze momentarily drifting to the kids, who are now in a heated debate over the superior ice cream flavor.

"But honestly, their paths mostly cross in fleeting moments. Like when Berry has Aliana in tow for practice, or I'm at my dad's office, or sometimes I catch them outside the locker rooms after a game, waiting on my dad."

We pause our chat to order, then Rayne turns back to our little negotiation with Walker. She strikes a deal: Victory at the game means ice cream at the hotel. He's initially resistant, but the mere mention of cotton candy wipes away any hint of discontent, his mood instantly lifting.

As we return to our spot, with the kids leading and full of energy, Rayne leans in and reveals, "Berry always has Aliana by his side. Every home game, nearly every practice, even during the preseason, she's with the team more than my dad. That girl's going to know football inside and out before she even hits her teens."

Imagining Aliana schooling some unsuspecting boys on football tactics in the future brings a smile to my face. I can almost imagine her, standing confidently, with a touch of sass in her voice, correcting one of them on a play.

"Berry did have a nanny, Faye, but she unexpectedly quit," Rayne continues, her voice filled with disbelief. Frustrated, she throws her hands up in the air. "Just up and left. Can you imagine? If I were in his shoes, I would've been furious, gone straight after her."

I shake my head, feeling the weight of her words. "That's really tough, just leaving like that without any warning."

Rayne nods, her lips pressing into a thin line, the sting of betrayal still fresh. "In any case," she sighs, her shoulders easing up, "my dad wanted me to watch over Aliana since she was supposed to attend this away game. But only if they win, of course." She chuckles. "So, of course, I said yes. How could I refuse my dad, right?"

A smirk forms on my lips as I take note of the fondness reflected in her stare. "How long have you known Berry?"

We settle back into our sideline seats, the kids finally sitting still as the players return to the field, engaging in their pregame routines. My gaze inevitably drifts to Luke, the one person I can't seem to ignore.

"About five, almost six years now," she says, her gaze wandering across the field. "Berry's one of the seasoned players. I met him when I moved back home after my divorce. I was pregnant at the time." Her voice falters, a shadow passing over her face as she recalls the past. She swallows hard before continuing. "Yeah, it was a tough time. My ex and I were always at odds, and I found out I was pregnant right when I was planning to leave him. But I always say, if there was one good thing to come from that marriage, it was Walker." Her eyes soften, filled with a tender light. "He might remind me of Tucker, but my love for him is beyond words."

Out of nowhere, Aliana's voice breaks through our conversation. "Payson, look, look! Excitedly bouncing, she and Walker point at the towering jumbotron. Blinking a few times, I try to process what's got them so animated.

Oh no.

Catcalls and energetic hollers reverberate through the air as Rayne observes, "Well, damn, seems like there's more happening between you two than 'nothing.'"

"Mama, 'damn' is a bad word," Walker interjects, his tone matter-of-fact.

Rayne quickly corrects herself, "You're absolutely right, sweetie. I won't use that word again." Their banter continues softly beside me, but I'm suddenly elsewhere, anchored to the spot by the image towering above us. On the jumbotron, I stand out in all my glory, with my face and every freckle exposed to the gaze of the stadium. Luke and I are frozen in time, just inches away from each other, with my lip nervously caught between my teeth, our eyes locked in a moment that seems like ages ago—when he whispered about our deal.

Rayne wasn't just making a passing comment. In that snapshot, Luke's gaze is so intense, so focused, it's as if we're alone in this buzzing stadium. The butterflies in my stomach and the heat on my cheeks amplify under his gaze, as if being watched by a crowd.

Then, my gaze drifts down to the name of the person who posted the picture. My heartbeat quickens, and my breath catches, as if my heart wants to escape my chest.

Troy M.

My breath quickens, the echo of my blood flow pounding in my ears. There's no way, right? There is no way that's the same Troy. There could be a million different Troys out there. Just as my mind starts to spiral, the jumbotron flicks to a new image, and my thoughts evaporate along with the picture.

Time races by in the second half of the game, the steady countdown of the clock making the minutes seem to fly. The kids, once a bundle of ceaseless energy, are now absorbed, their gazes fixed on the unfolding drama on the field with a concentration that rivals my own sudden, surprising captivation.

The clock is ticking, and with only five minutes remaining, the tension is high. Luke had mentioned earlier that this was a tough team to beat, yet he was confident in their victory. True to his word, they're leading, but it's a narrow escape, hanging by the thread of a single touchdown. The teams cluster around the fifty-yard line, directly in front of where we're seated.

Maddox, the quarterback, takes command, barking out plays that are gibberish to me. Yet, my eyes are glued to Luke —his movements are a spectacle of agility and focus. He zips across the field, a masterclass in athleticism, catching Maddox's pass with such precision it's like watching poetry in motion.

My chest tightens with a mixture of pride and anxiety. The crowd's roar crescendos, a wave of sound that crashes over us, making my skin prickle with electricity. I glance at Rayne, whose focus is completely on the field, her hands clenched into tight fists. The kids are on their feet, jumping and shouting, their excitement infectious.

Luke's intensity is noticeable even from afar. I can see the determination etched into his features, the sweat glistening on his brow under the stadium lights. He dodges and weaves through the opposing team, each movement calculated, each step purposeful. The clock ticks down mercilessly, and with every passing second, my pulse thuds louder, syncing with the rhythmic drumming of the crowd's cheers.

As the final play unfolds, time seems to slow. Luke makes a break for it, sprinting toward the end zone with a speed and grace that leaves the defenders in his wake. The ball sails through the air, a perfect arc that lands squarely in his hands. He crosses the goal line, and the stadium erupts in a deafening roar.

At that moment, all concerns about Troy and the intensity of the game vanish. I'm left with a single, overpowering emotion: awe. Luke stands there, victorious, his face lit up with pure, unfiltered joy, as if everything else had vanished, leaving only his triumph.

With a sly grin and a theatrical fan gesture, Rayne teasingly declares, "My friend, that man is incredibly talented."

I bite my lip, my pulse racing. If only Rayne knew the half of it, how Luke's scoring talents weren't limited to just the field.

As we start making our way out with the kids in tow, Rayne's still on it. "The moves he pulled today, those touchdowns, the cheeky winks he threw your way," she recounts, a mischievous glint in her eyes. "He was definitely putting on a show just for you."

I let out a half snort, half chuckle. The idea that Luke's

game skills were all for my benefit seems like a stretch. He was probably just trying to up the ante and show off. But as I brush the thought aside, a tiny, nagging doubt lingers. Did my presence push him harder than just the desire to win?

CHAPTER 24
LUKE

"Man, that was a frickin' unreal play. Can't believe it actually landed," Percy buzzes as we head toward the hotel bar. He's all hyped up for hitting the clubs, but my mind's set on a different kind of celebration.

And there she is, the center of my evening's plans, leaning casually against the bar, sipping what I'd bet is a spicy margarita. Don't ask me how I know—it's like I've got this radar now where she's concerned, picking up signals without even trying.

She's a vision at five feet, six inches, with golden curls cascading down her back, and my jersey draping over her frame, the name *Sutton* emblazoned across it. My heart pounds harder, a wild, erratic rhythm that echoes the chaos inside me. My breath catches in my throat, and my palms grow slick with sweat, forcing me to wipe them on my jeans.

Emotions I shouldn't be entertaining, desires I've got no right to harbor. Yet, here I am, riding a tidal wave of adrenaline and something far more intense. Tonight's game might just be the highlight of my NFL career, and it's clear as day—it wasn't our little experiment just pushing me. No, having Payson in the stands did something profound, sparked a drive in me that wasn't just about showing off. Mentally, I was locked in, fully present in every play. My focus wasn't on that text, not on Troy, not on any of that. It was about the game, my passion, and somehow the woman I'm inexplicably drawn to more each day made every moment on that field electrifying.

"You gonna keep staring like a lovesick puppy, or are you gonna go say hi?" Percy nudges me, breaking into my thoughts. He stares at me challengingly, almost daring me. "If you don't, I might just—"

"Not a chance," I interrupt, blocking him with my hand. He smirks even more, fully conscious of how his words impact me. My feet carry me toward her, my pulse beating like a war drum in my chest.

I quietly position myself behind her, and as she leans back, our bodies mold together seamlessly, igniting every nerve ending. "You trying to kill me, Penny? You look damn good with 'Sutton' on your back." A groan escapes my lips, loud enough for her to hear.

When she looks back and we lock eyes, it feels like everything changes beneath me. The noise of the bar fades into the background, leaving just her and me in this charged, intimate bubble.

She gives me that look—oh, she's definitely in one of those moods. The kind I'm all too happy to indulge. "Depends. You think Percy's up for a little . . . cleanup duty?" Her tone is playful, teasing.

Wrapping my arms around her waist, I pull her closer, my breath hot against her ear. "That's just wishful thinking. You know you'd need a *Dexter* enthusiast for that. You've got one right here," I murmur, my thumb tracing small, deliberate circles on her skin, feeling her respond beneath my touch. Her lashes flutter in response. "Plus, getting Percy involved would prevent me from honoring our deal."

She responds with a slight wiggle against me, making my cock as stiff as a double shot of whiskey. I shake my head and put my hand in my pocket. "We look good, don't we?" I say, bringing my phone around her shoulder so we can both see the screen. My phone lit up with a picture after the game. I typically receive media attention after my games, but it's rare to see a woman among them—except for that one night. But this picture? I had to admit, I liked it. It hit me at that moment: I'm seriously into this woman. Not in the way you like your therapist, or your little sister's best friend, or even just a friend. I mean, really into her. I'm not sure when or how it happened, but now I have this urge to claim her as mine.

And yes, the thought terrifies me, but also, it doesn't. The fear of not knowing the truth from that night years ago, or her not feeling the same, of opening up and being vulnerable —that's daunting, almost more than sharing my darkest secrets. However, I observe the identical guardedness in Payson that I possess. We're alike; we both put up walls. But tonight, with our deal, I'm ready to challenge that, to show her why she should let down those barriers that separate us.

She smiles, full of teasing and sass, and I love it. My hand seems to have a mind of its own, playfully slapping her on the ass. She gasps, her eyes growing wider. With a grin, I walk up to the bartender and ask for a beer for myself and another spicy margarita for her—she's almost done with her first drink.

"So, come on, give it to me straight—how'd I do out there today? Catch your eye at all?" Percy slides in with that trademark charm of his, finding a spot right between Rayne and Payson. Payson rolls her eyes, obviously onto Percy's game, yet she doesn't completely shut him down.

"You?" she says, and he looks expectant, like a dog waiting for praise. She just shrugs nonchalantly. "I've seen better." Percy's jaw drops, his face is a picture of mock horror, and I laugh as he clutches his heart, then dramatically points at me while I hand Payson her drink, our hands touching ever so softly. She mouths *Thank you*, paired with a cheeky wink.

And just like that, I have a hard on. And will all fucking night. My mind fixates on the idea of us being alone in my room. The desire to run away with her, to act on the fantasies playing in my head, is immediate and overwhelming. I'm ready to cash in on that deal, right this second.

"Admit it, I was way more of a spectacle out there than this guy," Percy says, playfully jabbing my shoulder.

I brush him off, focusing entirely on Payson. When she speaks, she subtly draws in her bottom lip, and I have to suppress a groan. "Well, that touchdown of his was something . . ."

With her words hanging in the air, I silently encourage her to go on by raising an eyebrow. She lets out a laugh, a sound that feels like sunshine breaking through clouds. Seeing her so at ease, especially around my rowdy teammates, is a relief. Whether it's witnessing Payson's light-hearted exchanges with Percy or her sweet moments over ice cream with Berry, she melts something within me, igniting a craving for more—more of these moments, with her.

"It was hot." Just those three words from Payson yank me back to the present. Her blue eyes are locked on my lips, then travel slowly to meet mine, her tongue peeking out, swiping her lip.

"*Payson.*" I groan.

She just smiles and my chest feels a flutter of arousal. Is she feeling this too? Does her heart race for me the way mine does for her? The potential for something more between us has suddenly become intensely real, like a fire sparked by a single moment.

Percy's eyes dart from me to Payson. Reluctantly, he takes a sip of his beer and admits, "I guess that touchdown was all right."

I chuckle, trying to shake off the intensity of the moment with Payson. "Thought you might say that; you practically did just a minute ago."

Percy rolls his eyes, turning back to the bar to order another round while striking up a conversation with Ray. I catch Ray's eye and offer a nod. She returns the smile, but her attention quickly shifts past me to someone else nearby.

Berry.

With a grunt, he interrupts the moment, pushing Percy aside to stand over Ray. "How was Aliana today?" he asks, his voice a seriousness that fills the air.

"She was great. Behaved well," Ray replies, smiling, but her expression shifts as Berry seems to retreat into his thoughts. With a sudden slap on the bar, he walks away. It is impossible to miss the change in Ray's demeanor as her shoulders slump.

"That girl's got it bad for him," Payson observes, leaning slightly into me, her shoulder brushing against mine. Without thinking, I move closer to her, our faces mere inches apart, her freckles standing out more than usual.

It's fucking adorable.

"You think?" I ask, curious.

She nods, a glimpse of her usual confidence shining through. "Absolutely. Women's intuition," she asserts with a small, knowing smile.

"You were on fire today, Sutton. Looks like our experiment paid off," she comments, her eyes twinkling with pride as she takes a slow, deliberate sip of her margarita.

"Sure did, didn't it?" I reply, my voice thick with gratitude and admiration. Her contagious smile draws us closer with a magnetic force. Tonight, she's all flirt and fire, and I'm utterly mesmerized.

This side of her? It's as irresistible as her confident, whip-smart sass.

My fingers lightly touch her wrist, moving along her arm as I move a stray strand of hair away from her face. When her eyelids flutter at my touch, I am left frozen, feeling over-whelmed by the intensity of emotion in her gaze. The woman in front of me is truly exceptional. She's not just helping me level up on the field; she's transforming me as a brother, a son, a man. She's pouring her heart into me, even without knowing the shadows that haunt my past.

Without fail, she's always making the journey to my place nearly every weekend. I haven't had to meet her halfway once, and that speaks volumes. She's got this big heart, you know? Although she may not always show it, she consis-tently puts others before herself. It's just part of what makes her, well, *her*.

"Is your phone still safely stored in your room?" she asks.

With a smirk, I nod and casually say, "Yep. I haven't touched it since our conversation this morning."

She laces her fingers with mine, momentarily surprising me, but I quickly embrace the warmth of her gesture as we make our way to the brown leather couches.

Settling down, the urge to pull her onto my lap, to escape into a hidden corner just for two, nags at me. Yet, holding her close, even in this simple way, quenches this thirst I am having. We lose ourselves in the murmur of life around us—the camaraderie of my teammates, the banter of coaches, each in their own bubble of existence.

Then, like a scene straight from a movie, Percy makes his entrance. With one smooth movement, he catches Payson in his lap, taking the spot I had set aside for her. She stiffens at first, then hesitantly relaxes, a small detail Percy happily ignores, wrapped up in his own world. He lacks understanding of Payson's subtle responses to unexpected male attention—a puzzle I'm continuously attempting to unravel. We only touched on the subject of her dad that night on the golf cart but haven't gone any further in our conversation about it.

Our eyes meet, and I observe the identical need mirrored in her blue gaze. She slowly captures her plush lip between her teeth, intentionally teasing me and awakening a wild desire. The primal force I typically harness on the field is now here, at the brink, ready to unleash.

But Percy throws a wrench in the works, waving his finger above him. "Hold up, hotshot." Payson's laughter, light and infectious, fills the space between us, and I notice—despite myself—how she naturally gravitates toward his touch.

Suppressing the desire to deck Percy is a battle in its own right. As I divert my eyes to Maddox, my hands form tight fists and my jaw clenches. With glasses resting on his nose and red hair slightly wet, he is completely engrossed in his Kindle, tucked away in a corner. With his legs crossed, he could easily be mistaken for a scholar instead of the NFL quarterback he actually is.

"See? I told you I would have you on my lap this weekend." Percy's gloating voice breaks through the commotion. Payson leans in closer to Percy, challenging me without saying a word. She's playing a dangerous game. I understand it's all in good fun, but witnessing another man wrap his arms around her in a bear hug, her laughter so carefree. Fuck, jealousy spreads uncontrollably, twisting my insides as it ignites like a wildfire.

Fuck this. I confidently stride over and firmly grasp her wrist. With her pressed against me, our hearts race in unison. I see the hesitation in her gaze, that internal struggle. She's battling the pull, but I've made up my mind—I'm not standing by. I lift her up, her body molding to my hold, and sling her over my shoulder.

She exhales her familiar huff, lightly smacking my back a couple of times before growing silent as Percy's voice follows us, cautioning, "Don't have too much fun. We have an early morning."

The boys throw in their two cents with chuckles and catcalls, but honestly, I couldn't care less. Let them think what they want. The early morning can wait because tonight is all about me and Payson.

Once the elevator doors slide shut, Payson's feet find the floor again. In a swift motion, she pivots to face me, her eyes ablaze with anger. "You madman," she snaps, her hand landing on her hip in a defiant pose. "You can't just carry me around whenever the mood strikes you."

I shrug, trying to play it off. "Why not?" I meet her gaze head-on, challenging the heat there.

Her head shakes and she murmurs, "What if they begin to think there's something happening between us?" Her tone drops to a secretive whisper, as if the walls could spill our secret.

I inch toward her, reducing the distance that lies between us, and she withdraws, pressing against the corner elevator wall. "And what if they do?" I ask.

Surprise briefly flickers across her face before she quickly adopts a hardened expression. "There's nothing happening between us," she insists, but her voice wavers.

I quirk an eyebrow. "Absolutely nothing?" I challenge, my tone dripping with doubt.

One step closer, and she remains motionless, trapped by

my intense gaze, while my hands instinctively rest on her waist. "Are you certain about that?" I murmur against her neck.

Payson's body goes rigid, her determination falters in the face of this crucial moment. She's allowing the tension to escalate, overwhelming both of us with its intensity.

"Come on, Penny," I urge, speaking more softly but still with insistence. "Tell me the truth—nothing at all between us?"

I lock eyes with her, witnessing a whirlwind of conflicting emotions. I can see the struggle, the push and pull. And then, summoning a gentle strength, she finally utters words, her voice barely a whisper.

"No," she confesses, squeezing her eyes shut. "I know there is."

The words hang in the air between us, reshaping the space, redefining everything.

Payson's chest rises and falls rapidly, creating a charged atmosphere between us. With her lips slightly parted, she gazes up at me, her eyes shifting to mine and then to my lips, silently inviting me. In an instant, my hands frame her face, and my lips crash onto hers.

I half expect her to push me away, to remind me that this can't happen. But she doesn't. Instead, her arms find their way around my neck, pulling me closer. Her tongue teases mine, seeking, demanding more, and I'm all too willing to deepen the kiss, to lose myself in the taste of her. It's fervent, insatiable, and yet, it's not enough. I crave more—her, in all her bare essence, beneath me, but this time with full awareness and sobriety coloring our connection.

A soft gasp escapes her as her head tilts, granting me better access. I trail my lips from her mouth to her neck, relishing each sigh and shiver. My hands venture under her jersey, the heat of her skin against my fingertips elicits a low groan.

"Luke, we shouldn't be doing this," she whispers hesitantly, her voice a gentle protest against my mouth. I don't miss a beat, guiding her hand down, pressing it against my hard cock. "We're way past should or shouldn't, babe. Remember that deal?" I murmur, each word laced with intent.

Her fingers tighten around my cock firmly, a bold and intentional touch, and I feel myself on the brink of losing control. It's like she's got the dial on my control, and with one little squeeze, she's cranked it all the way to the edge. The heat, the want—it's all-consuming, a wildfire she's stoked to life with nothing but her touch.

Our kiss ignites again, and Payson's whimper vibrates against me, her hips grinding into mine. "Fuck, baby, you're wet for me, aren't you?" The words slip out, more a groan than a question. She nods, tugging on my hair, confirming everything. My hands can't stay still; they're hungry for her, roaming with a mind of their own, feeling the weight and heat through the fabric that still separates us. The urgency is unbearable—I need to see her, all of her, no layers, no holding back.

But then the world crashes back. The elevator quivers, approaching our level. Our lips part as two businessmen step in. Payson's cheeks grow even redder as she quickly leaves through the door, laughter following her like it's a joke. I'm right behind her, hot on her trail.

Her giggles fill the hallway as her blonde hair dances, creating a pure, wild sound that makes everything else vanish. I'm by her side in a heartbeat, finding her propped up against my door, and that lip bite—it does things to me, deep, heart-racing things.

With fiery eyes and crossed arms, she looks at me, challenging and inviting me at the same time. I inch closer, feeling our heartbeats syncing, each labored breath she takes pulling me in deeper.

"What now?" her voice a breathless whisper.

With our faces just inches away, my smirk is reflexive. "The deal?"

CHAPTER 25
PAYSON

His words? Straight-up wildfire.

God, has it always been like this? This explosive? Somehow it feels like we're truly seeing each other for the first time.

The moment we step into Luke's room, the outside world fades away. It's just shadows and us, with the city lights peeking through his massive windows, casting a sultry glow over everything. With a devilish grin, he effortlessly draws me near, his cock pressing against my body.

My body pulses with energy, every nerve alive, following the elevator ride. With his confident stride, he enters the room and our lips collide, igniting a spark that sets my entire world ablaze. His sandy-blonde hair slips through my fingers as I cling to him for stability. I can't get enough of his taste, his touch, the raw intensity radiating from him.

Luke Sutton.

The person I promised to keep distant is now the one who I crave the most of. Here I am, completely consumed by him, with my heart and soul. I have no intention of resisting the powerful pull that exists between us.

While making our way through his room, his foot gets

tangled in something, causing us to burst into laughter as he pushes me against the wall. "Aren't the housekeepers supposed to handle this?" he mutters, pushing his shoe away.

"Guess what? It's your shoe," I tease, my voice a soft whisper. "You have the option to pick it up yourself."

Rolling his eyes dramatically, he gives my ass a cheeky slap and smirks. "I'll be using my hands for something else shortly," he answers, his eyes aflame with desire.

Tilting my head, I feel his warm breath on my neck, his lips gently touching the curve, igniting my senses. "Quite the confident one, aren't you?"

His laughter vibrates through my chest. "You have no idea," he murmurs, lips brushing mine with a gentle nip. "Penny, why are you becoming so fucking irresistible?" he whispers, causing my pulse to quicken. "And," he goes on, his voice low and filled with promise, "you're about to discover how much I truly relish it."

When he drops me on the bed, I can't help but giggle. I inch closer to him, my fingers brushing against the sheets as my knees sink into the mattress.

With each crawl closer, his expression shifts, hazel eyes turning carnal, drunk on lust. Witnessing his unraveling, completely unhinged, understanding that I possess that control over him—the man who catches the attention and desire of every woman—fills me with an exhilarating rush. Fierce pride pulses as strongly as my heartbeat.

"What?" I whisper, unable to hide the smile on my face. His eyes stay on mine, mirroring my gaze.

With a warm smile, he lightly brushes his finger against my lips. A smile that has the power to make me realize I'm on the verge of falling for him. When did that start? Emotions are not my thing. But then, why does this thing with him send my heart tumbling?

He shrugs. "It's nothing . . . " He pauses. "Your smile. I like it. It's like an extraordinary sunrise—rare, beautiful, and every time I see it, I feel like the luckiest guy alive."

My eyes unexpectedly soften. Tears? Not now, yet Luke's heartfelt comment sends my heart soaring, bolstering my confidence. This man, he's something else.

The sincerity in his gaze causes my heart to constrict, and I can't hold back any longer. I close the gap between us. Urgency courses through me as I hastily remove his shirt, and he does the same with mine. My red lace bra catches his eye, causing a smirk to appear on my face. The power of lace to make a man lose control is exhilarating, but it's the electric connection and heat between us that sets my body ablaze.

Turning Luke into a primal beast isn't my goal. No, I want him at my mercy, to flip the script. To prove that not every woman craves a man taking the lead. With a firm grip on his shoulders, I maneuver this giant of a man onto the bed, causing him to laugh. With confidence, I take off my jeans and underwear.

With his eyes wide, he looks up and says, "Goddamn, Payson."

I sit on his lap, feeling his unmistakably aroused cock through his briefs. A little shift draws a groan, his hands flying to my hips to steer. But tonight, I'm calling the shots. With a shake of my finger, I set the record straight. "Nuh-uh, not tonight."

"Penny, you the one in charge around here?" he teases, a glint of respect and challenge reflected in his eyes.

I nibble on my lip, savoring the rush of control. It's empowering to dictate the pace, to be the one in command. Many aspects of my life seem unattainable, but right now, I possess the control. It's rare and exhilarating.

Once more, his thumb grazes my lower lip, wordlessly

inviting me, and I oblige, lightly biting and then tenderly sucking as he pulls away.

"Goddamn it, baby," he hisses out, the words barely escaping his lips, thick with longing and frustration, before he tugs me down into a hard, all-consuming kiss.

The kiss is electric, a clash of desire and defiance. His hands explore my body with desperation and hunger. I take control of his wrists, keeping them pinned above his head. Straddling him, the intense heat between us is almost unbearable. His breath catches, and I feel his heart racing beneath my fingertips as I press against him, both of us lost in the storm of our need.

His fingers slip under the lace of my bra. "Penny," he murmurs, the word laced with intense emotion. "Look at you." His touch on my skin, tracing my peaks with an intimacy that feels sacred, leaves me breathless.

Then his mouth, oh, his mouth, is playing, savoring, urging me to move in sync with him. With a flick of his hand, my bra is gone, and I am laid bare, aching with delicious tension that deepens as his mouth returns to my breasts, devouring them. I could spiral over the edge from just that, but I need more, we need more. I pause, despite the protest of every nerve in my body.

I finally managed to peel his briefs away. They were stubborn, but victory was mine, even if it meant I stumbled back, our shared laughter breaking the tension. Then, there he was in front of me, his cock standing tall and proud, like Mount Everest itself. I was momentarily speechless, completely in awe.

Good lord, was this man always this damn big?

Our eyes meet, and there it is—that boyish grin, sparking another shared burst of laughter between us. Shaking his head, he reveals a tender and vulnerable expression. "It's never been like this," he said.

Like what? This easy? This right? The fun seamlessly intertwined with a sense of intensity that felt as effortless as taking a breath. Right now, I burn for him—every inch of him.

I plant kisses on his chest, moving down to the soft hairs above his waist, consumed by a fierce desire. His tousled sandy-blonde hair against my lips feels as familiar as my own heartbeat. Then, he gently pulls my hair and whispers, "Are you certain?" It's not just the words; it's the tenderness, the respect. It speaks volumes about the trust he's earned, here and now, with this intimate part of me.

I nod eagerly, heat flaming my cheeks, unable to contain the anticipation. He chuckles, and my eyes lock onto him, hard and ready. I'm mesmerized by his thumb swiping a bead of cum, rolling it around the tip of his cock.

"Baby, my control's hanging by a thread here. Come on, let me feel those lips."

Swallowing down my nerves, I go for it, desperate to taste him. He's gentle, allowing me to take my time, easing himself inside my mouth, and I'm so . . . full of him. Once I find my rhythm, everything falls into place. I explore tentatively at first, then with growing confidence, savoring the connection, the give and take.

My tongue flicks the underside of his crown. "Awh, Penny. Fuck . . . " he moans. His encouragement fuels me, and my confidence soars. This is nothing like past experiences— rushed and indifferent. Luke is focused on my needs, making sure I feel empowered and in control, while showering me with compliments.

He rocks into my mouth, his hips moving involuntarily with the sexiest sound of desperation I've ever heard. It echoes through my ears, urging me on as I slip my hand to cup his balls. Luke jolts back, popping out of my mouth, more swollen now, angry veins decorating his shaft. "Okay, yeah, baby, this isn't going to work. As much as I would love to have that sweet mouth on my cock, I can't wait anymore. I need to be inside you, now."

The urgency in his voice mirrors the pounding of my chest.

My back hits the bed, and he's there, hovering, his breath heavy and ragged. His eyes take a slow, torturous trek over me. Part of me wants to cover up, but I don't. He's looking at me like I'm something precious, like he can't get enough, making me feel powerful and exposed all at once. His deep-set brown eyes lock onto mine and he moves his head in disbelief as if he can't believe what he's seeing.

With a gentle touch, his voice so gentle and sincere, causing my stomach to flip, he softly says, "Payson, what are you doing to me?" It's rare for him to use my name, and when he does, it hits differently, making everything feel more intimate. More real.

Before I can get lost in that thought, he's kissing me, greedy and desperate, like he can't hold back anymore. His lips blaze a trail down my neck and over my chest, igniting every nerve ending. When he grazes my nipple with his teeth, my whole body reacts, pressing closer to him, craving more of this wild, reckless sensation.

"*Luke*," the name slips out of me as my fingers dig into his shoulders. He freezes, and a groan escapes me, frustration boiling over. Luke chuckles, hopping off the bed to grab a condom. They spill everywhere, and I can't decide whether to laugh or be annoyed. He leaps back beside me with a wild, predatory energy, making me let out a startled squeak.

"Planning a marathon, are you?" I arch an eyebrow, watching him fumble to get himself ready. My pulse races, nerves and excitement churning inside me.

His gaze connects with mine, smoldering with confidence.

"You bet." He smirks. "And I plan on using every single one. *Tonight.*"

My mind goes blank.

Leaning in, his hot breath brushes against my ear. "Ready to feel every inch of me, Penny?"

I'm nodding like crazy, way beyond any pretense of this being just some kind of deal.

Making a subtle adjustment, we're instantly on the edge, our breaths synchronized, and the room filled with anticipation. He holds us in that breath, that heartbeat of waiting, before finally pressing in.

My whole body tenses as I let out a breathy "Oh, my G-God," gripping the sheets tightly as if they are my lifeline. But then, as I start to find my pace, to find some ease, Luke's there, his hand gentle on my face, turning me back to look at him.

"Just breathe, baby," he murmurs, his skilled fingers bringing pleasure to my clit, eliciting a needy moan from me. He keeps moving, touching, soothing me deeper into the mattress, into this moment with him. "That's it, just breathe."

As Luke finds that perfect angle, filling me completely, he groans into the crook of my neck, his breath warm and ragged against my skin. "So good, Penny," he mutters, his voice a low, smoldering growl that sends a trail of goose bumps down my arms, melting away any resistance.

He starts moving, slow but deliberate, each thrust more intense than the last, making my eyes flutter shut as I savor every moment of the delicious stretch. "You good?"

I manage a simple nod, my throat too tight with pleasure to form words. Then he's diving deeper, his body pressing into mine with a ferocity that leaves me breathless, making me feel enveloped and pinned in the most exhilarating way. I bite down on my lip, fighting to stay silent, acutely aware that any of his teammates could be just outside these walls. But it's a lost cause because my stomach dips at the sight of him inside me.

Every move he makes, every touch, is intensified, as if I'm experiencing each sensation anew, both familiar and astonishingly powerful.

"So. Fucking. Sweet," I moan, lifting to meet his moves. Then, his hand, the one that was entwined with mine, trails down my body until it finds my clit.

I cry out. His hazel eyes drown in desire. His body, every muscle like it's carved from stone, flexes with each breath. He lets out a low hum, moving suddenly, and my leg finds a new home over his shoulder, hitting a spot that makes us both groan.

At that precise moment, a burst of understanding jolts me —I've never longed for someone like this before. The intensity of our connection is almost unbearable, a raw need that consumes us both.

Luke's pace becomes relentless, each thrust driving us closer to the edge. I grip his shoulders, nails digging in, desperate to hold on as the pleasure overwhelms me. When he leans forward, bringing my leg tight against him, using every bit of leverage, it's like he's reaching parts of me I didn't even know existed.

Sex like this? It's never been on my radar before. Sex was just that for me, sex. It was two people getting their needs checked off. But right now, with Luke, *it's more.*

There's sweat on his forehead, a testament to the intensity, our skin slick as we move together.

"You feel that, baby? You feel how well you take me?" he groans, each word punctuated by his movements. Luke pauses for a moment, then his hand cradles my jaw, drawing me into a breath-stealing kiss—rough, insistent, his tongue mingling with mine. As he settles more fully onto me, there's a shift. The urgency transforms into something more measured, more profound.

Together, we find a rhythm that's just ours. The kisses soften, become exploratory, as if we're both searching for something deeper. Our foreheads touch, his gentle touch overwhelms me with emotion.

This is new territory for both of us. It's intensely intimate, disarmingly real.

Yet, I can't help but chase that peak again with him, my fingers digging into his lower back, as if I could hold onto this moment, keep us right here on the edge together.

"I have been dying for this," he whispers, nudging his nose against mine before sealing the confession with another kiss. "I've wanted it, you, for weeks now." It's as if he can read my mind, because he quickly adds, "Not only about the sex."

There's a piece of me that understands I need to be clear, reaffirm the boundaries of our arrangement—this is strictly a deal he's cashing in on, nothing else.

Yet, with everything that's unfolded this weekend, with the way his words resonate within me, I find myself wanting to believe there's truth in his sentiment, that there's something deeper forming between us.

As Luke wraps his arms around me, pulling me close, our movements sync up perfectly. I clutch onto him, our bodies coming together. With his face nestled into my neck, I ride through a wave of an orgasm, while he reaches his own, his breath warm against my sweat-damp skin. My name falling from his lips like a prayer, a soft chant of gratitude. When he touches me, the name he calls me—Penny—feels like it's engraved in the depths of my being, radiating a love and warmth I've never felt before. A feeling I want to hold onto long after this moment fades.

Watching Luke lose it like that, all because of me? I'm

willing to go to great lengths to watch that again. The way we're still touching, still floating back to reality together, it's something else. But once he pulls away from me, it's as if a part of me leaves as well, leaving me feeling slightly hollow.

It's never been like this.

Then he's right there next to me, playing with my hair, staring at me as if I just hung the moon. It's a look that fills me up, making me realize just how deeply I am starting to feel for this man.

"Perfect," he murmurs, and I find myself nestled against him, as if there's nowhere else in the world I'd rather be.

Tenderly, he moves a strand of my hair away, his hand lingering on my face, making my heart skip a beat. He leans in, almost whispering, and teases, "How about another deal?"

My eyebrow shoots up, but his grin tells me I'm already halfway sold on whatever he's pitching. "How about we go for another round of this?" he suggests, his own eyebrows doing that funny dance that somehow, coming from him, seems utterly charming. I can't help but laugh.

I push against him playfully. "Oh, you mean sex?" I tease, but my hand betrays me, lingering on his muscle-bound chest.

He nods. "And how about we top it off by ordering some Mexican food and licorice?"

My heart, my poor, sweet heart.

I prop myself up a little, struggling to control the flood of emotions inside me. Luke's respect, both during and after, is something else entirely. Our last time was fast, nothing like this. And honestly, all those hit-and-run encounters I've had before? They never left space for anything like this—no lingering, no real connection, just fleeting moments. But here with Luke, I find myself craving the after, the staying.

I give him a nod, shifting to straddle him, and his hands

instantly find my waist, squeezing gently in a way that sends a message all its own. "I mean, who am I to turn down another round and free food?" I manage, trying to keep it light, even though there's a thrumming depth to what I'm feeling.

He laughs, that sound that's quickly climbing the charts to be my favorite.

Then he's tickling me out of nowhere, flipping things around until I'm the one underneath, the mattress catching me. I can't help the laughter, the surprise of it all, and then he's right there, hovering, with that *gotcha* smirk.

"It's a deal."

He pulls me back into his orbit, and suddenly, everything else fades away.

"You were incredible on the field tonight. How did it feel? Was the experience altered, perhaps, by the experiment?" I ask, lounging across from Luke on his hotel bed, our late-night snack of salsa and chips between us. The clock is ticking toward midnight, and I can't remember the last time I felt this content. The evening extended wonderfully, not only with an encore of orgasms but also because Luke decided to mix in an episode of *I Love Lucy* as part of another "arrangement"—a nod to intimacy. And frankly, missing out on Lucille Ball is not in my books.

Luke pauses mid-chew, contemplating his response, a chip half-dangling from his hand. "It was definitely different," he finally admits, shaking his head in wonder. "The constant buzz of wondering about incoming texts before or even during halftime vanished. I was fully there, in the moment, attuned to the coach's directions and my teammates' energy. It felt . . . " He searches for the right word, the pause stretching. "Freeing."

A grin sneaks onto my face. This whole experiment thing —it could've gone one of two ways, right? A total win or a complete disaster. Obviously, I was rooting for the win, which, judging by the magic on the field, we kinda nailed. But now, off the field, it's like we're still in it, the experiment not fully wrapped up yet.

I shake off my hands, crumbs flying, as I bounce off the bed, heading for the tiny kitchen table in nothing but his jersey. But before I can get far, Luke's arms are around me, pulling us both back onto the bed in a smooth move. I'm lying there, his chest against my back, and then his lips are at my ear, whispering, "You in my jersey, Penny, might be my favorite fantasy." His breath is hot against my skin. "Seeing you in it earlier, I was this close to just ripping it off you right there."

His words? Straight-up wildfire. They set every inch of me ablaze, priming me for another round with him—the kind of man who turns sin into an art form. I throw him a look over my shoulder, meeting those eyes that practically scorch me with their intensity. But I play it cool, tossing out a casual, cheeky smirk. "More like the best fantasy of your life."

His laughter booms, deep and infectious, as he yanks me back into a bear hug, landing a kiss on my neck. The contact sends shivers down my spine. Slipping out of his hold, I catch his hand with a playful smack on my ass.

"What? Guess you could call me an aficionado of sorts when it comes to that ass," he teases, his voice dripping with mischief and desire.

Yep, no doubts there. He was all over it, especially after round two when he had me from behind. Not that I am complaining or anything. I wander over to the table, catch sight of his phone, and, on a whim, grab it, bringing it back to the bed with us. Just as I'm about to settle in, cross-legged, Luke has another idea, pulling me straight into his lap. Despite his usual boldness and resilience, I can tell that this upcoming step is major for him. He's opening up, letting all his guards down to show a side of him that's raw, vulnerable. That's a move not many would dare make. But Luke? He's stepping into it, showing a level of trust and growth that's both rare and remarkable. This not only reflects his growth in our sessions but also the type of individual he's transforming into.

"I'm proud of you, Luke," I say, because it's the honest truth, and I want him to know that.

A soft smile spreads across his face as he replies, "Thanks, Payson," with a hint of emotion in his eyes.

I smile, acknowledging his words as I power on his phone. The screen lights up, revealing his screensaver—a family photo. It's a bit of a surprise, not because he doesn't value family, but I guess I half expected something like a Playboy model to grace his background. But that's not Luke, is it? While he projects a particular persona to the world, I am exposed to an entirely different side of him during our sessions. A side not many get to see, and I consider myself incredibly lucky for that.

Pressed against his chest, I detect him moving closer, his breath irregular. So, I do what I know works best to calm him down, employing a technique I discovered that night at Dream Scoops.

I twist a bit to face him, grab his cheeks, and pull him into a kiss that could start fires. Our tongues get tangled, and he lets out this low groan. While we part ways, our foreheads pressed together, I quietly reassure him, "We're in this together. No matter what's in those texts, I'm the one seeing them, not you. Remember, today is about you not diving into that phone."

He nods, understanding the drill. When I turn around, his chin settles on my shoulder and he appears to be a bit more calm. "Close your eyes," I say, sensing his grin against my neck.

"Just get it over with, Penny."

So, I dive into his phone. Suddenly, I notice that he saved my name as a cute combination of *therapy* and my nickname, Pennybacker, making me blush.

All right, Payson, keep it together.

Digging deeper, my attention is drawn to a group text received from his family. They're all pouring out pride and joy over his latest game, and they're spot on—he played out of his skin. It's clear as day the Suttons are all about love, and even though it sometimes feels like his mom and I are dancing on thin ice, I've got nothing but love for them.

And then, I spot the third thing that grabs my attention. My heart stops, freezes, and it feels like the ground beneath me just swallowed me whole. My hands become sweaty and I feel the blood rushing to my ears, causing everything to sound muffled and far away.

"Is it over yet?" Luke asks, giving me a light squeeze. But all I can do is shake my head, immobile. My mind starts to spiral. Is this that Troy? The one I saw on his mantel that day? The one Milli said was his childhood coach? My heartbeat is racing so hard it feels like it might burst out of my chest. My hands are trembling, and I'm trying my best to stay calm for Luke. I take a quick, shaky breath and open the texts. I decide to skip the history lesson and zero in on today's messages—one pregame and one from halftime.

Before the game, Troy's pushing hard.

TROY

Boy, these games count. The Super Bowl is coming up. Don't disappoint me.

And at halftime, it's all cheers.

TROY

> Hell yeah, Luke. This is the deal we talked
> about. We'll be on good terms if you do
> things my way, like Benny would.

But wait, there's a plot twist—another text pops up, fresh as I'm scrolling. Luke mentioned there are usually just two from Troy, but here's a third, sneaking in under the wire while I was busy reading.

TROY

> Oh, that blondie? Ditch her. She's nothing
> but a distraction. Not Benny's type either.

Blondie? What the hell? Is he referring to me? And what is the deal he's talking about?

"Penny, if you don't say something soon, I'm going to start worrying," Luke says, and I know he's serious by the way his body has tensed up.

My heart is beating so fast, I'm sure Luke can hear its pounding. My stomach becomes knotted and I feel queasy.

Clearing my throat, I stay true to our plan and delete the messages, but there's this one thing that's been eating at me, nagging at the back of my mind ever since that day in Luke's penthouse. I can't help myself—I have to ask.

I turn my head over my shoulder, my eyes finding his. He senses something is coming, something he won't like. His body tenses, and his jaw clenches slightly. But I need answers —real, deep, truthful answers if we want to ever fully get to the root of his anger issues.

"So, Troy . . . " I bite my lip, pausing, my pulse racing. "Was he a coach of yours?" I ask, my breath catching as I wait for his response. I already know the answer, but Luke doesn't know that I do. He nods, and it's all the confirmation I need.

A heavy weight settles over me, pure frustration boiling in my chest. My hands clench into fists, and my jaw tightens. Having a coach who pushes you to be your best—that's one thing. But this Troy guy? He's playing a different game. He's doing more harm than good, slicing through Luke with words that, no matter how much he might deny it, are etched all over his face, leaving their mark.

My heart pounds with a fierce protectiveness, anger surging through me. I can see the damage Troy's words have done, the way they've chipped away at Luke's confidence, leaving scars that run deep. This isn't coaching; it's cruelty.

With a deep breath, I speak firmly, "Luke, you deserve better than this."

He flinches slightly, the impact of my words hitting him hard. But then, for a moment, there's a flicker of something—recognition, perhaps. His shoulders tense, the strain of keeping everything bottled up evident in the rigid lines of his body.

Luke and I are a paradox—so alike yet fundamentally different. Our backgrounds, our journeys, and our destinies are worlds apart. But here we are, bound by the shared agony of being dragged down by someone close to us. To me, it's clear-cut abuse. For Luke, it's the constant, corrosive undermining.

Without a word, I set his phone aside and move to straddle him. His arms encircle my waist, pulling me impossibly close. His forehead pressed against mine, his eyes shut tight against the storm inside him. I can see how hard this is for him, and it makes my chest ache. All I want is to erase the pain etched into his features, to make him see he's worth infinitely more than Troy's dismissive jabs. I bury my face against his neck, inhaling his scent as his hands trace soothing circles on my back.

"Baby, it's okay. I'm used to it," he murmurs, the resignation in his voice breaking my heart a little more with each word.

I retreat and tightly grasp his shoulders, my voice both intense and shaky. "That's just it, Luke. You shouldn't have to get used to it. Nobody should."

Not even me.

"Luke, what deal is he talking about?"

He shakes his head, as if trying to shake off a bad memory. But I don't let him. I cup his face gently, my thumb brushing against his cheek. "Tell me, give me something here." Those hazel eyes find mine, and they pierce straight into my soul, like an arrow hitting its mark. He finally lets out a sigh, and I notice his nose twitching in nervousness. I grab his hands, squeezing them to let him know I am here, that he's safe with me.

"How about Benny? Can you tell me who he is?" I watch as Luke sucks in a breath, and I know I've hit a tender spot. He takes another breath, his eyes closing as if to shield himself from the pain. "Benny, he," he begins, but then his voice falters. "Fuck." The word escapes him like a desperate plea, and that's all it takes for me to pull him closer, my forehead resting against his.

"You can trust me, Luke. But if you don't want to, I completely understand."

His head shakes, his voice breaking, "N-no, I can."

He takes a deep, shuddering breath, and for the first time ever, I witness Luke Sutton break down in tears. If this were a year ago, I might have made a snarky remark like, *suck it up, buttercup.* But not now. Everything has changed. This has changed Luke, shaped him into the man he is today. He wipes at his tears, his movements rough and desperate.

"Sorry, it's just I haven't really opened up to anyone about Benny."

I nod, understanding this all too well. The need to share something so deeply personal, to spill every detail without fear of judgment or feeling like a failure for needing help from someone else.

"Was he your friend?" I ask gently. He nods, his tears starting to dry up a bit. "He is my best friend." Without missing a beat, he adds, "Was my best friend." I give his hand another reassuring squeeze, and before I can respond, he starts to open up, the floodgates of his emotions releasing. "He was actually our neighbor growing up until he moved away, but we still grew up together. We went to daycare together, hung out every chance we could, played sports together whenever possible . . . until we couldn't anymore." His eyes drift from mine to the window, growing hollow as he recalls the last part. Despite my urge to ask what happened, he continues, "Benny passed away a few years ago." His fingers dig into mine, and I can feel the pain radiating off him like waves crashing against a fragile shore.

"I'm so sorry, Luke." The words escape my lips, heavy with sincerity. My heart clenches as I see the torment etched in his eyes, a silent testament to the pain he's been harboring. Luke isn't over the loss, that much is clear, and it's evident he hasn't had a chance to grieve properly. He nods, his body trembling as a tear slips down his cheek, and I feel my own heart shatter in response.

He cups my face, his touch both tender and desperate. I want to show him everything I'm feeling, but my gaze falters, slipping away from his intense stare. He quickly redirects me, his hand firm yet gentle as he lifts my chin, forcing our eyes to meet again. "Don't feel sorry for me," he softly utters, his voice a fragile mix of regret and determination. "It was my fault, and I take full responsibility for it."

He thinks he's responsible for Benny's death? The notion is absurd. But before I can protest, Luke's thumb glides over my lip, soothing the bite I didn't even notice.

"Can we just let it go for the rest of the night?" he suggests. Leaning in, he kisses my jaw and trails down my neck, each gentle caress whispering volumes. "We should savor this moment," he murmurs softly, accentuating his words with a gentle kiss on my mouth. "Soak in us." My heart skips a beat at the word *us*. His gaze meets mine, heavy with promise. "Let's make that our world tonight."

I find myself nodding, and before I know it, he's lifting me, his strong arms inviting me to clasp my legs around him in a dance as old as time. He carries me to the kitchen table, the cool surface jolting my senses as I meet it. I lift an eyebrow, a silent question lingering, but he's already answering, dropping to his knees with a look that spells out all kinds of intentions. "Still got an appetite, baby," he murmurs, and it's clear he's not talking about food.

I laugh, shoving him playfully, letting the mood lighten. He needs this. We both do. And as the night progresses, a question gnaws at me, refusing to be silenced.

What was the deal he made with Troy? And why does he think he's responsible for Benny's death?

CHAPTER 26
PAYSON

Come on, Penny, play with me.

"All right, you can't just say it was fine, Pay," Milli mutters, dropping into a seat with a groan. We're in the middle of this country line-dancing joint—a place I'd normally avoid. But truth be told, I've been missing my girls. It feels like ages since we caught up, and here we are, teetering on the edge of another week. December's breathing down our necks, finals looming like storm clouds.

After a chat with Josie earlier in the week, seeing the progress Luke and I were making in our sessions, she gave me a nod, a simple gesture that meant the world. The taste of freedom was so close I could almost touch it.

I breathe out and drink some of my beer, which has a potent and stale taste. A margarita would have been preferable, but this dive isn't known for its cocktail menu. Our arrival here was met with skepticism because it's uncharted territory for us, and line dancing isn't our strong suit. Yet, here we are, spurred by Milli's enthusiasm.

Gratitude overwhelms me as I lay eyes on them. Despite

the stress and uncertainties, there is a deep comfort in these moments, in their company.

Attempting to appear indifferent, I casually glance at the mixed crowd of college kids and young adults grinding or doing line dances, saying, "Fine. It was okay."

Honestly, it wasn't just okay—it was kind of incredible. Borderline mind-blowing, and I'm not just saying that because of my first NFL game, which was pretty awesome too. But last weekend? It was a moment when I let go of everything, putting aside all my worries from school and home, seeking some peace. I was overwhelmed by a sense of liberation that was both thrilling and freeing in ways I couldn't even begin to describe. And it made me wonder if this was how Luke felt when he ignored those messages from Troy.

The highlight wasn't just experiencing New York for the first time; it was witnessing Luke peel back layers of himself he'd kept hidden. His willingness to talk about Benny and his own challenges sparked a surge of hope and determination inside of me. There was something there—something I could work with to help him through what he'd been battling for so long.

But I also couldn't shake the worry gnawing at the edges of my mind about where things were going with Luke. Yet, something deep within me was altered by that night with him. When I woke up the next morning in my hotel bed, the feeling of peace was unexpected but comforting. Later, on the plane, my body became instantly alert and my chest tightened when I saw him. Panic coursed through me, knowing that being caught was the worst possible outcome, but then I met Luke's unwavering gaze. His calm presence was like a balm, soothing my turmoil. For once, everything felt right, and I clung to that fragile serenity.

As my phone vibrates, I reach for it, catching Milli's eyes

narrowing. Her skepticism is written all over her face. I laugh, shaking my head. "Okay, it was beyond satisfactory—it was truly amazing, better?"

She chuckles. "Precisely."

"Which one was responsible, the company or New York itself?" Brooke asks, her gaze piercing despite the telltale way she bit her lip, a smirk wanting to let loose. The question lingers in the air, weighted with unspoken truths. My heart races. It was both, but admitting it felt like stepping over an invisible line I wasn't prepared to cross. These girls are my support system, the last people I want to keep secrets from, but the idea of confessing that Luke and I had explored unknown territory feels overwhelmingly intimidating.

Plus, it wouldn't be fair to Luke. We may be unsure of our situation, but one thing is certain: We have no intention of ending whatever is happening between us. And honestly? I was okay with that. You know that quote about people surprising you when you least expect it?

Once again, my phone vibrating causes my thoughts to scatter. I glance down, my fingers trembling slightly as I swipe the screen.

LUKE

Penny, I think I miss you.

He thinks? A laugh bubbles up, but it's cut short by a throat clearing. I raise my eyes and notice Brooke and Milli, both wearing sly smirks, watching me intently.

PAYSON

You think?

"Is it Percy?" Brooke peers at me above her beer. Inch by inch, she edges closer as she slides off her bar stool. Without thinking, I instinctively hide my phone from her prying gaze, causing her to laugh.

"What? Just because I'm taken doesn't mean I'm blind. Ever heard of 'look but don't touch'?" She shrugs, glancing at the crowd. "Percy has that laid-back surfer boy vibe, but if you're into the brooding, inked, big guy type, Berry is also an option."

I chuckle at her spot-on comments, wondering how she knows his teammates and their names so well. Right before I can reply, my phone starts ringing again.

LUKE

All right, I miss you. Happy now?

A smile tugs at my lips, impossible to hide.

PAYSON

That all depends. What exactly is it that you miss?

Once I press Send, my phone buzzes with a flurry of messages from Luke. Each one ignites a flame within me, my heartbeat accelerating with every word.

LUKE

What do I miss? Everything, baby.

Let's start with . . . well, that sweet pussy. My mouth is salivating over here.

And then there's that ass. Can't get enough of it.

What about the way you say my name when I'm deep inside of you? Yeah, that too.

Oh, and your smile? Lights up my whole world.

That last message sends my heart into overdrive. Luke has this way of shifting gears—from bold to tender in a heartbeat—and I find myself savoring every side of him.

PAYSON

Is that all?

The question hangs between us, almost a challenge. My curiosity intensifies and my stomach knots with apprehension as I wait.

LUKE

Now that you mention it, yeah.

I miss having you close, in my arms.

Wait, what? My heart doesn't just skip; it stumbles, racing with a thudding echo in my chest.

Milli's voice breaks through my daze, bringing me back to the here and now. "How did you become so well-informed about my brother's teammates?" She voices the question that I lacked the courage to ask.

With a shrug and a knowing smile, Brooke hints at her secret understanding. "Before Payson left for New York, I did some investigating."

Milli's nose scrunches, a familiar gesture that resembles her brother. "Isn't that more Payson's thing, though?" she remarks, matter-of-factly.

With a soft thud, Brooke's elbows land on our barrel table, her gaze wanders over the swaying crowd enjoying "Boot Scootin' Boogie."

I raise my shoulders. "No, it's not Percy. Don't worry about it," I deflect, sliding off my stool. The beer buzz is kicking in, lending me carefree courage. As I make my way to the heart of the dance floor, the song picks up, and I completely immerse myself in the beat, letting the music and the moment sweep me away.

The crowd arranges itself into a neat horizontal line, a dance formation I'm clueless about but eager to master. My girls are right there beside me, their excitement palpable. To any onlooker, we might blend seamlessly into the scene with our cowboy boots, flared jeans, and plaid shirts—a stark departure from my usual style, yet it feels just right for tonight.

Right when the dance starts, I get an alert on my phone. Luke again, I bet. But this time, I tuck it away, deciding he can wait. The rhythm takes over, and I lose myself in the music. We stomp, kick, and clumsily bump into each other, each misstep met with bursts of laughter. The pure, unrestrained joy is intoxicating. I hadn't realized how much I needed this—the simple act of dancing with friends, shedding layers of stress with each giggle and clumsy move.

We eventually drift back to our barrel table, breathless and glowing, gulping down water between shared grins and playful nudges. "I need a bathroom break," I announce, my legs still tingling from the dance floor's energy. Navigating through the crowd, my phone vibrates again. I roll my eyes, half expecting another message from Luke. Guilt washes over me—it might be Mom. Her constant updates of *I'm fine* have been bothering me. Is she really fine? Or just saying that? With New York, RA duties, and finals on my plate, going home hasn't even been a thought.

When I step into the women's restroom, I can't resist anymore and peek at my phone, the screen lighting up with yet another message.

LUKE

Your turn.

Opening Luke's selfie leaves me breathless. In his boxer briefs, with his hair tousled just right, there he is. Leaning casually against the sink, he smirks with that familiar curve of his lips. God, his body is simply stunning—impressive shoulders and abs carved out of stone, with a seductive trail of hair. A wave of heat surges through me, and I can't resist saving the picture—it feels almost criminal not to.

I quickly respond while leaning against the wall by the paper towel dispenser.

PAYSON

What's this supposed to be, a blast from the past? High school?

LUKE

More like us. Interested in a deal?

Us, huh? He tosses that word around like it's nothing, but it hits me deep every single time. The mere thought of him, us, makes my heart skip a beat and my body throb.

LUKE

Come on, Penny, play with me.

PAYSON

That's what she said.

I wait for a snappy comeback, but it doesn't come. Instead, the silence feels like a challenge. Nervous tension coils within me as I consider my next move. Snapping a selfie in the bathroom isn't a crime.

I let out a sigh, catching sight of my reflection in the bathroom vanity mirror, I can't help but smile at how absurd the situation is. Both of us doing bathroom selfies? It's ridiculous, but it also makes me laugh. Overflowing with playful energy, I decide to undo a couple of buttons on my plaid shirt, revealing my white lace bralette. The man clearly has a liking for lace, not that I can blame him. It's clearly my favorite too. It accentuates everything perfectly. I can almost picture Luke's reaction.

I place one of my cowgirl boots on the sink, leaning forward to draw attention to my cleavage. Tilting my head and sticking out my tongue, I snap a photo and send it to him.

Before my foot even touches the ground, my phone starts ringing. Luke's name lights up the screen. What in the world? Curiosity piqued, I swipe to answer, drawing out a playful "Yeah, Lukie?"

I can practically sense him rolling his eyes over the phone. "Not now, Payson." His voice is tinged with frustration.

With my back against the wall, a grin forms on my face. "And why is that, huh?"

His response is a low growl, the kind that sends a delicious thrill through me. "Just . . . get to the biggest bathroom stall."

The command, wrapped in that deep, resonant growl, sets my insides on fire. My pulse quickens, skin tingling with desire, craving his touch.

"Why?" I can't help but question—his request is so unexpected.

His reply is short, firm. "Now."

With a racing heart, I cautiously enter the final stall and lock it. The stall is surprisingly roomy, yet it's not the graffiti on the walls that shocks me—it's Luke's next command. "Strip."

I freeze. "No chance am I getting naked in this bathroom, Luke," I hiss.

He responds with a calm yet challenging tone. "Don't start backing out of challenges now, Penny." Despite my eye roll, the very idea of what's unfolding sends my fingers to the button of my jeans almost against my will.

Luke's laughter lightly comes through. "Come on, baby, trust me on this." I hear a shuffle, then a moment of quiet. "I'll guide you," he adds.

Reluctantly, I admit, "Okay, fine," but I want to make my

position known. "Just remember, this is about a challenge. I don't leave things half-done.

He chuckles. "Believe me, baby, there's nothing 'half-done' about tonight."

With a smirk, I shake my head. This man and his way with words.

"Find a wall," Luke instructs. With each step, my pulse quickens as I move to the wall farthest from the stall door.

"Now, pull your pants down those sexy legs of yours until they are at your ankles."

I hesitate, doubt racing through my head. Why am I doing this? But then his tone softens. "I'll do it alongside you," he comforts, his tone erasing my hesitations.

With a deep breath, I grip my waistband and gradually slide my pants down, savoring the cool feeling of the air on my skin. My heart hammers, making every inch feel like a never-ending stretch of time. When the fabric finally pools at my ankles, a shiver runs through me.

What is happening?

Putting my phone by my ear again, a new message pings and I catch a glimpse of yet another picture of Luke. That all-too-familiar bare chest, but now? Those boxer briefs he teased in earlier are gone. He's stark naked on the bed we've known so intimately, gripping himself.

"See that, baby? I'm set. Your turn now." His voice, a sultry whisper, makes my knees weak. "Just imagine."

I close my eyes, letting the fantasy take hold. I'm right there with him, tracing my fingers along his entire length, experiencing the throbbing sensation beneath my touch. The thought ignites a fire inside me, my breath hitching. My lips release soft moans as I fantasize about his warm skin, his lips, his tense muscles, and the needy sounds he makes exclusively for me.

Suddenly, my eyes pop open and my hand automatically

reaches down, shifting my underwear to the side, baring my skin to the cool breeze. I feel a jolt of pleasure as my fingers glide over my clit, leading me to catch my breath and my body to respond with tension and trembling. My skin prickles with goose bumps, my nipples hardening in pain, my legs spreading apart against the cold wall of the stall, seeking stability as I widen my stance, inviting the sensations.

"Penny, picture me," he whispers, his voice a tender stroke that elicits a pleading whimper from my mouth. With each stroke, my fingers explore deeper, teasing my clit, promising the ecstasy I desire.

"*Luke*," I moan, his name a desperate plea, a lifeline to the flood of passion taking over me.

Even though he's miles away, the intensity of the ache makes it seem like he's right beside me.

"Imagine my fingers," he tells them. I shut my eyes and hear the sound of his spit—no doubt for his hand. "Picture my fingers forcefully pressing into you." His groan, heavy with longing, vibrates through the phone. "God, what I wouldn't give to have you here," he says between grunts, his urgency palpable. "Having you in this bed." His breath hitches, and I can almost see his hand moving with a rhythm that's both desperate and deliberate. "*My bed.*"

Increasingly insistent, my touch traces circles on my sensitive, swollen clit. A gasp slips out of me, the sensation of becoming slicker, ready. Just as Luke's voice claims, "Where you belong," I heed the call. One finger slips inside, igniting a desire for more, swiftly followed by another. "Oh God, L-Luke," I breathe.

"That's it," he murmurs, his voice thick with desire. "Look, Penny." I hear a grunt, then. "Look what you do to me."

With each word he speaks, my fingers move in sync, increasing in speed as his voice grows more powerful. My back arches off the stall wall, the cold surface forgotten in the heat of the moment.

My breaths quicken, the climax builds, unstoppable, as I imagine his hands, his body, his need entwined with mine. Luke's voice interrupts my thoughts as the pulsating in my clit matches the rhythm of my heartbeat. "Tell me you're almost there," he says, his words accentuated by his own sounds of near release.

I instinctively nod, momentarily forgetting he can't see me, and murmur a breathy "Yes," while my fingers skillfully dance, leading me toward a peak I've never reached in such a place.

"That's it, listen," he urges. Needing both hands, I set the phone aside to dive deeper into the sensation. I slyly slip my free hand beneath my shirt, searching for my nipples and applying just the right amount of pressure. Luke's voice comes through again, asking, "Do you see how you affect me, babe?" My body responds, my hips seeking an unseen rhythm as I chase that climax, desperate to sync it with Luke's.

"Luke," I pant, my voice quivering from the intensity of my orgasm. His moan, rich and resonating, amplifies my pleasure, drawing me deeper into a state of euphoria. Every nerve in my body comes alive and electric, causing me to tighten . . . tighter . . . tighter, until I completely shatter. His release follows, a raw, guttural sound that merges with mine, binding us in this shared, breathless moment.

Luke's unwavering confidence shines through his words, even as the waves of ecstasy fade away. "Now, go back out there and make it clear who you belong to."

A wild smile stretches across my face. I am here, kneeling with my pants down, out of breath and smirking. The sheer absurdity of the situation makes me want to burst into laughter, yet there's also a freeing liberation in this unfiltered vulnerability, in the trust I have in Luke.

I should pull myself together, straighten my clothes, and step back into the world as if nothing happened. But as I adjust my clothes, giddiness overtakes me. Maybe it's the way Luke said it, or the undeniable truth in his words—there's something about being his, even for just this moment, that sets my heart racing.

As the night goes on, I am hit with an unexpected realization: Luke has managed to claim a part of me that I never intended to give away.

CHAPTER 27
LUKE

She's my rock. My protector. My safeguard.

LUKE

Say yes?

As I'm about to snap a photo of my jersey, which is sprawled across my kitchen table, a voice from the corner of my penthouse interrupts, "You do realize you're way out of your depth, right?" My gaze lifts from my phone, halting the shot I was about to take. Miles and I make eye contact, and he chuckles, remarking, "I mean, in her case."

I narrow my eyes for a moment, but then I go back to what I was doing, brushing him off with the response, "I'm not sure what you're suggesting," as I redirect my attention to my phone, effectively ignoring him.

"Really? You don't? Then who are you texting over there, huh?"

My eyes scan the name on my phone. Payson.

"Your face says it all—you're in deep trouble." A soft chuckle escapes him, drawing my gaze back to him, and he gets up, making his way to the kitchen. "Payson? Who the hell else would I be talking about? There is no other woman out there that can handle your ass."

Without warning, my head starts shaking as a smirk starts to appear.

"You can't hide anything from your ride-or-die," he remarks, oozing with his self-assuredness, and to be honest, I can't blame him.

We've always had this uncanny ability to read each other —except for that blip last year when he and Milli were sneaking around. But that's water under the bridge. Right now, his insight hits the mark. The truth is, my feelings for Payson have become even stronger since we got back from New York.

There was something off when we split up that night. Walking into my place, an emptiness swallowed me whole, gnawing at my insides. Payson easily filled the void. It's wild how spending time with someone you once couldn't imagine getting along with, someone you despised, can be like revisiting a book you thought you knew by heart, only to discover new layers.

All I crave is to spend time with her. To get past that tough exterior of hers. I want to prove that she can let go and trust me completely, just as I have learned to trust her. We haven't completely reached that point, but I'm making progress in showing her that she can be herself and have a great time with me.

It's insane to think that my whole life used to revolve around fame, football, women, and winning the Rookie of the Year award. However, you know how things change. All the trappings of the spotlight? I still give them recognition, but they're no longer my top priority. And while football will always be my number one passion, no doubt, there's only one woman who has captured all my focus. She's as bold and fiery as they come, a real *I Love Lucy* type that has me totally hooked. And that Rookie of the Year dream? It feels like a sure thing now, more than ever, thanks to the strides Payson and I have made together.

Once I send the picture message to Payson, I focus completely on Miles.

"So, what's the story? You showing up here on a Sunday and all?" I ask.

Despite being deep in his medical studies, Miles shocked everyone by choosing pediatrics instead of pursuing a career in the NFL. It came as a surprise, but he has the potential to be an exceptional pediatrician.

"You're clearly on a mission of some kind. You don't just show up out of the blue," I say, narrowing my eyes, trying to read his mood—a skill I usually have down pat, but right now, he's like Fort Knox. He waves me over and sinks back into my couch, his eyes drifting toward the floor-to-ceiling windows of my living room.

That's his tell—avoiding eye contact when he's got something big on his mind. I recognize it because I do the same.

For a split second, my mind races to the worst possible scenario, and I blurt out, "Is it your cancer?"

The weight of the question lingers between us until he abruptly redirects his gaze to me and shakes his head in denial. "No, nothing of that nature."

I exhale a sigh of relief, not ready to revisit those deep, troubled waters. It's been months since we've hung out, and while I'd always be there for him, Milli's got that base covered. I want this visit to be about the good times, a break from the heavy stuff.

Standing up, he retrieves his phone from his pocket before returning to sit next to me, his blue eyes meeting mine. "I haven't mentioned this to anyone else yet. You're the first I'm talking to about it."

I nod, fully absorbed. When he hands over his phone, my

anticipation spikes and then freezes me as I see what's on it. The word *beautiful* doesn't do it justice. In the middle of the ring lies a diamond, and not just any diamond. This one is shaped like an open book, with sparkling facets that resemble a love story. The band is adorned with inscriptions, small yet significant, that hold special meaning for Miles and Milli alone.

Taking a deep breath, I savor the image for a moment longer until Miles's voice, tinged with hopeful vulnerability, interrupts, "You think she'll like it?"

His question lands with quiet impact. This isn't just a piece of jewelry; it's a testament to their journey, a symbol of intentions and dreams, wrapped in a unique design. Miles is laying his heart bare, seeking reassurance for a step that's as bold as it is beautiful.

"Yeah, man," I choke out, my voice wavering as I fight back tears. "She's going to love it."

And I know she will because it's not only beautiful but also custom made. It's them.

Just for a moment, I envision myself in Miles's situation, getting ready to ask the big question. My heart pounds just thinking about it, mirroring the nerves that Miles must be feeling. The idea of being devoted to one woman and imagining a future filled with infinite possibilities is both strange and thrilling. Could I see myself making that leap, laying everything on the line for someone? In the past, I would've quickly rejected the idea. However, now I feel a subtle yet undeniable transformation, opening my mind to unexpected possibilities and potential futures.

Miles paces, his anxiety palpable. "God, what if this is a mistake?" he mutters, his voice trembling. He pulls off his hat, revealing the stark reminder of his chemo treatments, then quickly covers it again, as if trying to hide his vulnerability. "What if she says no?" His worry spirals out, his eyes filled with fear. "What if it's too soon?"

I reach out, gripping his shoulder firmly, anchoring him in front of me. We make eye contact, and I pull him into a solid hug. He unwinds immediately, tension melting from his body. I take a step back, chuckling, and give him his phone. "First off, it's definitely not too soon. You and Milli, you guys are like a timeless story. Plus, haven't you heard? Long engagements are a thing. Couples do it all the time."

He looks at me with hope in his eyes. "Really?"

I give him a pat on the back. "Seriously, how can you not know this?"

He simply shrugs, a wry smile slipping through. "Maybe because my life has revolved around textbooks and lectures, except for your sister."

"She's going to love it, man. You have nothing to worry about."

With a sigh, he keeps staring at the ring before admitting, "Yeah, you're right. It's so . . . her. I mean, I walked into the jewelry store, and this was the first one the guy showed me. I just knew—right then and there—that it was the one."

Relief and excitement shine in his eyes. "I've never felt so sure about something in my entire life, yet it still is terrifying, you know?"

I give a nod, sensing a surge of empathy. "Of course, it is. It's a huge step. But you're ready for this, and she is too. You've got something special."

While I'm busy packing up my football gear, preparing for the game, he playfully teases me in return, his face lighting up with a grin. "Brace yourself, that girl will sweep you off your feet so intensely you'll be caught off guard. It'll be like the most amazing Hail Mary pass in football—unpredictable, exhilarating, and when it happens, you'll realize it's what you've been waiting for."

His words catch me off guard, causing me to pause and my response to fade away. He's not referring to just any girl, he has a particular one in mind. And the truth? I'm silently wrestling with the fact that she's already in the process of knocking me off my feet.

The second the door to my penthouse shuts, she's backed up against the wall, and it's as if I can finally relax and take a deep breath. I hold her close, our bodies aligning perfectly. The heat from her, even through our clothes, ignites something primal within me. A week—it's been only a week since I've felt her like this, but the absence tormented me with the ferocity of years.

Out of nowhere, she leans into my chest and firmly utters, "Wait." Even with her forceful shove, I hardly budge. She rolls her eyes, that signature gesture that drives me wild, and murmurs something about me being as stubborn as a wall.

"Baby, is there anything that could possibly take precedence over this?" I place my hand on her neck, softly guiding her head to expose more of her velvety skin to my kisses. Tracing the outline of her neck with my tongue, a deep, primal growl resonates within me, fueled by raw desire.

Even though she pushes against my chest, I refuse to let her go—not right now. Using a gentle yet firm touch, I brush her hand away and close the distance between us. I press her back against the wall, my hands tangled in her golden locks. She lets out a gasp as I eagerly press my lips against hers, craving more of her.

Nevertheless, she forcefully pushes me away, ending our kiss.

I maneuver my arms to frame her against the wall, and I lean in so close that our foreheads meet. Her breath is fast, almost as untamed as my pounding heart.

Her eyes lock with mine. "I did make it to your game, right?" she jokingly teases.

Leaning forward slightly, I let out a small chuckle. "Hell yeah, you did. And babe, you rocked my jersey better than anyone ever has on that field." Her shrug tries to dismiss my compliment, but the blush creeping up her cheeks tells the real story.

With one more push, she manages to make me retreat slightly, giving her the opportunity to swiftly maneuver under my arm and run toward the kitchen island.

I laugh, a deep, genuine sound. "Penny, you can run, but you can bet your ass I'll find you!" I yell after her. She huffs slightly, with her hands on her hips. She's either preparing to assert her authority or challenging me to confront her. I'm on board, regardless of the choice.

When she presents that challenge to me, she says, "And what exactly are you going to do once you catch me?"

Sporting a wicked grin, I take a step forward only to be met with her forceful arm, her expression quickly becoming grave. Her eyes are fierce, a new layer of Payson I'm beginning to love.

Wait, *love*? There's no chance that I'm in love with her.

Am I?

But as soon as my eyes find those pretty blues, the realization hits me like a punch to the gut, leaving me breathless. This woman has become so deeply ingrained in my thoughts that it's almost unbearable. She inspires me to envision a future beyond football and motivates me to become a better person.

The moment she smiles, I feel a comforting warmth in my chest. This woman, she's more than just a temporary fling.

She's the type of woman who sneaks up on you, slowly, until you realize she's your forever.

"Well," she begins as I approach the kitchen bar stool. I raise an eyebrow, intrigued yet suppressing my own unfiltered thoughts. "There's something we need to handle," she says. Before she can elaborate, I yank her onto my lap. Because I can and because right now, I just want her close.

Chuckling softly, I gently rotate her, positioning her to straddle me. I grasp her neck with my hands and forcefully kiss her as if my life relies on it. Our mouths fit together seamlessly, as if they were made to be a perfect fit. With her arms around my neck, she grinds against me, emitting a low moan that signifies that she needs this as much as I do.

With hesitation, I draw away and gently hold her face, our foreheads touching, our breaths intertwining.

"I thought we had to address something?" I ask, my nose brushing hers.

She lets out a deep, rich laugh that makes my heart swell and my head feel light. "Yes, but there's someone who's distracting me," she says, her eyes shining.

I raise an eyebrow, leaning back slightly, my eyes finding hers. "A good one, I hope?"

Pretending to think, she bites her lip. Unable to resist, I start to tickle her sides. Squealing and squirming, her infectious giggles fill the air. "The best," she admits between laughs.

I pause, letting her laughter fade. "The best?" I say, grinning from ear to ear. "Penny, I always knew I was good, but, the best in your eyes?" I let out a low whistle and shake my head.

With a wide and teasing smile, she playfully shoves me against my chest while rolling her eyes. "Sutton, don't let that inflate your already big ego."

I widen my smile, gripping her hips and pulling her

toward me for another intense kiss. "It's too late for that," I whisper.

Her lips curl at the corners as they meet mine. "You won't hear it again, so don't expect to."

With a wink, I respond, "Baby, trust me, I'll hear it again."

"You're so full of yourself," she retorts, laughter in her voice.

"And soon you're going to be full of me, baby. Let's get the ball rolling," I say, attempting to sound self-assured despite my racing heart and sweaty palms. She notices—she always notices.

It's both hellish and comforting. Out of everyone, she's the one I'd want to see me like this.

She's my rock. My protector. My safeguard.

She takes my hand, steadying me. "You ready?" she asks gently. I silently nod, lacking trust in my ability to speak. Straddling me, she snatches my phone from the kitchen island. I explore with my hands, moving from her waist to my thighs, and finally to the back of my neck, in search of something grounding.

With her face lit up by the phone screen, she whispers and holds my hand tightly, assuring me, "I'm right here."

I lean my head on her chest, taking a deep breath. "I know, baby, and God, I'm so grateful."

She momentarily freezes but then loosens up and caresses my back with her hands. I shut my eyes, allowing her warmth to drive away the disorder.

Moments later, I hear her whisper, "I'm finished."

Two words that calm my breath and relieve the tension in my shoulders. Since New York, our experiment, things have been better than I ever imagined. However, I feel guilty for ignoring Troy's messages and not replying. It makes me feel like I'm failing him, failing Benny. But when I find Payson after my games and she deletes them, all the guilt and turmoil about the past dissolves with her simple words, *I'm finished.*

With a tender touch, she puts my phone aside and starts stroking my back again. Overwhelming feelings of gratitude and love flood my chest. When did I start depending on her this much? Was it last weekend? Maybe after our breakthrough in New York? Or was it during one of our sessions, when she chipped away at my walls, making me realize I could truly trust her?

All I know is, I trust her. And as terrifying as that sounds, it actually isn't. The emotions, our communication, my comfort around her, her smile effortlessly making me grin, and the power of her touch to bring me peace. And that laugh—it makes my heartbeat race. All those little things that define her, make her who she is . . . I love every single one.

God, I do love this woman.

Payson Pennington.

The idea overtakes me like a powerful current, submerging me and leaving me breathless. What if she doesn't feel the same way? What if she pulls back, decides she's done with our sessions? Just last weekend, I insisted we keep things light—sessions, phone chats, texting, watching *I Love Lucy* reruns. No pressure, no heavy stuff.

But now, those words feel hollow. I want more, need more. The fear of her not feeling the same haunts me, a relentless ache. The thought of losing her, of not having her touch, her laugh, her wit, her smile—it's unbearable.

Just as I try to sort out my mind, her lips forcefully meet mine, her nails digging into my neck in a fervent rush. It's like she's pouring every ounce of emotion into that kiss, and my heart swells, almost bursting from the intensity. My thoughts scatter, consumed by the raw heat of the moment.

She pulls back just enough to whisper, "Where were we?"

I can't help but smirk. "Me, filling you up?"

With a sultry look, she leans in close, her eyes filled with desire. With a seductive purr, she confidently declares, "I've got a better idea," and forcefully places her hands on my thighs, moving toward unbuttoning my jeans. "Up," she commands. Just one word, but it holds such power coming from her.

"Yes, ma'am." I chuckle, standing up to follow her lead. She helps me out of my shorts, her fingers grazing my skin, making my cock spring to attention. With a teasing squeeze to my balls, she boldly slides my boxers down, causing me to gasp and my heart to race. She just smirks and sinks to her knees, her eyes locking onto mine.

God, she looks fucking perfect.

Playful, mischievous, and still wearing my jersey. Honestly, I never want her to take it off—she looks too damn good with my name on her back. Brushing her hair aside, I notice her leaning in closer with parted lips. Everything around us fades as it becomes just the two of us.

I caress her hair, savoring the sensation of it gliding through my fingertips. She tilts her head, inviting me without a word, and I let myself go—no overthinking, just feeling. With one swift motion, she takes me in her mouth, and I'm instantly lost in her heat.

"That's it, baby," I murmur, caught up in the moment, her intense gaze pulling me deeper.

Her mouth wraps around me, tight, hot, and perfect. Our movements synchronize, each thrust and tug escalating until her name escapes my lips, and we spend the entire night entwined in my sheets.

CHAPTER 28
PAYSON

As my eyes slowly open, I feel a warm hand around my waist, pulling me gently toward a comforting chest. In that particular moment, everything seems absolutely perfect. Yet, with each blink, a troubling whisper in the depths of my consciousness stirs, alerting me to a sense of unease.

My life has never been this perfect, content, or easy—especially considering I haven't heard from my mom since I got back from New York, which was just a brief text. On our previous call, she expressed happiness for me when she found out about my trip to New York with my client. She didn't press for details, which I appreciated. She picked up on my joy and mentioned being able to hear it in my voice. And I must admit, I am happy. I'm just living my life—doing sessions with Luke, acing my classes, and preparing for finals. According to Mom, things at home are starting to look better, and she even hinted at Dad's progress. My jaw nearly dropped when she said that, but I didn't question it. Rather, I inhaled deeply, prepared to shift my attention toward my own life and away from the events occurring back home.

As I sigh, something unexpectedly prods me from behind. With an eye roll, I smile and push back against him, playfully wiggling in response. "Please tell me that thing isn't ready to go again?"

With his breath warming my neck, he pulls me in closer, nuzzling. "Mm-hm, yeah, around you, he's always ready," he mumbles.

I squirm again, relishing in the way his grasp on my body became firmer. "What was that, Lukie?" I tease. Suddenly, I find myself on top of him, with his hands firmly gripping my hips, bringing back memories of last night. My heart swells as I look down at him, captivated by his hazel eyes studying my face. His tousled hair makes my fingers itch to run through it. That damn boyish smirk appears, followed by one of his bright, daring, heart-stopping smiles. For a second, my heart actually stops, then races again, because for the first time, my chest clenched at the sight of him—not because he's some hotshot NFL player. This tightness, this all-consuming feeling in my gut, whispers a truth I can no longer ignore: I'm falling for this man.

Luke Sutton.

And that alone terrifies me. I've always been cautious with men, concerned they will turn out like my father. But with Luke, he's effortlessly closing that distance. Instead of making me want to retreat, it's drawing me closer to him.

Every moment with him, I crave more—the sessions, discovering the little things about each other, the light kisses, and shared laughter. His lips move from my collarbone, up my chest, and reach my jaw, the roughness of his stubble grazing my skin. He says quietly, "Morning wood is unavoidable."

With a quick motion, he grasps my waist and flips us over, positioning my back on the mattress. I chuckle. His fingers slide through my hair, brushing it away from my cheek, and that's when I notice something different in his gaze. I've witnessed his range of emotions, from anger to confidence, vulnerability to desire—I've even seen his eyes sparkle like fireworks when he catches sight of me at his games. But right now, those deep brown eyes are soft and warm, filled with a delicate tenderness.

He shakes his head out of nowhere, as if trying to clear his mind of some thoughts. Before he can utter a word, his hardness makes contact, causing my eyes to flutter in response to the friction. My legs, slick with anticipation, open instinctively despite the lingering soreness from our wild night. The need to feel his body against mine, his arms around me, and him inside me overrides everything else.

"Quickie?" I ask, wrapping my arms around his neck and playfully tugging his hair, a mischievous grin spreading across my face.

He growls, a deep, primal sound that reverberates through me. "Don't test me, woman. I could make you come in less than a minute."

With an arched eyebrow, I sense the growing heat between us. "Are you challenging me?"

His mouth presses against mine, and I am swept away by the powerful kiss, the seamless merging of our lips. No man has ever felt this right.

"Can you back up your theory with evidence?" I murmur, my body aching for another release before I head back to campus.

He smirks, his intent clear, but just as he starts to move, my phone rings.

I start to rise, but Luke holds me down, his weight pressing into me. The persistent ringing of my phone demands my focus. "Just give me a second," I breathe out.

Frustrated, he groans, yet still kisses the crook of my neck, making me almost disregard the call.

"Not fair," I mumble, feeling my resolve crumble. His sly grin tells me he's well aware of my weakness for his neck kisses. The phone's persistent ring cuts through our intimate haze again. Reluctantly, I separate myself from him. My fingers fumble as I reach for the phone, my body already missing his touch. A random number flashes on the screen.

With a pounding heart, I hesitate. Despite the odd feeling, I answer. "Hello?" I stammer, my voice trembling slightly.

There's a brief pause before a young female voice comes through. "Is this Payson Pennington?" I nod instinctively, then realize she can't see me. Clearing my throat, I reply quickly, "Yes, this is she."

Silence lingers on the other end, a void stretching infinitely, and I wonder if the call has dropped. Just as I'm about to ask, the pleasant daze I was in moments ago shatters violently. "Payson, your mother is in Prairie Creek Community Hospital," she says.

My pulse catapults into a frenzied rhythm, and a cold sweat erupts across my skin. Luke firmly grasps my hand. Our gaze connects, and my tears begin to gather, on the verge of overflowing.

Not here. Not now, Payson.

I tightly close my eyes, trying to hold back tears, while feeling an overwhelming sense of dread in my core. My voice trembles with emotion when I open them, barely a whisper. "W-what do you mean, my mom is at the hospital?" Luke's eyes widen, then transform into a determined, encouraging look as he tightens his grip on my hand, a source of strength in the chaos.

"Ma'am, your mother was brought to the hospital last night by ambulance, around midnight. She has remained unconscious since her arrival. Her vitals are stable, but she . . . " The voice fades, and I practically scream, "She's what?"

Panic takes hold of me, prompting me to forcefully remove my hand from Luke's and move around the room with wild, frantic energy. "Oh God, is she, is—"

The woman interrupts me, responding in a gentle tone, "Sweetie, it might be best if you come in. She's going to need you here." The call ends abruptly, and I'm left staring at my bare feet, my arms wrapping tightly around my naked body as tremors of fear course through me.

Oh God. This is not happening. My mother is in the hospital.

Payson, what are you doing? Get moving!

I fall to my knees, frantically gathering my scattered clothes from the previous night. My movements are hasty and desperate. What mess has my dad created now?

This can't be happening.

A wave of intense guilt hits me.

Is this my fault?

I feel like I'm suffocating, choking on it, unable to breathe. Suddenly, warm, muscular arms wrap around me, and the items in my hands tumble to the floor. I shut my eyes, attempting to calm my uneven breathing. The familiar scent of cologne, aftershave, and a touch of menthol provides a fleeting sanctuary as his strong presence anchors me.

Luke continues to rub my back. He whispers, "I'm right here, baby," and I grab onto his shirt, my trembling fingers unable to let go. With my legs tightly wrapped around his waist, he lifts me up, as if I'm holding on for dear life. Sobbing, I press my face into his neck, my tears drenching his skin. Every sob is like a sharp stone, scraping my heart and leaving behind traces of pain.

In one quick motion, he pushes away the mess on his dresser, causing it all to come crashing down. The dresser's cool surface grounds me in the here and now, pressing against my skin. Stepping back a bit, he softly holds my face in his hands, our eyes connecting. His gaze, a potent blend of strength, patience, and unwavering reassurance, elicits a trembling breath from me.

His thumb gently strokes my jaw as his voice remains steady and confident. "Everything will be okay," he murmurs. I nod silently, my throat constricted, my thoughts focused on the safety of my mom. Each word Luke whispers wraps around my frayed nerves, soothing them while he utters, "Just breathe, baby."

How does he do that? How can his simple words penetrate the chaos of my thoughts and ground me in my own being?

"Come on, I'll drive you to the hospital," Luke says with a resolve that makes my heart ache. I retreat, my mind and heart in turmoil. He can't do that—he has practice; his life is here in Dallas. Stoneton isn't far, but he can't just drop everything for me.

I'm not his girlfriend; I'm not his priority. Yet, the way he supports and looks at me makes me feel like his top priority. His constant presence and concern go against the boundaries I've established. Trying to regain control, I slip from his grasp and jump off the dresser, feeling my chest tighten.

With a firm yet gentle grip on my wrist, he draws me into his embrace from behind, wrapping his arms around me. "Payson, I'm taking you," he asserts, his words filled with an intensity that sends my heart racing.

I nod, surrendering as he says, "Good, now let's get you to the hospital."

As I get dressed, Luke moves purposefully to whip up protein shakes for us. It may seem like a simple act, but it speaks volumes. How did we end up here, in this moment where he feels like both my strongest support and my greatest downfall?

CHAPTER 29
LUKE

With each beat, my heart pounds against my rib cage, creating a deafening echo in my ears. Sweat drips from my palms, my trembling fingers gripping my jeans tightly. Memories resurface without warning, reigniting the fear and helplessness I felt ten years ago.

The memories.

The red, white, and blue-colored lights.

The yellow tape.

The piercing screams from Benny's mom and mine.

The breathalyzer.

Clinging to my hand, Payson and I burst through the hospital doors. Her earlier calm is gone, replaced by a frantic, scared woman. I've never seen this side of her, and though it's not something I hoped to witness, her letting me drive her here shows she's letting her guard down. It's comforting to see this vulnerable side because it means I'm the one she's leaning on now.

Each sob that comes out of her mouth feels like a heavy burden on my chest, making it difficult to breathe. Her palpable fear is nearly suffocating. While my own anxiety mounts, I disregard it and center my focus on her. This is Payson. She needs me. I can't let my past interfere. We're hit by the sterile scent of the hospital as the harsh fluorescent lights glare down, reflecting the stark reality ahead. With desperation, her grip tightens, nails digging into my skin. I squeeze back, a silent promise that I'm here, that I won't let go.

Inside, the chaos of the emergency room swirls around us, but it's as if we're in a bubble of our own terror. Nurses rush by, doctors call out orders, but all I can focus on is Payson. Her eyes, usually so bright, are now filled with dread. I want to say something to reassure her, but my throat is tight, words trapped beneath the heaviness of my own fears.

As we approach the reception desk, I steady my voice and provide a detailed explanation of the situation. The nurse nods, her face a mask of professional concern, and directs us to a waiting area. Payson sinks into a chair, her body shaking with silent sobs. I sit beside her, my hand never leaving hers. I've never felt so helpless, watching her break down, knowing there's little I can do to ease her pain.

Memories from the past resurface, but I choose to ignore them. This isn't about me. It's about her. She needs me now.

Although she has her dad, I suspect her mom's situation may be influenced by him—something I won't utter aloud. I must allow Payson to approach me and trust me with those weighty truths. And if it turns out her dad was involved in any of it? God help him if he ever hurt Payson—I'd make him pay.

Overprotective, Luke?

Maybe so, but I don't care.

Milli and Brooke could be here for her, too, but selfishly, I want to be the one by her side.

Payson releases my hand and rushes toward a nurse in the

corridor. "C-can you t-tell me where Nancy Pennington is?" she falters, her words cracking.

The nurse pauses and blinks. "Nancy Pennington?" she repeats. Payson nods vigorously. "Yes, N-A-N-C-Y P-E-N-N-I-N-G-T-O-N," she spells out, her tone quivering. The nurse checks her iPad as Payson describes her mother. "She's about five foot four, with curly blonde hair, and usually smells like pumpkin spice," she says, barely holding back tears.

Fuck. This is why emotions, why love, cut so deep. It's a blade to the heart knowing I can't make this right. Knowing I couldn't change a thing back then.

The nurse finally meets our gaze. "Ah, yes, she was admitted at—"

Payson interrupts, "Midnight."

The nurse nods, eyes locking with Payson's. I can't tell if she's nervous about leading us to her mother's room or worried about her condition. A sense of dread settles over me, but I still take Payson's hand as the nurse instructs, "Follow me."

A few steps behind the nurse, I glance at Payson and whisper, "Baby, it's going to be okay." She squeezes my hand, eyes forward, fighting for composure. I recognize that look—the slight slump, the weight of thoughts like, *What will happen?* and *Is this my fault?* pressing down. I've felt that same heavy anxiety in hospital halls before. Though I hoped never to return, for Payson, I'd walk through it again without hesitation.

The hallway is eerily quiet as we pass doctors, nurses, and occasional groups in the intensive care unit. I wonder if this is Payson's first time here. Her expression suggests shock, though she might have visited a hospital before under less serious circumstances.

I shake my head to clear these thoughts. It's strange—before, I believed there was nothing more irritating than

Troy's incessant messages and misplaced anger during games. But this situation eclipses all that.

We stop outside Room 17, her mother's room. The nurse kindly informs us, "Only immediate family can enter the ICU."

With anxiety churning in my stomach, I nod while Payson purposely looks away. With a face full of pain and confusion, she retreats into herself, displaying a more intense reaction than I've witnessed with our sensitive matters.

With a sympathetic expression, the nurse murmurs, "If there's anything you require, don't hesitate to tell me."

Payson's eyes remain unfocused, so I respond, "Thank you . . . " My voice wavers as I take a quick peek at her name tag.

Reassuringly, she offers a smile. "It's Nicole."

I manage a grateful smile. "Thank you, Nicole." She nods and departs. Every fiber of my being wants to whisk Payson away, to shield her from this harsh reality. But I know I can't.

Payson releases her grip on my hand and lowers her head with a deep sigh. I take a step toward her without thinking, but she blocks me with her arm, and my heart breaks into pieces. She's not just withdrawing; she's locking me out. I understand—I've done the same—but it doesn't ease the sharp ache that spreads through me.

Gradually, her head rises and our eyes lock, causing my chest to constrict. I feel my hand closing tightly, my teeth grinding together, as my primal instincts fight to break free. I'm usually more in control, but seeing her like this—hands balled into fists, eyes hollow yet tear-filled, posture defeated —overwhelms me.

Just as I am about to talk, she directs her attention to the small hospital window that provides a view of her mother's room. She quickly covers her mouth, trying to hold back tears, her whole frame shaking. Suddenly, she faces me again, her cheeks wet with the flow of tears, her body trembling with raw emotion. The sheer intensity of her blue eyes keeps me rooted in one spot. She wants to speak, words faltering, head shaking.

"Fuck it," I mutter, rushing toward her. Grabbing me tightly, her fingers sinking into my side, she abruptly lets go, pushing me back and taking my heart with her.

"Y-you should go," she stammers, her voice trembling. I move toward her again, intending to wait just outside, but she raises her arm to stop me. "Right now," she insists, tears streaming down her face. "You need to leave now!" Her voice rises almost to a scream, and I flinch.

Not wanting to leave her without support, I step forward and cradle her jaw with my hands, leaning closer. Her eyes close as I gently kiss her forehead, hoping this gives her the strength to face what's inside, just as I needed similar support a decade ago.

With a heavy heart, I start down the hallway but glance back to see Payson opening the door, murmuring a tearful, "Oh, Mama." My heart fractures once more, mourning not only for Payson but also for the little boy I was ten years ago, the one who is still grieving today.

CHAPTER 30
PAYSON

It's time to acknowledge the truth.

You're doing amazing work this semester, Payson. Keep it up! So PROUD of you! Don't forget to study for finals this coming week!

I close my eyes, letting Josie's words wash over me, trying to hold onto the small comfort they offer. It's a fleeting warmth, something to cling to in the midst of the chaos, but it quickly slips away, lost in the cold, gnawing fear that has taken root inside me ever since that phone call.

Graduation, freedom—it all seemed so close, like it was finally within my grasp. But how did it all disappear so fast? How could everything I've worked for be obliterated in a single, horrifying moment?

Deep down, I always knew this was possible. I felt it in the pit of my stomach, a dark premonition I tried so hard to ignore. But I didn't want to believe it. I didn't want to face the reality that my dad could do something so monstrous, that he could hurt her like this. But here we are. And now, even though I want to focus on my future, on getting out of this mess, all I can think about is the terror that lurks in the corners of my mind.

What if he comes back? What if he finds out I'm here? The thought sends a shiver down my spine, making my pulse quicken with fear. I'm trying to be strong, to focus on what matters—my mom, getting her safe, getting us both away from him—but the fear is like a weight on my chest, making it hard to breathe.

The police can wait. I know my dad doesn't care—he's made that clear by his silence, by the fact that he didn't even bother to call, didn't even have the decency to report what he did. That was our neighbor, Jean. I found out through a text from her, urging me to call so she could explain everything. But I can't bring myself to hear it from anyone but my mom. I need to hear her voice, to know she's going to be okay, to know we'll both survive this.

With shaking hands, I type out a quick thank-you to Josie and set my phone down on the table beside my mom's hospital bed. We've been here for over a week now, and it's Sunday—the day I should be focusing on my future, my goals, my session with Luke. But instead, all I feel is a crushing wave of helplessness, fear wrapping its cold fingers around my heart.

I've isolated myself from nearly everyone except my therapist. I can't bring myself to contact my friends or Luke, even though I desperately want to.

Whenever my best friends text me, I make up an excuse and say I'm with my mom. It's the truth, and they never probe further. They are unaware that my father is abusive. The only information they've received are murmurs from Stoneton—a blend of false assumptions and fragments of truth. I desperately want to confide in them, to scream out my pain and fear, but what would that achieve? Sympathy? Empty platitudes that *everything will be okay*? Things have never been okay, and this hospital stay is just another stark reminder of that harsh reality that is my life.

How much longer will this go on?

Will it ever come to an end?

Maybe if I had checked on her, my worst fear wouldn't have become a reality. The thought of letting her down and not being there for her when she needed me most brings anxiety to my throat.

I shift my books and place them next to my phone, then make my way to the window in my mom's hospital room. Although there isn't much to see, the first snowfall of the season brings back that familiar feeling of childhood happiness. Yet, as I watch the large snowflakes settle, a numbness washes over me. I feel like I'm on the sidelines, watching the world progress as I stay stuck in this unchanging hospital room, with familiar faces coming and going, and my mom in a medically induced coma.

I shower here, eat hospital meals, and keep up with my studies. And this is how it will remain until my mom wakes up and I can see for myself that she's truly all right. She must be. That first day, when Luke and I arrived and I saw her—bruised black and blue, with cuts on her cheeks and lip, her arm in a cast, surrounded by a maze of IV lines—I knew this had to be rock bottom. She has to realize this, understand that it can't happen again. I'll make sure of it, even if it's the last thing I do.

I hear a soft knock at the door. When I quickly look behind me, I see Nicole, the nurse I know, holding two vases of flowers. I express my gratitude with a smile and motion toward the wall covered in beautiful floral arrangements. She places the vases next to the rest and whispers, "Someone must truly cherish you two special ladies."

Warmth spreads through my heart like the first rays of sunrise, and my vision blurs with tears as I think about how much Luke has shown up this week. I pushed him away last week—something I regret but needed to do. I needed this time alone with my mom to figure out what's next. But seeing the flowers arrive has been a constant reminder of Luke's care, showing more than words ever could.

The new bouquets catch my gaze, their vibrant colors standing out against the sterile hospital walls. As I spot the white card hidden among the flowers, my heart starts to flutter. When I reach for it, I notice this message is different. It's not the usual *I miss you, hope you're okay, call or text me.* Instead, it simply says, *Turn your TV on. Xoxo, Luke.* Those hugs and kisses at the end make my pulse race a little faster.

Payson, it's only a card, not a love confession.

Still, no man has treated me like this before, and Luke went beyond just giving flowers. He arranged for my books to be delivered from my dorm room and made sure I had my favorite foods. He went as far as having the nurse deliver a brown paper bag to me one day. I couldn't contain my laughter when I found a T-shirt that looked oddly familiar—it was one of the therapy shirts he wore to a session. Inside, I found a card that read *Figured it might keep you warm.*

But why the TV? What's he planning with that?

Driven by curiosity, I grab the remote and turn on the TV. The screen takes a moment to light up, and during that silence, a sweet and familiar voice enters my ears. In an instant, my head snaps toward my mom as she speaks for the first time in over a week. "Is that *I Love Lucy*?" she mutters.

I chuckle as tears spill down my cheeks—not just from hearing her soothing voice again, but from the realization that Luke somehow arranged for an *I Love Lucy* rerun to play on this hospital TV. I'd mentioned in passing to a nurse that I wished I could watch it; did she relay that to Luke? But how would she have his contact information? Did he leave it with her?

Regardless of how he pulled it off, I don't spend another second pondering. I dash toward my mom and give her a tender hug, being cautious of her arm. "Hi, Mom."

She responds with a gentle squeeze and softly whispers, "Hello, Pay Bay."

God, I didn't know if I would ever hear those two words again. I'm left breathless.

Taking a step back, she gently wipes my tears away and questions, "How did you even get that old show on the TV?"

In a state of overwhelm, tears, sobs, and laughter escape me all at once as I manage to whisper, "Luke."

"It's so good to see you, sweetie," she says as I lean in for another hug.

My voice trembles as I respond, "You too, Mama, you too."

"So, are you going to tell me about this Luke situation?" my mother asks, taking a delicate sip of water through her straw, her gaze fixed on me as we sit side by side on her small hospital bed. It's odd witnessing her in this state—serene, silent, as if nothing occurred despite the fact that it did.

"This is Luke Sutton we're talking about, right?" My eyes narrow suspiciously. How does she know that? Then she grins—a sincere, affectionate grin, the first I've witnessed from her in what seems like forever. "I might have seen his name on your phone during our movie night."

I respond with a questioning look. "I'm not entirely sure what you're referring to, Mom."

That knowing smile, the type only moms can manage, is her response. "Oh, Payson, there's no fooling your mother. I know better."

I exhale deeply, knowing she's right. We spent the better part of the morning just holding each other, quietly savoring the comfort of our shared presence. The nurse entered and examined her vital signs, finding everything to be normal. We purposely avoided talking about my father and the details of the situation. I wasn't ready to broach those topics, not even after the nurse asked questions to ensure the coma or my father hadn't affected her neurological functions. The moment we were alone again, I swiftly changed the subject to avoid the conversation. But now, as the hours have slipped by, my curiosity tugs at me. I'm eager to understand the full story.

"Well, are *you* going to tell me what happened?" Her eyebrow curves in that well-known, daring fashion. I playfully shrug, participating in our familiar game of back and forth. "You know the rules—I share, then you share."

Closing her eyes momentarily, she firmly holds onto my forearms, pulling me as close as the hospital bed permits. "I might need your super strength to get through this," she says, her mix of tears and laughter shattering my heart into a million pieces, each fragment stabbing at my insides.

I briefly hesitate to push forward, but I understand she requires this gentle push, just as she once encouraged me to begin therapy. Maybe saying it out loud, she'll realize the severity of the situation this time.

God, my dad—what must he be feeling right now?

I know I shouldn't be concerned with his feelings, not after what he did to her. But he's my father. The truth is, I can't just switch off my love for him, regardless of his faults. It's heart-wrenching, like a constant ache in my chest, exacerbated each time I'm caught in the crossfire of my parents' tumultuous marriage. Guilt and obligation intertwine like thorns, suffocating my soul in an unending storm.

"Mom, I'm here for you," I say.

While resting on my forearm, she smiles but then retreats and clears her throat. "You first," she insists, her gaze shimmering.

If sharing my troubles can lighten her load or give her the strength to face what happened, I'm all in. So, I dive into everything about Luke. Initially, I couldn't tolerate him, but now things have changed. How he missed our initial therapy session but later showed up at my favorite coffee shop, apologizing. As I recount the story, she snuggles even closer and I press a soft kiss on her forehead, resting my head on top of hers. While she laughs at our initial struggles, her demeanor quickly changes when I detail his recent acts of kindness toward her and myself, exposing the continuous support he has provided me.

While I describe my recent visit to New York, particularly the moment on the rooftop, she gently holds my hand. Our gazes meet, and I notice her eyes are filled with tears. "Payson, baby." She pauses, a tear falling onto my shirt. "As stubborn as the Suttons can be, that man loves you."

My breath catches—*love*? The word feels both foreign and familiar. But I feel it in the way my heart beats faster, the dizziness I experience, the tightness in my stomach whenever he's near.

For a moment, I wonder—could Luke actually love me?

But I push the thought aside. He's my best friend's brother, the man who once, and maybe still, despised me. How could he ever love me?

I don't respond, just wipe a tear from her cheek. She squeezes my arm and, with a glow in her eyes, says, "I'm happy for you. I'm so grateful I got to see this."

I raise an eyebrow. "See what?"

She chuckles, clutching her chest. Passing her water, she takes a sip and happily says, "My daughter is happy, healthy, and in love."

I shake my head, my throat tight like it's tied in a knot. There's that word again.

"You can't be that naive, can you, Pay Bay?" A Soft laughter escapes her.

"I'm just so . . . " She pauses, struggling to speak. I hand her the water again. "Thankful to see you like this—smiling, really living," she says, her tone softening.

My brow furrows. Has she never seen me truly happy before? Although I haven't been constantly joyful, I've been here, putting in my best effort.

"Especially before I share something I should have told you years ago."

My pulse quickens, my gaze automatically shifting toward her. I'm frozen, waiting, holding my breath.

"Tell me what?" I ask, anxiety gripping me. "You're scaring me, Mom." Tears prick my eyes. I hate crying, especially in front of her—the strongest woman I know.

Her gaze shifts to our linked hands before she starts speaking. Her next words send my world reeling.

"I had an affair."

I widen my eyes, and it feels as though the ground beneath me has opened up, threatening to swallow me whole.

She did what?

The room is completely quiet, except for the constant ticking of the IV machine.

She cheated on him? *On Dad?*

"You had an affair?" The words barely escape my lips, a tremor running through each word as if saying them aloud makes them more real. Sinking into the bed, my legs grow increasingly weak and unsteady. She wrings her hands together, a silent plea for understanding that only intensifies my anguish.

"An affair?" The word bursts out of me, my voice cracking

as it rises, a near scream tearing through the room as I spring from the bed. Confusion gives way to a tidal wave of fury, crashing over me with a force I can barely contain. She's fidgeting now, her gaze flitting everywhere but to me, as if she's searching for an escape from the truth.

I know getting upset won't help her, won't change what's already been done, but this revelation—this truth—is like a knife to my chest. I've been here, by her side, consumed by the guilt of what he did to her, trying to piece her back together. And now to find out that everything—the pain, the fear—was set in motion by her betrayal? Even though nothing justifies his violence, it's still too much to bear.

"Look me in the eyes," I demand, my voice trembling with raw anger.

Finally, our stares meet, hers a dimmed shade of blue. "Please, tell me this isn't true," I say, but there's no need for her to respond. I can see the heaviness of the secret she has been holding onto for years, even from across the room. Nevertheless, her actions are inexcusable, especially considering how she always believed he was worth fighting for and promised me that I would understand when I found someone special.

Special, my ass. Anger surges through me, causing my fists to clench involuntarily and my knuckles to whiten.

But does she deserve this? To be beaten almost to death? To be constantly assaulted or too afraid to show her face in public because of bruises and cuts? Absolutely not. No one deserves that, least of all her. My mother. The one person I looked up to, yet she had an affair. Each breath I take comes in shallow, ragged gasps as the weight of the truth presses down on my chest, making it hard to breathe. My mind spins, struggling to wrap around what's happening.

If her infidelity caused all of this, why didn't they simply divorce? Why continue living like this? My fingers tremble, the tension in my muscles making me feel like I might snap at any moment.

She delivers yet another shocking revelation. "I am also going to Aunt Bethany's."

I flinch, my jaw slackening. You'd think the first one was enough, but no, she seems determined to keep the shocks coming. The loud thumping of my pulse drowns out the silence that follows her words.

"What do you mean you're going to Aunt Bethany's?" The question hangs in the air, sharper than I intended. Nicole appears in the doorway, worry etched on her face. She doesn't need to ask—she already knows something's wrong. I manage a quick wave, forcing out a quiet "We're fine." She hesitates, then retreats, leaving just the two of us in the room.

I turn back to my mother, the reality of her words sinking in like a stone in my chest. She's leaving. It feels like a betrayal, even though I know deep down it's what she needs. Still, I never pictured it like this—miles away, in another state, without me.

For years, I've imagined her escaping the nightmare of my father, but in those daydreams, she was always close by, within reach. I thought we'd find her a place nearby, somewhere safe but still close enough for me to visit, to make sure she was okay. But now, the thought of her moving so far away, of being alone without her, is unbearable.

I shake my head, trying to clear the mounting panic. This wasn't how things were supposed to go. I've been the one holding everything together, standing between my parents' battles, carrying the weight of our fractured family. And now, she's leaving, and I'll be left to pick up the pieces alone.

With a sigh, my mother's gaze shifts back to her hands. Why can't she look at me?

Is she blaming me? For what happened here? Because I

wasn't here this time to stop it, to prevent him from going further? Guilt rolls my stomach—over the lies, over the betrayal.

Finally, she looks up at me. "I am going to spend some time out there."

I release a sigh, sensing my chest constrict. "California?" A bitter and sarcastic chuckle slips out. "So, you're just going to run off to fucking California?" My hands tighten, nails piercing my palms.

Her eyes widen slightly, and she chides, "Manners, Payson Jane."

"Middle name now? That's supposed to scare me?" I mutter under my breath. A jolt of pain shoots through my temples, causing my jaw to tense up. She doesn't have the right to sit there on her hospital bed and scold me for swearing, not after what she's done. I shake my head, trying to make sense of everything, but it's pointless. What's the use? She's leaving, and my dad—God, I don't even know where he is or how he's doing. For all I know, he could be in another state by now.

With a sigh, I bow my head and close my eyes. The room spins slightly as I fight the urge to cry.

This can't be happening. This isn't my life.

But it is, Payson. It's time to acknowledge the truth.

In my element, I strive to conceal my emotions and maintain a neutral demeanor as I face my mother. Despite my attempts to remain calm, my voice quivers. "How long?"

She hesitates before replying, "For as long as I need. A month, maybe a few months. I'm not sure."

I take a deep breath, trying to steady myself, but it feels like I'm breathing through a narrow straw.

"I know you don't understand what I did," she starts.

"Understand? How could I?" I spit out. "You were the one who turned everything upside down."

With her eyes averted, she absentmindedly fiddles with her arm sling.

"For years, I've had your back. I used hurtful words against Dad because of his actions. I've been weighed down by a sense of guilt for what's happening to you and our family, and it's all because—" I stop, biting my lip and shaking my head.

"I needed to find myself," she murmurs. "I was suffocating at home."

She was suffocating? I was the one fucking suffocating. What did I do to deserve this? To wake up every morning wondering how the day would turn out? How would Dad be? How I would protect myself if it was me— I stop my thoughts as my head turns to my mom.

"Suffocating?" I echo, incredulous. "What about me? You're just going to leave? Go off on some self-discovery trip?"

Every thump of my heart echoes through my body, pounding in my chest. I know I'm the one who has always pushed her to leave him, to do something different, to make a change—but not like this. Not where she leaves me completely behind.

Her words bear down on me like a physical force, making me lightheaded as I rub my temples. Unshed tears sting my eyes, but I won't allow them to drop. Not here. Not now.

Her barely audible voice utters, "I'm sorry."

"Sorry isn't enough," I reply. I retreat, needing space between us. The air is oppressive and suffocating, giving me the feeling of being trapped by the walls.

"Payson, please . . . " She extends her hand, but I instinctively withdraw, my body recoiling. "What your father did . . . " She shakes her head, sparing me the details. "This is my decision. This is my plan." I arch an eyebrow, still seething, as she concludes, "I told your father I was leaving for California—that's why all this happened. He was furious, upset, and you know how that ends up." She gestures toward her battered body, and briefly, my anger is replaced by a deep hurt for my mom.

God, admitting that even hurts. How do you deal with a situation where one parent is abusive and the other is unfaithful? What does that mean for me? What if I turn out just like them? My forehead breaks out in a cold sweat, and my hands start shaking uncontrollably.

"That night, I was ready to go—bags packed and everything. But then, everything changed so abruptly, and ending up here in the hospital only confirmed my decision to stay with my sister. It wasn't just the best choice for me or even for our marriage, but for you, Payson."

Me? Now she decides to do the right thing? I should feel grateful, maybe even happy, that she's taking action, but how can I? How can I look at her the same way after learning the truth?

"You deserve a strong mom, a healthy dad; you deserve everything beautiful in the world and more." She exhales deeply, clearly drained—not just physically after a week in a coma but emotionally, having no one to confide in. Her words hit me like a punch to the gut, and I find myself doubling over slightly, clutching my stomach.

I close my eyes tightly, attempting to understand everything.

"Payson, I'm doing this for you."

A sob chokes me as I shake my head in disbelief. "I just . . . I don't understand any of this. Why couldn't—" My voice falters, and the tears I've been holding back finally spill over, hot and unrelenting.

"Why couldn't I just have normal parents? Why was I the one caught in the middle of your marriage, burdened by guilt for all these years? The one who felt like I was failing you both, when really, you were failing yourselves." The words tumble out, raw and choked with emotion. My chest heaves with each ragged breath.

We share a silent moment, burdened by everything that lies between us. Every muscle in my body is aching from the effort of keeping it intact. I pause for a moment, taking a trembling breath in an effort to calm down. "I need some time," I finally say.

Nodding, her face reflects the pain and regret she feels. "Take all the time you need."

I lean in to give her a kiss on the forehead. There's a story hidden beneath her tears, one she'll share when she's ready. For now, I accept her silence and walk out of the room, my legs feeling like they might give out at any moment. Each step is an effort, but I force myself to keep moving. I need to get out of here, to clear my head, to figure out what the hell I'm supposed to do next.

I close the door and slump against the wall, slowly sliding down to the floor. Hot, relentless tears blur my vision. Just the thought of returning to my dorm and facing my friends' inevitable questions makes my chest constrict. With trembling hands, I pull out my phone and book an Uber. I need to be with the one person who will offer me comfort by asking nothing in return.

CHAPTER 31
LUKE

Warm water cascades down my neck and back, mingling with the stress of the past week. The steam in the shower surrounds me, but it does little to relieve the tension. Tonight's game has taken a toll. My body aches, but it's my mind that truly suffers. Leaving Payson in that hospital feels even worse than that night ten years ago.

Leaning on the tiled wall, I shut my eyes, attempting to silence the incessant beeping of hospital monitors that echoes in my thoughts. The muscles scream in protest, yet the hot water only soothes the surface pain, leaving the deeper wounds unaffected. My mind wanders while the game replays, caught in a loop of concern and remorse, dragging me back to that moment.

"Benny, Luke, will you two just shut up? I'm trying to drive here!" Troy's voice thundered through the car as he slammed his hand on the steering wheel, the sudden outburst making me flinch. Benny remained motionless, gazing wearily at his dad. He had seen this side of Troy before. But for me, it was a shock. I had only known Mr. Maverick as

the upbeat coach, always quick with a smile and a high five, clapping backs and shouting encouragement on the field.

But tonight, he was different. His face was tight, eyes hard and glossy with an emotion I couldn't place. The car seemed to shrink around us, the air heavy with unspoken tension. Despite the warm fall night, I felt a chill. This wasn't Mr. Maverick who cheered us on and believed in our potential. This was someone else—someone on edge, barely holding it together.

It scared me. Benny nudged my arm, pulling my focus away from Troy. Benny's hand was outstretched, shaking slightly. My gaze narrowed, trying to understand what was happening. Then Benny initiated a simple game of rock, paper, scissors. Realizing this was what my best friend needed, I played along, our hands moving in sync.

All of a sudden, a piercing screech of "Dad!" shattered the moment, and everything became a blur.

Suddenly, the temperature of the water drops, jolting me into the present. I gasp and clutch my chest, memories of that night threatening to overwhelm me. I blink, my vision blurry with unshed tears.

Fuck. I don't do this.

Benny wouldn't want me standing here crying—over what? Over him? Over what happened that night? Did I cause this whole mess? I shake my head, refusing to believe it, yet in a second, my fist flies to the tile wall. Pain shoots through me in an instant. Fucking hell. I clench and unclench my fist a few times.

Fuck, that hurt.

Where was Troy, anyway? Usually, he had texted me by now, or at least Payson had deleted his messages. However, today had been eerily quiet. Too quiet. I can't tell if that's a good thing or if Payson and I have actually succeeded. Was deleting his messages really that simple? Would he truly leave me alone after all these years?

The echo of a gentle knock in my apartment startles me out of my thoughts. My eyes narrow—who would be here so late? This time, the knock is louder and is followed by a tearful voice calling out, "Luke."

Hastily wrapping a towel around myself, I rush to the door, my mind racing. When I open it, I am met with the sight of Payson, her eyes red and swollen, tears flowing down her cheeks. My heart breaks into fragments. Damn it. It's impossible to handle seeing her like this.

Instantly, I wrap my arms around her, sensing the quiver in her body as she clings to me. Her hands collide with my exposed chest, her agony scorching through my flesh. Closing the door, I effortlessly lift her while her legs wrap around my waist. The overpowering urge to console her fills me as I bring her to my bedroom.

With a gentle touch, I situate her on the bed's edge and lower myself to my knees in front of her. I hold her face tenderly in my hands, her tear-streaked cheeks and baby-blue eyes reflecting her deep anguish. "Stay here. I'll be right back," I assure her. A tear rolls down her cheek as she nods.

Fuck. I knew this was going to be hard on her. Fuck. Fuck. Fuck.

With a racing pulse, I dash to the medicine cabinet. I fetch Tylenol to combat her inevitable headache, melatonin to aid her sleep, and water and peppermint herbal tea for added comfort.

With a slight shake, I carefully arrange everything on the nightstand.

Payson looks at the objects, and her crying intensifies, shattering my heart once more. I've felt heartbreak, but witnessing her like this is a whole other level of pain. I softly touch her face, using my thumb to wipe away the tears. "Baby, tell me what you need." She shakes her head, her shoulders shaking with the force of her sobs.

Desperation drives me to act swiftly. I nearly stumble in my haste to get the medication, pressing the pills into her hand. She takes them, and we both crawl into bed. She lies on top of me, her body trembling against mine. With slow, comforting circles, I caress her back and softly say, "I'm here, baby." Over and over, willing my presence to bring her some measure of peace.

Payson

My body feels utterly drained, exhausted to the bone, as though I've been dragged through hell and back. But his strong arms, caring eyes, and tender murmurs have been my lifeline during this endless night. Rolling to my side, I find myself locked in a gaze with his deep, handsome hazel eyes. The sheer tenderness in them grips my heart so tightly it aches.

Can this man truly love me? The thought invades my mind, a desperate whisper of hope clawing at my heart.

If he could, he would. And Luke?

He didn't have to open his door, his arms, or offer this unwavering support. Emotional support—something I never believed he, or any man, was capable of. But this side of Luke, this relentless presence, makes me want to gather it all up and never let it go.

Tracing my lips with a hand that trembles, his eyes follow every movement until they meet mine, filled with an overwhelming flood of emotions. "Hi," I murmur, my voice shaky now that the tears have stopped. God, what must he think of me? I probably look like a complete wreck. Just as I'm about to avert my gaze in embarrassment, he swiftly flips me around and I find myself straddling him. It's as if this is his favorite way to connect with me, to keep me close. His fingers grip my chin as he maintains a serious demeanor, with his lips forming a firm line.

"Don't, don't do that." His voice is firm, almost desperate. "Don't shy away from me."

"Remember, this is about trust," he reminds me, pointing between us. I shake my head, confusion and doubt swirling inside me. That was about his therapy sessions, helping him. Not me, not my own chaotic mess. Just thinking about what's happening now, and the uncertain future, is enough to bring another onset of tears.

Is it possible that I'll end up like my parents?

Will someone still love me even if they know about my abusive upbringing?

God, what if I turn out like Josie, developing a weird obsession with kittens that scares off my clients.

Luke gently pushes aside my disheveled hair, undoubtedly a mess, along with my tear-streaked raccoon eyes, and says, "I understand if you don't want to talk, but I'm here for you."

Has there ever been someone who truly stood by my side? When have I ever been vulnerable enough to allow someone into my life? He cradles my face, wiping away another tear that has broken free, seemingly never ending. It's as if all the emotions I've held back for years are now flooding out.

"Whatever you need, I'm here for you. If you need a shoulder to cry on, I'm all in. Craving your favorite food or licorice? I'll dash to the nearest store. Want to binge *I Love Lucy* reruns? I'll make popcorn and grab a Diet Coke. And when you need someone to lend an ear, know that I'm here." His voice softens, oozing with sincerity.

"I am here," he echoes, his words igniting a war of goose bumps on my skin. My chest tightens as I offer a grateful smile and an unsteady nod. This man is so different from everything I've always known. Just months ago, he seemed so self-centered, always *Luke this, Luke that*. But now, I see the real him, the one beneath the facade.

He's the kind of person who doesn't shy away from his mistakes, a man who was worth the chance I took months back. He took a risk and shared his most personal secrets with me, entrusting me with his vulnerability. For the first time, I feel an overwhelming urge—a desperate need—to reciprocate. I don't know what's pushing me; maybe my guarded walls have finally crumbled enough to let Luke in. Maybe it's because he had the chance to tell Milli about me being here in his penthouse, but he didn't. He kept it to himself. Maybe it's because, at the core of it all, I am no longer just falling for this man—I love him.

He softly asks, "What is it?"

A lump forms in my throat, rendering me unable to speak, so I shake my head.

What will he think of me? Of us?

I let out a weary sigh as Luke's hands wrap around mine, his silent support more comforting than words. Overwhelmed with emotions, tears flow from my eyes as I try to utter the word, but my voice falters and the simple, three-letter word chokes me. "D-Dad," I finally manage to whisper.

Luke's eyes close slowly, pain etched on his face. "Payson," he says, his tone heavy with hurt. Suddenly, I collapse into him, my tears streaming uncontrollably onto his bare chest. He envelops me in a tight embrace, absorbing each sob. He soothes me, rubbing my back as I shatter in his arms for the second time.

With each tender stroke, he calms me and helps me catch my breath. I stay there, pressed against him, our hearts beating together. Moving slightly, he murmurs, "Breathe, beautiful," before placing a kiss on my forehead. The gesture makes me close my eyes, giving me that last fragment of strength. I know I need to explain more. So, I do—I spill everything. I reminisce about the shifts that began when I entered high school as a freshman, the days when my dad was kind, and our Sundays were treasured with *I Love Lucy* reruns and unplanned lessons on history. It was pure bliss, until it wasn't anymore. When everything turned upside down, I was the only one who could reach him.

I can feel Luke's tension radiating through his grip, his hands twitching and his body trembling as if he's barely containing the urge to move. He repeatedly shakes his head, trying to comprehend the news, but then I bring up my mom moving to California to stay with Aunt Bethany after leaving the hospital.

His frustration deepens, his breaths coming in ragged bursts. As I finally pull away, understanding flickers in his eyes, paving the way for his next words. "My penthouse is open," he offers.

I quirk an eyebrow, until he continues, his touch gentle but urgent as he rubs my arms. "For winter break. You're more than welcome to stay, because, you know . . . " His voice falters, his breath hitching as his other hand clenches in his hair so tightly I fear he might hurt himself. I carefully uncurl his fingers and connect them with mine.

I understand, I truly do. I see why he's so upset. I've been carrying this burden for years, and only when my mom was hospitalized did things start to change.

"Baby," he mumbles, his eyes briefly closing before snapping open with a fiery intensity. "You must realize, what he did was not right." I nod in agreement—I'm painfully aware. "Even if your mom did cheat." Another nod as I wipe fresh tears from my cheeks. "You have to understand that this was their decision, not yours. You have your own life, your own responsibilities. Their choices and responsibilities are theirs alone, no matter what happened in the past." He says these words with a heavy sigh, his head turning slightly, and something flickers in his eyes—recognition, perhaps.

I nod again, speechless. What else can I say? I'm uncertain if my mom will ever disclose her reasons or if she intends to keep it a secret indefinitely. The thought of her betrayal and the pain my dad endured makes me collapse into Luke's arms again.

Luke's voice, a gentle balm to my wounded soul, asks, "What do you need, Payson?"

For my dad to be my dad.

For my mom to have been faithful.

For my life to stop unraveling.

I hold him tighter, and in that moment, without a word, he knows what I need. I fall into the most peaceful sleep of my life, soothed by the steady, comforting rhythm of his heartbeat.

CHAPTER 32
PAYSON

Payson, now is the time.

The following days passed in a blur of busyness. Surprisingly, I handled all my finals and still found time to talk to Josie. She delivered exciting news: Luke and I can continue our sessions in the spring semester. My heart swelled with overwhelming joy and peace. Knowing that graduating early was truly within my grasp brought a serene calm over me. Even if I have another full year, it's still better than facing two more.

And I couldn't contain my excitement at the thought of more time with Luke. Ever since I reluctantly left his penthouse after two blissful days, he has showered me with affection: heartfelt messages, beautiful flowers, and even a Mocha Haven coffee waiting on my nightstand this morning.

Let's just say I was a puddle of goo when I left his penthouse.

I hear my phone ping, and I grab it from the center console of my Kia.

LUKE

Penny, you going to take me up on my offer to stay at my penthouse over the break?

> Don't say no.

> You'll shatter my heart if you do.

> I miss you, Penny.

With an amused smirk, I try to overlook the fact that this man has already seen me today.

LUKE

> I ache for your cuddles, your infectious smile, your joyous laughter, and those breathtaking blue eyes that bring warmth to my mornings and nights.

> Forget it. You have no choice. I will do everything in my power to bring you here and never let you leave. ;)

I giggle at the caveman message, feeling a heat from his flirtatious words. All right, game over—where is the real Luke Sutton? The arrogant man I've known for years has vanished, replaced by this charming flirt. Just then, another text interrupts.

Stoneton Girls

MILLI

> LOOK LOOK LOOK . . . [Picture of engagement ring]

My jaw drops. No freaking way. Miles proposed to Milli?

BROOKE

> NO FREAKING WAY, Mills.

PAYSON

> WHAT? He proposed?

MILLI

Yes, and guess where it happened?

Brooke and I respond simultaneously: *Dance studio.*

MILLI

Yes!

BROOKE

This calls for celebratory margaritas!

I chuckle.

Milli sends us a picture of the entire dance studio at NRU, adorned with rose petals and candles. My eyes widen, and a smile forms on my lips at the romantic scene. I wonder what it must feel like to be her in that moment, to love someone so deeply that you want to bind them to your life forever.

Witnessing my mother tied to my father, enduring his abusive actions, filled me with dread and unease, causing me to fear that any man could replicate the same behavior.

But in the past few days, I've realized that none of this was my fault, and I shouldn't have felt guilty, torn between them, or like a failure. Knowing this has given me the confidence to be here. To seek answers. To try to move forward.

My heartbeat pounds loudly as a shadow moves inside my parents' house, filling me with tension.

Payson, now is the time.

Knowing what I need to do, I quickly text Luke back that I would take him up on that offer. How could I not? A few weeks with him? Just the two of us in his penthouse, no sessions, just time spent together watching reruns of *I Love Lucy*—and lately, *Dexter*. Us trying each other's favorite foods while lounging on the couch, talking about life—it would be foolish to say no.

Before closing my messages, I send another text to Luke. Even though I didn't share my plans with my girls, with Luke, it feels right to be open, even if it's just a simple message.

PAYSON

Going to see my dad.

Reluctantly, I turn off my Kia and drag myself toward the front door. However, for some unknown reason, my feet have different intentions. They pull me toward a path I haven't ventured on in years. It isn't avoidance but the heaviness of bittersweet memories that has kept me away.

Within moments, I'm several blocks away, standing in the peaceful center of Time Walk Heritage Park. The brisk air stings my cheeks, but I welcome the bite, a reminder that I am here, now. The world seems to tilt as I close my eyes and spin, immersing myself in the peacefulness of the park. Each beat of my heart echoes the past as memories of time spent here with my dad rush through me.

"Daddy, did you know that the Great Wall of China is very long!" I chirped, my small hand swinging in his as we ambled along our favorite path for our Sunday walks.

With a chuckle, he nodded his head as we headed back home.

"Like, the Great Wall of China was built over many years, and it's so long that it stretches over thirteen thousand miles!" He chuckled again at my wide-eyed wonder, then gave my hand a reassuring squeeze.

"Okay, how about this, Dad? Did you know that dinosaurs lived a long, long time ago?" Once more, his laughter resonated, accompanied by a gentle smile. "Yeah, I think most people know that, Pay Bay."

I beamed up at him. "But did they know that dinosaurs roamed the Earth about two hundred and thirty million years ago, way before any humans were around?"

Approaching our house, I saw the first signs of spring as flowers bloomed. "Perhaps not everyone is aware, but paleontologists certainly are," he responded.

My questioning look only made him laugh more as we reached our front door. "Dad, I absolutely love these days."

He kissed my forehead tenderly. "Me, too, Pay Bay."

Moments before we entered, I turned my gaze upward to him. "Dad, I hope we always remember this moment." His face briefly showed a trace of sadness, but it was soon replaced by his familiar smile. My dad always preferred to smile, and it made me smile too.

"Trust me, I could never forget these moments with you, sweet girl."

"Why are you here?" With a gruff growl, my father stands in the doorway as the front door creaks open. Blinking multiple times, I struggle to accept the contrast between the broken man before me and the father I once recognized. Gone are the warm memories of him smiling, our shared laughter over historical facts. In their place are hollow eyes and a scowl etched deep into his face. He seems like a hollow version of the person he used to be.

My heart sinks. My skin crawls. I think I am going to throw up.

Briefly, I contemplate avoiding the confrontation altogether. But then I remind myself: This is necessary. I need this fight for redemption to move forward with my life, to finally put myself first for once.

In an effort to remain calm, I clear my throat. "I came to see you, Dad."

With a sarcastic snort, he turns away and goes back inside the house. Anger flares within me, but I follow, scanning the once-familiar surroundings now marred by empty beer bottles and trash. Holes puncture the kitchen wall—likely from his fists, judging by the bruises. I cringe, overwhelmed by the degradation.

"Where did everything go?" I finally ask.

Cracking open a new beer, he gives a nonchalant shrug. "I tossed it," he says with indifference.

When did he start drinking so heavily? It's worse than I thought. Guilt gnaws at my throat, making it a struggle to take in air. Without any hesitation, I quickly run down the hallway to the bedrooms. First, I reach my parents' room. Only a bed remains. With panic mounting, I rush to my bedroom. "What do you mean you threw it away?" My heart trips over itself as I stop at the doorway.

Everything is gone—from my bed to my favorite green curtains to my pictures on the wall. It's as if someone had erased my existence.

He did this. He took it all away, discarding everything like crumpled paper into the trash.

The air is squeezed out of my lungs as a sharp pain tightens in my chest. The panic rises within me as I hear him come to a halt in the doorway—my father, the one entrusted with our safety, with her protection. His cold, detached eyes sweep over the vacant room, and when our gazes connect, something inside me shatters. The deep rage I've concealed for so long finally breaks free, ending the silence between us.

"WHAT THE HELL DID YOU DO?" I scream, my voice raw with fury, my eyes burning with unshed tears. The heaviness of these words surpasses the emptiness in this room; they bear the weight of unanswered questions and wounds he has caused.

At six foot two, he looms over me with a smugly satisfied look on his face. He nonchalantly shrugs, provoking another surge of anger within me.

"I didn't expect you to come back after witnessing your mom and seeing her in the hospital."

I am completely at a loss for words. What happened to the dad I knew from childhood? The one who would buy my mother flowers every Sunday? What about the dad who would lend a hand with my history homework? Nausea rises in me. Is this what my life has become?

"Therefore, I discarded everything. What's the point of keeping it?"

Because it was *mine*. My memories. My things to hold on to.

His words are cold, callous, each one landing like a punch to the gut. He doesn't need to say it, but I hear the unspoken truth loud and clear: What's the point of keeping us?

He turns away, already dismissing me, heading toward the kitchen as if this conversation means nothing. But it means everything.

I can't let him walk away. I follow, the frustration inside me building like a ticking time bomb, seconds from exploding.

"Those were my things!" I cry out, my voice trembling, my hand gripping my chest, as if I can prevent my heart from breaking apart.

"They were inside my home," he responds, each word growing colder, stealing away the final traces of warmth from this space. His indifference cuts deeper than any wound, turning this house—my home—into a hollow, unfamiliar space.

"Just because she cheated on you, just because your marriage fell apart, just because you think it's okay to abuse her, doesn't mean I should suffer the consequences! It doesn't mean you get to throw my stuff out!" My voice quivers, torn between anger and sadness, overwhelmed by the pain of betrayal.

Is this really what he wanted for his family? To tear us apart at the seams? To become the monster he is now? I've spent years refusing to see him that way, clinging to the hope that there was still a shred of decency in him. But after seeing Mom in the hospital—the bruises, the vacant look in her eyes—it's impossible to deny the truth any longer. He's exactly what I feared he was.

He moves toward me with a predator's precision, his stormy eyes betraying a cruel malice. "You assume," he mutters, his pace controlled and ominous, "that those words," he takes another stride toward me, his aura oppressive, "carry any weight," he stops just inches from me, his exhalation scorching my flesh, "in my eyes?" With a force that makes me flinch, he slams his hand down on the kitchen island, his voice dropping to a low, venomous whisper. Trapped against the sharp edge, I have nowhere to go. My heart pounds, not just in fear, but also in the agony of knowing that the father I once knew is gone, replaced by a heartless stranger.

I close my eyes tightly, expecting the worst, but instead, a burning pain shoots through my face. Shocked, my breath catches and I am momentarily unable to move. Tears start to well up as the relentless throbbing in my cheek continues to spread. My mind reels, struggling to process the reality: My dad just struck me. For the first time. With a twisted satisfaction, his glinting eyes assure it won't be the final time.

With desperation driving me, I dodge to the side and slip beneath his arm, but his quickness is honed by years of cruelty toward my mother. With a forceful hold, he grabs my waist and presses my back against him. For a moment, I can't breathe; his forearm presses against my throat, cutting off my air supply. Panic overwhelms me as I frantically grab at his arm, attempting to release myself, my heart pounding in a frightening rhythm.

He's choking me.

Gasping for air, my heart beats frantically, my vision blurs, and my body goes numb from lack of oxygen. "Your mother was my everything," he begins, his voice overflowing with seething rage. "Pay Bay, you were my everything." The nickname feels like a stab in the heart. "Until you weren't. Your mother cheated on me with one of her colleagues." His comment is sharp and bitter, a hiss of pure venom, as his arm tightens around my throat.

I squeeze my eyes shut, trying to focus on his voice, clinging to the sound in a desperate attempt to block out the terror that this could be the end.

I don't think he realizes how much pressure he's putting on me, the chokehold that's close to making me lose consciousness. "She runs off to California, can you believe it? And with Bethany, of all people," he sneers, his laughter dripping with disdain. "She doesn't even like her sister."

With every furious movement, I clutch at his arms, my voice a trembling whisper, "Please, Dad. Please, let go. You're hurting me," I say, but my pleas fall on deaf ears as he directs our attention to a family photo on the fridge—a photo that had gone unnoticed until now.

Using his other hand, he gestures and points, his finger like a spear of blame. "You see that family?" he growls. "That damn family was perfect." He tightens his hold even more, making my body freeze with panic. "We were perfect."

But that's the thing, Dad, no family is perfect.

It's a truth I've come to understand deeply. Just because a family looks "perfect" doesn't mean they don't have their own problems or challenges. You're only witnessing the surface, unaware of the intricate complexities within.

I remain silent, barely even risking a motion. "Until your mom thought there was a better man out there," he bitterly remarks. His arm constricts so intensely that black dots flicker across my vision.

Move, Payson. Move.

And I do. I take a deep breath, closing my eyes, summoning all my strength. Using a swift motion, I strike his groin with my elbow. Letting out a grunt, he doubles over and releases his grip on me. "Goddammit, Payson," he yells, clutching the kitchen island.

I stumble a few steps, coughing harshly as I try to catch my breath. I gaze at him—the man who was once my idol, the one who never missed a chance to hold my hand, who used to entertain me with historical trivia, who would sit with me and watch reruns of *I Love Lucy*.

He is completely gone now.

He's truly gone. Sobbing uncontrollably, tears stream down my face, I burst through the front door. My throat burns, each breath a painful rasp, and my face throbs with the remnants of his violence. A crushing truth takes hold, sinking deep into my chest: My dad will never change. This is who he has become. The weight of that realization sinks in, and my heart is gripped by a deeper sorrow—I may never get him back.

CHAPTER 33
LUKE

Anxiety twists in my gut, tightening like a constrictor around its prey. My hand grips the doorknob, caught between the urge to act and the fear of overreacting.

Just relax.

How? Ten of my messages had gone unread. My heart races, my mind filled with countless what-ifs. Payson seemed fine when she left my penthouse yesterday morning. Our text conversation was brief, but my anxiety skyrocketed when she brought up seeing her dad. Was I comfortable with her confronting him alone? Fuck no. After what went down with her mother, who could say he wouldn't lash out, do the same to her?

That fear replayed endlessly last night, through practice, and as I tossed and turned in bed. How can someone who was meant to provide love and guidance fail her? Her father should have been the first man to teach her about trust and love. Instead, he showed her fear, anxiety, and a reason to be afraid of a man's touch.

Desperation eats away at me—I have to prove that not all

men are like her father, to show her she can trust me. I would never hurt her, and she has all of me. Without even realizing it, she has complete control over my being, soul, and heart.

Gathering my courage, I finally open the door to her dorm room. Two things happen the instant I step inside. First, my heart stops—literally halts—at the sight of Payson. Then my body freezes, rooted to the spot.

"Luke?" Payson's voice is hoarse, breaking into a weak cough.

Her tear-filled eyes meet mine, telling stories of pain etched on her face. My mouth opens, but no words come out, my thoughts a chaotic jumble.

What the—

My thoughts come to a sudden stop as I scan her from top to bottom. She's curled up on her dorm room bed, arms wrapped around her knees. She has red, puffy eyes, a swollen face, and a faint bruise on her high cheekbone. Blood roars in my veins, and my fists clench so tightly that my knuckles turn white.

It catches my eye immediately—the black and blue bruises on her neck. My heart begins to pound once more, fueled by a fierce, protective anger.

That bastard—but then she lets out a small, cry-like gasp, snapping me out of my fury and anguish. I rush to her side, and she instantly wraps her arms around mine, burrowing into my lap for comfort as she has many times before. Her sobs come in broken waves, each hiccup a raw, gut-wrenching sound that tears at my heart. This woman has endured so much, more than I realized when I was trying to bring her down every time I saw her. I wish I could end all her suffering right here and now, but I know that's not possible—*yet*.

So, in this second, I vow to be everything she needs. I will give her the love and care she deserves—and more. My pulse pounds with determination as I gently rub her back with one hand and stroke her hair with the other. The soft kisses I place on her head are my silent promises. Whispers escape my lips, filled with emotion, reassuringly saying, "It's okay." We stay entwined, her fragile body pressed against mine, my arms a fortress of strength and support. The room is silent except for her soft sobs, and I know words are futile. I understand Payson; when she's ready to share, she will, without pressure.

With each passing hour, her tears diminish, leaving her looking exhausted and me feeling emotionally drained. The sight of her face, pale and marked by tears, wrenches my heart. And at that moment, it occurs to me that maybe she doesn't need to talk right now. Maybe what she needs is a way to take her mind off things, a simple act of kindness to reassure her that I am there for her in a way that goes beyond anyone else before.

I squeeze her hand, feeling the softness of her skin, and turn to her on the bed. "Let's go." Her brows knit together in confusion, and I gently push back a strand of her hair, the softness of it a stark contrast to her turmoil. "Trust me," I urge. She closes her eyes, her uncertainty palpable.

I sit up, trying to appear lighthearted and spontaneous despite the strain in my cheeks from forcing a smile. It's likely the last thing she wants to do, but I know it can help. Obsessing over problems can trap you in an endless cycle. It's crucial to take action—any action—to break free from that cycle and keep moving forward.

Slowly, she swings her legs to the edge of the bed. She anxiously observes her hands as they fidget. With a trembling touch, she cautiously reaches for her throat and cheek, flinching at the slight discomfort. Kneeling beside her, I softly grasp her hand and press it against my mouth.

"I've got you, baby."

I move toward the bathroom vanity, where her items are scattered among Milli's, a chaotic mix of familiarity and intrusion. I retrieve the bag labeled MAKEUP and kneel in front of her. My hands shake slightly—I've never done this before. What if I mess things up?

Luke, get it together.

Taking a deep breath, I feel the air entering my lungs and soothing my nerves. "Tell me if this hurts, okay?" She nods, her throat visibly tense as she swallows, her eyes brimming with unshed tears. Using a tube labeled CONCEALER, I gently apply small dots on the bruise on her cheekbone and neck, concealing the hidden shades of black and blue. While I gently blend the concealer with a makeup sponge, her eyes meet mine, brimming with a vulnerable trust that makes my heart flutter like a trapped butterfly's wings.

Unleashing tears, they cascade down her face and absorb into the sponge. With every tear, I take a moment to kiss her damp skin tenderly, as if my lips could erase her pain. She trembles uncontrollably as her emotions overwhelm her, collapsing into my arms.

After her sobs turn into quiet hiccups, I come to the realization that makeup won't do the trick today. With my hands still trembling, I search through her things and discover the Lone Star scarf and ball hat I had given her—simple protection for the battles of today. I gently help her into comfortable leggings, a warm NorthRidge University sweatshirt, and a light vest. With each deliberate motion, I assist her into her familiar white Nike sneakers, ensuring stability and comfort with every step.

Finally ready, we step outside, the crisp air biting at our skin. Her hand grips mine tightly as I lead her to my Range Rover. Silence fills the car as we navigate the winding road, heading to a secluded location I'm well acquainted with— shielded from prying eyes.

Following a short drive, I reach the reserved parking area for players and unbuckle my seat belt. I lean over and unfasten Payson's seat belt, noticing her gaze fixed on the Lone Star Stadium. She looks at me, raising an eyebrow curiously. I chuckle. The idea had struck me suddenly, and after a quick text to our GM asking for a favor, he gave us the green light as long as I practiced a few throws.

Extending my arm across the center console, I intertwine our hands, relishing the warmth of her touch. "Please trust me," I plead softly. She nods, releasing a deep, shaky exhale, and a rush of relief and validation washes over me, tingling through my body. Her trust—something I've been yearning for, craving with an ache deep in my chest—is unfolding before me. I didn't think I would ever witness this moment, but here it is, occurring right in front of me.

Holding her hand, I quickly gather a couple of blankets before we go. Walking together, we head toward the stadium, enjoying the chilly December breeze.

During this time of year in Texas, the weather is always uncertain—never consistently cold or warm, with occasional unexpected snow or rain. Today, the sky is overcast, the temperature biting in the high forties.

Holding Payson's hand, I enter through the players' gate and rush to the control room to bring the stadium to life. Flipping switches and turning knobs, I spot Payson near the players' tunnel as I glance down from the press box. Not wanting to lose another second, I race back to the field, grabbing the essentials I need for a few practice throws.

Entering the stadium, Payson has one blanket spread out on the ground and another wrapped around her shoulders. She nods in the direction of the net that Maddox usually practices with, and occasionally I use it to work on my throwing skills.

I give her a questioning look, catching her silent cue to

get to work. Yet, she doesn't realize that my real reason for being here isn't to practice throws; it's all for her. I wanted this moment for her, not my training. I lower myself, locking eyes with her, her vacant stare piercing my heart with a painful tug. Without hesitating, I grab her hand and tilt my head with an encouraging, "Come on."

She hesitates, her eyes glued to me, until I flash that knowing smirk—the one guaranteed to get her moving. Biting her lip, she lets out an exasperated huff and mutters, "That's unfair." Moments later, we're standing in the middle of the field, tossing the ball back and forth.

At first, she hesitates and lacks confidence, but I offer reassurance, saying, "That's what I'm here for, baby."

Positioned right behind her, I direct her hands to achieve the perfect throw. With the diminishing daylight and chilling air, our connection strengthens, surpassing the warmth of the sunniest day. That undeniable connection remains constant, unwavering.

We continue exchanging the ball, our breaths becoming ragged gasps. Face to face, I release the ball as it falls. I can almost feel the weight of the words she's about to utter, words that will demand all my strength.

"Baby, you don't need to say it. It's okay," I murmur, stepping closer to her. My hands tremble as they gently stroke her arms. "I'm right here. That's all that matters."

Her head shakes, the internal struggle evident, and it breaks my heart to witness her in this state—scared to expose her pain, unwilling to let others shoulder the weight.

She lifts her gaze, her eyes filled with unshed tears that glimmer. "He hit me," she whispers, her voice barely audible. Her eyes squeeze shut as tears escape and run down her cheeks. "My dad, he—he tried to strangle me," she stutters, her fingers unconsciously holding onto the scarf covering her bruises.

As her words sink in, my mind seizes on one: *Strangle.*

He strangled her? Her own father?

A cold fury rises within me, seeping into every fiber of my being. The image of anyone, especially her father, causing her harm stirs a relentless resolve in my heart. My vision sharpens, narrowing in focus as my body tenses, ready to confront any threat to her.

I yank her into my arms, holding her as if my very life depended on it, feeling her sobs shudder through her fragile frame. But then she's pushing me away.

This is it. When she withdraws—again—I see it in her gaze, a mixture of fear and resignation. I refuse to let her face this alone. Moving closer to her, she intercepts me, her hand quivering like a leaf in the gust. Her lips form a tight line as she silently mouths the words, *Just stop*, her face growing stern with unwavering determination.

A red-hot flood of rage courses through my veins. Damn it, that fucking bastard.

Her gaze shifts, but we quickly make eye contact again, both holding back tears. "Luke, do you know you're the first person I've ever been able to tell any of this to?" Her voice falters as she continues, "The first person I've really let in, shared my past with." My fingers itch to pull her close, to envelop her in a protective cocoon and shield her from the world.

"I can't believe it," she whispers, shaking her head and clutching herself tightly. "Typically, I keep my emotions to myself and share them with my therapist, but with you," her piercing eyes focused on me, "it's different. You make me speak freely, lowering the walls I've painstakingly built to keep everyone out." She lets out a bitter laugh, a harsh sound that echoes in the stadium. "I even keep my parents at arm's length; it's been that way for years."

Despite her initial hesitation, I inch closer, feeling the

tension emanating from her. With steady yet tentative hands, I gently hold her face, searching her eyes. "Payson, don't you understand?" I whisper, my voice trembling. "That's exactly what I want—to be here for you, to be someone you can feel completely safe with."

"No, Luke." She shakes her head, biting her lip as if to keep from crying out, and steps back, my words hitting her like a physical blow.

Tears flow along her cheeks, each one striking my heart like a hammer. "Trust me, you don't want any part of this. *Of me,*" she chokes out, her voice breaking.

She pauses, and a hollow laugh escapes her lips, laced with a sorrow that chills me to the bone. "What even are we? I'm your therapist, and you're my client. Sure, we've had our moments, shared things, but that doesn't make us anything more." Each word cuts through me like a dagger, leaving a searing pain in its wake.

Yet I know Payson pushes away those she cares about most when things get tough. But she has to see—I'm not the type to give up easily, not on her. She's the one for me. All this time, she has been right in front of me.

"I'm a disaster," she confesses, starting to pace while snowflakes drift down around us. Each heavy flake matches the sinking feeling in the depths of my soul.

Halting abruptly, she turns to me and admits, "My life is a complete mess." Her bright blue eyes are sad, hollow, scared. A painful ache spreads through me as I witness her suffering.

There's a sudden tightness in my chest. What I'm about to say might change everything, but I can't hold back any longer.

Stepping forward, I block her path and softly cup her face in my hands. Each snowflake gracefully lands on her nose and eyelashes as the snowfall intensifies. "Then let me be a part of that mess, baby," I say.

Skepticism clouds her gaze. My pulse beats heavily in my temples, each thud mirroring the urgency in my heart.

Say something, baby. Something, anything.

Her eyes shut tightly, and her fingers dig into the fabric of my shirt. "L-Luke, n-no. That's not what I meant," she stammers.

I rest my forehead against hers. "I truly meant every word," I whisper, our breaths intertwining. Those beautiful eyes connect with mine. This is my opportunity to bare my soul, to reveal everything I've kept inside.

"Did you know that the majority of people start their day by checking the time? But for me, the moment my eyes open, my thoughts rush to you. I ache to see you lying next to me, to lose myself in your beautiful blue eyes."

Her breath hitches, and she tightens her grip on my sweatshirt, her eyes closing again. "After every game, win or lose, you're the one I want—need—by my side the moment I step off the field. Whether we're celebrating a victory or seeking comfort in each other's arms after a loss, watching reruns of *I Love Lucy*, it doesn't matter. You're my person, Payson."

With my fingertips, I brush away a stray tear from her cheek, savoring the warmth of her skin. "And every time you get nervous, you fidget with your hands or take that no-nonsense stance. You let out that adorable little huff—the one that makes my heart skip a beat. It makes me want to kiss you, to hear it again and again, because I love every single thing about you."

Her body shivers slightly, and I instinctively pull her closer, feeling her heartbeat sync with mine.

"That's the thing, baby. I love it—all of it. Whether you're giving me a piece of your mind one moment or helping in our sessions the next." I pause, savoring the moment as her eyes flutter open, meeting mine with a softness that makes my heart swell. "I love you, Payson." She gasps softly, a sound that sends a warm shiver through me. "And I know you might feel like your life is a mess, like you're a mess, but that's what I adore about you. It's what makes you, you, Payson. I love that woman. I love you."

I run my thumb gently along her cheek, our faces close in the biting cold as snow swirls around us. "Baby, let me be a part of that mess. I don't care what it involves, as long as I'm in it with you."

Time seems to stand still as she takes a deep breath, her warm breath caressing my skin, and a comforting sensation surrounds me. My heart pounds in my chest as I brace for her response. Words fail her, but her actions speak volumes. She wraps her arms around my neck, pressing her body firmly against mine. She swiftly lifts her legs, wrapping them around my waist, her body melding with mine as she nods.

In each other's arms, we stand amid the falling snow, creating our own secluded world. She leans in, her cheek grazing mine, and whispers, "Okay."

Relief floods through me, washing away my anxieties. While I long to hear those three words from her, her acceptance is enough for now. I don't need her to say *I love you*—I just need her to keep trusting me, to let me in, to not push me away. This time, she doesn't. She's discovering that I'm here for the long haul, that I crave this connection, our lives intertwined.

Our gaze locks as our foreheads touch again, a chaotic sea of unspoken emotions surging between us. The sight of her leaves me momentarily speechless as I memorize every exquisite detail. "I love you, Payson," I say again, my voice quivering with intensity. In an instant, her lips collide with mine, a fierce urgency in the kiss that leaves me breathless. With a tight grip, her fingers weave in my hair as she pours her soul into this moment, her nails leaving fiery marks along my neck.

"Maybe I need to say that more often if I get this kind of reaction from you." She playfully shoves at my chest, but the slight tilt of her lips reveals how much she needed this. The irresistible magnetic force between us draws me back to her lips. My fingers hold onto her waist, then glide over her ribs, causing gentle tickles and eliciting her beautiful laughter. That sound, her laughter, feels like the sun finally shining after endless gray skies. It sets off a real smile that rapidly grows on my face.

Then she whispers, "Say it again."

Without a second thought, I twirl us in the falling snow, the world fading into oblivion. With every ounce of passion and devotion in my heart, I shout at the top of my lungs, "I LOVE PAYSON PENNINGTON!" The words I never thought I'd say now flow freely, and it feels pretty damn amazing.

CHAPTER 34
PAYSON

You deserve better.

MOM

Finally feeling settled at Aunt Bethany's. Love you, Pay Bay. Call me soon.

Exhausted, I fall into Luke's living room's soft egg chair, enjoying the comfort it provides. A grin appears on my face as I recollect how it had ended up here. Luke, known for his preference for luxurious minimalism, would never have selected such a whimsical item for his penthouse. However, he was aware of my love for Milli's egg chair and got one specifically for me.

Be still my heart.

Luke has taken every chance during winter break to tell me how much he loves me. This is something I never thought I'd hear from someone other than my dad. Yet, each time he says it, my stomach flutters with fierce, wild butterflies. It's more than just words; it's a reassurance that I don't need to fear letting another man in. It serves as a reminder that my dad is not representative of all men.

With each passing day, I can no longer deny that I am in love with Luke. I haven't expressed it, but I knew it deep down when he took care of me in my dorm. His voice, eyes, and actions exuded gentleness, softness, and tenderness, making me feel deeply loved, cared for, and secure.

The forceful knock on Luke's door interrupts my thoughts and startles me into the present. I narrow my eyes at the door, suspicion curling in my chest. Who could possibly be here right now? Luke is never home on game day for the Lone Stars, everyone knows that. The silence stretches until the doorbell rings, the sound a jarring note in the quiet apartment.

Reluctantly, I sigh and tug at the hem of my crop top, the one emblazoned with the words, *Lucy, you got some 'splainin' to do!*—a relic from my childhood when life felt simpler. My dad had given it to me back then, and as I grew older, I couldn't let go of the memories it held. So I transformed it into a crop top, clinging to the remnants of a time when everything made sense.

The shirt, like my feelings for him, is a complex mix of emotions—anger, confusion, and sadness, tinged with bitter-sweet nostalgia. Yet, it also brings a strange comfort, a fragile shield against the newer, more painful memories that I'm not ready to face. It's not a solution, but for now, it's enough to keep me afloat.

My stomach churns with dread as I hover my hand over the doorknob, taking a trembling breath. The world freezes as I summon the courage to open the door. My breath hitches, and my heart slams against my ribs. His once vibrant green eyes now appear dull as they meet mine. His hollow cheeks and the tired shadows beneath his eyes reveal a tale of sleepless nights and hidden agony. My gaze drifts down-ward, catching sight of the worn suitcases at his feet, their presence confirming a decision long overdue. His damp hair clings to his forehead, the droplets like tears he refuses to shed.

Once again, our eyes lock, and the intensity is overwhelming. Before I have a chance to process, fear and a relentless ache force me to shut the door abruptly. Yet in an instant, his hand emerges, not with force, but with a gentle touch, ensuring the door remains open as if his entire being relies on it. "Payson, please." The crack in his voice, the raw desperation in that single word, freezes me in place.

"Pay Bay," he murmurs, and the familiar nickname cuts through me like a knife. My eyes squeeze shut, trying to block out the memories, the pain, the love that still lingers despite everything.

How dare he use that name after everything he's done? He's lost the right to that intimacy, that closeness he once took for granted. Fueled by anger, I forcefully open the door and take cover behind it, using the thin wooden barrier as protection. In a momentary lapse, I perceive the realization in his eyes, as he understands the fear he has caused me. That realization should evoke some pity or sympathy in me, but it doesn't. A father should never be a source of fear for his daughter.

The silence between us is thick and suffocating. I watch him carefully as he avoids my gaze, the same way he's avoided so many truths. It's easier to breathe with his eyes turned away, easier, but not easy. I know that if I meet his eyes—if I see even a single tear or a hint of genuine regret—it could unravel everything. My carefully constructed walls could crumble, leaving me vulnerable to the very pain I've worked so hard to overcome.

But I've learned from Lori's therapy sessions that I need to focus on my own growth. At twenty years old, it's time to let go of the burden of being the fixer, the peacemaker in a home where the lines between parent and child were always blurred. It's been painfully difficult to step back after years of being their emotional crutch, but I understand now that it's not my job to heal them. I need to prioritize myself, to find who I am outside of their chaos.

So I stand there, behind the door, with a heart hardened by necessity, choosing to protect the fragile progress I've made. Let him deal with his own demons. I'm done carrying them.

Abruptly, he seizes his suitcases, barely whispering, "This was a mistake."

A bitter laugh escapes me as disbelief and anger surge simultaneously. "Is this some kind of joke?" I snap, my voice trembling with the effort to keep it steady.

When our eyes meet again, the raw pain in his gaze cuts through me, reflecting the turmoil swirling inside my own heart. I feel tears coming, but I quickly suppress them, reminding myself that this moment is about my needs and finding closure. Although it's difficult to breathe under the weight, I won't show him my weakness.

"You can't just show up here," I say, my voice laced with fury, "and then turn tail and run like a coward." My hands grip the door frame, knuckles white, as if it's the only thing tethering me to the ground, keeping me from being swept away by the storm of emotions surging inside me. "Not after everything you did. So be a damn man, and say what you came here to say," I demand, my words sharp and searing, burning in my throat like embers that refuse to die out.

He shrugs his shoulders in defeat, remaining silent, and the ensuing silence eats at me until I can't stay quiet anymore. "Why are you here? How did you even know I was here?"

In a thick and almost unbearable silence, he finally utters, "Luke."

That single name sends my heart stumbling. *Luke.* Panic

begins to rise, tightening my chest. Luke had been texting me all day, just checking in like he always does. But now, a cold fear grips me—what if something happened? What if my dad—

My thoughts are a storm of dread when he suddenly reaches for my hand. I flinch back, instinctively pulling away. He tightens his jaw, his face showing the effort as he searches for the perfect words. "I apologize, Payson," he says, the weight of his words hinting at their sacrifice. Trying to steady his emotions, he takes a breath. "Luke is why I'm here."

The room seems to close in around me as those words sink in, leaving me grasping for understanding. Why Luke? Why would my dad be here because of Luke?

Before I can form a coherent thought, my father speaks again, cutting through the fog in my mind. "Can you believe it? Surprisingly, that boy was able to reason with me," he mumbles, his tone reflecting a combination of disbelief and grudging acknowledgment.

"He went to the house."

My pulse races, my mind spinning in a frenzy. Luke—at my house. With him.

"When?" I whisper, more to myself than to him. My heart pounds as the reality sets in. Luke faced him . . . for me.

My father's gaze drops, and I see something in his eyes that I haven't seen in years—regret. "I-I don't understand," I stammer, my voice trembling with the effort to piece this together.

Gradually, his shoulders drooped. "At first, I didn't either. But . . . Luke held nothing back. He spoke the words I needed to hear—words that no one else would have the courage to say. Part of it was harsh and deeply hurtful. But he was right," he admits, his voice cracking as he struggles to continue. "He made it clear . . . if I ever wanted to have you in my life again, I had to get help.

"He made a promise to protect you, even if it meant protecting you from me."

The room is silent, the air thick with everything left unsaid. A tear slides down his cheek, carving a path through the rough lines of his face. His head shakes slowly, as if he's trying to deny the weight of his own emotions. My chest tightens with the instinct to reach out, to wipe away the tear and pull him close. But I stay rooted to the spot, my fingers curling into fists at my sides, a fragile boundary I can't afford to cross.

It doesn't lessen the sharp ache gnawing at my insides, watching him crumble in front of me. This man—my father—who for years has only shown me anger, bitterness, and hurt, now stands before me, raw and exposed in a way I never imagined. Vulnerable. Fragile. And for the first time, I see the sorrow he's buried beneath the rage, a sorrow that makes me want to believe there's still something left to salvage between us.

But I can't let myself move. Not yet. Not when the scars he left still sting, not when I'm still learning how to breathe on my own again.

"To hear someone say that they need to protect my own daughter from me?" His voice cracks, the weight of the words pulling his hand from his suitcase to rub his face wearily. A sigh of weariness slips from him. "It broke me, Payson. This is something you should have never had to endure," he pauses, his voice getting lower, "this bullshit."

He locks eyes with me, carefully observing my face before his gaze settles on my neck, where the bruises in shades of black, purple, and yellow are slowly fading away. I touch my neck on impulse, causing my dad to quickly avert his gaze and bite his cheek hard. I can tell this view is hurting him, but I no longer have any concern. This might be exactly what he requires to confront—the pain he's inflicted.

While I acknowledge my mom's infidelity and do not support it, it's evident that both of them played a role in their troubled marriage. Instead of seeking help or confronting their issues, she stayed in an abusive relationship, and my dad continued his destructive behavior unchecked. It was only when my parents hit rock bottom—my mom in the hospital and my dad getting physical with me—that any significant change occurred.

"I wanted to share with you that I'll be leaving."

Leaving?

"I'm going to find support," he states, his voice surprisingly calm as his wet hair is tousled by his fingers. His attention returns to me, marked by a deeper level of seriousness. "Despite my reservations, Luke gave me some contacts. His words were, 'If not for yourself, then do it for Payson. She deserves better.'"

"He said that?" My heart does a triple-take.

He nods solemnly. "Yes, he did. And he's right—you deserve better."

Luke really said all that? He went that far for me? My mind spins. The care he's shown, the steps he's taken—all for me. He really does love me, doesn't he? My thoughts fixate on Luke, causing my father's voice to fade into the background. Right now, the enormity of his actions eclipses everything else, filling me with a deep, resonating appreciation for the man who loves me enough to intervene so decisively.

God, I'm such an idiot. All this time, I've just been sitting here, waiting, as if something was going to happen by itself. Waiting to tell this man that I love him. That I am in love with him, and have been for a while. I need to tell him how grateful I am, how incredible he is, and most of all, how proud I am of him. Even with everything going on in his life, he's here, offering me his support in my own chaos.

I gulp, my throat tight, as Dad says, "I came to say good-bye. I don't expect closure, or even a hug, but you should know—I'm going to work on myself. I want to be the father you remember. The one you can rely on, the one you aren't afraid to touch." His voice breaks, filled with a pain that cuts deep.

With his head down, he grabs his suitcase, and just before leaving, he turns and says, "I love you, Pay Bay. It might be a long shot, but I hope we can rebuild. I'm so proud of the woman you're becoming, and I'm blessed to have such an amazing daughter. I want you to be happy, proud, to call me your dad again."

With each footfall away from the door, something inside me shifts. My heart sinks, but there's a surprising lightness in my chest that I haven't felt in years. As my back presses against the cool wood of the door, I realize that my tears aren't about guilt or the usual heartache. It's all about change—his, hers, and now, mine.

These tears represent my dad's decision to heal and my mom's choice to prioritize herself.

And now, it's my turn. The tears that start streaming down my face as I hurry to Luke's room aren't just about the pain; they're about gratitude, about all that Luke has stood by me through. Gripping my phone tightly, I'm ready to pour my heart out and tell him that I love him. However, as I swipe to his contact, a moment of hesitation takes hold of me. Maybe it's not just words he needs—maybe, it's time I show him just how deeply I love him.

The afternoon flew by in an instant, and for a moment, I feared my dad's unexpected visit would derail everything. I imagined myself curled up in Luke's bed, lost in an *I Love Lucy* marathon. Surprisingly, though, it had the opposite effect; it motivated me. That brief encounter with my dad, followed by the news from my mom that she was settling safely in California, somehow gave me the clarity and drive I needed to finally focus on myself.

My eyes do a sweep across the living room, lingering on the array of T-shirts strewn across the couches—each a canvas showcasing Luke's quirky humor. I chuckle softly, reminiscing about the countless times he's sported shirts like I'M TACKLING MY ISSUES, ONE PLAY AT A TIME or the pun-laden I'M THE REASON THEY CALL IT A "TIGHT" END. Initially, his odd choice of apparel irked me, but now, it endears him to me in a distinctly Luke-ish way.

As my gaze continues to roam his space, thoughts of declaring my feelings for him swirl in my mind. This is uncharted territory for me, and initially, I was at a loss for how to proceed. When Luke confessed his love for me, it wasn't with a grand gesture; it was spontaneous, perfectly in the moment. That's the authenticity I crave for this confession.

The opening credits of *Dexter* flicker on the screen, and the sun dips below the horizon, allowing the lights of Dallas to begin their nightly illumination of Luke's penthouse. I've already set the mood, turning on the fire by the mantel to cast a warm glow across the room. In the spirit of the evening, I've prepared holiday margaritas, and a Mexican feast awaits us. It's from the same restaurant where Luke and I ate after our hike session, the one he raved about, declaring it his favorite. So naturally, I ordered it again.

The final piece of the evening's ensemble hangs on the bathroom door in his bedroom—the lingerie outfit I chose a while back. While I didn't know when I would wear it for him, now seems like the perfect setting. He knows green is my favorite color, and it feels almost unjust not to let him see his eyes light up. Closing my eyes in a deep breath that feels like my first in ages.

With the knowledge that Luke could come home any moment, I quickly go to the bathroom to put on lingerie. I nearly bump into the mistletoe I whimsically hung earlier; laughing, I snatch it down as I glide into my outfit. In the bathroom, I add a green velvet robe—a perfect complement.

The sound of the doorbell jolts me from my thoughts. Puzzled, I pause momentarily, wondering who could be ringing the doorbell at this hour. Ignoring the confusion, I determine that it is unimportant. With my robe swishing around my legs, I skip toward the door.

With bated breath, I swing the door open, hoping to catch a glimpse of Luke's familiar hazel eyes that always seem to see into my soul. Instead, what I find is a pair of unexpected dark, stormy blue eyes staring back at me.

CHAPTER 35
LUKE

Trembling hands, pounding heart, and a wide smile. My excitement is overflowing because we just won the most critical game of the season. Deep in the playoffs, this victory over the Lions was vital. Our team was unstoppable. I had a feeling Troy might reach out after this win, but he didn't. He hasn't in weeks. Oddly, it doesn't bother me. It has been freeing not hearing from him these past few weeks.

I've realized that I don't need his messages to perform at my best. I no longer require his words for motivation. I've found my drive, my own reasons to excel. Benny's pride in me fuels my spirit. Knowing that one of us made it to the NFL, achieving our shared dream, means everything. It wasn't until Troy remained silent for weeks that I saw this clearly.

My hand jiggles the doorknob to my penthouse, and I swing the door open with a cheerful, "Honey, I am home!" But as the door slams shut behind me, my heart plummets— a familiar pair of blue eyes meets mine. Those eyes have haunted my dreams, mirroring my hurt, pain, and grief. But now, there's no pain or grief, only seething anger. I swallow hard and set my bag on the ground, my pulse quickening.

"It looks like quite the setup here, doesn't it?" Troy says, his grin sharp and conniving. My jaw tightens as I take in the scene—the Mexican food, the margaritas, *Dexter* playing on the TV. My eyes land on a collection of shirts I've worn in my sessions with Payson.

Payson. My heart lurches when I see her. She's by the fire, draped in a green robe that's far too revealing for Troy's eyes. A surge of anger courses through me as my gaze locks onto his.

"What are you doing here?" I demand.

Troy shakes his head, his features filled with a mocking disapproval. "Naturally, I had to stop by and offer my congratulations," he says, his last words laced with sarcasm.

Locking eyes with Payson, I notice the anxiety in her wide eyes and restless fingers. Every part of me wants to rush to her side, to hold her, to tell her to leave, but I remain rooted, confronting the man before me.

"Plus, I figured you missed me?" He picks up one of the shirts I've worn in my sessions with Payson. His smile is twisted, nothing like the one I used to know, but the one that changed all those years ago.

My brow furrows in. What does he mean by missing him? Before I can ask, he interrupts, stepping closer. Payson's foot shifts slightly, ready to react to any threat. I won't let her get involved physically. Not after everything she's been through.

"Well, seeing as I gave you time off from our deal, I needed to make sure it was still in motion."

What the hell is he talking about?

"You know, me not texting you all these weeks." My mind spins until he adds, "And clearly, things are going . . . well." He glances at Payson, his eyes roaming her body with a predatory gaze.

"I thought little was going on between you two, but that picture I took in New York?" He shakes his head. "I definitely knew something was up."

Wait a minute, he's the one who took that picture of Payson and me? The one she told me was displayed on the jumbotron? What the hell?

That bastard. I'm about to step toward her, but she moves her head side to side, and I see it—that look in her eyes. She knows something I don't. Troy turns toward her abruptly, making her flinch. She straightens instantly, holding her ground. Troy studies her, as if unraveling a puzzle. "Hmm, she's pretty," he observes, then shifts his gaze to me. "But we both know you can do better." He walks over to the mantel and picks up a familiar picture frame from years ago. "We both know Benny would have preferred a brunette."

My hands ball into fists, consumed by anger and hurt, craving an outlet—preferably Troy's face. Years have passed since we've been near each other, and for good reason. His presence always reignites the unresolved tension and unspoken grievances between us, benefiting no one.

Troy's fingers clench the picture frame as he speaks. "Even as a child, Benny always had dreams for his future. He wanted two kids, a wife, the white picket fence—the whole damn thing." He pauses, staring at the photo. Then, in a sudden burst of rage, he hurls the frame to the ground, shattering it into pieces.

Payson gasps and rushes toward me. I instinctively pull her behind me, shielding her.

"But that dream's destroyed now, isn't it, Luke?" Troy asks coldly, kicking aside the shattered glass. Bending down, he picks up a shard, his movements tense. "You're not sticking to the deal, are you? You do what I say. No talk backs, no issues," he commands, pausing for effect. "But I know you haven't been sticking to our deal because I haven't sent you a text in weeks." He chuckles, a cruel sound, and his hand strikes one of the margaritas, sending it spilling everywhere.

Behind me, Payson's grip tightens, her anxiety seeping into my own. Troy, once the beloved coach and father figure, the man everyone admired, has changed. He and my dad used to be inseparable—until that night ten years ago, when everything fell apart.

"First, you ignore me," Troy declares, waving the shard of glass in his hand at Payson and me. Payson's breath comes out in short, fearful gasps. "Then you think you can just break our agreement?"

Consumed by fury, he flings the glass at the wall, the piercing sound resonating as blood oozes from his clenched hand. "You were meant to adhere to my instructions, marrying the person I selected and living the life I had planned for Benny," he hisses, his words saturated with venom. His furious gaze locks onto mine.

"Luke," Payson whispers, her voice trembling. I squeeze her waist, silently urging her to stay calm. Her breath against my neck steadies me for a moment.

"Because of YOU!" Troy bellows, making me flinch. "Because of you, damn it!" His voice cracks, the strain palpable. He paces back and forth like a caged animal, fists clenched so tightly that his knuckles turn white. A muscle twitches in his jaw, barely containing his seething rage. "You ruined everything! For me, for him." Each word is a dagger, piercing me with blame and bitterness.

But did I really? Was that night truly my fault? Each time I look back, I remember the car veering as Benny and I played rock, paper, scissors. Troy had asked us to calm down, but I couldn't ignore the gloss in his eyes, the way his hands fidgeted on the steering wheel, then moved to his neck, then his hair. It was as if he couldn't control his movements, his emotions.

And then we were airborne, the car rolling five times into an abandoned field. Blue and red lights flashing, the ambulance where I sat watching a cop use a breathalyzer on Troy. I witnessed him getting the green light, knowing he was deemed innocent. Free to go.

Free of murder.

Slowly shaking my head, I struggle to believe what I'm hearing. Just then, Payson's gentle hands glide up my arms, her touch light but steadying against the storm of accusations. Two significant events occur in that instant: I take a deep breath, feeling calm, and a surge of clarity enables me to confront the harsh truth I've been avoiding. It may have taken me a while, but I know the truth. For years, I've kept this secret, afraid that if I revealed it, Troy would do something unforgivable, like falsely accusing an innocent child, as he's always done.

The truth hid in every text, insult, and warning.

My veins throb with a sharp and clear rhythm. It wasn't my fault, and it certainly wasn't Benny's. With newfound resolve, I meet Troy's inflamed eyes. "I didn't do a damn thing!" I scream back, my voice echoing defiantly in the tense air, shattering the heavy silence between us.

I softly grasp Payson's hand, briefly finding comfort in her supportive touch. "I'm okay," I assure her, and perhaps myself. With a nod, she becomes a silent symbol of strength and lets go of my hand, allowing me to proceed on my own.

With each step toward Troy, my resolve hardens. Our eyes lock, his narrowing with confusion and dawning realization. This man had overshadowed my thoughts for years, dictating my guilt. No more.

"You've got it all wrong, Troy," I say, my tone steady but heavy with the weight of years of suppressed truth. "That night—it wasn't my fault, nor was it Benny's." I stop just inches from him, watching the twitch of uncertainty that flickers across his face. *"It was you."*

A beat passes, a moment suspended in time. Then, with a derisive snort, he laughs. "Me?" he echoes, his words a mixture of incredulity and scorn. He leans closer, his breath hot with fury. "What the hell are you talking about?"

I can't bear to meet his eyes, my gaze instinctively falling to the floor as I prepare myself for the consequences of the truth I'm about to expose. It's a confession I've kept buried so deeply within me that even now, its release feels both inevitable and terrifying.

"You were drinking," I murmur, the admission escaping before I can stop it.

Troy briefly widens his eyes in shock, then smirks smugly. "Oh, yeah? Who says?" he taunts.

But his confidence wavers. I notice the glimmer of fear in his eyes as they dart nervously around the room, unable to settle on mine. His hands betray him, fidgeting and tugging at the fabric of his pants. The slight quiver in his voice gives him away; he's shaken, and he knows I can see through his bravado.

"What are you going to do, run to Mommy and Daddy? Call them? Have them save you?" Troy sneers, his contempt masking the panic simmering just beneath the surface.

I shake my head, my determination hardening. "No, but I will call the police," I declare, my voice ringing with a newfound confidence that feels both strange and empowering. "You think you have it all figured out, don't you, Troy?" I exhale deeply. "You thought I would be your little puppet forever, didn't you? And why?" I pause, letting the weight of my words sink in. "Because of that car accident? Because the one time you told me and Benny to be quiet, we crashed just seconds later?"

I laugh then—a harsh, joyless sound that mirrors the contempt bubbling within me. "You thought you could tell the police it was all my fault? That I wasn't listening, that I was distracting you?" I shake my head, a mix of incredulity and bitterness. Interestingly enough, I also heard the police officer. I saw him test you, and you were over the limit, Troy."

I kick at the glass scattered across the floor, each shard a painful reminder of the anger and hurt that's been festering inside me for years. I let this man control my life. I stayed silent when I should have spoken up. But now, standing here with the words pouring out of me, there's no holding back.

"It's amazing what having resources and people readily available to do favors for you can accomplish, don't you think?" There's a subtle spark of recognition in his eyes, as if he's aware that I've discovered his secret act of bribing the cop that night. I stride toward the fireplace, the flames dancing and casting a fiery glow that mirrors the blaze in my eyes. "It's taken me years," I pause, turning to face Troy. His eyes follow my every move, wary and tense. "It's taken me ten fucking YEARS!" I explode, the words ripping from my throat. "To finally realize that I didn't cause that accident."

That I didn't cause Benny to die.

"YOU DID." Each word I hurl at him feels like a weight lifting off my chest, making it easier to breathe, as if with each accusation, the suffocating burden lightens.

"You drank that night. You were the adult, the one responsible—you drove us home after the game."

Troy's face contorts with denial, his hands clenching unsteadily as he shakes his head. "No, no, no, y-you have it all wrong."

He continues to move his head, his hand rubbing the back of his neck as he paces the room, agitated. "No, you're wrong. You two were messing around in the back, and when

I took my eyes off the road, it—" He cuts off abruptly, the unfinished thought hanging heavily in the air.

Watching him, my heart tightens with a mix of pity and anger. His hands are fidgeting incessantly, sweat beads forming on his forehead. He bites his lip, his eyes darting everywhere but on me, unable to hold my gaze.

"You're right," I concede, my tone even but firm. "We were messing around in the back. However . . . " I pause, carefully choosing my next words, "You looked back at the road, but we didn't wreck then. It was a few more miles down the road—you were swerving. I remember clearly because Benny gets carsick, and he had asked you several times to stay off the rumble strips. Our laughing, our messing around? It was my way of distracting him, trying to keep his mind off the nausea your driving was causing."

My eyes drift away from Troy's defiant stare and find Payson. She has wrapped her arms around herself, hugging tight as if to keep from falling apart. Her whole body trembles with silent sobs, and she bites down on her lip hard enough to draw blood. Tears carve clear paths down her cheeks, glistening in the dim light, making her look like a fragile porcelain doll about to shatter.

God, this is the last thing I wanted her to see. These are my demons to wrestle, my past to reconcile—not hers to bear.

Despite her own distress, she notices my gaze. Her tear-filled eyes meet mine. They are pools of raw emotion—pain, fear, and a glimmer of understanding. She shakes her head ever so slightly, a silent plea for me not to pull back, not to let the guilt consume me. Her vulnerability serves as a reminder that I'm not alone in my regret, like a guiding light in a storm.

"It was enough . . . until it wasn't," I confess. Until that final, fateful moment when I heard the horn's blare cut through the night like a verdict. In that moment, the world lost control, and the car flipped end over end, creating a dizzying and terrifying sequence before violently hurling us into the middle of an empty field.

I can't help but let out a sarcastic laugh. "And you know what you told the cops?"

Troy halts his pacing abruptly, his attention snapping back to me, the weight of accusation palpable between us.

"You accused me and then insisted that you hadn't consumed much, blaming a faulty breathalyzer. The cop believed you. He actually believed your damn lie. And why? Because you two were buddies? Because you bribed him with your money that you loved to flaunt around?"

With my gaze fixed on the floor, my voice trembles as I continue, "And you want to know the absolute worst part?" Troy avoids my eyes, probably because he's scared I've figured out the truth. "I believed you."

I hear a soft gasp from Payson, and I know she's finally piecing it all together. After countless sessions, she's witnessing firsthand the agony I've been battling for years.

"I fucking believed you," I say. "You made me think that if I didn't follow through on your threats, you would turn my world upside down, that you could harm my family.

"You constantly reminded me of what Benny would want, what he would do, what he wouldn't do." I shake my head, and Troy finally meets my eyes. Guilt and fear are clear in his expression. "But you know what? I know Benny would be proud of me. Proud that I went to the college we always dreamed about, that I made it into the NFL draft, that I found the love of my life. I've done it all. Benny may not be physically present, but he is here," I state, touching my chest and sensing my heart race. "He's right here, he's always been here, and he would be proud of me. Because I am proud of myself."

Time stretches painfully before Troy finally breaks the silence. "Y-you are wrong," he stutters, his voice hollow and frail in the tense room. Repeating his denial, his knees buckle, and he crumbles to the ground. His hands slap the floor, unable to steady his trembling body. He sobs, his frame shaking uncontrollably as he gasps for breath. "No, no, that didn't happen. I remember, it wasn't me," he chokes out between ragged breaths.

I should feel sympathy for him, empathy for his plight—I know I should. But my heart aches more for Benny, who never got the chance to demand more from life, all because of this man, his father, standing right here.

One lesson I've learned from my sessions with Payson is the importance of confronting fears directly. It might be uncomfortable, it might cause pain to those around me, but it's necessary. I have to face the truth for my sake, to clear the path forward. For my peace, so I can finally move on.

My heart pounds with each step, the sound echoing in my ears as I close the distance between us. A knot is forming in my stomach, every breath getting heavier from years of pent-up feelings. Slowly, Troy lifts his gaze and locks his eyes onto mine with a chilling intensity. I briefly wonder if he can sense any of the anguish that has plagued me for years. The constant submission to his desires, transforming myself into the son he no longer has, has left throbbing scars that ache with each passing moment.

The immense guilt I held weighed heavily on me, a persistent, tormenting presence that tainted every moment of joy and accomplishment. It was a parasite, feeding on my happiness, leaving behind only emptiness and regret. To this day, my parents remain oblivious to the deceit; they know only of a tragic accident, with Troy at the helm. They were never involved in the investigation process, never asked too many in-depth questions. After all, it was all an "accident," according to Troy. Something he told my parents repeatedly in the hospital, a mantra meant to cement the lie.

My legs tremble slightly as I stand before him, my eyes searching his for any sign of remorse, any sign that he understands the hell he has put me through. But his stare remains hard, unyielding, and I realize I must be the one to break this chain, to free myself from the past.

"It was your fault. There's nothing wrong with what has been said tonight." I bend down to meet his gaze directly, our eyes locked in a tense standoff. "Now you have two options: get the fuck out of my penthouse and out of my life, or I can have the cops do it for you."

His eyes brim with tears, but a simmering anger lurks just beneath the surface, a volatile mix of grief and fury. In a flash of rage, he throws a fist at my face. The blow hits me hard, causing me to fall backward onto the floor with a sickening thud. A burst of pain spreads across my cheek, a piercing sting expanding outward, and the metallic taste of blood lingers on my tongue.

Despite the pain, I let out a laugh, more out of defiance than amusement. "That's all you got?" I challenge him, pushing myself back up to my feet, the room spinning slightly. I wipe the blood from my face with the back of my hand, smearing it across my knuckles.

"Benny would be so disappointed in you." I shake my head slowly, the weight of disappointment heavy in my voice. "He would be so disappointed to see you putting blame somewhere else, not holding yourself accountable." My words hang in the air, a stark contrast to the raw emotion etched across his face.

His rage falters for a moment, replaced by a flicker of guilt and confusion. The tears that had threatened to spill over now flow freely, carving silent paths down his cheeks. Yet, his fists remain clenched, knuckles white with unresolved anger.

I take a step closer. "You think this anger will absolve you? It won't. You need to face the truth, just like I did. Benny deserves that much. We all do." With determination in my voice, I add, "Make your son proud, Troy. Just this once."

He stares at me. His eyes, once so warm and inviting, now seem distant, the gates to his soul firmly shut. As he kneels there, surrounded by the elegance of the penthouse—the walls adorned with abstract art and the scent of expensive cologne lingering in the air—his posture remains rigid with indignation. It's painfully clear that the delusions he clung to about that long-ago accident revealed the depths of the man he has transformed into.

Troy is a mess, his body wracked with hiccupping sobs, his head shaking in denial. His hand, bloodied from the shards of glass, trembles as he clutches it to his chest, unwilling or unable to accept the reality of that night.

My voice is low and cold as I deliver my ultimatum. "Get out of my fucking penthouse and take whatever shred of dignity you think you still have," I hiss, my words slicing through the tense air. "And if I receive any more texts, if you dare to darken my doorstep uninvited again—remember, I have powerful allies too. Allies who wouldn't hesitate to see you behind bars."

I straighten my back, standing tall as I deliver my final blow, the words echoing off the walls of my penthouse. "That guilt I felt all these years, the one that gnawed at me, making me believe it was all my fault—it's yours now. Enjoy drowning in your own sea of sorrows and lies."

With a dismissive flick of my wrist, I add, "Now get the fuck out of my place." My voice booms hollow yet resolute.

Troy doesn't hesitate; he's practically sprinting, his figure a blur as he disappears out the door. I watch, almost disbelieving, as the door slams shut with a definitive thud, sealing his exit. My eyes remain fixed on the door, savoring the finality of this moment—the end of an era.

Payson's at my side in an instant, her hands gently cradle my face as she examines me, looking for unseen wounds. "You okay?" she asks, her voice laced with concern. Her fingers gently tilt my face toward hers, ensuring I meet her gaze.

At that moment, something shifts within me. The burden I've been carrying for a while vanishes, as light as a feather, floating away. With her caring eyes locked onto mine, I find the courage to speak the truth, and as the words escape my lips, I feel a deep sense of liberation: "I am now, baby."

Payson's lips curve into a soft, understanding smile, and she pulls me into her chest. She embraces me with her warmth, her steady heartbeat calming my own.

Payson eases back, her hands softly placed on my shoulders. "You did the right thing," she murmurs, her voice a soothing balm to my wounded soul. "You defended yourself. Defended Benny. That takes courage."

I nod, the truth of her words sinking in. "I couldn't have done it without you," I admit, my voice choked with emotion. "You've been my rock through all of this." She smiles again, a tear slipping down her cheek. "We've got each other. That's all that matters now."

Wrapped in each other's embrace, we stand, the penthouse making the outside world seem far away and insignificant. What was once an uncertain and fearful future now holds countless opportunities.

EPILOGUE
PAYSON

I Call It Love, #88

"This is so unfair. We always prepare our margaritas as a team," Milli argues, her lower lip quivering in an exaggerated pout. Her eyes, usually bright with mischief, narrow slightly as she watches Luke and me whisking up a batch of New Year's Eve margaritas in the heart of the Sutton family kitchen.

The house is alive with the hum of celebration. And when I say everyone is here, I mean *everyone*. Brooke, along with a few of Luke's teammates, are sprawled in the family room, laughter echoing as they share stories. Luke's parents, along with their close friends, fill the living room, voices mingling with the steady countdown on the TV, each second ticking us closer to midnight.

Milli shields herself from the emotional blow of the moment by crossing her arms and remarking, "You can't just replace me with him."

With a playful wink, Luke counters, "Sorry, but she can actually." Milli huffs in response, and I can't help but smile—a small, secret smile that I hide behind the rim of my glass.

What could I say? How could I choose? The truth is, I can't. They both mean everything to me, just in different ways, ways that words struggle to capture.

Not so long ago, the thought of spending New Year's with the Suttons would have seemed absurd, a fleeting fantasy at best. Back then, the only reason I would have set foot in this house was Milli—her laughter, her warmth, her way of making the world seem just a little bit brighter. But now, everything's changed. Radically. Beautifully. And even though I can't quite wrap my mind around it all, my heart knows this is where I'm meant to be.

Even if the real reason I find myself here, surrounded by colorful party hats, shrill blowers, and glittering New Year's decorations, is Luke and Mrs. Sutton's gentle yet insistent invitation, I still can't shake the nerves. Mrs. Sutton knows. She knows about my relationship with Luke and the fragile state of my home life. Her knowledge feels like a silent pressure, a constant hum beneath the surface of this celebration.

The moment Luke's car rolled into the driveway, I felt a wave of nausea rise within me. My instinct was to turn back, to retreat. But then Luke reached over, his hand warm and reassuring in mine, and whispered, "She really wants you to be here." And for some reason, I believed him. Tonight, Mrs. Sutton's warm smiles and small, thoughtful gestures have wrapped around me like a comforting blanket, easing the tension I've carried for so long. Did it make me question what I'd done to deserve such kindness? Absolutely. But thanks to Lori and our sessions, I'm learning to let go of those doubts. To accept things as they come, and trust that I'll figure it out along the way.

"You're just jealous of my margarita skills. They're top-notch. Just ask Payson," Luke says with a smug, knowing smirk. I smile, shaking my head as memories of our private margarita-making tradition flood back—especially that Christmas margarita at his penthouse.

I wouldn't tell Milli, but truth be told, that margarita was perfection. But it wasn't just the drink that made it memorable. It was the way Luke opened up to me that night, his raw honesty that made this holiday season bearable, even without my family by my side. In that moment, sitting there with him, I realized how much he had gone through—far more than I had ever imagined. The pain he had carried, the burden that had weighed him down, was staggering. And yet, knowing all of this, he still found the strength to be there for me, to make me feel safe and cared for in a way that I hadn't felt in a long time.

Despite everything, Luke and I managed to continue our therapy sessions into the spring semester. It was a godsend, really—finding another therapist-client connection with someone new would have been daunting, almost unbearable. As long as we both play our parts, we can maintain our professional boundaries during sessions, slipping back into those familiar roles where the lines are clear. But outside of those walls, it's different. Out here, Luke showers me with the kind of attention that feels like sunlight after a long, dark winter. He says he can finally breathe freely after years of suffocation. And I understand him completely.

I can finally look ahead, he had whispered to me one night, his voice tinged with a mix of relief and wonder. *Without my past holding me back.*

Our spirits mirror each other in that way. Both of us are caught in this dance of seeking redemption, trying to shed the weight of what once was, and embracing the possibility of what could be.

As I stand beside Luke at the kitchen counter, I can't resist playfully bumping my hip against his. He responds with a cheeky slap on my ass, his grin flashing with mischief.

I arch an eyebrow in response.

"You started it," he replies, a twinkle in his eyes.

From the corner of my vision, I notice Milli watching us, her expression hard to read. For a moment, she just taps her finger thoughtfully against her chin, her gaze flickering between Luke and me as if trying to piece together something she never quite expected to see. Then, slowly, a smile spreads across her face, small but genuine.

"This is so weird . . . " she murmurs, shaking her head. "But still, it's so freaking amazing." Her smile grows as she looks at us, a mixture of wonder and amusement lighting up her features. "Who would have guessed that you two would become a couple?"

I smile softly, knowing Milli's words carry a certain truth, yet also aware that she doesn't have the full picture. The night Troy entered Luke's penthouse was the turning point when everything changed, as Luke exposed the hidden pain fueling his resentment. With a trembling voice, he finally disclosed the reason behind his deep-seated animosity toward me.

It was something that had never fully registered until that moment—back in high school, when Milli and I, tipsy and carefree, had called him only for the connection to fail. Luke had been frantic, lost in his own memories. When we stumbled back home later, his eyes grew dark at the sight of us, wild with the thought that I had driven drunk. The image had sent him spiraling, back to that night with Benny—the screech of tires, the flash of headlights, the awful finality of a car swerving off the road. To him, I had been just as reckless as Troy, putting my own whims above everyone else's safety.

But what Luke didn't know, what he couldn't have known, was that I hadn't driven at all that night. Milli and I had taken an Uber, a detail that could have cleared everything up in seconds if only he'd asked. But that moment never came. He left for college soon after, and the distance between us grew—a chasm brimming with misunderstandings and unspoken words. Every time we crossed paths, it was as if we were locked in a battle neither of us could win.

In a tender voice, Miles whispers, "To be precise, you did it a million times," while placing a gentle kiss on her forehead.

Wrapping her arms around his neck, she faces him with a graceful ease, her warm smile lighting up her entire face.

"I definitely did, didn't I?" she murmurs, wiggling her eyebrows teasingly. Their laughter mingles in the air before their lips meet, first in a soft caress, then deepening into something more.

Just then, Mrs. Sutton's sharp yet amused voice cuts through the moment, punctuating it with her characteristic wit. "Milli, just because you're engaged now doesn't mean you get to act like a lovestruck teenager in my kitchen," she chides. With a sly smile, she steps closer to Luke, standing on her toes to plant a warm kiss on his cheek.

"Hey, sweetie," she utters, her voice softening with the gentle affection of a mother.

Milli remains undeterred by the interruption, her eyes gleaming mischievously. Her hand rises, the kitchen light catching the diamond on her finger, causing glimmers to dance around the room. It's a stunning ring, one that captures the eye—and suddenly, I find myself imagining a ring like that on my own hand someday. It's a thought I never expected to have, but life has a way of surprising us. People change, desires evolve, and that's okay.

"All right, then," Milli teases. "We'll just take this to the living room . . . " The daring lilt in her tone is unmistakable, and she shares a conspiratorial glance with Miles. Laughing together, they make their way to the living room, leaving behind a trail of lighthearted whispers.

Once the laughter subsides, Mrs. Sutton shifts her gaze to Luke. "Mind if I cut in?" she asks.

Luke narrows his gaze, meeting his mother's eyes with suspicion. "I'm not sure, Mom," he responds.

With a delicate touch, she grasps his shoulder and gently swivels him around until he's facing her fully. Then, with a tap on his nose, as if he were still the boy she used to guide through childhood's little troubles. "This will be good for us," she asserts. Her eyes, warm and knowing, meet mine, and for a brief moment, something unspoken passes between us.

As she holds my stare, she gently steers Luke out of the kitchen. Even after he's gone, she doesn't look away; instead, she turns her full attention to me. A fleeting thought crosses my mind—I could follow Luke, escape this unexpected moment. But before I can move, her hand touches my arm with a tenderness that surprises me. "Stay," she says, her voice gentle, her smile the most sincere I've ever seen from her. Her kindness feels like an invitation, closing the usual distance between us in an instant.

It's not that Milli's mom ever actively disliked me. I was a constant presence in their home during our childhood, practically a second daughter with how close Milli and I were—and still are. We even share a dorm room now. But something shifted as we grew older, as our teenage years brought changes neither of us was fully prepared for. When I started to change—when my parents changed—everything felt like it was falling apart. I tried to hide it all behind late nights, wild parties, and sarcastic remarks, wearing my rebellion like armor. But of course, it showed. Mrs. Sutton saw right through it, even if she didn't know the full story. And though I can't entirely blame her for the disapproving looks or the subtle, cutting remarks, they still stung.

When Milli came home late, or drank too much, or wore

something a "Sutton" shouldn't, I could see the way Mrs. Sutton's eyes flicked toward me, the unspoken accusation lingering between us. I was the bad influence, the one who led her daughter astray. And maybe she wasn't entirely wrong. But in this moment, as I stand here, her hand still resting lightly on my arm, I draw in a deep breath. She doesn't really know me—not the real me, the person behind the mask. And maybe, just maybe, it's time I let her.

"You know, I've never seen my son so captivated," Mrs. Sutton observes, her voice calm yet thoughtful. Her eyes rest on Luke, and I find myself following her gaze, both of us watching as he chats animatedly with Percy, his face lit up with an ease that seems so rare. "When Luke called me about the whole Troy debacle, I was beside myself—hurt, upset, overwhelmed by every shade of distress imaginable."

Her words unfold like a confession, revealing a side of her I hadn't expected. The genuineness in her eyes is unmistakable, almost startling in its raw honesty. "But do you know what helped me survive that emotional storm?" She doesn't wait for an answer. Instead, she turns to me, her gaze steady, and her hand gently cups my cheek. My throat tightens with emotion as I am caught off guard by the unexpectedly maternal and tender gesture.

"You." One word—simple, but it knocks the wind out of me. "It was the fact that he had you," she continues, her voice like a soothing balm to a long-open wound. "You were his anchor, the one who steadied him when everything else was falling apart. You guided him through the darkness and brought him back to a place of comfort."

With a gentle stroke of her thumb, she begins to break down the emotional barriers I've built. "He loves you," she whispers, her voice so soft, so full of truth, that it cradles my heart with a warmth I didn't realize I was yearning for.

I know Luke loves me; he declares it daily, his devotion as

unwavering as the sun's rise. He seizes every opportunity to express his feelings, and being loved by him is the sweetest joy I've ever known. Through his actions, he shows me what love truly means—treating me with the respect, care, and tenderness that every woman deserves.

I slowly shut my eyes . . . the tears finally letting loose. Her touch is gentle as she wipes them away, each stroke of her fingers filled with surprising tenderness. Before I can fully grasp the moment, she pulls me into a tight embrace, the suddenness of it causing my breath to hitch, my chest tightening. Her whispers reach my ear, soft and filled with empathy, her voice trembling ever so slightly. "I know your parents aren't with you this holiday season. And I am so sorry for that."

She pauses, permitting the gravity of her words to settle between us, the emotion in her voice cutting through the usual barriers. Then, in a voice both firm and tender, she adds, "But I won't apologize for having you here, for seeing the love my son has for you, and for witnessing the wonderful friend you continue to be to Milli."

As she slowly releases me, her hands slide gently from my shoulders, leaving behind a sense of comfort that lingers. Through the blur of my tears, I catch her examining my face —likely noticing the makeup now smeared like a raccoon's mask—but all I detect in her eyes is care, a genuine concern that touches me deeply.

"Above all," she begins, her voice softer now, "I want to apologize if I ever made you feel small, criticized, or unwelcome in any way. Milli was my baby, my precious girl, and I had such clear ideas of how I wanted her life to unfold. When things didn't go as planned, when I lost control of those dreams, I guess I became . . . overbearing. At least, that's what my husband always says." She lets out a light, self-aware laugh, a hint of vulnerability peeking through. "But that's behind me now. I see how foolish I've been, blind to the incredible bond you've shared with Milli, and now with my son. He's so incredibly lucky to have you—not just as his therapist, but as his girlfriend."

Her words hit me like a wave, and I can feel my chest pounding, my pulse soaring with an unfamiliar sense of acceptance. My hands tremble, slick with nervous sweat, as tears break free and stream down my cheeks. I hadn't realized how deep the ache of her approval ran within me, or how much I needed to hear these words. For so long, I felt lost, unworthy of love, always doubting that I could ever be good enough for someone like Luke. But now, wrapped in her affection and the sincerity of her apology, I glimpse something I hadn't dared to hope for: the promise of belonging.

Just then, Luke strolls back into the kitchen, a teasing grin on his face. "Aw, Mom, you made her cry," he says, his tone light, but the way he slips his arm around me, drawing me close to his side, speaks volumes. It's a gesture of quiet protection. One that I've come to love.

A gentle smile stretches across his mother's face, a look of deep understanding shining in her eyes. "Happy tears, right?" she asks, her voice soft and warm, her gaze filled with a kindness that tugs at my heart.

I can't help but mirror her smile, nodding as a wave of emotion swells within me. "Happy tears," I confirm, my voice catching slightly. I shut my eyes, allowing myself to fully savor the sweetness of the moment.

"Good," he murmurs, his breath brushing against my skin. Then, with a playful grin, he turns to his mother. "Now, Mom, if you'll excuse us." His eyes twinkle mischievously as he winks, and then, with a gentle squeeze of my hand, he intertwines our fingers and leads me down the hallway. The sound of our footsteps blends into the soft hum of the house, creating a sense of quiet intimacy as we move through a few rooms, finally stopping at the door to his old bedroom.

"Just a second," he says, flashing me a quick smile before disappearing into the bathroom. Left alone with only the remnants of his youth, I take a quick second to explore, my fingers grazing the cool metal of the trophies and medals proudly displayed on the shelves. Each one tells a story of his dedication and skill in football, a testament to the man he's become. The walls are lined with photos, capturing a younger Luke in the midst of his victories, his expression lit with joy and determination. As I take it all in, my soul swells with love for the boy who grew up to be the man I adore.

Then my eyes land on the last picture, tucked neatly among the others, a more recent addition that his mother must have placed there with care. I pick up the frame, my breath catching as I gaze at the image. It's us, all of us, standing together on the Lone Star Stadium field after Luke's championship game, the moment just after the NFL Honors ceremony, where he received Rookie of the Year. Luke's arm is wrapped protectively around me, his family surrounding us as he proudly holds the plaque. The memory floods back, vivid and alive—the months of shared sessions, the fiery arguments that eventually gave way to something far deeper. I smile, feeling a surge of love for everything we've been through: the bitter clashes, the passionate nights, the tender words that have slowly woven us together.

Suddenly, I feel a soft buzz in my pocket. My heart skips a beat as I see my mom's name flashing on the screen. Without hesitation, I swipe to answer, bringing the phone to my ear. "Mom?" I say, my voice a mix of surprise and anticipation.

"Hey, Pay Bay," she greets me, using the nickname she's called me since I was little. Her voice emits a soothing feeling that feels both familiar and new, a tone I'm still adapting to but one that fills me with comfort.

Since she moved to California, our calls and video chats have become more frequent, and each time, I notice the change in her. There's a lightness in her voice, a joy that wasn't there before. It's like she's found a piece of herself she didn't even know was missing. Her smile is brighter, her laughter more genuine, and her face—there's a glow that wasn't there when we lived in the same house. It's only been a few weeks, but the transformation is undeniable. Knowing she's thriving, even from miles away, eases a part of me that's always worried for her.

"Hey, Mom. Happy New Year," I reply, my voice softening with affection.

"Happy New Year, baby. I just wanted to call you real quick," she says, her tone light but filled with love.

In the background, I can hear faint laughter, the clinking of glasses, and a chorus of voices cheerfully shouting, "Happy New Year!" and "Love you!" The sounds are distant yet somehow enveloping, like they're wrapping me in the warmth of family, even though I'm not there with them.

A lump forms in my throat, and I swallow hard, trying to keep my voice steady. "I love you guys too," I say, my words thick with emotion. It's strange, the way distance has brought us closer, how her happiness brings me peace. And in this moment, with the echoes of celebration in my ear and the warmth of my mom's voice in my heart, I feel an overwhelming sense of connection—across miles, across time, across all the things that once seemed so big but now feel so small.

This is home, I realize. Not a place, but a feeling—one that follows me, no matter where I am.

"I had a thought . . . " Her voice falters, and I can almost see the hesitation on her face. "Maybe you could come visit over summer vacation?"

For a split second, my heart clenches, and a question

burns on the tip of my tongue: *Won't you be back by then?* But I bite down on my lip, swallowing the words before they can escape. Instead, I force a smile—an automatic reflex, though she can't see it through the phone—and say, "I would love to."

She's told me before that I'm welcome to return to the house anytime, for spring break or summer, or whenever I want. But the truth is, I haven't pressed her on the details of their situation—why she left, or what really drove her to . . . everything. Maybe it's because I'm more focused on myself now—on my own goals, my own future—than on the tangled mess of my parents' marriage. Or maybe, deep down, I'm just not ready to know the answers. Months from now, maybe even years, the truth might come out. But for now, I'm just relieved to hear the contentment in her voice, and maybe that's enough. Maybe my dad is finding his own contentment, too, in whatever way he can.

"Have you spoken with your father?" Her voice dips into a hesitant tone, the first time she's mentioned him since this all began. I knew this moment was coming, especially with it being our first New Year's apart as a family, but that doesn't make it any easier.

I close my eyes, letting the weight of her question settle on my shoulders. I take a deep breath, willing myself to stay calm, and then slowly exhale. "No, I haven't. Not since he showed up at Luke's."

A heavy silence falls between us, punctuated only by the faint background noise on her end. I can almost hear her thinking, wrestling with her own emotions. Finally, she breaks the quiet with a soft, contemplative "Hmmm."

"Maybe it's for the best?" she offers, her voice tinged with hope, as if she's trying to convince both of us.

I don't respond right away, the words caught in the tangled web of my thoughts. There's a part of me that wants to agree, to say that maybe some distance is what we all need right now. But there's another part—a smaller, quieter part—that wonders if this distance will only deepen the rift, turning a temporary separation into something permanent.

For now, I push those thoughts aside. It's enough to know that my mom is finding her own way, that she's glowing in a way I haven't seen in years. Maybe that's all I need to hold onto, as fragile as it might be.

I simply murmur, "Mm-hm," though a knot tightens in my chest. Deep down, I *want* to share her optimism—I want to believe that my dad is also making an effort, that he's changing in ways I can't yet see. I cling to the hope that one day, he'll reappear, transformed, ready to show just how much he's grown. But I know it wouldn't be easy. If that day ever comes, we'd have to rebuild everything from the ground up—trust, understanding, the fragile bond that once held us together.

My relationship with my mom is far from perfect, but I try to focus on the positives, on the progress we're making. Healing takes time, I remind myself, echoing the lessons from my therapy sessions. Boundaries—they've been essential, a lifeline. They're not walls to shut my parents out, but shields to protect my well-being, to remind me that my needs matter too. Even as I cautiously navigate this new distance with my mom and dad, I know these boundaries are helping me hold onto myself.

"You ready?" Luke's voice pulls me from my thoughts, grounding me back in the moment.

On the other end of the line, my mom chuckles softly, a hint of curiosity in her tone. "Ready for what?" she asks, and I can practically visualize her raising an eyebrow, intrigued by this new development.

I glance at Luke, who's standing in the doorway with that familiar, easy smile that always manages to put me at ease.

There's a gleam of playfulness in his eyes, the kind that makes me forget, even if just for a moment, the weight of everything else.

"Not sure yet, but I have to go, Mom. I love you," I say, wrapping up our conversation with a warmth that feels more genuine than it has in a while. There's a quiet pause at the receiving end, almost as if she senses the sincerity, before she responds, "Love you, too."

I stay still for a moment, letting the conversation linger in my mind, before Luke re-enters the room. The soft glow of the Christmas tree lights reflects off the tinsel, casting a cozy ambiance around us. My eyes catch the writing on his shirt, and I can't help but burst into a full, hearty belly laugh when I read the playful words.

Luke's shirt proudly showcases the slogan: MY THERAPIST: THE ULTIMATE MVP. He spins around, arms outstretched, causing me to laugh again as I approach him. The room feels warmer, brighter, as his familiar smug grin spreads across his face. He takes a theatrical bow, adding an exaggerated flourish. With a wink, he confidently declares, "I know, I did well."

I shake my head, closing the gap between us with slow, deliberate steps until I'm only inches from his face. My lips meet his in a soft kiss, a tender contrast to our playful exchange. "You did good," I murmur, letting the words linger between us before pulling back with a mischievous smile. "But . . . " I pause, my fingers inching toward the hem of my sweater. With a playful twinkle in my eye, I announce, "I did better."

Luke's eyes widen at the sight of me taking off my sweater, but he promptly stops me by grabbing my wrist. "Baby, not here. We can't do that," he says with a mix of amusement and caution.

I chuckle, rolling my eyes. "Oh yeah? Since when don't you want to get me naked?"

Pausing, he breaks into a smile and joins in my laughter. Eventually, he relents and aids me in pulling the sweater over my head, uttering, "Yeah, you're right." But as the fabric clears my face, his expression shifts. While observing the shirt I'm wearing underneath, his gaze grows stronger—the shirt that was supposed to be a gift for him before Troy interrupted us.

That confession never happened, and after taking a few weeks to process everything, I still hadn't managed to say *I love you*. But standing here now, I know I want him to understand everything—how much I care, how much he has changed my life, how deeply I love him.

I allow him to read what's written on the shirt's front, peeking over my shoulder, my heart races, each beat louder than the last.

Luke's eyes become gentle, brimming with affection and attentiveness. His mouth curves into a smile while he reads the message on the back, my special addition: I CALL IT LOVE, #88.

Time seems to slow. I hold my breath. Luke takes a moment, his hand moving from his jaw, to the back of his neck, and finally running through his hair. The uncertainty on his face adds a charming vulnerability to his normally confident demeanor, making him look nervous. I can feel the heat of his breath on my skin, the slight tremble in his hands as they grab my waist.

With a full turn toward him, he grabs the back of my neck, his lips find mine, rough, yet soft. It's an all-consuming kiss. One that makes my toes curl and my pulse race as I deepen the kiss.

"Goddammit, woman. Took you long enough." He murmurs and I giggle.

He pulls back, both of us now breathless. I wrap my arms around his neck, and I observe the shine in his eyes, tears on the verge of falling as he digests what my shirt says.

Bringing me closer, he eases the tension by pressing his forehead against mine. I can feel his heart pounding against my chest, each beat a silent confession.

"Penny, you saying you love me?"

I smirk slightly, giving a shrug. "Maybe."

"Speak up, don't be shy, baby. Let me hear it," he coaxes, his voice gentle.

With my heart pounding fiercely in my chest—a wild, exhilarating rhythm—I gather every ounce of courage and confess, "I love you, Luke."

He grins, his expression lighting up with joy and surprise, but for a few long moments, he doesn't speak. We just stand there, wrapped in each other's arms, basking in the gravity of my words. I observe his face, recognizing the tears welling up in his eyes.

"Happy tears?" I ask.

He nods, and his smile grows bigger, filling my heart with love like a ray of sunshine. "So unbelievably happy."

I hold him tightly, his joy echoing deep within my soul. "Me too, baby, me too," I whisper. For the first time, I feel an all-encompassing happiness flooding every corner of my being with warmth and light. As I gaze into Luke's eyes, I see not just a reflection of my own joy but also a shared promise of all that is yet to come.

Acknowledgments

Hey lovely readers,

First off, big virtual hugs for picking up this book! Writing it was like being on a rollercoaster of emotions, and knowing you're here for the ride makes everything worth it.

A heartfelt shoutout to my family for their endless encouragement and coffee. My children, you're my inspiration with your laughter and sweet interruptions. To my other half, you're the real-life romance that keeps the dream alive. Thanks for putting up with the late nights, the plot rants, and for being my forever plus one.

A huge thank you to my editors, Chelsea and Kelsey from Represent Publishing and Paisley from Perfectly Write Editing Services. You all have polished my chaos into something beautiful and kept me on track.

And to everyone who's been a part of this journey, you're all awesome. Now, let's dive into this adventure together with Luke and Payson, and remember, love always finds a way.

- Charli Cotner